"PARANORM **DOESN'T GET BET** —*Love*

PRAISE FOR THE NOVELS
OF NALINI SINGH

Archangel's Storm

"If you have never read Nalini Singh, if you have wondered what a great romance hero should be like, go get book one of the Guild Hunter series and read them all."
—*Vampire Book Club*

"*Archangel's Storm* gives us a pair of beautifully rich characters perfect in their flaws and imperfect in their strengths who lead us through a dark dance of pleasure, pain, and heady hope." —*Supernatural Snark*

Angels' Flight

"A great intro to Singh's series, if you haven't read her before, and a delicious addition if you have."
—*HeroesandHeartbreakers.com*

"Nalini Singh spins a captivating story while presenting vibrant relationships that catch the heart and the imagination. Her characters *matter* . . . A must-read for anyone familiar with the series." —*Errant Dreams Reviews*

continued . . .

Archangel's Blade

"Stuns with intensity . . . Left me raw and aching at the end in the best way possible." —*Romance Junkies*

"Mesmerizing . . . Fascinating world-building."
—*Bitten by Books*

Archangel's Consort

"Powerful, raw, intense, dark—and so intimate."
—*Smexy Books*

"Steamy and beautiful . . . makes me want to read everything Nalini Singh has ever written." —*Fresh Fiction*

Archangel's Kiss

"Stunning, original, beautiful, intriguing, and mesmerizing."
—*Errant Dreams Reviews*

"I'm so intrigued by this world, so captivated by Raphael and Elena, and Raphael's Seven, that I simply cannot wait until the next Angel book." —*Dear Author*

Angels' Blood

"Completely awe-inspiring." —*Fallen Angel Reviews*

"World-building that blew my socks off."
—Meljean Brook, *New York Times* bestselling author

"A fabulous addition to the paranormal world."
—*Fresh Fiction*

Archangel's Legion

Nalini Singh

JOVE BOOKS, NEW YORK

THE BERKLEY PUBLISHING GROUP
Published by the Penguin Group
Penguin Group (USA) LLC
375 Hudson Street, New York, New York 10014, USA

USA | Canada | UK | Ireland | Australia | New Zealand | India | South Africa | China

Penguin Books Ltd., Registered Offices: 80 Strand, London WC2R 0RL, England
For more information about the Penguin Group, visit penguin.com.

ARCHANGEL'S LEGION

A Jove Book / published by arrangement with the author

Jove Books are published by The Berkley Publishing Group.
JOVE® is a registered trademark of Penguin Group (USA) LLC.
The "J" design is a trademark of Penguin Group (USA) LLC.

For information, address: The Berkley Publishing Group,
a division of Penguin Group (USA) LLC,
375 Hudson Street, New York, New York 10014.

ISBN: 978-0-425-25124-9

PUBLISHING HISTORY
Jove mass-market edition / November 2013

PRINTED IN THE UNITED STATES OF AMERICA

10 9 8 7 6 5 4 3 2

Cover art by Tony Mauro.
Cover design by George Long.
Cover handlettering by Ron Zinn.
Text design by Kristin del Rosario.

1

Elena watched the ducks peck at each other in the pond in Central Park and thought about the last time she'd been here. She'd sat on this very bench, musing on the fact that even the ducks couldn't be nonviolent as her mind fought frantically to find a way out of the mess in which she'd found herself—a mess that had seen her tracking a mad archangel for another immortal as lethal.

Shimmering white-gold over her vision as she lifted her eyes to the sky, an echo of that fateful day. "Hello, Archangel."

Raphael folded away his wings, his eyes on the ducks. "Why do you find them so fascinating?"

"I don't. I just like this spot." Her own wings uncomfortably squashed against the seat built for humans and vampires, she rose to her feet. "Though I think you need to sponsor a new bench over there." She pointed to a beautiful spot across the way; it'd be shaded by the delicate green leaves of a flowering cherry tree in summer, the soft pink blooms in spring. Right now, with winter's kiss in the air, the tree was all bone, stark against the evergreens.

"It will be done," Raphael said with a cool arrogance that

made her want to drag him back to bed. "You realize you're capable of sponsoring many such benches?"

Elena blinked as she always did when she remembered she was rolling in it. Not in comparison to older immortals, of course, and way below Raphael's league, but her personal fortune was more than respectable when it came to a fledgling immortal. Earned in the hunt that had broken her back, made her bleed until her throat filled with the iron dark fluid, and brought Raphael into her life, the money was currently amassing ridiculous amounts of interest in her Guild account.

"Damn"—she whistled—"I need to start thinking like a rich chick."

"I will be most amused to watch this transformation."

Narrowing her eyes, she said, "Just you wait. Before you know it, I'll be one of the angels who lunch."

He laughed, her dangerous lover who wore his strength as a second skin and had a face of such violent masculine beauty that she was stunned anew each time she realized he belonged to her. Hair of darkest midnight and eyes of a painful blue found nowhere else on this earth, Raphael was a man blooded with power—no one would ever mistake him for anything but what he was: an archangel who had the capacity to snuff out a life as easily as she might crush an ant.

The wings that arced over his shoulders only deepened the sense of dangerous temptation. His feathers were white, but for fine filaments of pure gold that caught the eye and the light. Flawless wings, but for the astonishing "scar" of golden feathers where she'd once shot him. A few months back, his primaries, too, had begun to turn gold, only for the process to continue past yellow-gold and to a glittering metallic white. Now the sun caught on those primaries as he laughed, igniting an illusion of white fire.

"I'm afraid," he said after the laughter faded, "I have some news that may regretfully turn your attention in another direction."

Put on guard by his tone, she ignored the people in the distance whose mouths had dropped open at the sight of Raphael's amusement, the Archangel of New York not known for laughter. "What is it?"

"I have two pieces of . . . interesting news."

Elena's stomach dropped. "Lijuan?" According to Raphael's spymaster, the batshit old archangel was creating reborn again, if only in small numbers. Lijuan called it giving "life," but her walking dead servants were nightmares, a plague upon the world—and the worst thing was, many of them knew it, their eyes screaming for help even as their bodies shuffled to follow the commands of their mistress.

Then there were the strange desiccated bodies found near her stronghold that no one could figure out. The general consensus was that they were failed attempts at creating reborn, but whether that was good news or bad news was anyone's guess. "She's not—"

Raphael shook his head before she could complete her question, the black silk of his hair rich and dark. "My mother," he said, "has invited us to a ball."

Elena pulled a blade from one of the butter-soft forearm sheaths that had been a gift from Raphael. "Excuse me while I stab myself in the eyes—and disembowel myself while I'm at it." The last time Elena had attended an immortal ball, she'd ended up bathing in the blood of the reborn while Beijing burned around her. And oh yeah, let's not forget smashing to the earth after being ripped out of the sky.

"I'm afraid I cannot permit that," Raphael said, in what she thought of as his "Archangel" voice, formal and ruthless. "Who would then keep me amused at the ball? I may otherwise be driven to pluck out my own eyes and I believe you are quite fond of them."

"Funny." Sighing, she leaned her head against the muscled strength of his arm, his skin bared by the brown fighting leathers that told her he'd come from a sparring session, likely with Illium. "Why is Caliane having a ball?"

He spread his wing across her own in a susurration of sound that was a familiar intimacy. "Her city and people have fully awakened, and she wishes to formally greet the other powers in the world." A pause. "My mother may have been many things, but the one thing she has never been is impolite; as an Ancient, she is cognizant of her responsibility to take a part in the ruling of the world, even if it is from a distance."

Complex, intelligent, once-insane, Raphael's mother wasn't a woman who could be put easily into any kind of a category. The Ancient had left her son broken and bloodied on a forsaken field an eon ago, but she'd also risen perilously early from a centuries-long Sleep to save the life of that same son. "When's the ball?"

"In less than two weeks."

"I'll make sure my jewels are glittering and my nails done."

Raphael's lips curved again as she slid away the knife and held out her hands to display unpolished nails clipped hunter-short. The back of her left hand was bruised from a tussle with a recalcitrant vampire she'd retrieved for the Guild a few hours before, and her palms, when she flipped over her hands, proved to have a plethora of calluses.

Even her newly immortal body couldn't erase those calluses, not when she worked constantly with weapons. "I don't think a manicure is going to cut it."

"Should you ever touch me with court-softened hands, I will know an imposter walks in your skin."

Some women might've taken his words as an insult; they made Elena want to initiate a very public, very hot kiss. "So," she said, promising herself she'd indulge that particular need as soon as they were alone, "what's the other piece of news?"

"Perhaps I should take your weapons first."

Elena tried to think of what could be worse than attending a ball with the most powerful, most vicious angels and vampires in the world, and came up with, "My father wants to have dinner with us?"

"No, it is not Jeffrey." The suddenly brutal angle of his jawline made his opinion of her father clear. "Come, we cannot talk of this where we may be overheard." Stepping a little away from her, his wing sliding off her own, he said, "Do you wish to attempt a vertical takeoff?"

Elena thought of the number of witnesses, pitted that fact against the straining effort it would take for her to get aloft. That teeth-gritting struggle would betray weakness in a way that would reflect not only on her, but on Raphael—and an archangel could never be seen as weak, for the sake of mortals and immortals alike.

In all probability, she'd have made a different choice even a few months ago, she'd been fighting so hard to retain her sense of self in the new world into which she'd been thrust. Now she understood far more about the intricacies of the balance of power in the world, understood, too, that while Raphael might occasionally frustrate her with his protectiveness, he had no desire to clip her wings.

"No, not here." Walking into his arms, she folded back her wings, and he took them effortlessly into the air, his hold steel around her waist, his heartbeat strong and steady.

Crashing waves and the salt-laced sea, rain clean and bright, that was Raphael's mental scent and it lingered in her every breath, made her body ache. Always, he made her ache. Shifting slightly in his hold, she pressed her lips to his throat, felt his pulse speed up.

"Would you dance with me above Manhattan?"

Her breath caught at the sensual murmur, the idea of their bodies and wings intertwined in the rawly sexual act pure adrenaline in her blood. "Not yet. I don't think I'm that brave." Raphael might possess the archangelic ability to shield them from all sight, but *she* would still be able to see the city below. "I like dancing with you above the sea." Loved feeling the sheer power of him as they plummeted from lethal heights to hit the water. "Tonight?"

"I am seduced." Easing his hold above the cloud layer, he claimed her mouth for a darkly passionate kiss that made her breasts tighten, her body eager for the wild promise of the night. "Ready?" he asked when their lips parted, his body hard against her own.

At her nod, he removed his arm from around her waist and she fell through the gossamer kiss of the clouds . . . to unfold her wings and circle up on an updraft, the exhilaration of flight in no way lessened by the fact that she'd had a year to get used to the astonishing wonder of it. *Is it urgent?* she asked. *What we have to discuss?*

Not so urgent that we cannot fly.

Looking up, she watched him wing his way higher and higher with breathtaking ease, until he was a faraway dot in the sky . . . then felt her heart stop as he dropped, a sleek arrow

of white-gold that shot past her, accelerating until she could
see people screaming in the park below. A second before what
would've been terminal impact for a mortal, Raphael spread
his wings and shot back up.

You terrified everyone. Her own pulse was in her mouth,
her blood thunder in her ears.

*Humans need to be terrified every so often. It keeps them
from crossing lines that shouldn't be crossed.*

*You ever think maybe archangels should be challenged once
in a while?* she countered. *That it'd take care of the whole
arrogance issue?*

Anyone may challenge me.

When he executed a turn toward the Hudson, Elena followed, the river winds riffling through the strands of hair that
had escaped her braid. *How can people challenge you when
they're so afraid?*

It didn't stop you.

Well, he did have her there. But—*I've always had a dash
of crazy in me.*

Flying wing to wing with him, she swept out over the water,
following the river north, before turning to head to their house
in the Angel Enclave. Situated along the cliffs on the opposite
side of the Hudson from Manhattan, it was a magnificent building that offered sweeping views of the city, but for Elena, it
was simply home.

*Montgomery has prepared something special for you. Do
not break his heart.*

Elena grinned at the thought of the butler. *You know Montgomery and I have a mutual love affair.* Coming down on her
feet on the still-green grass of the lawn that ended in a steep
drop into the Hudson, she watched Raphael land, his wingspan
incredible.

"A storm," he murmured, his eyes on the clouds that had
begun to boil over Manhattan. "It grew quickly."

So quickly that she hadn't noticed anything while in the air.
"It's not another Ancient waking up, is it?" she asked, the tiny
hairs on her arms standing up at the memory of the last time
the city had suffered inclement weather.

"No," Raphael said to her relief. "It'd be an extraordinary

thing for two to rise within the span of a year—this is likely nothing but the first lash of winter. Still, we will watch to make certain. We cannot forget that the Cascade is in full effect."

"Yeah, and it's not exactly a flowers-and-butterflies kind of thing." The Cascade, according to everything they'd been able to discover, was a confluence of time and certain critical events that led to a surge of power in the Cadre. All of the archangels would grow in strength, some might be touched with madness, but none would remain the same. Neither would the world, for the archangels were part of its very fabric.

"Does the second thing you want to discuss have to do with the Cascade?"

"No." Those eyes of endless blue met her own. "Michaela has asked permission to remain for an extended period in my territory."

Elena's jaw dropped. "Oh, *hell* no." The female archangel had made it clear she considered Elena something lesser, a bug to be ground beneath her designer boot. "What makes her think I'd want her in my city?"

"I do not believe Michaela thought of you at all." Brutal words from her archangel, but Elena knew the anger wasn't directed at her.

"Michaela," he continued, his tone as cold as a scalpel slicing across the throat, "would've had a better chance of receiving my assistance had she not insulted my consort in the asking."

"The fact we're discussing this means you're considering her request."

"She wishes sanctuary because she is with child."

Shock rooted Elena to the spot. It suddenly made sense, why the woman many considered the most beautiful in the world hadn't been spotted in the media for at least two months, when she'd always loved that kind of attention. "What about the father of her child?" she asked at last. "I assume it's Dahariel?" At Raphael's nod, she said, "He's a powerful angel in his own right, second to an archangel."

"Michaela might've slept with Dahariel, but she doesn't trust him not to stab her in the back while she is vulnerable."

Elena couldn't imagine such a situation. She knew Raphael

would fight to the death to protect her if and when they decided to try for a child. "Will she be? Vulnerable?" Michaela wasn't an archangel simply in name—she had the blinding power to go with it.

"Yes." Raphael's eyes followed a squadron of angels coming in to land at the Tower, their bodies angled to slice through the rising wind. "Pregnancy can be difficult for archangels. Michaela's power will remain, but her hold on it may become erratic. It is why a consort is so necessary during this time."

"She can't have mine," Elena said, well aware Michaela was cunning enough to use her condition to further her aim of gaining Raphael for a lover. "Won't Dahariel consider it an insult if she chooses your protection?"

"No. He isn't yet her consort."

Much as she disliked Michaela, Elena couldn't help but think of the anguish she'd once witnessed on the other woman's face, the unutterable pain of a mother who'd lost a child. "We can't say no, can we?"

Raphael cupped her cheek, brushing his thumb over her cheekbone. "Your heart is too soft, Guild Hunter. I can and will say no if that is needed." His eyes glowed incandescent, the flames lightning blue. "I have not forgotten that she has attempted to hurt you more than once."

Instinct urged Elena to push him to decide exactly that; nothing good could come of having Michaela nearby. However, this wasn't only about the female archangel and her machinations, but about the innocent she carried in her womb. "I would never forgive myself if we said no and then she lost the child in an attack."

"Were the situations reversed, you know she would leave you in the streets to starve."

"I'm not Michaela." It was a line in the sand, one she would not cross.

"No, you're far more than she will ever be." He dropped his hand with a single hard kiss, his eyes returning to the gathering storm. "I'll consider her request—and I'll consider the rules should I grant it."

"I definitely don't want her in the house next door." There

was a difference between showing compassion for a vulnerable woman, and stupidity. "If—"

Something soft slammed to the ground in front of them.

Startled, Elena looked down to see a bloodied pigeon. "Poor thing." From what she could see when she crouched down, its neck had snapped in a sudden, violent death. "It must've suffered damage to its wings in the air, been unable to stay aloft."

"I do not think it is that simple," Raphael said, as she was thinking they should bury the dead bird in the woods that bordered the house on either side.

Looking up, she followed Raphael's gaze to see hundreds of tiny splashes in the Hudson, the air above dark with a swirling cloud that had become fat and black. Another bird landed on the very edge of the cliff, its wing lifting limply before it slipped off the rocks and into the water.

"This storm," Raphael said softly on the heels of a third bird hitting the ground at Elena's feet, its tiny body broken, feathers matted a dull red from the crushing impact, "is not so ordinary after all."

2

Elena stood inside their home, staring out at the world through the sliding glass doors of the library. That world had gone insane. Birds continued to fall from the sky, the "cloud" created of thousands upon thousands of their tiny forms. Elena's instincts urged her to do something, stop the terrible rain, but there was nothing she could do.

The river had quickly emptied where the birds circled, and Elena hoped most people caught under the edge of the massive cloud that now encompassed part of Manhattan would have the good sense to duck under shelter, or into the subways to escape the bombardment.

"Have you ever heard of anything like this?" she asked the archangel beside her.

"No. I—" Words slicing off in midthought, he slid open the doors. "Stay here."

"Where are you—" Her question caught in her throat as she realized the wings above and crashing into the Hudson were suddenly far bigger than those of the dying birds.

Angels were falling from the skies.

Though the urge to follow Raphael as he dove off toward

the water filled with broken wings was a drumbeat in her skull, Elena forced herself to use her brain. The birds were falling at speeds akin to a fastball, complete with sharp beaks that would shred wings if they hit at the wrong angle, and she wasn't powerful enough to survive many of those hits in the air, nor agile enough in flight to avoid them. She'd only be a liability out there.

But she could be an asset here. "Montgomery!" she cried, running out of the library.

The butler ran out into the central core of the house just as she reached it. "Guild Hunter?" He was dressed in his usual impeccable black suit, but his eyes held the same disbelief that was ice in Elena's blood.

"We need to set up an infirmary," she said. "Raphael is closer to this side of the river and likely to bring the fallen here." She looked around the central core—it was huge by any measure, but angelic wings took up space, and they had no way of knowing the number of injured about to come in. "We'll start here, but we might also have to rig up something in the yard. It'll have to be strong enough to block the birds."

"I'll get things under way." The butler disappeared in a startling rush of speed that was a silent reminder that beneath his dignity and plummy British accent, Montgomery was deadlier than any vamp she'd ever hunted.

Her cell phone rang as she was about to make her way to the cliffs—if she could help haul the injured inside, then Raphael could focus on rescue. Glancing at the screen as she ran to the doors, she saw it was her best friend. "Sara?"

"Ellie, we have angels hitting the streets." Stark shock, but below that was the steely strength that made Sara head of a guild formed of some of the most lethal men and women in the country. "Our people are rendering aid where they can, but I have reports of angels hanging broken off gargoyles on skyscrapers and stuck on church steeples."

Elena blew out a shuddering breath at the horrendous images. "Call the Tower." She rattled off a number that'd give Sara direct access to Aodhan. "If he's out of action"—*dear God*—"someone else will be there to cover."

Hanging up without further words, confident Sara would

understand, Elena ran across a lawn scattered with bloodied
birds, their eyes filmed over with the oblivion of death. However, the tiny corpses were far enough apart that it was clear
both the house and the grounds were under the very edge of
the affected zone. Fear a metallic taste on her tongue, she hoped
the deaths had been caused by the impact, and *not* by the reason
for the fall, because, unlike the birds, an angel could survive
countless broken bones.

"I have him!" she called out to Raphael as he came in, an
angel in his arms.

"He's not breathing, his back is broken, and his heart has
stopped." Putting the lithely muscled angel on the clifftop,
Raphael swept off, but his mind remained connected to her
own. *Tell Montgomery to take medical measures—the male is
too young to survive otherwise.*

I will. Hauling one of the angel's thankfully unbroken arms
over her shoulders—ignoring the conventional teachings about
broken backs because this wasn't a mortal—she gritted her
teeth and got to her feet. The victim's shattered body was
soaked from his fall, his wings dead weight. It was as well that
as a born hunter, she'd always been stronger than most humans.
Her growing immortality had only cemented that strength.

Still, she was glad to see Montgomery race out to take the
angel's weight on the other side, neither one of them flinching
as two birds hit their backs hard enough to bruise. "Medical
measures," she managed to get out as they traversed the distance to the house as fast as possible; she hadn't known until
now that there *were* any medical measures—at least of the
ordinary kind—that could be applied to angels.

More of the household staff, and a number of unaffected
angels from other parts of the Enclave, ran or flew past them
as they took the injured angel in through doors that led directly
into the central core. The space that a couple of minutes earlier
had been all shining wooden floors, an elegant statuette set
against the wall, was now a temporary hospital.

A young vampire Montgomery had taken on as his appren-
tice was throwing down large futons that must've come out of
storage, and a slender angel—Sivya—who was normally in

charge of the kitchens, was snapping open a large black leather
bag that looked like an old-fashioned medical kit.

As soon as they laid the angel on a futon, Sivya stabbed a
large-bore needle directly into his heart and depressed the
plunger. Elena had a thousand questions, but now wasn't the
time to ask them, Montgomery beside her as they raced back
out. When she saw wings of silver-blue rising into the air after
dropping off a victim, she felt an intense sense of relief . . .
mingled with horror as she realized exactly how many winged
bodies floated in the murky waters of the Hudson.

Another bird hit her as they ran, the beak carving a line
down her face, but she shook it off and kept going. On their
second trip inside, she heard a cough, saw the first angel they'd
rescued retching on his side. His left wing and legs were
mangled—but at least he was alive.

Leaving their current charge in Sivya's hands, she ran back
out with Montgomery at her side. It felt like an eternity, but she
would later find out the actual hell of what came to be known
as the Falling lasted five short minutes. Then the birds stopped
dropping from the skies . . . and so did the angels.

Four hours later and they finally had some real numbers.
Eight hundred and eighty-seven angels had gone down over the
city in that horrific period no one would ever forget. Eight
hundred and two of the fallen had been part of the two-
thousand-strong defensive force stationed at the Tower, the
remaining eighty-five composed of nonwarrior angels, visitors
to the city, and two couriers who'd had the bad luck to come
in just as things went horribly wrong.

"All of the injured," Aodhan told Raphael, as the three of
them stood on the railingless balcony outside Raphael's Tower
office, the sky above painted in the fiery palette of an agoniz-
ingly stunning sunset, "have been retrieved."

Raphael, his wings and clothes streaked with blood, glanced
at the angel who was made of fractured pieces of light. Each
strand of Aodhan's hair appeared coated with crushed diamonds, his wings so brilliant as to hurt mortal eyes under

sunlight, his irises shattered outward from the pupil in splinters of crystalline blue and green.

"You're certain?"

"Yes. I've checked the fallen against the master list we keep of all angels stationed at the Tower or otherwise resident in the area." Aodhan resettled his wings, light sparking off the faceted filaments of his feathers. "Illium has accounted for all visitors—and we've had no reports from the Guild's network of informants about unrecovered angels."

"How many did we lose?" Elena didn't want to ask the question; her hands fisted in rejection. Angels might be immortal in the eyes of humans, but they *could* be killed . . . the younger they were, the easier they died. A destroyed heart, a broken spine paired with significant internal injuries, decapitation: none of that would kill Raphael, but inflict the same physical insult on a newly adult angel and the outcome would be lethal.

Raphael's face was stripped of all emotion as he waited for Aodhan's response.

"Five," the angel answered. "It was the secondary trauma that caused the deaths, not the inciting incident."

"Tell me," Raphael ordered.

Aodhan's voice was quiet, his words violent. "An impalement on a spire where the heart and spine were both destroyed almost simultaneously—"

"Who?"

"Stavre. He was on his first placement. A bare hundred and fifty."

Jaw clenched against the injustice of it, Elena made herself listen as Aodhan completed the recitation, his tone without emotion, but she knew the words he spoke must cut like razors.

First, he named the fallen, then said, "Two died as a result of decapitation combined with major heart damage when they fell into traffic in front of vehicles that couldn't stop in time; another was decapitated after she hit the sharp corner of a building, her body breaking into multiple pieces on impact with the street; and we lost the last when he fell into a rooftop exhaust system." A pause. "The humans did all they could, but the velocity of his fall into the blades meant there was no hope of survival. His body was sliced into shreds."

Five out of the nearly three thousand angels in and around the city at any one time. It didn't sound so bad . . . until you realized that angels didn't reproduce as humans did. Only a single, cherished child might be born in the space of a decade. A century might go by without *any* new births. The loss of five angels in the prime of their lives was an unspeakable tragedy.

"They must have an escort home." At that moment, Raphael was very much the Archangel of New York, a leader icily furious at the loss of his people. "Contact Nimra," he said, naming an angel Elena knew to be a power within the territory. "She will understand what must be done."

And her presence, Elena realized, would be a sign of respect and honor from an archangel to his fallen soldiers.

"Sire." Aodhan inclined his head, the rain clouds that had begun to creep across the sunset doing nothing to dull the glittering shine of his hair.

"The injured?" Raphael asked.

"We're moving them all to dedicated floors inside the Tower. The transfer will be complete by midnight."

Raphael, his wings glowing in a silent testament to his rage, continued to stare at a city that had gone eerily silent. No horns blew, no brakes screeched, no one fought, the events of this day so nightmarish as to erase the petty problems of life.

"Status?" he asked after several minutes.

"Three hundred and fourteen required emergency medical intervention as a result of life-threatening injuries," Aodhan answered, "and will be down for months. The rest have broken bones, and most will need at least four weeks to recover."

Despite explanations, Elena didn't quite understand the drug used today, except that the closest human analog was epinephrine, though the two weren't identical. According to Montgomery, the drug was a last-ditch option, because while it could kick-start the self-healing process in a badly injured angel— when that angel's body might otherwise simply shut down—it had one very bad side effect: it extended the normal recovery time by months.

After seeing the stuff revive an angel who'd been all but decapitated, his head attached to his body by the gleaming wetness of his spinal column alone, and his lower body torn off to leave him a bloody stump, Elena didn't have any argument with the drug.

"The Tower-based healers were able to speak to a number of the injured who regained consciousness," Aodhan added, the world turning to twilight as the clouds succeeded in hiding the last rays of the sun. "They all report a sudden sense of dizziness, followed by unconsciousness before they could land."

Glancing at Aodhan when Raphael didn't respond, Elena spoke with her eyes. Unlike with Illium, her relationship with this member of Raphael's Seven was new yet, but he was one of the most empathic angels she'd ever met. Now, he gave a small nod and disappeared inside the Tower.

"Are you subverting another one of my men, Elena?" Raphael said into the quiet.

She came to stand beside him, their wings touching. An instant later, the rain clouds released their store of water in an unexpected deluge. It would, Elena thought, wash away the blood on the streets and the buildings, but the trauma of this day would never be erased. "I think nothing on this earth is capable of subverting your men." The Seven were as loyal to Raphael as hunters were to the Guild.

"But," she said, blinking the rain from her eyes as Raphael's wing rose over her in a protective curve, "I do have certain rights as your consort, including the right to stand with you against this thing, whatever it is."

His arm sliding around her waist, Raphael brought her against his body, the midnight strands of his hair even darker with the rain.

"I'm sorry, Raphael," she whispered, spreading the fingers of one hand over his heart, needing to feel the life of him as a ward against the awfulness of what had taken place. "I know an archangel can't be seen to grieve, but I know you grieve for the people you lost." Her own throat was thick, her eyes burning.

"They were under my protection," he said and it was all that needed to be said.

Elena didn't try to comfort him with words. She simply stood with him as the rain pounded over them both, cold and harsh as the death that had come so darkly to their city. Lightning burst in the distance, the roiling clouds turning the early evening into midnight. As if in defense, warm golden light began to flood the windows of every skyscraper within sight, but there was nothing eerie or "other" about this wild black storm. It was a simple, beautiful display of nature's power.

"Have you ever flown in something like this?" she asked, protected from the ferocious wind by the shelter of his muscled body, his wings.

"Yes." Raphael looked out over the downpour, the lights in the windows refracted by the hard rain coming in from the left. "It was above an island in what is now called the Pacific, the sky a rage of thunder, the lightning a violent dance. My friends and I, we made a game of dodging the strikes."

She wanted to smile at the image, but the wounds of the day were too raw to permit it. "An immortal game of chicken?"

"Perhaps." Blinking away the rain, he stepped back. "Come, we must see to the injured."

They stopped in at their Tower suite only long enough to dry off and change, before heading down to the infirmary. It made no difference that she'd already seen the damage—it was as bad now as it had been the first time. An angel with wings patterned like a sparrow's had lost most of his internal organs, his chest a gaping cavity, but at four hundred, he'd survived the damage and now slept in an induced coma that would help him heal.

Beside him was the near-decapitation victim, his life signs flickering. Kneeling beside the young male, Raphael placed his hand over the gruesome injury. Only Elena was close enough to see the faint blue glow that was an indication of Raphael's growing but nascent healing ability. He couldn't fix all the damage, but he could give the hurt man more of a fighting chance.

Two beds down lay an angel who'd lost both legs at the upper thigh and broken most of the remaining bones in his body, including those in his brutalized face. But whether through luck or through fate, his brain was still inside the cracked eggshell of his skull, his heart in his chest, his spine damaged but not fatally so—because Izak wouldn't have survived otherwise, being far too young to heal such trauma.

"Sorry! Sorry! I just got out of the Refuge. I—" A gulp. *"I wasn't supposed to tell you that! Please don't tell Raphael."*

Anger and worry combined into a knot in her throat at the memory of their first meeting. He'd been hanging upside down off the roof over the little balcony of her old apartment, all yellow curls and huge eyes as he tried to sneak a peek at a real-live hunter. To see someone so young and innocent lying broken and silent, his body a mass of bruised and torn flesh . . .

Elena wanted to do violence, make someone pay for this horror, but as of right now, they had no answers as to the origin of the nightmare, their enemy invisible.

3

It was well past the midnight hour when Raphael and his consort found their beds. He didn't need rest as Elena did, but she slept better if he was in the bed with her. When she woke to find herself alone—and she almost always woke in the middle of the night if he wasn't there—she came looking for him.

The first time it had happened, he'd thought she'd been wrenched from her rest by nightmare echoes of the horror that had ended her childhood, but she'd said she just missed him. Such simple words. Such powerful words. So now he slept with her, at least for certain critical hours of the night.

Tonight, though, neither one of them was ready to surrender to slumber. "Lijuan," she said at last, her head against his shoulder. "Are you thinking the same?"

"The possibility had occurred to me." The Archangel of China was rapidly becoming the Archangel of Death, her abilities touched with the putrefaction of a final ending that was without mercy or dignity, for all that she called herself a giver of eternal life.

Lijuan's version of life was a horrific shambling shell fed of human flesh.

"But?" Elena raised herself on her elbow so she could look down at him, the near-white strands of her hair brushing over his skin, a thousand fleeting caresses.

He spread his fingers on the warmth of her lower back, stroked along the delicate arch of her spine. His tough hunter was still so vulnerable in countless ways, could well have been among the fallen today, for it was the youngest who'd borne the brunt of the damage, and Elena was the youngest angel in the city.

"Jason," he said, crushing the thought before it could take damaging hold, "contacted me with a report an hour ago." His spymaster was currently on the other side of the world, but he'd spun into action within seconds of the deadly events in New York. "As always, he has ways of gathering information unavailable to the rest of us."

The fine rim of silver around Elena's irises glowed in the dark of their bedroom, a silent indicator of her growing immortality, though that immortality was not yet set in stone in any way. "What did he say?"

"That he knows for a fact Lijuan was in her own territory during the entire span of the Falling." Considering the certainty in his spymaster's tone, he added, "I have a strong suspicion Jason may have attained the impossible and tracked Lijuan to her innermost lair."

Elena sucked in a breath, and he saw she understood the danger. Should Jason be discovered, he wouldn't make it out alive; Lijuan knew too well how loyal the Seven were to Raphael. But, Raphael thought, his spymaster would take no unnecessary risks, not now, when Jason knew his loss would be a fatal wound on the heart of the princess who awaited his return.

"If it wasn't Lijuan"—dark realization in her eyes—"then . . ."

"Yes. The Cascade is apparently moving ahead with the speed of a—" He paused at Aodhan's mental touch. *A problem?* he asked the angel who, with Illium, was currently in charge of Tower operations.

The Archangel Caliane has informed me she wishes to speak to you, Sire.

I'll contact her from the house. Returning his attention to Elena, he touched the curve of her wing where the midnight feathers segued into indigo. "We might be about to get some answers," he said, telling her of Caliane's call. As the only Ancient who was awake and in the world, his mother knew much that had otherwise been lost to the pages of history.

"I'll stay out of view," Elena said when they reached the screen in his study, her skin glowing against the robe of cerulean silk he'd gifted her on the anniversary of her mortal birthday.

Irritation simmered to life in his blood. "Elena, you are my consort."

"You know how she gets," was her unshaken response where others would've quivered at the edge in his tone. "She'll be far more forthcoming if she's not feeling insulted by my presence." Leaning against the wall beside a framed piece of art, she blew him a kiss.

We'll discuss this later, he said and made the call. His mother continued to abhor technology for the most part, but she'd begun to accept the usefulness of certain aspects of the modern world. He hadn't expected otherwise; Caliane might prefer what she termed the more "civilized" mores of centuries gone, but she was an Ancient, and no one lived so long by miring herself in the dusty past.

Twin flames of blue on the screen, his mother's hair a river of black, her face the template used to cast his own. "Mother," he said, his heart yet unused to the fact that she breathed once more, that should he wish, he could fly to her, feel the touch of the hands that had rocked him in childhood . . . and left him broken on a bloody field far from civilization.

"Raphael, I have heard of the events in your city." Her fingers rose to the screen in a familiar gesture of love. "Your people?"

No other archangel would he have trusted with the truth, but for all that she'd done, his mother had never once backed anyone else against her son. "We mourn," he said quietly and saw the pain in her eyes.

It was from Caliane that he'd learned how an archangel should rule. Even when her madness distorted the truth of who she was, he'd never forgotten she was also the archangel whose people looked to her with love in their eyes. He wasn't Caliane—he inspired fear as often as not—but, like those who were hers, his men and women knew he'd fight with unrelenting fury to protect them.

"Five began their journey home this night." Raphael had led the flight out over the dark lick of the water until Manhattan was a silhouette far in the distance, Elena on one side and Nimra on the other. Every other angel in the city who could fly, but for the squadron needed to hold it secure, had been part of the silent cavalcade, and each had held a lantern that protected the candle within, lighting the way home.

Then they'd hovered in place as Nimra and the squadron he'd placed at her command pulled away into the starless night, the fallen carried in flower-covered biers that would reach the Refuge in twenty-four hours. It would've been faster to send the bodies home in a jet, but they were creatures of the wind and the sky, and so it was by the sky road that the fallen would return home.

"We mourn with you," Caliane said, a single tear rolling down her face. "I will send a squadron to the Refuge to act as an honor guard for those who are carried home."

"I thank you, Mother, but in this time of unrest, I believe you should keep your people near." Caliane remained Lijuan's most dangerous foe, and she had only two winged squadrons, having taken the people of Amanat alone into her Sleep.

Her expression altering from sorrow to one that betrayed an acute political intelligence, his mother sat back in her chair, her gown a vibrant turquoise that framed her dazzling beauty, until he could hardly believe the truth of her extraordinary age.

"I know you wish to ask me if I saw anything such as this in the previous Cascade," she said, "but I must tell you there was no Falling in my time." A sudden shadow across her expression, and he knew she thought of the madness she believed had touched her during that Cascade. "There were, however, other strange events."

Raphael waited while his mother thought. He knew the delay was no power play, no arrogant posturing. Caliane was simply very, very old, her memories hidden in long-forgotten corners of her mind.

"Once," she murmured into the silence, "an entire city of angels turned against each other for a single minute. Blows were exchanged, knives thrown—then everyone seemed to wake up and no one knew why they had acted so." A frown. "There were some who believed the chaos must have been caused by the use of a new archangelic ability, but there was never a repeat of the incident."

It was tempting to believe the Falling had been another such aberration, but—"I can't be complacent, not given the changes occurring in the Cadre."

"The one who dispenses death." Caliane's wings glowed a sudden, lethal, brightness. "She who styles herself an Ancient, you think she has a hand in this."

"It doesn't appear to be Lijuan's handiwork." Raphael's mind flickered with images of another time when his mother had glowed . . . during an execution that had broken her spirit and splintered their family. "But," he added, closing the lid on the memories of his father's violent death, "we've barely begun the hunt for answers."

"You will not permit this to keep you from my lands." It was an order.

He infused his response with unbending steel. "I'll make that decision when it is time." His mother had a way of forgetting that he was an archangel with a territory of his own.

Caliane's lips curved, the music in her voice reminding him of the songs she'd sung to him as a boy, songs that had held the Refuge in thrall. "You were always a stubborn child. The only way your father could get you to let go of anger, as an infant, was to scoop you up in his arms and take you flying. Oh, how you loved to fly with Nadiel." Love and a haunting sadness in her every word. "You always came back laughing, your hair wild and your cheeks red, my beautiful boy."

Raphael touched his fingers to the screen as she'd done, his heart aching for the losses that marked his mother. He didn't know if he could ever forgive her crimes, didn't even know if she was truly sane or if this was a fleeting lull, but he knew that he loved her. "I hope," he said as her fingers touched the screen on her end, "you will not tell such stories when we are in company."

Her laughter was a song, her eyes iridescent. "I promise you'll be a babe only in my eyes, always my son." Laughter fading into sadness once more, she said, "I am sorry, Raphael. To lose any of one's people is a deep sorrow."

Turning to Elena once the call had ended, he found her knuckling away a tear, his tough hunter whose shell was not so tough to those who knew her. *"Hbeebti."* He took her into his arms, the silk of her robe sliding over his skin.

"She loves you *so* much." Elena's whisper was rough, husky. "It's there in her every breath, every word. I can't imagine what it must do to her to know that she hurt you during her madness."

Raphael understood that his mother hadn't been in her right mind when she sent him plummeting to the earth, his wings shredded, but some part of him was still that broken boy who'd lain bleeding on the dew-drenched grass—as her feet danced away over the green blades speckled with viscous red. "I cannot forget."

"I know," Elena said, that painful understanding binding them on a level no one else would ever comprehend. "I know." Her mother had loved her, too, but Elena's most enduring memory of Marguerite was of her high-heeled shoe lying on its side on designer black and white tile.

Strange, how the memory of that shoe made her skin chill, her lungs struggle for air. But that was how it was. Some memories dug deeper, held on tighter.

"What happens now?"

"This city, my Tower, cannot be seen to be weak."

"Of course." Anything else might be taken as an invitation to conquer by certain others in the Cadre. "We have to convince them the Falling did far less damage than it actually did." Almost half of the Tower's defensive force was down for the foreseeable future: a staggering deficit.

"Yes." Raphael reached between them to tug open the tie of her robe, slide his hands inside. "As part of that," he said to her responsive shiver, "my consort must be seen to be indulging in her strange fetish for hunting vampires."

"Ha-ha." Undoing the buttons of the shirt he'd pulled on for the call, she pressed a kiss to the firm muscle of his chest. "I'll tell Sara not to strike me from the roster." Chasing delinquent vamps hardly seemed important in the wake of the tragedy that had befallen the city, but if it would help create the illusion of a Manhattan undamaged by the horror that had taken place in a few short minutes, then that was what she'd do.

She knew angelkind in general remained fascinated with her, the first angel Made in living memory *and* one who continued to hunt. According to what she'd heard from Illium, there were as many angels glued to news reports about her as there were humans and vampires. So why not use that notoriety to the city's advantage?

Raphael's hands stroked off her robe to leave her naked, her skin igniting under his touch. "You need to rest," she argued halfheartedly, a clawing need inside her to taste life in its most primal form. "You pushed your new ability to the limit in the infirmary."

Lips on hers, his mouth claiming everything she had. "There are," he said, backing her against the wall, "other ways of revitalizing the self."

Elena gasped as he lifted her, her legs locking around his waist to leave her intimately exposed.

He was hard and demanding that night, her archangel, his fury at the attack on his city a rage in his blood—but she was no fragile bird. Giving back kiss for passionate kiss, she took the pounding thrusts of his cock and demanded more, until there was no more thought, only the most beautiful firestorm of sensation.

Raphael had thought only to hold Elena close as she slept on the thick carpet in front of the study fireplace, their bodies and wings entangled, but he must have been more tired than he'd understood, because all at once, he realized he wasn't awake. Instead, he found himself on the forgotten field where Caliane had left him more than a thousand years ago, when he'd been a boy at the dawn of his existence.

A boy who'd thought to kill his mother before she became an even bigger monster than the one who had orchestrated the death of two thriving cities, the adults drowned, the children broken in ways even Keir, their greatest healer, couldn't repair. No immortal would go to the ancient ruins of those cities even now. There was too piercing a silence, created of the pain of thousands of souls, such silence as Raphael would never forget, the pain of it an icy wind.

Today, as he stood draped in a quiet heavy with the echo of memory, he saw blood on the grass, the crimson liquid that had dripped out of him as he lay splintered on the earth underneath a crystalline sky so blue it hurt. Yet he wasn't on his face on the grass as he'd been then, his wings torn and heavy on his body, parts of him missing. No, he stood on his feet and he was a man, an archangel, not that scared, determined, heartbroken boy.

Flexing his hands as if in readiness for battle, he took a step forward . . . and walked into a wall of whispers. Hundreds of voices, each one raspy and somehow unused, the words interlaced and incomprehensible. They came from every side, yet when he rose up into that sky of cutting clarity, he saw nothing but the gnarled bodies of the trees that surrounded the field, sentinels of such age that they had stood through eternity.

And still the voices whispered and murmured, pushing at him in waves that ebbed and flowed, until at last, he heard a single strong voice slice through the chaos. The other whispers died away, but did not fade altogether as that one voice asked him a question. *"Who are you?"*

Feet touching the grass once more, the dew wet on the very tips of his wings, he felt a roaring surge of anger. "Who are you to ask questions of an archangel?"

The murmurs rose again, the volume rising to a thunderous crescendo.

Archangel. Archangel. Archangel!

4

"Archangel." Elena gripped Raphael's shoulder, his skin strangely cool under her fingertips. "It's time to get up."

He always woke at her first touch, but today she had to call him a second time before his lashes lifted, the relentless blue of his eyes shadowed by a darkness that muted their vivid hue. "It's daylight," was the first thing he said, his gaze taking in the lacy streamers of light coming in through the study windows.

"You were in such a deep sleep, I thought I'd give you a few extra minutes." It was the only gift she could give; to protect an archangel was an impossibility. "It's barely dawn." Watching him get to his feet, this magnificent and lethal male who was her own, she rose and pulled on her robe. "You had an angry look on your face at the end. Bad dream?"

"Not bad so much as strange." He didn't speak again until they'd both showered and begun to dress, their bedroom drenched in dawn sunshine from the skylight and open balcony doors. "I dreamed of the field where I fought Caliane."

Tying off her braid, she busied herself checking her cross-bow, though she saw nothing of the weapon, every ounce of her being concentrated on Raphael. He spoke rarely about that agonizing day, and she hadn't pushed him, because the whole "time heals all wounds" thing? It was a load of bullshit. "Was your mother in the dream?"

"No." Walking to the balcony, his upper body bare, he spread his wings as if soaking in the sun's rays, the golden filaments hidden in the white sparking with a fire so brilliant, Elena found herself brushing her fingers along the living silk.

"What do you see, Elena?"

"There's a kind of fire in your feathers now." She almost expected to capture a piece of piercing white flame in her hand. "It's incredibly beautiful."

Raphael glanced at his wing, shrugged. "So long as they work." Folding them in, he turned to pick up one of her throwing blades and slid it into the sheath on her left arm. "The dream was not . . . what it should be," he said, as she made a minor fix to one of the sheath straps. "Of course, yesterday was no ordinary day. It's not inexplicable that I should dream of violence."

"It could be that simple." Elena held out her right forearm, sheath in place, so he could slide in the other throwing blade. "But I've seen way too much freaky stuff since you first summoned me to do your bidding to take anything at face value."

"You were abysmal at doing my bidding." It was a cool reminder. "I thought you the most fascinating creature I had ever met."

"You did not." She pointed a gleaming knife at him before slotting it into a thigh sheath strapped over her slimline black leather pants, her clothing designed to reduce drag in the air. "You thought I was a nuisance you might have to throw off the side of the building in order to teach me manners." As it was, he'd made her close her hand over a blade, her blood dripping to stain the roof, a being so terrifying she'd seen nothing of humanity in him. "You were kind of a bastard, if we're being brutally honest."

Lips curving, he picked up the long, thin blade she wore hidden along her back in a sheath built into her long-sleeved black top, the fabric tough enough to take the demands of a hunter's life. "You," he said, sliding the blade into place when she turned, "are the only individual who would ever say that to my face."

"Remind me to tell you sometime about how I decided I should get *Big Idiot* tattooed on my forehead." Facing him once more, she smoothed her hands over his gorgeous shoulders. "And what does it say about me that I thought *you* were fascinating and sexier than sin, even after you made me cut myself?"

"That you're a warrior who knew she'd finally met her match."

Elena snorted. "It says I'm a dumbo who doesn't know when to be meek and subservient and save my ass, that's what it says."

Smile deepening until his cheeks creased with it, Raphael curved one hand around her nape, using the fingers of his other to caress the sensitive upper arch of her wing with long, firm strokes. "Had you been meek and subservient," he murmured as her knees threatened to melt, "I would've never summoned you to do my bidding."

His kiss threatened to finish what his strokes had begun. Licking her tongue against his, her breasts crushed against the hard muscle of his chest, Elena wanted nothing more than to stay in this stolen minute, to forget the outside world, but the ugly reality that awaited couldn't be ignored.

"I've been away from the Tower for over six hours," Raphael said when they drew apart, his expression shifting in a way that reminded her he wasn't simply her lover, wasn't simply the man who wore her ring on his finger. No, he was an archangel, responsible for the lives of millions, mortals and immortals alike.

"Finish dressing." Releasing him, she headed for the door. "I'll bring up some food. You need to refuel after all the healing you did."

By the time she returned, the transformation was complete, the Archangel of New York a grim-eyed power beside her as they ate standing on the balcony. He'd chosen to wear a simple black shirt and pants, the cut pristine, rather than the leather combat gear he often chose. All part of the illusion, she realized, an elegant "fuck you" to whoever had dared attack his city and harm his people.

Elena watched him slice through the biting cold of the wind

only minutes later, the early morning sunlight sparking white fire off the altered filaments in his wings, and felt her heart tighten in a deep, chill fear. Never had she expected to find him, to fall so deeply, wildly, insanely in love—and sometimes, her soul-deep joy in their passionate entanglement terrified her, the fear of losing him as she'd lost her sisters, her mother, a stealthy intruder in her mind.

After yesterday, that intruder had forced its way to the forefront of her consciousness.

Fingernails digging into her palms, she returned to the bedroom to pick up her phone. She didn't currently have an active assignment, but she could put in some time teaching a class at Guild Academy—not as high visibility as a hunt, but perfect in its utter normality. However, as part of her contribution to Raphael's "fuck you," she stopped at a rooftop coffee stand set up by a human shrewd enough to realize angels liked coffee, too.

She made herself laugh at the barista's joke, heard phone cameras clicking quietly as the businesspeople from the building took advantage of her proximity to update their social media pages. *Take that and smoke it,* she thought to the unknown enemy who'd caused such carnage and loss. *You might have managed to kill five of us, but you haven't come close to breaking this city.*

Anger a rock in her throat as she thought of the biers even now on their way to the Refuge, she took off in a showy sweep that ignited more photo taking, the coffee held in hand.

The head trainer at Guild Academy was more than happy to have her take the advanced crossbow class, the staff used to adjusting the schedule to take advantage of active hunters who had some downtime.

Lesson complete, she'd just walked onto the roof in preparation for takeoff toward Guild HQ when her phone rang. "Eve," she said with a smile, "I was just thinking we needed to talk." Much to Jeffrey's anger and disgust—the damn hypocrite—Elena's youngest half sister was also hunter-born.

"E-Ellie, can you c-come now?" Sobs in Eve's usually ebullient voice.

Smile fading, Elena said, "Are you at school?" Both Evelyn

and her older sister, Amethyst, had been boarders at a private school upstate until the bloody events there this past spring. It was in the aftermath that Eve's hunting abilities had come to light, leading to a transfer to a private school closer to Guild Academy. Amethyst had chosen to come with her.

Eve sniffed. "Y-yes. I'm hiding."

"I'm on my way."

Her sister must've been watching for Elena from her hiding place, because she ran from around the imposing redbrick building just as Elena landed on the manicured lawn out front.

Eve had turned eleven a week earlier, but she appeared much younger today, her face blotchy, her sobs deep and silent and heartbreaking. "Sweetheart," Elena said, waving off a teacher who'd appeared on the front steps.

The suit-clad older man frowned but returned through the heavy wooden doors carved with some kind of a crest.

Gathering Eve's school-uniform-clad body in her arms, Elena gritted her teeth and achieved a vertical takeoff through sheer strength of will. According to every known fact of angelic development, she shouldn't have been capable of the maneuver yet, her body not having formed the necessary musculature, but the idea of being grounded and helpless was untenable—so she'd learned to lift. It wasn't graceful, and it *hurt*, but she could do it.

She caught the excitement at the school's windows as they passed. Good. No one would tease Eve for her tears now; the other students would be more interested in her stories of flight. "It's okay," she said when Eve, realizing her feet were no longer on the ground, clutched at her. "I've got you."

A few more sniffles before her sister began to crane her neck to see around Elena's wings, her hair whipping in the wind. By the time they landed at the Enclave house, her face was gleeful, cheeks happily windburned.

"If you're going to play hooky," Elena said, relieved to see Eve's tough spirit rising to the surface, "do it in style."

That got her a bright-eyed grin, the gray of Eve's irises a stamp Jeffrey had put on them both. "Can we do that again?"

"After we have a snack. Come on." Walking past the house, dead certain Montgomery wouldn't let her down, she took Eve to her greenhouse.

"Oooh." Eve touched her fingers to the petals of a wildly blooming daisy inside the heated enclosure. "Did you grow this?"

"Yep. You should see this one."

It was only three minutes later that Montgomery proved her faith in him once again.

"Hot chocolate and cakes for your guest, Guild Hunter," he said, placing the tray he carried on the little wrought-iron table Elena had situated in a cozy corner the first time Sara came to visit.

"Thank you," she said, aware of Eve standing politely by her side, hands folded in front of her. "I don't think you've met my youngest sister, Evelyn." Of her three living sisters, only Beth had been to the Angel Enclave house and she'd been so overawed she hadn't spoken a peep the entire time. "Eve, this is Montgomery."

An elegant bow. "Miss Evelyn."

Eyes wide, Eve stuck out her hand. "Hi."

Elena had never seen Montgomery shake anyone's hand. Expecting him to be scandalized by the idea, she found herself charmed instead at the solemnity with which he accepted Eve's hand.

"If you need anything further," he said, after the formalities were over, "I will be at the house."

Wiggling into one of the chairs at the table after the door closed behind Montgomery, Eve leaned in close to whisper, "Was he a butler?"

"The best one you'll ever meet." Picking up the gorgeous little teapot, Elena poured hot chocolate into delicate cups she'd never before seen, the edges curlicued and the white china surface painted with tiny pink flowers.

Perfect for a young girl.

"Wow. We have a housekeeper, but I don't know anybody who has a *butler*."

Elena grinned, thinking of her own reaction the first time she'd seen Montgomery, and put a cupcake on Eve's plate, the frosting swirls of yellow decorated with crystallized violets. "Now," she said, once her sister had finished the confection, "tell me what made you cry." She'd never have been so direct with Beth, but Eve was built tougher, for all that she was a child.

Face falling, her sister pushed a crumb around her plate. "I feel dumb now. I shouldn't have called you—I know you must be sad and busy because of the Falling." She squashed the crumb, staring at it as if it were the most important thing on the planet. "I was scared you'd fallen, and Amy was, too. Thanks for messaging me back."

"No thanks needed." Elena reached over to tuck the deep black strands of Eve's hair behind her ears. "Remember what I said? I'm always here for you." The angry bitterness between her and Jeffrey might've kept her a stranger from her half siblings for most of their lives, but that was a mistake Elena would never again make. "It was nice to get your message yesterday, and I'm glad you called me today."

A hiccuping breath, and Eve looked up, eyes huge and wet. "I know I shouldn't have, but this morning I told Father about how I aced an exercise at the Academy."

Elena's stomach twisted. She knew what was coming, but she listened anyway, because Eve needed to release the poison before it could fester—as it'd festered in Elena and in Jeffrey, until it'd worn a jagged hole through the once-strong fabric of their relationship.

"He's always so proud when I do well at school," Eve continued. "I thought he'd be proud of this, too . . . even though I know he hates hunters." Lower lip trembling, she swallowed. "I thought if I could make him happy, then maybe he'd be nice to you, too, except h-he told me to get out of his sight."

"Oh, Eve." Chest aching for her sister's hurt, she went around the table to kneel beside Eve's chair.

Sobbing in earnest now, Eve threw her arms around Elena, her face wet against Elena's neck. Elena said nothing, simply stroked her sister's back, let her cry out the pain. It was better this way. As a child, Elena had swallowed her own pain again and again until it had become a knot inside her she wasn't sure anything could unravel.

Some wounds were inflicted too young, scarred too deep.

It took time, but Eve finally cried herself out. Wiping her sister's cheeks with a napkin she dampened using water from the small jug Montgomery had left on the table, Elena kissed each in turn. "Jeffrey hurt you, and he has no right to do that, no matter if he's your father." Even as she spoke, she knew she had to tread carefully, make sure her scars didn't color Eve's view of Jeffrey.

Because notwithstanding the bastard he'd become as far as Elena was concerned, he'd apparently been a good if remote father to Eve and Amy. Not the same man who'd thrown Elena into the air as a child and danced with his first wife in the rain—that part of him was buried in the same grave as Marguerite—but a father Eve and Amy could rely on nonetheless.

Elena would never do anything to damage that bond, not when she knew what it did to a child to be estranged from the man who was meant to protect her at her most innocent and vulnerable. "The truth is," she said gently, her wings spread on the greenhouse floor as she continued to kneel beside Eve's chair, "Jeffrey's not rational on this one thing."

I have no desire to house an abomination under my roof.

Words Jeffrey had thrown at her during the final, ugly fight that had destroyed the last, brittle threads of the bond that had once tied them together.

"But *why*?" Eve fisted her hands, jaw jutting out as she asked the one question Elena had never been able to answer. "If I'm hunter-born and you're hunter-born, doesn't that mean that Father must be hunter-born, too?"

5

"No," Elena said, answering the question she could, "it means someone in his family was, and he carries the genes for it." A fact he'd consciously hidden from Elena until the emergence of Eve's ability had thrown a grenade onto that particular secret. "But the ability isn't active in him, like it is in me and you. Do you understand?"

A thoughtful nod, frown lines marring the creamy skin Eve had inherited from Jeffrey's second wife, Gwendolyn. "Like he's asleep and we're awake."

"Yes." Elena got to her feet, spreading her wings in a light stretch that had the white-gold primaries grazing a pot of chrysanthemums in bloom. "I think that's a good way to put it." However, their father couldn't keep on being asleep, continue his willful, damaging blindness. Elena would *not* allow him to hurt Eve as he'd hurt her.

"He might never understand, right, Ellie?" Eve said with her customary openness of nature a few minutes later, as they got ready to leave. "That's why he's always so mad at you."

Elena squeezed her sister's hand, her calluses encountering

the ones just beginning to form on Eve's soft palms. "Jeffrey and I," she said, "have other problems."

Slater Patalis had been drawn to their suburban home because of Elena. Until that awful, cruel day a lifetime ago, they'd been a family of six. Jeffrey, Marguerite, and their four girls. Mirabelle, with her hot blood and wild affection. Ariel, even tempered and bossy and protective. Elena, who wanted to do everything her older sisters did, and Beth, too young to truly remember now who they'd been together before Slater Patalis walked through the kitchen door.

Where the murderous vampire had butchered Ari and Belle in a horrifying reign of blood, tortured their mother over and over . . . tortured the woman who was, and would always be, Jeffrey's greatest love. Beth hadn't been home, but Elena had. And though it was all her fault, *she* was the one who'd survived.

"He loves you," Elena said, as the memories bruised her from within, hoping she wasn't about to lie to her sister. "It might take him time, but he'll accept your hunting."

Dropping Eve back at school and taking responsibility for her absence, Elena flew straight to the tony brownstone Jeffrey used as a private office, only to find it closed, his assistant nowhere in evidence. Figuring her father would call her soon enough, Elena didn't bother to slide a note under the door and headed toward Guild HQ. Once again, her phone rang before she made it there. Answering in the air, she found Sara on the other end.

"Ellie, I know you probably can't take this with what happened yesterday, but—"

"I'm actually on my way to see you, wanted to ask if you had a hunt for me."

"Good, because we have a serious problem." Taking an audible breath, she said, "One of our hunters has gone off the rails. We might be talking murder if we don't stop him."

Elena landed on a nearby roof, her pulse suddenly in her mouth, her palms clammy, Sara's words having unlocked a hidden vault: Bill James had been a celebrated hunter, Elena's mentor . . . and a serial killer. One so good at hiding his crumbling psyche that none of his friends had realized what was happening until the first dead child. "Who?" she asked, throat raw.

"Darrell Vance." Relief that it wasn't a friend had Elena lifting a trembling hand to her face. Perhaps it wasn't fair or right to feel this way, but she'd already had to execute one friend, would never forget the look of betrayal in Bill's eyes as he died in her arms, his blood hot on her skin.

"Ellie." Confusion in his voice. "Why, Ellie?"

Sara's voice broke into a memory that still woke her up some nights, mouth full of cotton wool and the words "I'm sorry" on her lips.

"Darrell had a hunt go seriously bad," Sara told her. "Vamp had second thoughts after being Made, went back to the mortal family he'd left, only to find his wife had remarried and another man was now raising his son."

Elena had seen this script before. "He killed the husband."

"No, that would've been bad, but—" When Sara had to pause as if girding herself for what was to come, dread began to crawl up Elena's spine. "He tore out the husband's throat, then tied up his son and wife, wrapped them in his arms, and set himself on fire."

Oh, Jesus.

"Darrell found them while they were still burning, tried to put out the flames, but you know how vamps burn. It's like they're doused in petrol."

Elena had once witnessed a vampire burn as a result of a hate crime. It had been horrific, the smell of roasting meat threatening to make her retch as she tried frantically to beat out the flames. But to find a woman and child in the mix? Her stomach twisted. "Darrell's fallen off the radar?"

"Yes. The way this went down wasn't his fault—he did the track in record time—but his head's probably so messed up, he can't see that. As it is, he attacked an innocent vampire and put him in the hospital two nights ago; a couple more punches and he'd have fatally damaged the heart. I found out a half hour ago when the vamp woke up."

Vampires might be strong, but an average untrained one didn't stand a chance against a member of the Guild. "Have you contacted the Slayer?" Elena asked, referring to the often anonymous hunter whose task it was to hunt those of the Guild gone bad.

"She took a bad injury in a recent situation, is out of commission. This one we'll have to handle without her—Ransom is lead; he has the sketchy details we have so far, and I know he wants you as his backup." An unspoken acknowledgment of the bond that had formed between them the day Bill died. "As it is, he's just come across something that'll probably need to be referred to the Tower, so you'll be doing double duty."

Raphael glanced at the mortal news channel running on one wall of his Tower office and smiled. It wasn't a smile of humor, but of pride. His consort had done exactly as he'd asked, the media mystified by the apparent nonchalance with which she'd bought a cup of coffee that morning. Pundits who'd the previous day termed the Falling a catastrophic disaster were now beginning to question their judgment. More and more often, he heard it being termed an accident of some kind that had "fortunately not caused lasting harm."

"Elena certainly knows how to leave an impression," Dmitri said on the other end of the phone, having been watching the same news feed.

Raphael's second and his consort had never seen eye to eye, for to Dmitri, Elena was a lethal chink in Raphael's armor, but today he heard grim admiration in the vampire's tone. "If we can continue to manipulate the media," he said, switching the screen to silent, "and maintain a stranglehold on any news that leaves the Tower, we can convince the enemy that the five we lost represent the only real damage." Those five would be halfway home by now, crossing over the blue-green span of a mercurial sea.

"Acknowledge a few serious injuries, or allow that information to leak." Dmitri spoke with the icy intelligence that made him a master strategist. "It'll take care of the images already out there of angels who fell into traffic or were otherwise publicly injured, and it'll explain the healers. Illium's very good at whispering the right words in the right ears."

Raphael sent the instruction to the blue-winged angel as he continued to speak to Dmitri, his eyes on the glittering steel and glass metropolis that was Manhattan. "We need to quietly bring in troops from outlying areas." No enemy who wanted to be taken seriously in the immortal world would launch an attack at any target but the Tower—in the game of archangels, to conquer was to strike at one another's base of power.

"I need you to assist Aodhan in organizing that shift." Aodhan was yet new to the territory, having previously been Galen's right hand in the Refuge. "I have Illium focusing on creating new working squadrons." With so many angels down, the current squadrons had become unbalanced in critical areas.

"Sire, do you wish me to return to the city?"

"No," Raphael said, conscious Dmitri's wife was still regaining her strength after her transformation from mortal to vampire. "Your continued absence serves my purpose for the time being." Everyone knew Dmitri was the oldest of Raphael's Seven, the one Raphael considered a friend. "When the war breaks, I'll want you by my side, but that time isn't now."

Not quite yet.

Elena landed in front of an old-fashioned two-story villa set in the middle of a derelict street twenty minutes after her call from Sara and stared. Surrounded by tall weeds and smothered in ivy on one side, the building in front of her could've stood in as the prototypical haunted house; in point of fact, the entire street had escaped any attempt at modernization. Even the streetlamps were wrought iron, the frames rusted, the glass cracked to splinter the pavement, not a single electrical or telephone wire in sight.

That was hardly surprising in a city filled with angels and vampires, not all of whom embraced change. If, however, this place belonged to an immortal or almost-immortal, it had been permitted to fall into remarkable disrepair. The older ones who liked to keep things the way they'd been at some point in the past, took great pride in maintaining the historical detail and beauty of their properties.

It didn't appear anyone had touched this house for decades. The paint, which might've once been white, was peeling and blackened from the dust of the city streets, the windows shattered, the eaves hung with cobwebs thick and sticky, the curtains within rotten shreds from what she could see from her position on the street. The wood itself was warped out of shape, until the house couldn't be in any way weather-tight—and an unusually tall tree had fallen onto part of the roof, caving in one side of the house.

"What the hell is this place?" she said to Ransom when he appeared from the other side of the porch.

Green eyes vivid against skin of copper-gold, he raised an eyebrow. "Are you talking about this multimillion-dollar piece of real estate?"

"Seriously?"

"When's the last time land went for sale in Manhattan?" he asked, shrugging wide shoulders hugged by the battered black leather of his motorcycle jacket, his legs encased in old blue jeans over scuffed heavy-duty boots. "This entire street is one parcel. Developers have fucking public orgasms dreaming about getting their paws on it."

Elena whistled. "Someone's sitting on a gold mine."

"He was. Now he's dead."

Heart slamming against her ribs, she jerked her attention from the rotting house next door. "Not—"

"No, it wasn't Darrell, but it's someone the Tower's going to be interested in." Ransom's blade-sharp cheekbones cut against his skin as he said, "We need to clear this fast and continue with the hunt."

Agreeing, she walked gingerly up the front steps, not trusting them not to collapse and dump her on her ass. "How do we get in?" Front door was boarded up, the nails corroded and the wood obscene with graffiti.

Angling his head to the left, the glossy black tail of his hair tied at the nape of his neck with a strip of rawhide, Ransom led her around the house. "Your angel friends okay? That young blond one who follows you around like a big, goofy puppy?"

Stabbing pains in her stomach, her mind rebelling against the brutal images of Izak's torn-off legs, his flayed skin. "He's hurt bad."

"Shit. He's just a kid."

Elena's throat knotted as she thought of the other young soldier who hadn't survived, whose family even now held vigil for the return of his body. "The angel you rescued from in front of the truck?" she said, forcing herself not to give in to useless anger. "It'll take time, but she'll heal."

Ransom blew out a jagged breath. "I didn't think she'd make it. She was . . ." He shook his head. "I had to collect her arm from under the tires, Ellie." Gesturing for her to take care over a broken board, he said, "What I found today? It's going to add to the shitpile."

Fuck. The city didn't need any further problems. "You tracked Darrell here?"

"Darrell didn't go loco right after that clusterfuck with the mother and the kid," was the surprising answer. "He came in, had counseling, said all the right things, and was assigned a slam-dunk retrieval to ease him back into things."

Reading between the lines, Elena realized the counselor had known something was off and asked for Darrell to be kept within reach.

"Vamp who owned this place was his assigned target." Ransom drew his guns from the shoulder holsters he wore under his jacket, the action deadly silent. "I figured I might as well use him as a starting point for the track, since Darrell did send in a report to say he was on the guy's trail."

Elena had her throwing blades in hand when they turned the corner. Half of the back wall was just gone, leaving a gaping entrance filled with street detritus, dead leaves, discarded hypodermic needles, and other things she didn't want to think about too deeply. Trying to keep her wings from trailing in the crap, she took a step inside . . . and a rat as big as a goddamn cat scurried over her boot.

Biting back her instinctive scream, she glared at Ransom—who was very conspicuously *not* grinning. "You couldn't warn me?"

"You're a tough-ass hunter who gets naked with a freaking archangel, has a miniature flamethrower—which, by the way, you should leave to me in your will—and a crossbow, all within easy reach." His cheeks creased, eyes glinting. "Rats quiver at your presence."

"Now I remember why you're only an almost-friend."

"Oh, Ellie, you wound me." He paused. "Did you stop and get the masks?"

"Yeah." Reaching into a side pocket of her pants, she passed him a collapsible mask. Like her, he was hunter-born, his sense of smell acute.

"Thanks." He pulled it on over his mouth and nose, tightened the elastic band. "Smell's worse upstairs."

Since it reeked down here—a disgusting miasma of droppings, spoiled food, and urine—Elena didn't waste any time following his lead. Tugging out a pair of latex gloves from another pocket as Ransom did the same, she nodded at him to lead, and they skirted past what looked like the mummified body of a feral cat, and out of the kitchen.

The hallway beyond was narrow enough that Elena had to lean slightly to the right to avoid scraping her wing over the dark brown thickness smeared on the wall, all her air coming in through her mouth now . . . because her brain had identified the major component of the putrid stink as that of a decomposing corpse.

6

Stopping at the foot of the narrow staircase that ran along one wall, Ransom murmured, "Keep to the left and wait till I'm at the top, then come up."

The stairs creaked under his weight, again under Elena's, but held.

Guns out, Ransom led her down the upstairs hallway and into a room so pungent with death her stomach would've revolted if she hadn't steeled herself against the gag reflex. The second slap was of humidity, something about the way the room was built acting to trap what little heat there was . . . and accelerate the decomposition process.

Immediately identifying the filthy mattress below the boarded-up windows as the source of the scent of putrefaction, Elena walked across, trusting Ransom to watch her back. The body was bloated with the gases of death, skin a sickly green, but the head remained attached to the neck, and the shirt-clad chest was unmolested, judging from a surface glance. That meant his heart was likely still inside his body.

Going down on her knee, Elena blinked rapidly to dry out

eyes that threatened to water from the pulsing waves of smell, ignored the maggots, and peeled back the corpse's lip.

Canines, sharp and gleaming white.

"He isn't a baby vamp," she said through gritted teeth, "so this isn't a Making gone bad."

"Look at the throat."

Wings rustling against God knew what on the dirty floor, she retrieved the slimline flashlight she kept tucked alongside the knife on her left thigh and pointed the beam at the victim's neck. "Hell." Thick pustules filled with bloody fluid covered the male's throat, all the way to the open collar of his shirt . . . and down.

"Smell's getting to me, Ellie," Ransom said, just as her own stomach began to churn.

"Me, too."

They both ripped off their masks to take deep gulps of the crisp winter air the instant they hit the street. Gloves went next, Elena's skin itching to breathe. When Ransom retrieved a couple of bottles of water from the panther-black body of his motorcycle, throwing her one, she took it with a nod of thanks.

"Vampires aren't supposed to get sick," he said, after emptying half the bottle.

Splashing some water into one hand, Elena wiped it over her face, knowing it would take multiple showers to get that foul smell out of her nose. "No, they're not."

"Chop off their heads, they die," Ransom continued. "Set them on fire, or cut out their hearts, they die unless they're strong and *old* old. But soon as they're Made, they don't get sick. One thing's for sure—Darrell definitely didn't have anything to do with this."

Elena agreed. "I'm going to have to bring in a consult from the Tower." One of the more experienced angels or vampires; maybe there *was* a weird vamp virus that got a minority of them and she simply didn't know about it. "Whoever it is will probably ask you to sign a nondisclosure agreement in blood."

Ransom pretended to plump up a vein while she made the call to Aodhan. "I think this is serious," she said to the angel, after describing the situation. "Ransom and I need to continue our hunt—can you spare someone to guard the body until it can be moved to a morgue?"

Aodhan asked her to give him five minutes but it was almost fifteen minutes later that he personally escorted another angel to the site. A bare five foot six and slender as a boy, the unexpected angel's uptilted eyes were a gentle brown, his lips lush in a face saved from near-feminine prettiness by the sense of sheer maleness that clung to Keir.

Her frustration at the wait dissolving into deep affection, she leaned down into Keir's kiss on the cheek. "You must have left the Refuge as soon as it happened." *It*. The Falling. An awful malice reduced to two simple words.

"Raphael had a jet prepared for me so I would not be tired upon my arrival," he told her, eyes painfully wise. "It was strange to fly in the belly of a metal creature when I have wings of my own, but he was right."

When Aodhan was unexpectedly recalled to the Tower a second later, Elena remained at the house to watch Keir's back, while Ransom continued to circle out from the house, searching for any sign that Darrell had made it this far. Stomach muscles clenched against the noxious stink, Elena led Keir to the corpse, where the healer examined it in silence, not saying a word until they were back out on the deserted street.

"A true infection." Troubled darkness in the lush brown of his eyes. "I must autopsy the body under better lighting, see if I can pinpoint how the infection was introduced into his body."

"Ransom and I were talking before you arrived, and we thought maybe the victim drank from the wrong person."

His expression grew darker, even more serious. "The bodies of our blood kin," Keir said, "are built to filter out impurities in blood—that is why a vampire can feed from any donor, even the most diseased." Strands of silky black hair fell across his dusky skin as he looked at the ground, lost in thought. "If that mechanism failed . . ."

A sudden brilliance of blue, Illium landing in front of her. Having contacted her while Keir looked over the body, he'd brought a body bag to transport the victim to the research labs underneath the Tower, a small biohazard container for her, as well as better masks and replacement gloves, and didn't argue when she made him use the safety gear.

"This house needs to be burned to the ground," he said when he returned with the body, his expression harsher than most people ever saw. "We can't take the risk that the cause of the infection might lie within."

Sensing Keir was anxious to examine the body, and aware Raphael had to need Illium, she told the blue-winged angel she'd take care of the situation and made a call to Ransom as soon as they lifted off. "I'm going to do a final run through the house." After which she had an idea about its destruction. "I need to finish this"—stop the disease here if it hadn't already spread—"so if you want to—"

"No, it's okay," he interrupted. "I'll join you. Trail's so dead it's in rigor—don't think Darrell made it this far. Background report should come in soon, so we'll have a better idea of other places he might frequent; may as well try to figure out what happened here in the meantime."

Freshly gloved and masked, she and Ransom went through the entire place one more time, looking for anything that might provide a clue. "Why did you say this track was a slam-dunk?" she asked, placing the hypodermic needles she'd noticed earlier into the biohazard container.

"Vamp wasn't a runner. He just got homesick every so often—his angel would give him three or four days, then send a hunter to pick him up." The quiet pity in his tone resonated with the same emotion inside Elena. "Records say he never resisted, was always polite and apologetic and full of stories about his plans to renovate the house."

It was a poignant image, of a harmless man who hadn't deserved death. As the five angels Nimra's squadron carried home in flower-strewn biers hadn't deserved it. Embers of anger burning slow and dark inside her, she didn't reply and the two of them finished the rest of the sweep in silence.

"I have to agree with the pretty boy—house needs to be toast," Ransom said, once they were back out in front of the dilapidated villa.

"You're calling Illium a pretty boy?" Elena snorted, glad to focus on something other than the heavy cloud of death that hung over the city. "Have you looked in the mirror lately?"

"I have scars, like any respectable male."

"Tough guy." Staring at the house where a vampire had died in what she hoped was a quick death, she put her hands on her hips. "Think Sara would be pissed if we just set it on fire and said 'oops' when the fire department arrived?"

"I don't think she's forgiven you for the whole being-chased-by-a-vampire-through-Manhattan incident." He rubbed his jaw. "Arson would make a good cover story, though. It's just the kind of place some firebug would light up."

An hour later and thanks to Sara's connection to every agency in the city, the house underwent a controlled burn initiated by the fire department. If only, Elena thought, they could as quickly erase the threat posed by a disease that had decimated the cells of a near-immortal.

Having flown to the Tower to drop off the biohazard container, Elena took the chance to duck into her and Raphael's private suite to shower and change. Ransom had roared off to do the same—not only were they stabbing blindly in the dark with the background report still MIA, neither one of them would be much good at sneaking up on a fellow hunter with the stink that clung to their clothes and skin.

"Might as well wear a bell," had been Ransom's succinct assessment.

She'd just finished scrubbing her hair and body clean several times over when her cell phone rang, Jeffrey's name on the screen. Grabbing fresh gear from the clothing she kept at the Tower, she let the call go to voice mail, having no intention of hashing this out over the phone.

Once dressed, her hair braided and her weapons in place, she got in touch with Ransom. "Do you need me right this sec?"

"No, I want to check out a tip on my own."

Figuring he needed to connect with one of his street contacts, wary people who trusted Ransom alone, she agreed to meet up with him at an Upper East Side address in an hour

and, walking out to the balcony, flew off into the cold wind
coming off the water. She'd spoken to Raphael while she'd been
in the shower, so she knew he was heading back to the Tower
over that water, Aodhan by his side and two integrated squadrons at his back, having just completed a critical drill.

Preparation, Elena thought, for an unprovoked and already
ugly war.

Words that might as well apply to her relationship with
Jeffrey.

The woman who opened the door to the brownstone office
had skin of gleaming mahogany, her hair cut in a glossy bob
and her body encased in a neat skirt-suit of jewel green. Nothing at all like the vamp-addicted brunette who'd been Jeffrey's
last assistant, her skin pale from too many donations in too
short a time.

"Do you have an appointment?" the current PA asked, her
throat moving as she swallowed.

"No. Tell Mr. Deveraux I'll wait for him in the back garden."
As she made her way to that tiny green enclosure through a
narrow access path, her mind filled with images of another
brownstone, another door. Sara and Deacon had changed the
layout and size of their house so that Elena would feel welcome,
and yet her own father had done exactly nothing to ensure the
same. Not that Elena was surprised, only furious at herself for
continuing to permit him to wound her.

Jeffrey appeared in the back doorway as she arrived.
"Elieanora. I have a meeting in five minutes." Curt impatience
in eyes of pale gray set in an aristocratic face and hidden behind
spectacles framed in fine gold, his pure white hair combed with
neat perfection, his stone gray suit sitting easily on his
shoulders.

No doubt, her father was a handsome man, the kind of confident male irresistible to women young and naïve enough to think
they could penetrate his icy exterior. He'd have no trouble finding another mistress to take the place of the one who'd been
brutally murdered during the hunt that had forever altered Elena's
life. Perhaps he'd already done so, already replaced the woman
who'd looked nothing like the elegant beauty who was Jeffrey's
current wife. No, the poor woman had been a pale imitation of

Marguerite . . . and a living symbol of the pain her father had never once acknowledged aloud after those first brutal days.

Instead he'd wiped Marguerite from their home in what Elena now understood had been a cold rage. His wife had betrayed him the day she wrapped that noose around her throat, and Jeffrey was still so *angry* at her for it. Elena could've forgiven him that rage, but what she couldn't forgive was that he'd thrown one of Marguerite's children out with the trash, too.

"You know why I'm here," she said, fighting to remain calm, to not be reduced to the level of a screaming teenager.

"You had no authority to take Eve out of school."

"Stop. I am not doing this dance with you today." She kept speaking despite the chill of his eyes. "The reason I went to Eve was that she was hiding in a corner crying."

Skin white over bone, a tic in his jaw.

"You know why," she said, merciless in her love for a sister who was yet an innocent. "She's your baby, and you told her to get out of your sight?" Elena made no attempt to hide her disgust. "You don't get to do that, Jeffrey, not to her. She thinks you hung the fucking moon!"

"Watch the language," he snapped, hands still in the pockets of his suit pants. "And my daughter is none of your concern."

"She's my sister, you bastard. Same blood, remember?" Voice vibrating with old anger that threatened to savage her intention to remain rational, she didn't back down. "You *made* us, and you know what, I don't even care anymore." It was a lie she wished would become the truth. "But Eve, she cares. So grow a pair and *be a man*."

"Elieanora!" Striding across the grass, he grabbed her shoulders and shook hard enough to make her teeth rattle. "I'm still your father and you will not talk to me that way. Marguerite taught you better than that."

It was the first time in over a decade that she'd heard him say her mother's name and for an instant, they both froze, before fury ignited in her blood. "Don't you dare bring her into this! You chose to stop being my father a long time ago."

Fingers digging into her shoulders, he ground out his next words. "I will always be your father . . . and I wish to God I wasn't."

Flinching at the vicious emotional blow, she finally remembered her hunter training and wrenched away, her wing smacking hard against his body as she twisted. "Yeah, me, too." How could he do this every time? Cut her so deep? "But me and you, it doesn't matter. Ancient history."

The father who'd loved her had died with her mother, the shell left behind this cruel stranger capable of aiming a kick at a child's soft heart. "You just think about whether you want to be having this same conversation with Eve ten years from now."

She shouldn't have done it, not with having already strained her wings once today, but she made a vertical takeoff, ignoring the words Jeffrey spoke as he reached for her. And when tears poured down her face, she told herself it was from the pain in her muscles. It wasn't a total lie, her body screaming at the abuse.

Two minutes later, a tendon tore with an audible snap, and she realized she was now not only useless to Ransom, but that, in her unthinking fury, she might have made a fatal mistake.

7

She barely made it to the Tower, her knees slamming hard onto the concrete of the balcony outside the suite she'd left only twenty-five minutes earlier. When a tiny blue feather fluttered to the hard surface as she leaned on her palms in an attempt to fight the bright pain of the impact, she knew she wasn't alone.

Illium landed beside her an instant later, his hands going to her shoulders and his wing sliding across her own. "Ellie, you're hurt."

She shrugged him off, still able to feel Jeffrey's grip on her arms. "How long have you been following me?"

"Only a minute—it didn't look like you were going to make the landing."

"Well, I did, so go," she said. "Go. *Go!*"

An instant after the words were out, she raised her head to apologize, but Illium was already dropping off the balcony. Hating herself for allowing Jeffrey to mess her up until she'd hurt one of her closest friends, she crawled and dragged herself into the living area of the suite, collapsing flat on her face the instant she was concealed from the windows, the carpet against her cheek and the crossbow digging into her hip. Reaching down, she managed to get it off, along with the miniature flamethrower, placing both on the left side of her body.

A whisper of sound not long afterward told her Illium hadn't been offended—he'd simply gone for stronger weaponry. "Guild Hunter." Words deadly and cool from the Archangel of New York. "You've hurt your wings."

Fingers digging into the carpet, she admitted her mistake. "I did two hard vertical takeoffs today."

"Lie still. I will attempt to fix the damage."

"I'll be fine," she said through the screaming agony. "The others—"

"Will be bedbound for weeks or months, regardless of my actions. Your stupidity, meanwhile, I may be able to mend immediately."

Lashed by his tone, she struck out. "I didn't ask for your help!"

"No, instead you did your best to ensure I'd have to deal with a dead consort *when you are meant to be helping to protect the city by evidencing your strength.*"

Jaw clenched against the anger dammed up inside her, she didn't say a word, and a bone-melting warmth invaded her wing muscles a second later, trickles of it reaching her knees, as if Raphael's ability had sensed the fractures that cracked her kneecaps. The pain began to dim almost at once, and she realized he'd become far stronger than he'd been even a month before . . . but that didn't alter the fact that, in stark contrast to the violent physical abilities manifesting in the rest of the Cadre, Raphael's new power was a pacific one.

Ironically, his ability to heal might end up being a lethal weakness.

"There *will* be a war," he'd predicted weeks earlier as they watched midnight come to their city, the night winds thrusting covetous fingers through his hair. "It's inevitable during a Cascade—from all we know, one or more of the Cadre will either touch madness or gain a power that so eclipses the abilities of the others, he or she will seek to seize the world. I can't afford to stagnate, to have only the strength that has always been at my command."

"Your power negates Lijuan's," she'd pointed out. "And she's the biggest threat."

"A negative power won't be enough to win, and, while she may be the biggest threat, she isn't the only one." The cold-eyed candor of a man who'd held his territory for half a millennium. "Neha creates fire and ice, Astaad is rumored to control the sea, and there are whispers Favashi holds the winds in the palm of her hand. For the Cadre to remain in balance, I cannot stand in place."

Now, the guilt that had been gnawing at her since that conversation combined with her impotent anger at Jeffrey to create a caustic mess in her gut, corrosive and damaging. Raphael would never blame her, but it was Elena who'd made him a little bit mortal, a little bit weaker—exactly as Lijuan had once warned.

"You tore a tendon." The ice in his tone hadn't thawed. "Do that again and I'll leave you to heal on your own. Perhaps then you'll develop some respect for your body."

"I was pissed off and I acted before I thought," she said, giving him one truth even as she hid the more noxious one that continued to eat at her. "I know it was childish and dangerous— you don't have to tell me."

"Jeffrey?" Raphael said, allowing her to sit up, which she did without a twinge of pain.

"He hurt Eve." Raphael knew her well enough to understand what that meant.

Chrome blue eyes flat with renewed fury. "Is she well?"

"Yes."

"Good." Twisting her braid in his fist with that single word, Raphael tugged back her head and took her mouth in a kiss that was hot red passion and the cool brush of an archangel's anger. *If you did not love him,* he said into her mind, his hand closing possessively over her breast, *I would sever this man from your life like the diseased limb that he is.*

I'm not sure if I love him or hate him, she confessed as he took her down to the carpet once more, *but Beth, Amy, Eve, they need him.*

A gasp, her back arching; Raphael had burned away the

laces that held her top together to bare her breasts to the air. His mouth touched her sensitive flesh an instant later, his teeth grazing her nipple. Hissing out a breath, she dug her nails into his shoulders and tried to flip him using her legs, wanting the advantage . . . but her lover was an archangel, and he didn't want to be moved.

He bit down deeper, until it skated the edge of hurt. *When you decided to continue flying, did you think about the fact I might have to scrape you off the street?* Releasing her breast with that angry question, he ravaged her mouth and, at the same time, ripped open the fly of the cargo pants she'd changed into a half hour earlier.

His fingers speared through her damp flesh, her panties who the hell knew where. "I'm sorry," she gritted out as he rubbed his thumb deliberately hard against her clit, knowing it would send her over the edge . . . only to relax the pressure right when her body hovered on the brink of excruciating pleasure.

"Fuck." Chest heaving, she stared into a masculine face that held more than a hint of cruelty right this instant. "That was mean."

"I'm feeling mean, Guild Hunter." He touched her again, thrusting two fingers inside her and using his thumb to play with her clitoris as he bent his head to her exposed breast once more, his teeth marking her soft flesh. *Very mean.*

Body quivering as he denied her an orgasm for the second time, Elena snarled and raked her nails down his back, tearing the fine black fabric of his shirt. Blood scented the air, Raphael's head snapping up to reveal eyes gone incandescent, his wings glowing above her. Slamming his mouth down on her own, he tore open his pants and she felt the blunt hardness of his cock pushing against her . . . but he didn't thrust, clearly still in one hell of a mood.

Do it! Biting down on his lower lip hard enough to break skin, she locked her legs around his hips and jerked her own upward.

A single hard inch, and then all of him as he thrust deep, stretching her tight flesh with his thickness. Elena came without warning, her body clenching around his so possessively that he broke the kiss to brace his fisted hands on either side of her head. Refusing to lose that connection even as her body spasmed in a near-painful orgasm, she grabbed his face, initiated another kiss that was all tongue and heat and fury.

His cock slid over her oversensitized muscles as he pulled out his entire length, only to slam back in so hard she felt him in her throat. Then he was coming inside her, the intimate wetness pushing her over the edge into a pleasure so vicious, it tore her to pieces.

"You're still wearing all your knives."

"I should've used them," Elena muttered from her position trapped beneath Raphael's body, his cock still inside her, and his breath hot against her neck. "Bastard."

"You drew blood, so I believe we're even."

Arms wrapped around his neck, she kissed his temple. "I'm sorry I scared you." It wasn't the done thing for an archangel to admit fear, but he was hers, and she'd hurt him without meaning to; it was up to her to fix her mistake.

His wings shifted, but he didn't extricate their bodies. "I didn't know fear until you, Elena. Use the power wisely."

It was a punch to the heart, that naked admission. "Well," she said in an attempt to make him smile, "if it gets me this well fucked . . ."

Rising onto his elbows, his hair a turbulent mess and his lower lip already healed, he pinned her with a gaze kissed with more than a touch of male arrogance. "Have I not been satisfying you?"

God, he was sexy. She wanted to tear off his clothes and drive him wild when he got that look on his face. "Given that I screamed the greenhouse down the night before last," she said, her toes curling at the reminder of how he'd taken her from behind, her hands braced on her workbench, "I think you know exactly how well you've been satisfying me." She moaned as he withdrew from her body, her tissues deliciously swollen. "Though angry sex does have something going for it."

A faint curve of his lips at last, his head dipping to press a kiss over the bite he'd taken of her breast, the mark red yet. "Yes." He rose, did up his pants, and dragged her to her feet. "It may become my favorite way to work out our differences."

"Not if you do this to all my clothes," she said, realizing the ripping and tearing sounds had been for real. "Damn it. I just changed." Sudden panic, a glance at her watch. "I still have fifteen minutes to make the meet with Ransom." Racing into the bedroom, she stripped off her weapons, slithered out of her clothes, and—after a quick dash into the bathroom to wash some hotly personal fluids from her body—returned to re-dress.

An insane three minutes later, and Raphael, wearing a black shirt identical to the one she'd shredded, slid her longest blade down her back again. "The hunt might run late," she said. "So don't send the squadrons out looking for me."

"Either you have forgotten your prior engagement," Raphael said as she rapidly rebraided her hair, "or you're attempting to avoid it."

It came to her in a rush of memory—heavy embossed paper, a polite invitation it had taken her hours to draft, a response elegant and formal but with a delicate, whimsical drawing of a lemur in one corner. "They didn't cancel?"

"Elijah offered, but I told him we'd like to see him and Hannah at our table." Folding his wings tightly to his back, he walked out onto the balcony, the winter air a cold blast as she followed. "I think it's time we began to build some true friendships among the Cadre. Other alliances are already forming that may be destructive in the war to come."

Rubbing at her bare arms, she tried to remember if she'd left spare full-length sheaths at the Tower. However, it wasn't only the wind and the thickening cloud layer that had the hairs rising along her arms. "You're thinking about Neha and Lijuan." The two powerful archangels were neighbors, had always had a cordial relationship.

"It could be a lethal liaison."

Elena thought of a Manhattan under siege from a hail of fire and ice, while the reborn fed on mortal flesh in a bloody plague across the city, and felt her gorge rise. "Jason said he's positive Neha hasn't been taken in by Lijuan."

"Neha also has a twin in her territory who may yet lead her

army against Neha," Raphael pointed out. "And she blames me for the death of her child." A reminder that no matter Neha's acceptance of Jason into her territory in the recent past, certain wounds continued to fester. "Lijuan, meanwhile, has been very polite about keeping both her reborn and her forces away from their shared border."

Put that way Elena could see the alliance forming in front of her eyes. "Elijah and you—you're friends already."

"Of a sort. He has always offered his support to me in matters of the Cadre." Acknowledging a passing squadron led by Illium, who looked every inch the blooded fighter she so often forgot him to be, Raphael shot out a random bolt of energy.

Elena sucked in a breath as Illium gave a single command and the squadron split to avoid the bolt . . . which Illium deflected with the sword he'd pulled from his back. It hit the Tower without causing damage, and Illium saluted them with a grin before continuing onward. "That wasn't angelfire." An archangel killer, angelfire could shatter concrete.

"No, it was a weak strike meant to test the squadron's alertness." Eyes on the city, Raphael returned to their earlier topic of conversation. "If Elijah and I are to create a true friendship, an alliance that'll hold in the fighting to come, then I must not only invite him into my territory, but trust him on a level beyond."

"You're going to tell him the full effects of the Falling?" Open surprise in his consort's tone.

"No." He trusted none of the Cadre enough to share the compromised status of his defenses. "Elijah may have offered the olive branch of friendship, but he has also held his territory for longer than I've been an archangel. He is as ruthless as any of us."

"How bad is it?" Elena asked quietly. "Now that you've had a chance to assess all the injuries."

"We've begun the process of transferring in men and women from outlying areas to bolster our defensive force, but Tower personnel are chosen for a reason. They're the best of the best, each personally tested and selected by Galen." Furthermore, his weapons-master made it nonnegotiable that each fighter return to the Refuge once every two years for intensive training.

"The outlying areas—they won't be left vulnerable?"

Checking the gun she carried in an inner thigh holster, having swapped out one of her blades for the sleek piece, Elena slid it back, the fine lines of her face troubled in the stormy light. "Since we're taking their people."

It was exactly the kind of question a consort was meant to ask, one that challenged without judgment. He knew Elena often thought she didn't know the "rules" of immortal behavior, but knowledge of pomp and ceremony was useless without the heart to love their people and the courage to speak her mind. "It's considered cowardly to nibble away at a territory and no archangel wishes such a stain on his or her honor."

"Well," she said, as a spit of rain hit her cheek, the sky holding the deluge for now, "I guess that's good news."

"In a sense. But there's no shame in being clever about your invasion." Immortals valued intelligence as much as strength. "To soften up a city for an attack by engineering an event such as the Falling? It would be considered a good strategy in the aftermath."

"The diseased vamp." Eyes of winter gray met his, the rim of silver faint in this light. "It can't be a coincidence."

"We'll know nothing for certain until Keir completes his tests, but I've told all senior angels and vampires to report any aberrant or troubling behavior. No such disease can be permitted to gain a foothold anywhere in the territory." He looked to the clouds once more. "Complete your task for the Guild, Elena. Be visible in the doing. Our objective remains the same—not to give our enemies any indication that the city has been so grievously wounded."

"Far as I'm concerned," Elena bit out, "if the Falling was a planned attack, it wasn't clever but cowardly. Murder from a distance."

Words he'd expect from a warrior.

A fleeting kiss, her weapon-roughened fingertips on his cheek. "I won't be late."

He watched her leave in a sweep of midnight and dawn, her wings unlike any other, and he knew he'd damn his own honor and take vengeance on the world should anyone dare lay a finger on her.

8

Ransom was sitting on his bike staring at a taped-up fold-out map when she landed beside him only four minutes behind schedule. His black leather jacket undone to reveal a dark green tee, paired with leather pants and the heavy black boots he'd been wearing earlier, mirrored sunglasses hiding his vivid green eyes, he looked like an ad for the bike company, far too pretty to actually be dangerous.

Except, of course, for the guns strapped to his thighs, the blades and extra firepower he wore hidden underneath his jacket. "Anything from your sources?" she asked.

"Zip," he said, without taking his eyes off the ancient map he refused to give up, even though, like every hunter, he had a Guild-issued smartphone with full GPS capability. "But at least we now know Darrell isn't crawling around in the underground."

Not in the mood to tease him today about his infamous map, she glanced around and forced herself to return the polite smile of the vampire who passed on the sidewalk, his cane and hat as dapper as the suit that encased his short, bowlegged form.

Copper dust and cinnamon spice, with an underlying hint of burnt oak.

Complex and interesting and unique.

"I always wanted to ask something," she said in a deliberate attempt to get her mind off the repulsive nature of the attack against the city—and after Raphael's comments about "softening up" a city, she had few doubts that that was exactly what it had been. "Do you scent the same things I do?"

Ransom made a face when she described what she'd picked up from the passing vamp. "Yeah, except I don't say shit like 'cinnamon spice with a hint of burnt oak.' I say 'dude smells like an electrified tree with a side of doughnut topping.'"

Choking on unexpected laughter, she leaned her arm on his shoulder and looked down at the map, aware of two stroller-pushing nannies stopping to sneak photos of them from the other side of the quiet street. "So who are we going to see?" A whiff of citrus, strong and clean. "Nice shampoo."

"Lemons, smart-ass. My gran says it's the best way to get rid of bad smells. Darrell's grandmother, on the other hand, owns that building there"—a nod to the right—"and if Darrell is close to anyone, it's likely to be his gran."

"I didn't realize you knew him."

"I don't, not really. We were on one hunt together three years ago." Folding away the map, he gave it to her to slide into the daypack he wore. "He didn't say much, but I picked up that his gran pretty much raised him—a quick online search gave me this address for her."

"We still don't have the background report?" With a hunt this time-critical, they needed the information yesterday. If Vivek had been in charge . . . but he wasn't.

"Apparently"—a clenched jaw that told her he was about to deliver bad news—"there was some kind of computer meltdown. Guild's working manually to put the report together."

Frustration churning in her gut, she stepped back so he could swing off the bike, keeping her eyes open for any movement from behind the curtained windows of the regal old home that was their destination. Complete with fancy cornices marred by not a speck of city grit, the entire place was painted a gleaming white.

"Ms. Flaherty is indisposed," a maid told them when they reached the door.

"This is about her grandson, Darrell." Ransom showed the stately white-haired woman his Guild license. "I think she'd like to know."

A hint of what looked like true concern on her face before she gestured them into a room off the hallway. "Please wait in the morning room."

Wings just fitting through the doorways, Elena walked to stand in front of a window that overlooked the street, while Ransom prowled around the room after dropping his daypack on a chair upholstered in burgundy with swirls of gold, the arms and back carved of honey-colored wood.

They heard the quiet hum of what might've been an elevator several minutes later, then the maid wheeled Ms. Flaherty into the room. Darrell's grandmother wore a peach-colored turban on her head, her body thin underneath a flowing caftan of soft violet, her mocha-colored skin papery thin. However, the hand she reached up to squeeze the maid's appeared strong, her brown eyes alert and clear.

A face, Elena thought, that held as much strength and character as beauty. Not a woman who'd break under the troubling news of her grandson's mental state—if she didn't already know. Could be Darrell had come home to hole up, try to get his head on straight. It'd be the best possible outcome.

Folding her hands on her lap rug after the maid left, Ms. Flaherty looked straight at Elena. "Is my grandson dead?"

"As far as we know, he's alive," she said at once, because if Ms. Flaherty didn't know of Darrell's whereabouts, any other answer would be a torment.

The tiniest slump of her shoulders before the elderly lady took control of the situation. "Stop looming and sit." She didn't speak again until they'd both obeyed. "So, if he's not dead, then he must be in trouble. How bad is it?"

"He hasn't crossed the line yet." Ransom had apparently come to the same conclusion as Elena about Darrell's grandmother: she might appear weak but this lady wouldn't thank them for pussyfooting around. "We need to haul him in before he does something the Guild can't fix."

"He put an innocent vampire in the hospital," Elena elaborated, when Ms. Flaherty turned to her. "The beating was merciless."

"Lucky for him, he chose a vampire just out of his Contract, with dreams of cruising the world and no time for hassles with an official case." Ransom leaned forward, arms braced on his thighs. "The Guild Director convinced him to accept a payout in lieu of laying charges, which means the Guild doesn't have to officially suspend Darrell's license, but he hurts anyone else and he's done."

"That's not my boy." Ms. Flaherty's body vibrated with unhidden outrage. "Darrell does his job. He doesn't abuse those he hunts."

"The things we see in the course of the job?" Elena held the elderly lady's sharp eyes. "It can cause cracks that don't heal without intervention, and Darrell recently walked into a nightmare."

Ms. Flaherty's fingers trembled on the lap rug, but her voice didn't crack when she spoke. "I haven't seen or heard from him in a week, and he always calls me every couple of days, especially since I've had this dratted cold I can't seem to shake." A deep breath that caught, but she waved off their concern to point a finger at Ransom. "You find my boy before he comes to harm. Don't you let him down—you're his Guild. He always said you were like family."

"We *are* family," Ransom muttered once they returned to the bike, neither one of them of the opinion that Ms. Flaherty had lied. "Why didn't the idiot just come in when he realized he was losing it? He knows no one would've blinked an eye if he needed more counseling—or, hell, if he wanted to get drunk every day for a week. We would've gone with him, carried him home from the fucking bar."

"He's in a bad place, not thinking straight." Elena refused to fail at bringing Darrell home. Maybe she couldn't halt an archangelic war, or make her father into a decent human being, but this one fracture she could and would mend. "Since we don't have specifics, how about we start trying the usual Guild haunts?"

"That's what I w—" Grabbing his phone at the chime, he gave her the thumbs-up. "Sara's been talking to his friends, sent us a list of his other known hangouts. One of his buds already scoped the apartment, found it empty." Sliding on his sunglasses, he e-mailed the list to her phone. "You take the top half, I'll take the bottom, see if we can pick up a trail. If you think you have him, call me—with his head screwed up as it is, he might forget we're family."

"You call me, too." Scanning her half of the list after getting his nod, Elena noted a gun shop, a clothing resupply store that catered to hunters and cops, an apartment that apparently housed a discreet pro, and the New York Public Library. "He must like to read." Somehow, that small, unexpected fact made him more human, more real.

"Yeah. Always has a paperback in his back pocket." Tugging on his helmet, Ransom straddled the bike, flicked up the kickstand with a boot, turned the key, and kick-started the engine. The machine roared to purring life. "Get on. I'll run you over to a building you can use as a launchpad."

"No, thanks. I'll have to spread my wings to keep them off the street and next thing I know, I'll be clipped by some cabbie in a bad mood." Elena wasn't going to flirt with being grounded again. Not to mention she'd then have to deal with one extremely pissed-off archangel.

Devil-may-care grin on his face, Ransom gunned the bike. "Come on, Ellie. I bet we stop traffic."

"Be visible in the doing."

She had a feeling Raphael hadn't considered this when he'd spoken those words. It was no doubt a bad, bad idea, but damn if it wouldn't get a stupid amount of coverage, maybe give the city something to smile about.

"They should make motorcycles for angels."

It was a kick to the gut, that splinter of memory. The words had been spoken by the young angel whose funeral cortege would reach the Refuge after darkfall, his statement directed at a friend as the two of them sat with their legs hanging off a Tower balcony to the left of where Elena stood. She'd smiled at the time, but now the words incited a renewed wave of angry sadness.

This one's for you, she thought and swung her leg over the thrumming machine. However, she didn't sit—that would leave her wings touching the street. Instead, she placed her hands on Ransom's shoulders and stood on the footholds. She had to spread her wings a little to avoid tangling them in the bike, but it wasn't as bad as she'd feared. "You're going to have to deal with considerable drag."

"My sweet girl eats drag for breakfast." Then they were off, the wind slamming into her face and her wings as Ransom executed a turn and roared down the street to the wide-eyed astonishment of everyone they passed. Laughing, Elena threw back her head and enjoyed the ride as that young soldier would've, had he only been given the chance.

She and Ransom had unquestionably made an impression by the time he brought the bike to a gentle stop in the silent street behind an older building. "This do?" he asked, nodding at the external fire stairs that led all the way to the roof.

"Yep." Hopping off the bike, she checked her wings. "Still in one piece."

"Told ya."

Bumping his fist to her own, he roared down the street.

I do believe that is the first time any angel has ridden a motorcycle.

Grinning at the kiss of the wind and the rain inside her mind as she climbed up the fire escape, she said, *I bet that gets our would-be invader's panties in a bunch.*

An . . . interesting image, but as a distraction from the state of our defenses, it was inspired. If, however, I didn't know Ransom was much in love with another, I'd now have to kill him.

No touching my friends, remember?

I wouldn't have to touch him to kill him.

Very funny. Having made it to the roof, she flared her wings and, sweeping off the edge of the building, flew in the direction of the gun shop as Raphael returned to Tower business. She'd debated heading for the pro first, men being men, but according to Sara's intel, Darrell hadn't visited the woman in over two months. The gun shop, however, was one he went to every time he was in town.

The owner, bearded and with a serious beer gut, was happy to cooperate once she reassured him he hadn't somehow earned the wrath of the Tower. "Darrell? He's a good customer, nice guy, too, but I haven't seen him for, let's see . . . going on a week now." A chuckle. "He really stocked up that last time."

When Elena heard what Darrell had bought, her head almost exploded. *He has an arsenal,* she messaged Ransom and got *#%&!* as a reply, then a call.

"Indoor shooting range was a wash. Literally." Ransom's tone was taut. "Burst water pipe five days ago, but the owner says Darrell came in every day before the damage, was a crack shot with multiple guns."

"Shit." If Darrell had moved from fists to guns this fast, they could be talking massacre.

"I'm heading to check out his mother's place. They're not close, but if he was angry, he might've turned up there."

Elena's next stop, the resupply store, had her slamming up against an ex-cop who gave her a blank face and said he didn't gossip about customers. Too fucking worried to put up with bullshit, Elena laid her cards on the table, no sugarcoating. "Darrell is in trouble. The kind of trouble where he might pick up a gun"—not to mention the freaking *assault rifle* he'd bought—"and put it to his head or someone else's."

"And what?" Flat cop eyes. "The Tower cares?"

That was his problem? "The Guild cares." She slapped down her license.

"I heard you were still hunting," he said, after examining the badge, "but I guess I figured that was horseshit."

"Yeah, well, it isn't." She slid away the license. "Now, Darrell?"

"Saw him three days ago."

"What did he buy?"

"No, it wasn't here. I saw him at the corner bar couple of blocks over with a stacked redhead. Legs up to her ears." A shrug. "I figured the man was enjoying his time off, and who was I to bother him."

The pro's apartment, too, Elena realized, was only two blocks over.

People pointed and whispered the instant she stepped out

of the store, this part of town busy, but no one crowded her. All it had taken for her to get her space was shooting a crossbow bolt into the boot of an idiot who wanted to get up close and personal. He'd lived, despite his whining, and now she had a rep. Exactly as she liked it.

"Ransom," she said, cell phone to her ear as she walked, just like every other New Yorker on the street, "the pro. Redhead with long legs?" Curving around a businessman engrossed in his miniature tablet, she heard a crash and turned to find him staring openmouthed at her, his expensive gadget on the ground.

"Tourist," sniffed a passing black-suited executive, her hair a sleek blonde bob and a cup of take-out coffee in her hand.

The acerbic comment made Elena grin, then they'd moved past one another.

"Wait," Ransom said. "I was just looking up her photo—yes, that's her. Double D chest, too."

"Should've known you'd notice."

"I'd have to be dead not to notice that. I got a nibble about a bar on—"

"I can see your bike." Hanging up, she jerked up her head. "Bar staff know anything?"

"They saw him three days ago, that's it."

Crossing the street without a word, they made it to the pro's apartment building in under a minute. Her doorman, his eyes bugging out at the weapons bristling from their bodies, didn't put up a fight at their questions, divulging that the woman hadn't left her apartment for forty-eight hours and counting.

"And Honey, she never misses her book club. That was last night."

Elena's eyes met Ransom's at the doorman's coda, the acrid taste of fear on her tongue. There was a very good chance that Honey Smith was no longer able to read a book, able to do anything, her decomposing body lying irreparably broken in her apartment.

Elena was so sick of being too late.

9

Having taken the stairs to the roof, Elena swept down, intending to look through the windows of the apartment, only to find the blinds shut. She returned to meet a gun-toting Ransom in front of one of the doors that lined the stylishly decorated and dimly lit penthouse floor. Her own gun out of its holster, she moved quietly to the other side of the door wide enough that her wings wouldn't be a hindrance in a fight.

"I don't smell decomp." It was a bare whisper.

Elena didn't either, but what if their quarry had been smart and changed the temperature inside? "Air-con," she mouthed and saw Ransom's lips flatten into a thin line.

"Ask or go?"

"Go soon as we have an in." Ransom slid away his weapon. "Can't take the risk he has a gun to her head if she isn't already dead, and he's in there with her."

Motioning for her to keep out of sight, he put on his shades and pounded on the door. "Hey, sweetheart." It was just loud enough that the resident, if she was alive, would worry about her neighbors. "Open up. We had a date and I paid in advance!"

Hearing rustling sounds from inside the apartment, Elena

scowled at Ransom to pull away from the door in case Darrell
shot through it. When he stayed put, she gritted her teeth and
prepared to shove him out of the way the instant she picked up
anything that sounded even vaguely like a weapon.

Except the next thing she heard was the door being unlocked
and pulled open, the security chain jerking it to a stop. "Shut
up, you drunk moron," hissed a clearly irate woman. "You've
got the wrong apartment."

"You Honey Smith? I made the appointment through your
website."

"I'm not taking new bookings." Unhidden frustration. "You
must've made a mistake."

"I have a fucking confirmation number."

"Show me."

"Here." Lowering his hand into a pocket, Ransom slammed
out with some kind of a metal tool and the security chain was
gone.

The redhead screamed as they came in, guns out . . . to find
themselves facing the wrong end of a Glock semiautomatic
held by a tall, lean man in jeans that hung low on his hips and
at least three days of beard growth on his face. "Honey." The
black-satin-robe-clad woman slid behind him at the curt order.

Ransom was the first to lower his gun. "Shit. We thought
you fucking lost it, man."

Darrell didn't lower his own gun an inch until Elena slid
hers back into the holster.

"The Guild," she said to Honey, in an effort to defuse the
tension, "will pay for the damage."

The other woman rolled pretty hazel eyes set in a Botticelli
face. "I'll send them a bill. Now shut the damn door and come
in before you get me kicked out of my apartment. I'll make
coffee."

"Ellie found out about the weapons," Ransom said to Darrell
after the redhead disappeared down the hallway. "We were
afraid you were planning to go on a rampage."

"I thought about it." A flat statement, his skin several shades
lighter than his grandmother's, eyes a dark gray. "It was when
I started working out the best vantage points for a sniper that
I locked all weapons except this one in my gun safe, changed

the combination blind so I couldn't open it without a blowtorch, and came here."

"Whatever your excuse," Elena said, tone hard because Darrell needed it to be hard, "you should've checked in with the Guild—and your gran."

It was her final statement that got his attention, his eyes tortured. "I knew she'd be able to tell I was in trouble, and she's so sick. I didn't want to worry her."

Elena threw him her phone, unable to forget the trembling of Ms. Flaherty's hands. "Do it now."

The smell of coffee filtered into the air just as he finished the call, and Honey padded back to the entranceway. "Y'all planning to come in and visit, or just stand around looking badass?"

Elena grinned, deciding she liked the other woman, just as Ransom folded his arms high on his chest. "I'm always up for looking badass."

"Except for the hair, right?" Darrell said, a glint in his eye.

Ransom showed him the finger and all at once there was no more tension.

A half hour and a cup of coffee later, Darrell turned himself in to the Guild, ready to undergo a psych evaluation and to actually cooperate with the counselor. It was a small win for the good guys, but Elena would take it. Now she had to fly home and do her best to help Raphael forge an alliance that could mean the safety of hundreds of thousands, the scale of death that might result from an archangelic war incomprehensible.

After a day that had involved countless subtle strategic moves as he positioned his city in readiness to defend against an attack from an unknown enemy, Raphael stood beside his consort on the lawn of their home, watching Elijah and Hannah come in to land. The other pair had decided to stay at an undisclosed location about an hour's flight from the Enclave, though they'd notified Raphael the instant they crossed over into his territory.

"It's like a courtship, isn't it?" Elena murmured, her flowing gown of blue-green silk a cool kiss of spring in the arms of winter. "Both of you being so well behaved and formal."

I understand the allusion, hbeebti, *but perhaps you can find another term.* He brushed his wing over her own, pleased to see she appeared to carry no residual soreness. *I have no desire to court Elijah.*

Amusement in a face that showed only the faintest touch of immortality, the transition far too slow to protect her from the dangers on the horizon. Yet Elena was not one to sit in safety. No, his hunter would fight beside him, come what may. That was who she was, as he was an archangel who'd battle to the death to protect his own.

"Elijah" he said, once the visiting couple had folded away their wings, "my consort and I welcome you."

"We are glad to be here, Raphael." Elijah's gaze met his before he turned to acknowledge Elena with a formal bow of his head, his aristocratic profile the inspiration to countless sculptors over the millennia of his existence, his hair golden against skin of a paler gold.

Raphael made the introductions, was unsurprised when Elena greeted Elijah with warmth and poise, despite her reservations about "not knowing which fork to use," as she'd put it. Then, before he could warn her that protocol between two consorts dictated she must call Hannah by her title of Consort until invited otherwise, she smiled and said, "I'm so happy to meet you at last, Hannah."

Elijah's consort beamed and held out her hands instead of taking insult, her exuberant black curls swept back with jeweled combs, the ebony of her skin glowing in the red-orange of sunset. The storm clouds had passed with only a single heavy shower and the air tasted of ozone, clean and fresh, erasing any final traces of the blood that had soaked into the earth on which they stood . . . but the scar remained. No one would ever forget the day the angels fell.

"I say the same, Elena." Hannah's response was made in a voice clear and musical, the two women's hands touching. "I came to the Refuge especially to see you, you know, but Raphael was remorselessly protective and did not trust me at all. He was right—had I seen your wings up close, I would've hounded you until you agreed to sit for me."

Face alight, Elena drew the shorter woman in the direction of the house, Hannah's gown of deep bronze brushing against her own. "I was as graceless as a baby bird when I first woke and irritable about it," she confessed. "I'd have been a dreadful subject."

Raphael didn't hear Hannah's answer, the two women having moved a small distance away, but their mingled laughter floated on the air. "I'm not so sure we've done the right thing in bringing together the only two consorts in the Cadre," he said to Elijah as they followed in the women's wake.

"Ah, but could we have stopped it?"

Exchanging a glance with the other archangel that would've been understood by no other in the Cadre, he led the other man through the main doors, the dinner to take place in the sprawling formal living area/dining room off the hallway. Soaring ceiling, hand-polished floor of rare wood, and arching windows that drenched the room in sunlight or moonlight depending on the time of day, it was a room meant to impress.

Elena had taken one look at it, in the days after she moved in, and said, "We're eating at the table by the library windows, where I can talk to Your Archangelness without needing a megaphone."

Did you bring your megaphone, Guild Hunter? he asked, aware of Montgomery and his staff clearing away, having quietly carried in champagne and canapés.

A narrow-eyed glance over her shoulder. *Where exactly would I put it in this dress? I couldn't even figure out a way to wear panties without ruining the line of the slinky thing.*

Raphael's blood heated as Hannah said, "Elijah, look," her voice potent with wonder.

Grabbing her consort's hand, the dark-haired woman tugged him to the glorious painting of the Refuge that dominated the far end of the room. It ran across the entire wall and was a study in painful blue and piercing white over rocky gray, but for the wings of the angels flying above the city, each painted in intricate detail.

"This is Dahariel." Hannah brushed her fingers reverently over wings patterned like an eagle's, and Raphael knew her admiration wasn't for the named angel but for the artist who'd captured him on canvas. "And, oh, it's Galen with three of Jessamy's little ones."

"This is the Hummingbird's work."

"No, it is Aodhan's," Hannah said in response to Elijah's murmur.

Scowling, Elijah leaned closer to the work. "Where's the signature?"

"Neither one signs their work in the usual fashion." Hannah scowled back at her consort. "We must find the clue in the image."

You are wearing no panties with another male in the room? Raphael ran his hand down Elena's spine and over her lower curves, searching for lines and finding nothing but firm feminine flesh. *You truly aren't.*

Elena's shoulders shook, deep creases in her cheeks. *Oh, my God, you're scandalized!* Eyes tearing up in the effort to fight her laughter, she pressed her hands to his chest and stared down at the floor. *Should I tell you I did find a way to wear a knife? In a thigh sheath.*

Of course you did. What do panties matter so long as you have your steel.

Stop it! Her shoulders shook harder, the diamond-studded pin that anchored the knot at the nape of her neck catching the light as her touch seared him through the crisp white of his formal shirt. *I'm trying to be elegant and graceful and consortlike.*

Cupping her nape, he squeezed. *Our guests are about to turn.*

Refusing to look at Raphael for fear any eye contact would set her off, Elena walked with the other couple into the living area of the large open-plan space.

"This is a lovely room." Hannah took a seat on an elegant gold settee, as Elena had learned the piece of furniture was called, her wings flowing gracefully around the back support. The other woman's feathers were a deep, luxuriant cream with blushes of peach on the primaries and appeared so lushly soft that Elena was tempted to commit social suicide, sneak a touch.

"The little tables there," Hannah said as Elena fought the uncivilized and very unconsortlike impulse, "who was the designer?"

"I'm going to have to fess up and admit ignorance." Elena showed her empty palms from the opposite settee. "I'm afraid I'd get a D in that aspect of consort life."

"If you are to get a D in such things, then I'm afraid I must confess I'd get an F in defensive training." Sparkling eyes, a conspiratorial whisper. "Elijah has resorted to teaching me how to stab people in the eye with my paintbrushes."

"That's a really excellent idea if you always have paint-brushes at hand." Elena tapped a finger on her lower lip, her mind on the other tools of Hannah's craft. "I've seen Aodhan with a paint scraper—you could sever someone's jugular with that."

"I knew your consort was a smart woman, Raphael." Elijah took a seat beside his own consort and, despite his slight smile, Elena couldn't help but be alert to the lethal power that pulsed in his very skin. It made her realize what her friends must see when they looked at Raphael, and why other rough-and-tough female hunters had toasted her on her "brass balls" in going to bed with him.

Elena put her hand over his on the fine velvet of the settee when he sat down next to her, their wings overlapping. *I'm glad we're doing this, even given the circumstances.* While a political alliance had to be their first, critical goal, Elena also knew she couldn't rebuff the warm overtures of a woman who not only understood the pressures of being consort, but whose friendship could take her through the millennia to come.

Because one day, if they survived the coming conflicts, she'd pick up the phone to call Sara, only to remember her best friend was no longer there, her bright light having faded into the final goodnight. Sara called her a silly goose for worrying so much about a time that could be decades into the future, but Elena's heart broke at the idea of not having Sara's warmth and love in her life.

"Elena," Hannah began.

"Ellie," she said, swallowing the knot of pain in her chest and remembering her promise to Sara that she'd give Hannah a real chance, rather than keeping her at arm's length out of loyalty to Sara. "All my friends call me Ellie."

"Ellie. I am honored to be given the right."

The conversation continued to flow effortlessly through the hours that followed. Conscious of Hannah's preference to stay out of angelic politics, Elena had been willing to stifle her own hunger to sit in on the coming dialogue between Raphael and Elijah and lead the other woman to her solar for quiet discussion. Hannah, however, waved off the invitation when she made it after dinner. "In such a dark time," she said, voice soft but eyes resolute, "a consort must stand beside her archangel."

The discussion segued into weightier matters almost immediately, and, but for a poignant minute of conscious silence when Raphael received word from Galen to say the fallen were home, the focus was on the consequences of the Cascade.

"I hear," Elijah said, as the clock ticked over midnight, "you've gained the ability to negate Lijuan's power."

The air seemed to go motionless, silence filling the room; it was the first time either of the two men had come even close to touching on their own new abilities.

10

Trust, Raphael. Elena met eyes the hue of Prussian blue, except no pigment could ever be as intense, as pure. *It has to start somewhere.*

"Yes." No indication in Raphael's tone of the momentous step denoted by that single word. "I can cause her pain and a certain level of harm, though whether I can deliver true death remains a question."

"I, too, have gained an intriguing new ability," Elijah said, sending his consort a look so openly affectionate that Elena found herself seeing the man behind the power for the first time. "It's one that initially caused Hannah some consternation."

"Otherwise known as unadulterated terror." Hannah's tone was dry. "What," she said to Elena, "would be your reaction if one sunny morning, you walked, blissfully unknowing into the greenhouse you told me of, and found a family of pumas had settled in overnight?" Hannah nodded at Elena's wide-eyed look. "Yes, that's exactly what I found in my studio."

Raphael looked to Elijah. "You can speak to animals?"

"I don't know about *speak*, but I can certainly make cats

large and small attend my commands. My first command, of
course, was that they vacate my consort's studio and stop snarling at her." Hannah's gentle laughter filled the air before he
added, "I can also command birds of prey. They are now sentinels in my territory."

Big cats and birds of prey? Elena knew South America had
plenty of those, thanks to the expansive sanctuaries sponsored
by Elijah, a point that once again proved the archangels' new
abilities had their roots in who each member of the Cadre was
as an individual. *That's an army on its own.*

Yes.

"Neither one of us, it is clear," Raphael said aloud, "is
defenseless against an attack. But"—his eyes locked with Elijah's golden brown gaze—"we'd be stronger together."

Elijah's response was solemn. "Your friendship is one I
welcome. I have no desire to live in a world overrun by Lijuan's
monstrosities."

"Or," Hannah whispered, her hand sliding into Elijah's, "in
one where angels fall from the sky."

The other couple didn't leave till dawn, the information
shared as the city slumbered and Montgomery slipped unob-
trusively in and out with wine, then coffee, and finally orange
juice, going far beyond what either couple had expected, the
birth of a trust that had Elijah telling them what he'd discovered
about Titus.

"It appears he has gained power over the earth—my man
says Titus can now cause earth tremors. If his ability continues
to develop in the same vein, he may one day soon be able to
collapse the ground under the feet of an invading army."

In turn, Raphael shared Jason's information about Astaad's
domination over the sea, and possibly other bodies of water.
"There are also rumors Favashi can control the winds," he
added, "though I have no confirmation. Michaela and
Charisemnon remain a mystery."

"I, too, have been unable to discover what they may have
gained," Elijah said, skin taut over the bones of his face and

jaw tight. "But knowing what I do of Charisemnon's appetites and Michaela's cruelty, it can be nothing good."

Raphael could do nothing but agree, his distaste for Charisemnon deeply hewn. The other archangel took girls barely budded to his bed, having somehow convinced his people that such was an honor to the children chosen. As for Michaela, he was deadly certain she'd egged Uram on when it came to making the fateful decision that had turned the other man into a blood-soaked monster, her effect that of the spider that eats its mate.

"I'll share anything further I learn of the others if you'll do the same," Elijah said when they walked out onto the lawn, offering his arm to seal the pact.

Raphael accepted the offer, his hand closing over the top of Elijah's forearm and the other man's over his, theirs the clasp of warriors. "It is done."

"This might've been my first official gig as your consort at our home"—Elena hid a yawn behind an open palm as they watched Elijah and Hannah fly high into the sky—"but I call that an unqualified success."

"Elijah's cooperation causes me concern." Sliding an arm around her waist, he drew her to his chest. "No archangel shares so readily."

"Readily?" Mouth falling open, Elena cupped his face in her hands. "It took you two *six hours* to get to the point. It was like watching a couple of tigers circling each other, deciding whether to be friends or to bite."

"First a courtship, now tigers?" He ran his hand down her spine, and when she yawned once again, drew her toward the house, her wing brushing the underside of his arm. "You must rest. Hannah may be able to take a night without sleep, but you are a babe in immortal terms."

"I shouldn't be this tired," she muttered. "I pulled all-nighters at Guild Academy, for crying out loud, then aced my exams the next day."

Spreading his hand on the silken curve of her hip, he leaned down to kiss her scowling mouth. "You are becoming immortal, Elena. Not a single cell in your body ever truly rests."

A pause, her feet halting on the grass. "Doesn't it ever bother you?"

Surprised at the piercing vulnerability of the question, he tilted up her chin so he could see her eyes. "That my consort needs sleep?"

Elena realized he hadn't understood her question. "Yes," she said, "and the fact that she will for a long time yet." As a human, she'd been stronger than most; it made her weakness as an immortal even more difficult to accept. "Right now, Hannah, with her lack of offensive skills, could beat me in a fight, simply by holding on until I was too tired and weak to go on."

Raphael raised an eyebrow. "No, she could not, because should it come to a fight to the death, you would slice off her head in the first ten seconds, cut out her heart in the next twenty, then burn her body to make sure she'd never again rise."

Blinking at the cold-blooded response, she stared. "You really think I'm capable of that?"

"If Hannah should prove a threat to me or the others you love, yes." A faint smile, his kiss a flagrantly sexual branding, his fingers thrusting into her hair to send pins scattering to the grass, his body all hard ridges and heat against her own. "Your love is a fierce thing, Elena, a thing with claws and teeth when it comes to protecting those you claim."

He was right; she'd take on that batshit crazy Lijuan herself if it meant saving the lives of the people she loved. "Does *that* bother you? That I'm so bloodthirsty?"

Laughing, he reached down and swung her into his arms with an easy strength that made her feel like a gently reared Southern belle out of a period drama. "I'll answer that upstairs. After I see your knife sheath."

Oh, God, he sounded like he was purring. "Sleep is overrated," she whispered, wrapping her arms around his neck and kissing the delicious slope of it. "I'd much rather get naked with my man."

The instant they were behind the closed doors of their bedroom, he threw her on the bed and divested her of her dress and shoes, leaving her wearing only the slim knife strapped to her thigh. When she reached down to get rid of it, he shook his head and, holding her gaze, stripped off his own formal clothes to reveal a body that made her whimper before he got on top of her.

A kiss to her hip, his tongue flicking out to taste her skin; his fingers tracing the strap of the sheath; his wings spreading; the exotic, erotic taste of angel dust on her lips; her breath locked in her throat.

Then his mouth was a heated dampness on her navel.

"Raphael." His name came out a caress as she tangled her hands in the midnight silk of his hair to hold him to her, her love for him a huge thing inside her.

He kissed her hip again, licking out at the bone in a light flick that made her tremble. A very male, very Raphael smile against her skin. When he shifted up over her, she was ready for his kiss . . . but she was never truly ready for Raphael's kiss. He made her burn, the pleasure a hot, liquid burst that shimmered over her skin in rolling waves. "I could kiss you forever," she murmured against his lips, sucking at the lower one, playing with the upper, his body weight a luscious pressure. "I love feeling you against me."

"You say such things, Elena. You will make me your slave." Wings spreading wider above her, he cupped the side of her face and leaned into the kiss, deepening it until their tongues tangled in sweet, hot battle, Elena's breath lost. Gasping in just enough air to continue, she stroked her hands against the taut muscle of him, and returned to the kiss.

More? It was an intimate question between lovers.

"Yes," she whispered. "More."

One arm braced above her head, he gave her what she wanted, continuing to kiss her while caressing the highly sensitive upper arch of her wing with his free hand. She shivered, sliding her own hands to his nape, then down, her fingers brushing his wings. He loved it when she kissed her way down the inner arches where his wings grew out of his back, and she loved that she knew that about him, about her lover.

"Stop that, *hbeebti*," he said, their lips parting on a wet kiss of sound.

She smiled, her nipples flush against the hard wall of his chest. "You like it."

"Too much. And today, I wish to pleasure my consort."

Pressing his thumb down on her jaw to part her lips, he kissed her again, angel dust glittering in the air.

"Mmm." She rubbed against him. "Did you make a change to your special blend?" Angel dust, he'd told her, was normally rich and exquisite, but not sexual. Elena had only ever tasted Raphael's blend, and it was always oh-so-sexual—today, it also held a dangerous bite.

Kisses down her throat. "I wouldn't wish my consort to suffer ennui."

"Oh!" It took some time for her brain cells to unscramble after he took one of her nipples into his mouth, rolling it over on his tongue like it was a plump berry, then turning his attention to the other. Chest heaving when he lifted his head to lave a kiss just below her breasts, she managed to say, "Ennui, yes, that's exactly what I feel right now."

His eyes glinted. "So, my consort challenges me. Very well."

Shivering, because his voice . . . it was fur over her senses, across her tight, damp nipples, along her lips, she watched him dip his head, place a wet kiss on her navel. He blew a breath over the wet, kept going past her renewed shiver. "Now," he purred, "it is my turn to be intoxicated."

Her spine curved off the bed at the first touch of his mouth on her most private flesh. As she knew her lover, he knew her. Every tiny, nerve-laden curve. Now, lifting her thighs up over the wide breadth of his shoulders, he cupped her buttocks in his hands and kissed her with an intimacy that stole her senses, making her feel delicious, decadent, beautiful.

Hands buried in his hair, she held on to him as her body shuddered again and again, the orgasm a slow, exquisite ride. He licked her to the end, stroking his hands over her thighs to shift her legs to either side of his body, his fingers lingering on the strap that held the knife to her thigh. "My warrior." Another kiss to her navel before he rose up over her again, his arousal nudging at her pleasure-swollen dampness.

She gripped at his upper arms, muscle and tendon flexing under her touch as he clamped one hand over her hip, the other braced on her wing—an added pleasure—and thrust his cock inside her. Moaning at the erotic storm of sensation and needing him even closer, she drew him down to her mouth. He came, his hand sliding up her body to mold her breast as he stroked in and out of her in a deep, lazy rhythm that said he had nowhere else to be, his attention only and absolutely on her.

Her body sparked to new life under the relentless focus of her archangel to clasp him in sensual pulses. Breaking the kiss so she could watch him find his own pleasure, she caressed her fingers down the line of his throat, over his shoulders, and to the rising arch of his left wing. He shuddered and thrust home when her fingers closed over that arch. *"Elena."*

Raphael's pleasure, his kiss, sent her over a second time . . . and it wasn't until they both stirred again that Raphael reached down and undid the strap of her knife sheath, putting it and the knife on the bedside table. "Beautiful as this sheath is," he said, touching the leather, "I much prefer the one which holds my blade."

Elena thumped a fisted hand on his shoulder, laughter bubbling in her veins and her body boneless. "I'm happy to know I beat leather that finely worked."

"Always." Lips curving in a smile that made her body tighten on the "blade" still inside her body, he bent his head to her lips.

And a certain blade and sheath once more proved their perfect fit.

Leaving Elena happily exhausted and asleep in their bed, Raphael flew not to the Tower but toward the house that belonged to Jeffrey Deveraux and his family. A single expertly timed burst of angelfire and he could eliminate the mortal male from the face of the planet, while leaving his wife and children unharmed.

Or he could simply fly down and thrust his hand through Jeffrey's rib cage to tear out his shriveled, useless heart. It would be intensely more satisfying than spilling the other man's blood from a distance.

Except taking either action would break Elena's faith in

him, while doing nothing to seal the gash Jeffrey had torn in her psyche. It'd continue to rip open at unexpected moments, as it had this morning. It had taken every ounce of his considerable control not to respond in anger when he'd realized the import of Elena's question—and that it was the same thing she'd asked him in more subtle ways in the past months.

Anger would've bruised and confused her, for his consort didn't recognize the fear that drove her to ask such questions, a fear that could be encapsulated in seven simple words that formed a vicious sentence: *Will this flaw make you reject me?*

What Jeffrey had done, it had scarred Elena on a level beyond the conscious. She knew she held Raphael's heart, she *knew*, and yet a wary, wounded part of her worried he'd change his mind one day, find her no longer worthy of loving.

Raphael. It was a murmur half drugged with sleep. *Why are you growling in my head?*

Teeth gritted, he made the deliberate decision to turn away from the Deveraux house and toward the Tower, not confident he could hold to his resolve not to murder Jeffrey if he saw Elena's father. *My apologies,* hbeebti. *I didn't realize you could sense it.*

'S okay.

Sleep, he said, and because he couldn't bear to think of her in pain: *As you dream, know that you are loved.*

'Course I am. I'm yours.

The sleepy mumble was enough to soothe his rage, telling him that despite the fears that haunted her, Elena understood the truth of who she was to him so deep within her, she remembered it even heavy with sleep. *No more growling in your head,* he promised, but she was already gone, lost in slumber.

Sire, said another voice an instant later.

Yes, Aodhan?

Augustus will reach the meeting point in an hour.

Thank you. He'd already met with Nazarach and Andreas, two of his angelic commanders—each in charge of running a particular section of his territory. Augustus would be the third. Step by quiet step, he was making certain every one of his commanders knew to prepare their regions for a long absence in the near future. He'd need them in New York when war screamed into being, a war that had been inevitable from the instant Lijuan created the first reborn.

Should her perversions of life be permitted to run free, they'd infect the world, turning it into a charnel house before it became a monument to death given flesh.

Seven hours later, after five hours of deep sleep, followed by an hour's teaching at the Academy and some high-visibility flying around office buildings, Elena landed at the Tower to find Raphael wasn't yet back from a meeting with one of his commanders. Aodhan, however, was in the office from where Dmitri had run Tower operations before he left the city with his wife.

Seeing her, the angel held out a paintbrush, its handle wrapped in a piece of paper.

She accepted it, mystified. "Thank you, but why?"

"The Sire asked me to make sure you received it."

Tearing off the paper, Elena found seven simple words written on the slim wooden handle: *Each consort has her own unique weapons.*

God, she thought, her entire face a smile, her Archangel had serious moves.

Happy, plain old heart-deep happy, she stored the slender brush carefully in a zippered side pocket of her tight cargos, where it would be in no danger of falling out. Seeing Aodhan's quizzical look, she realized she hadn't had a real conversation with him since his transfer to the Tower, this angel who was beautiful in the most inhuman of ways. Fractures of light, that was Aodhan.

His eyes splintered outward from an obsidian pupil in shards of crystalline blue-green, his skin alabaster stroked with gold, his hair so pale as to be colorless . . . and yet so bright it was as if each strand had been coated in crushed diamonds. The illusion of light was echoed by his wings, until in sunlight, he dazzled the eye beyond the human ability to bear, his beauty a painful blade. Though Illium had wings of blue, and Venom the eyes of a viper, it was Aodhan who was the most "other" of Raphael's Seven.

He was also the most remote, his unseen scars leaving him averse to any physical contact. Elena couldn't imagine a life devoid of touch, yet Aodhan had lived an eon divorced from that simple, necessary sense of connection. It had to have been something beyond vicious to have scarred him in such a violent way, but that was Aodhan's story to tell and he hadn't chosen to tell it to her.

"How are you liking New York?" she asked.

Walking out onto the balcony with her, he stepped to the very edge to look down at the city below. "I'm not yet certain." Wings glittering in the sunlight, he appeared to be watching the streams of yellow cabs below. "I've never before experienced a place such as this. The Sire's domain was not thus the last time I was stationed here."

Elena hadn't realized Aodhan had ever before been stationed at the Tower, but of course it made sense, given that he was close to five hundred years old. "It's certainly one-of-a-kind." She loved the energetic chaos of the city, but knew it wasn't for everyone; though since Aodhan had requested the transfer after centuries at Raphael's Refuge stronghold, something in New York had resonated with him.

"Most people still don't know you're here." It had surprised her when Aodhan's arrival hadn't made the splash she'd expected. Then she'd discovered he never flew at a height where he could be discerned by mortal eyes. Those who glimpsed the light sparking off him during the rare instances when he dropped below the cloud layer assumed it to be a trick of the light, or a stunning spark off the metal body of a passing aircraft.

"Illium enjoys dancing with the world. I prefer to watch it."

"Don't you want to explore the city, fly above the streets?" She could understand why he wouldn't want to land where he might accidentally be touched, but that didn't mean he couldn't see New York up close and personal.

Aodhan gave her a searching look, those eyes of shattered glass refracting her face into a million fragments. "You are right, Consort. I should be seen in the city, especially at this time—there are those who have forgotten my power because I don't choose to display it."

Elena had no doubt Aodhan was as lethal as the rest of the

Seven. "I wasn't thinking about the politics of it. I'm more worried about you." From what she knew, of the immortals in New York, he was close to Illium alone . . . but there, too, he maintained a painful distance.

"Even when we were young, Aodhan was serious where I was full of mischief, but he had laughter in his soul and enough wickedness to be my true friend in all things. I miss him."

11

"No one," she said now, the piercing sadness of Illium's words echoing in her mind, "can go through life alone." Not even a woman who, as a girl, had seen her mother's high-heeled shoe on the hallway tile, and vowed never again to give anyone that much power over her heart. Sara alone had managed to break through, and that after years of trust.

Then had come an archangel as dangerous and as fascinating as the wild winds above a storm-darkened sea. "It isn't only hurt you avoid by avoiding bonds"—she tried to make him see the truth it had taken her almost two decades to understand, this angel so haunting in his aloneness—"you also miss out on the painful joy that comes with throwing your heart wide open and going hell-for-leather."

A pause, then words that were stones thrown into the tranquil mirror of an unbroken lake. "Are you not afraid?"

"Terrified," she admitted, thinking of the violent stab of vulnerability that had hit her just that morning. "But you know what? Fuck fear. I won't allow it to steal my life from me—and you shouldn't, either." No, she didn't understand the hell that had shaped Aodhan, but she'd been through her own hell, had firsthand knowledge of the cage such horror could create. "Fly hard and fast, Aodhan. You never know what you'll see. And what's the worst that could happen?"

Aodhan's response was quiet and bloody. "I could crash to the earth, my wings broken and my body a fleshy pulp."

"But imagine what you'd experience in the interim . . . and ask yourself if safe aloneness is all you ever wish to know."

Leaving the solemn angel to his thoughts when he didn't respond, she squared her shoulders and made her way back inside the Tower, and to the first of the strictly guarded floors that held the wounded angels. The majority remained in the healing comas Keir had induced, their bodies shattered into pieces, but the faces of those who were conscious lit up the instant she came into view.

Calling her "Consort," they asked her for news of what was happening in the city and with their squadrons and apologized for being unable to rise from their beds. It was the first time she'd had real personal contact with many of the fighters who defended the Tower, and it humbled her that they saw her visit as an honor, for she was "consort to their liege."

Thankful for Keir's quiet whisper that so concisely explained a response she'd been struggling to understand, Elena settled in. As she spoke to the injured in the hours that followed, she began to comprehend another aspect of her responsibilities when it came to her position by Raphael's side. She was no doubt the weakest angel in the room in terms of power, but that wasn't who the men and women around her saw, wasn't what they needed from her.

"Take a deep breath," Keir murmured when she walked out to the corridor after seeing the brutal injuries done a dark-eyed angel who'd proudly shown her the sword he'd been given by Galen himself—a sign of the weapons-master's respect for his skills. The angel's left wing was nothing but tendon clinging to bone, his face pulped on one side, his arm severed at the shoulder.

Hands on her knees, she sucked in gulps of air and, when she could speak again, said, "Will he heal?"

"Yes, though it'll mean months of hurt for him." A gentle hand on her hair, a healer's touch. "In the hours past, have you come to understand why they respond to you as they do?"

A lump of emotion in her throat, Elena rose to her full height, topping Keir by several inches. "I'm their conduit to Raphael." She hadn't understood until this instant that the general fighting troops had the same awe of Raphael as many mortals. Even among angelkind, an archangel was a being to be feared and respected.

Dmitri, Aodhan, Galen, Illium, all of the Seven, they were only a rung below the Cadre as far as the troops were concerned. The fighters would go to any one of them without hesitation when it came to issues to do with the Tower's defenses, but would never think to bother them with anything else. "*I'm* meant to be the one who looks below the formal, structured surface and to the individuals beneath." The one who kept her finger on the living heartbeat of the Tower, made certain people were happy.

"You feel foolish that it has taken you until now to apprehend this."

"Someone couldn't have clued me in?" Not that she would've known what to do—she didn't now—but at least she would've tried. "It's been months!"

Keir's frown was a silent rebuke. "No one expected you to take up these responsibilities for years, if not decades, yet. You are a young consort; it is understood that you have much to learn . . . but the trauma of the past days has altered that timeline." Shadows heavy on the fine bones of his face, his tone holding a haunting sadness.

"I don't know how to do this." It was a confession torn out of her soul. "Not long ago, I told Aodhan to take risks, but God, Keir, I think I'm at my limit. I'm not sure my heart is big enough to encompass thousands." Some of whom would inevitably die in battle. The pain of the loss wouldn't be a distant, manageable one if she knew their names, their dreams, their hopes. Each death would be a kick directly to her battered heart. "I've lost too many people already."

"Courage, Elena." Brushing his fingertips over her cheek, he led her back to the infirmary. "Of that I know you have an imprudent amount."

It took all of her courage to visit the one person in the infirmary she'd avoided till the last possible moment. "Izzy." The young blond angel, his curls having been shaved off to reveal his fractured skull, had a sweet crush on her. Even so badly hurt that she couldn't believe he was awake and aware, his brutalized face glowed when she took a seat by his bedside.

It was impossible to do anything but smile back, he was so adorable in his devotion.

"I thought you forgot me." Shy words, his cheeks going pink as she flirted with him in an effort to take his mind off the excruciating pain of his injuries.

"Our bodies are capable of healing the most horrific wounds," Keir had said, "but the cost is pain. No drug to numb pain will work on angelic bodies, though we've tried to find such for centuries upon centuries. I, too, can only soften the hurt, not eliminate it, and while the babes and the ones over three or four hundred can be placed under for a long duration, the younger adults wake constantly and thus are too often conscious."

Fifteen minutes later, she was careful not to accidentally cause Izak any further hurt when she pressed a kiss to the single unbroken patch of his face. "Rest, heal. I'll come by again soon." Maybe she was scared at what was being asked of her, but if Izak could smile through his agony, she'd damn well find the guts to be what he needed her to be.

"When you create your guard," he said abruptly as she turned to leave, "will you at least consider me?" Eyes huge with entreaty. "I know I'm young and I don't mind having the least—"

"Wait." She tilted her head to the side. "You know I don't have bodyguards." It had taken more than one drag-down fight with Raphael to carve that rule into stone, and Elena had no intention of altering that fact.

"No, not guards. A *Guard*."

This time, Elena heard the capital *G*.

"Like Raphael's Seven," Izak continued, aching hope in his expression. "You're a consort. Elijah's consort has a Guard."

Elena didn't know what she would do with a Guard, but

saying no to this fragile, broken, hopeful boy was out of the question. "Consider yourself the first member."

His smile lit up the whole room.

It was well after nightfall when she left the infirmary and went up several floors to find Raphael ensconced in a strategy session with his Seven, those not physically in the city having called in on visual feeds. She could've gone in, taken a seat, and listened, but she needed to clear her head after the intense emotional strain of the past day.

Digging out her cell phone, she messaged her best friend. *The munchkin asleep?*

Snoring like a champ. Want to come over for coffee?

I won't interrupt you and your love bunny?

My love bunny has abandoned me for his workshop. He's making some super-special nifty weapon for another woman. Good thing I love you or I'd have to kill you.

A smile breaking through the sadness and anger inside her, she sent a message to Raphael's phone instead of interrupting his thoughts, then flew to Sara's. The last time she'd been by, the roof had been a construction site, but today, her best friend waved at her from the now flat surface, two steaming mugs and a baby monitor sitting on the battered wooden coffee table in front of an equally battered sofa.

"Nice," Elena said, taking in the currently empty planters set in the corners, the wall around the roof high enough that Zoe could play here without any risk she'd fall.

"You'll have to help me pick out some plants in the summer." Sara held up a mug of coffee and, when Elena took it with a sigh, patted the sofa next to her. "No proper furniture yet, so your wings will be a bit squished."

"It's actually so soft, it's not bad." Sinking in, Elena propped up her boots on the coffee table, taking care not to jiggle the monitor. "How's Darrell?"

"Messed up." Sara brought up her legs to sit cross-legged, her hands cupped around her mug, her skin a rich, smooth brown against the white ceramic. "But I think he'll be okay. You and Ransom got to him in time."

They sat in comfortable silence for several minutes, their eyes on the stars above, the sky holding the sharp clarity of the coldest of nights, their breath frosting the air. When they did talk, they meandered from topic to topic, their friendship old enough that they could skip from their worry about the predicted archangelic hostilities to a discussion on Sara's sideswept bangs to bursting out laughing when they both muttered, "Men," at the same time.

Then Sara, having curled up against the arm of the sofa, poked at Elena's thigh with a sock-clad foot. "Stop it."

Startled by the burst of inexplicable anger, Elena stared. "What?"

"Stop thinking about what'll happen when I'm gone." It was an arrow to the heart. "You ever think about the fact that maybe I'll have to watch *you* die?"

"I'm becoming immor—"

Her friend snorted. "Since when has the immortal world been a happy-happy-let's-hold-hands-and-sing-'Kumbaya' kind of a place, huh? Weren't we just discussing a war, genius?"

Mouth dropping open, Elena blinked and realized Sara was right. Her life was no less dangerous now than it had been during her time as a hunter. In fact, it could be argued she swam in far deadlier waters as Raphael's consort. "Well, damn."

"Exactly. So don't let me see that look in your eyes again." Sara clicked her mug to Elena's. "You know what I've learned from my baby girl? To enjoy the now. It'll be gone soon enough, and no one knows what the next hour, much less tomorrow, will bring."

Elena decided she should engrave those words on her brain, saying as much to Raphael two hours later as they lay skin to skin in their Enclave bedroom. He'd come to her with a grim look in his eyes and battle plans on his mind, his touch so tender, tears had wet her cheeks. "That was a pretty wonderful now," she whispered afterward.

"Yes." A deep masculine murmur.

Her head on his chest, she soaked in his warmth, knowing they were lucky to have these hours together, possible only because of his trust in his Seven. Word had come from Jason that the other members of the Cadre were currently confirmed as being in their territories, which gave New York some breathing room.

"I visited the injured," she said, knowing the respite was a temporary one—like Raphael, she didn't believe in coincidences, especially a coincidence that brought death to angels and vampires alike. "I managed to speak to everyone who was conscious."

"I know." His hand fisted in her hair. "You acted as a consort should, despite the cost. I'm proud of you, *hbeebti*."

Chest tight at the simple acknowledgment, she ran her foot over his shin. "I also seem to have acquired the start of a Guard."

"Oh? Who have you chosen?"

"Izzy," she said, and told him how it had happened.

Raphael laughed. "I will, of course, have to throw the boy into training with the toughest men in my employ as soon as he has recovered. He may regret volunteering."

"I don't actually expect him to do for me what the Seven do for you."

"Would you dent his pride?"

Elena sighed, having the sinking feeling she'd inadvertently ended up with a *real* Guard. "How was I supposed to say no to someone that adorable?" She lifted her head to scowl at her lover. "It'd have been like kicking a puppy then stomping on his heart."

Raphael folded one arm behind his head, his biceps flexing. "He's not as much a babe as you believe."

"No?" Leaning in, she grazed her teeth over the firm muscle.

His fingers curved over her bare breast in return, neither one of them in any hurry. "Izak's been in training with Galen since he was younger than Sam."

Galen with *babies*? "Impossible," she said, even as she recalled Hannah pointing out the opposite in the painting downstairs. "Galen eating babies I can understand, but training them?"

Open amusement. "I think you miss our weapons-master."

"Ha-ha."

That got her a long, lazy kiss, their tongues licking against each other, his thigh pushing possessively between her own.

"When Galen was first courting Jessamy," Raphael said with a brush of his thumb over her nipple when their lips parted, "he began to teach flight skills to the little ones. Over time, it has become a tradition—Galen is always the one who gives basic flight instruction to the babes, and some, like Izak, never stop training with him."

The idea of Galen, with his wings akin to a northern harrier's, leading a squadron of babies—not all of whom could fly exactly straight—had Elena shaking her head. "I'm sorry, I need to see to believe this. It's like you just told me the sky turns purple every Wednesday."

Sensual laughter twining around her, Raphael's mood no longer black. "For his age, Izak is exceptional. In comparison to older fighters, he has much to learn, part of the reason Galen organized a Tower placement."

"So he could study under more experienced men." It was similar to what the Guild did, pairing up a neophyte hunter with an experienced one for the first year after graduation.

Raphael nodded. "Izak may be comparatively weak at present, but he'll grow with you and so will the bond between you." His eyes closed when she reached out to stroke the most sensitive part of his right wing, her damp flesh rubbing against the hard muscle of his thigh. "Aodhan was a stripling, Illium even younger, when I accepted them into what became my Seven."

She was leaning in to kiss him again when his eyes snapped open, languid relaxation erased by cold-eyed focus in a single heartbeat. "Keir is on his way to see us."

Elena thought of the decomposing vampire found in that house now burned to the ground, the wounded angels in the infirmary, the five carried to the Refuge on flower-covered biers, and knew the news could be nothing good.

12

Looking out toward the glittering mirage of Manhattan from their balcony a couple of minutes later, she saw the dark shadow of wings over the Hudson. "Is Illium providing escort?" Even with the wild blue and shimmering silver lost to the night, the angel had a distinctive style of flight.

"I've ordered that no one fly alone at night—or should they be heading into an isolated area." A hard glance. "That applies to my consort, too. You left the Tower tonight before I could speak to you about it."

"No arguments here." Tugging at the belt of her robe, she said, "I should put on proper clothes."

"This'll do." Raphael, dressed in jeans and a white T-shirt, ran his knuckles down the side of her face. "Keir is one of the few men whom I will allow to see my consort naked of her armor."

Because, Elena thought, the healer had seen every part of her broken body—and he'd helped bring her back.

"As for your Bluebell, his heart is already yours."

Her fingers clenched on the belt. "Raphael, he's not truly . . . not that way, is he?" She couldn't bear to hurt Illium.

"I think," Raphael said, as the night wind brought with it the whispering promise of snow, "Illium needs to heal and you are safe."

Elena rubbed her face. "I hope that's all it is." Regardless, she did change into jeans and a simple green-and-white-checked shirt, Raphael doing up the buttons on the wing slits for her before they walked down to open the library doors and step out onto the lawn.

The two angels made a quiet landing a minute later.

Keir's face was solemn, his face showing a strain Elena had never before seen on him, certainly not when she'd left the infirmary earlier that night. Gut twisting, she took his arm and led him inside to find the fire lit and the table by the windows set with coffee and tea, as well as a tray of fruit, nuts, and a rich, creamy cheese. Crackers lay neatly on a different platter, alongside a thin flatbread flavored with herbs.

Thank God for Montgomery.

Nudging Keir into an armchair in front of the crackling flames, she poured the healer the tea she knew he liked, as Illium fixed him a plate. "You have to eat," she said, when he would've waved off the food.

Expression drained, eyes devoid of their natural warmth, he didn't respond.

Elena wasn't ready to admit defeat. Taking the plate from Illium after setting the tea on the little side table beside the healer, she nodded at the blue-winged angel to go speak to Raphael, while she took a seat in the armchair opposite Keir. Putting a piece of cheese on a cracker, she held it out. "Please, Keir."

Gaze flicking to her, he took the morsel. "So, the patient looks after the healer."

"The patient knows that if she gets herself damaged again, she's going to need you, so it's self-serving."

A glimmer of light in his expression. "And if I don't eat?"

"This healer once told me I had the unbreakable will of a mule." It had been a compliment, Keir's delight at her progress unhidden.

His beautiful lips curved slightly at last and he ate the cracker, took the next one. She managed to get that and some flatbread into him, as well as a peach she sliced into pieces. "You did this for me once, remember? When I was bored and grumpy after you told me I had to stay in bed." It had been in the aftermath of Lijuan's ball. "Stupid balls. They should be banned."

Soft laughter, the peach eaten quarter by quarter while Illium and Raphael stood at Raphael's desk, talking quietly about the ongoing holes in their defensive line. The firelight glinted off the white-gold of Raphael's feathers, and since he was right next to Illium, the filaments of silver in Bluebell's wings also catching the light, the difference in effect was crystalline.

"White fire." Keir's intrigued expression told her he was back. "Extraordinary."

It was, Elena thought in wonder, a resonance to the shifting fire that gave Raphael's wings a sense of movement though he stood in place.

Settling back in his chair, Keir said, "I haven't seen such an effect in the others who are Cadre."

Elena forced herself to look away from Raphael, her antennae on alert. "Do you know anything of what's happening with Michaela's abilities?"

Keir shook his head. "She doesn't trust me, though she knows I would never break my vows as healer. It is also true that I have always favored Raphael." Putting down his tea, he looked at her with his old, wise eyes. "As I favor the consort who has brought him back from the cruel edge of immortality."

Elena set aside the plate on which she'd cut the peach, and leaned forward after a quick glance to ensure Raphael remained absorbed in his conversation with Illium. "Lijuan warned Raphael I'd make him a little bit mortal."

"You have." Quiet equanimity. "And you worry you've weakened him. You have."

Elena flinched.

"Elena." Shaking his head, Keir waited until she met his gaze again. "Even an archangel needs a weakness—absolute power is a corruption. Of that, Lijuan is the perfect example."

A rustle of wings, Illium and Raphael walking across to join them before she could point out that while the latter might be true, Raphael needed to be at full strength to beat Lijuan and her ilk.

Raphael wasted no time or words. "What did you discover, Keir?"

"The disease that killed the vampire, it is akin to the pox."

Elena sucked in a breath as Illium came to lean against her armchair, his eyes liquid gold in the firelight and his wing warm against her own. "The disease that has so often killed tens of thousands of mortals?"

"Yes." Keir held up a hand when they would've spoken again. "It isn't identical—it has a more virulent effect on the internal organs, turning them to liquid, yet doesn't appear to be as infectious. It requires more than a speck or two of blood to transfer. A few droplets, perhaps even a small feed, though I cannot be certain on that last point."

Raphael shook his head. "You wouldn't fly to us when you are so clearly exhausted if you had good news."

"You've known me too long." The healer took a deep breath. "My tests show the disease has an incubation period of six hours. After that, it appears to progress at vicious speed—the victim would've been too debilitated to go for help by the time he understood he was ill. Terrible as that was for him, it's good in the wider scheme of things."

"So there's a very high chance he wouldn't have had an opportunity to infect others."

Keir nodded at Illium's words. "The bad news is the pox shows every indication of being designed to attack vampires." Turning to Raphael, he said, "Your instincts led you true—I detect an intelligence behind the disease. It is no natural thing."

"First my angels fall from the sky, and now this." Raphael's expression was brutal. "There is no longer any question the city is under attack."

Illium said something in a language Elena didn't understand, but his last word was cuttingly identifiable and the same one on the tip of Elena's tongue. *"Cowards."*

"Agreed," Raphael said, his voice ice. "We've focused on Lijuan because she's a known enemy, but we must not wear blinders."

They all nodded.

"Such cowardice eliminates Titus," Raphael continued. "He's a warrior in the oldest sense and unless there are indications he's been touched by madness"—a glance at Keir, the healer shaking his head—"then he wouldn't stoop to stratagems that skate so close to the line of what is permitted in a war."

"Astaad," Keir said softly, "despite his occasionally secretive ways, believes absolutely in honor, and I think such actions would stain it. He continues to feel a deep shame over his violent actions toward his concubine during your mother's waking, though we all know he wasn't in his right mind at the time."

"Neha's too busy holding off her twin to bother about us." Worried what the Archangel of India would do in her continued grief about the execution of her daughter, Elena had read every one of Jason's reports as they came in. "Is Elijah two-faced enough to offer friendship with one hand and stab us in the back with the other?"

"Eli has a noble heart and the inclination not to cause you or yours harm," Keir said to Raphael, then glanced at Elena. Obviously noting her surprise, the healer smiled. "He is the rarest of archangels, one who didn't show signs of such violent power as a youth or as a young male."

From the way Raphael was staring at the healer, he didn't know this particular story, either. "You will not stop now, Keir."

Laughing, the healer said, "Eli was a seasoned and loyal general in another archangel's army on the day of a great battle against—" Cutting himself off, Keir shook his head. "I will tell you that tale another time. It is far too long and interesting to shorten so precipitously."

Fascinated, Elena waited for him to continue.

"Eli," Keir said into the silence, "had just cut down the last of the enemy and raised his sword to declare victory when it hit: a sudden and total ascension that sent him screaming into the skies. It was extraordinary, as all ascensions are extraordinary, but what is most important is that when he returned from the sky to the earth, he was no longer a general but one of the Cadre."

Raphael said what Elena was thinking. "He was Caliane's general."

"Yes, so unless you betray him, he will not first betray you. He would've hunted your mother in her madness had she not disappeared into Sleep, but he would've taken no pleasure in it, for he has never forsaken the vows he took to cause no harm to her and those of her blood."

"Caliane's never mentioned him."

"Did you ask her?" An arch question. "You know her age. It's very possible she hasn't quite assimilated that you are now Eli's peer, for he was an archangel before you were born, and in her eyes . . ."

"I'm a child still." Raphael thrust his hand through his hair. "I wish you'd shared Elijah's past with me earlier. It would've made certain negotiations much less fraught."

Keir stood to pour himself a fresh cup of tea. "You are your mother's son, Raphael. Until you had judged and decided to accept Eli's friendship for yourself, it would've done no good."

"There isn't," Illium said into the thoughtful pause that followed, "much difference between death and disease. Lijuan remains a prime candidate."

Raphael stared into the flames. "Not for the Falling," he said at last. "I cannot believe such a large-scale act didn't need a closer hand, and Jason confirmed she was in her own territory at the time, busy with her reborn. For the vampire pox, however, she could've simply sent in a carrier of the disease."

"It could even be a mortal." Keir retook his seat, his expression intent. "My gifts tell me the disease is passed through blood, and a donor would be in the best position to infect many." Frowning, he shook his head. "Yet if it is thus, we should have more bodies—the dead vampire had been so two days at least."

"If the victims die at such speed," Illium said quietly, "they might be locked up rotting in their homes."

It was a horrible image, and Elena was glad for the distraction when Montgomery appeared in the doorway, his eyes sending her a silent message. "Guild Hunter," he said when she excused herself to walk over to him. "There is an urgent call for you from the Guild Director."

Taking the portable house phone, she said, "Thank you."

Ten seconds into that call, and her gut churned. Because Ransom had just found those other bodies, and Illium had been right: they were locked up inside their home, rotting slowly from a malicious disease that had ended their chance at immortality.

All four of them landed on the tiny drive of a run-down house in a dingy part of the Bronx within the hour. Having been waiting outside, Ransom led them into the building without anything more than a nod, his cheekbones slicing against his skin from the way he clenched his jaw. She smelled the reason for his rigid self-control as soon as she stepped inside the house, the air putrid with disease and heavy with a warmth that told her the central heating had been on for the duration.

"How many?" Raphael asked, wings limned in a lethal glow.

"Five, and they've been dead a couple of days at least." Ransom went left, heading toward what was probably a bedroom, while Keir and Illium broke off toward the other side of the house. "I turned off the heat and opened the windows to release the worst of the smell."

Why is it always Ransom who shows up with these bodies?

Hearing the deadly supposition in Raphael's tone, Elena locked eyes with the man who was her lover . . . but who she knew didn't see other mortals the same way she did. *Don't get any ideas. Ransom grew up on the streets and still has all his old contacts. The people who talk to him, tell him things, wouldn't ever talk to anyone from the Tower—or even most of the other hunters in the Guild.*

"Who discovered the bodies?' Raphael asked aloud.

Ransom's answer was immediate. "I did. Got a tip about the smell, broke in when I recognized it."

He is lying.

He's protecting someone. It was what Ransom did when it came to the street people, who were as much family to him as his fellow hunters.

I can't permit news of this to spread, Elena. It would incite a panic. Either Ransom talks or I'll have to take the information from his mind.

Stomach tight, her hand clenched on the blade she'd dropped into her palm when they entered the house. *He's my friend.*

I trust Ransom to keep his mouth shut. The sea, clean and bright, the wind an icy blast. *I do not trust those he trusts.*

And if I ask you to let it go?

I won't.

13

Jerking at the vicious bluntness of Raphael's response, at the realization that she was helpless to protect someone she cared for deeply, she stopped Ransom in the bedroom doorway. "You need to tell the truth," she said, each word a razor in her throat. "Who found the bodies?"

A shake of his head, his jaw stiff. "If I do, I make that person a target."

"I will take this memory alone and do the witness no harm." Raphael came to stand beside Elena. "He or she will live and remember nothing of this night."

Ransom's eyes slid to Elena and in them she saw the harsh realization that if he didn't answer the question, Raphael would take the information anyway.

"I'm sorry," she whispered, ready for anger.

But Ransom shrugged. "He's an archangel, Ellie. We're just rats to him."

She knew he hadn't meant anything by it, had in fact been trying to comfort her, but Ransom's words brought home how little power she had in this relationship. Raphael could override her in so many ways, but she'd become used to having him listen to her, to being able to argue her points. Never had she expected to hear a flat negative, with no room for negotiation.

"You won't touch her other memories?" Ransom asked Raphael, while she was still reeling under the force of the cruel emotional slap.

"Questioning the word of an archangel is a good way to end up dead."

Raphael! Stop it. Furious, she met Ransom's green eyes. "He doesn't want anything but this particular memory." *Don't make me a liar,* she said mind to mind at the same instant.

A dangerous pause. *You question my word, too, Elena?*

Ransom is right. We are rats to you.

You aren't part of any other group. You are my consort.

Ransom spoke before she could respond and it was just as well, since what she wanted to say would probably only have thrown fuel on the ugly fight brewing between her and Raphael.

"Cici lives down the street," he said. "She came to buddy-watch the latest episode of *Hunter's Prey* like she does every week, and when no one answered, she used the key they gave her a while back when she needed a place to hide out from a violent ex. She knew something was wrong as soon as she got a whiff of the smell, but she figured maybe the cat had dragged in a dead rat or something while everyone was out."

Running a hand through his hair, he messed it up, tugged off the rawhide tie to put it back in order. "She's a tough working girl, has come up against knife-wielding assailants and walked out the winner, but I found her curled up in a ball sobbing when I arrived." A look at Raphael. "Janvier is with her. We were out riding together when I got the call."

That explained the unfamiliar red motorcycle out front, parked next to Ransom's black one. As for how Ransom knew the vampire who held the trust of senior Tower personnel, Janvier had some kind of a relationship—no one quite understood what—with one of their fellow hunters.

"Which house?"

"It's an apartment. I'll show you."

Remaining behind after Raphael left with Ransom, Elena forced herself to go through the house, while Keir focused on the victims and Illium stood watch outside to make sure no one decided to get curious.

Three males and two females lay dead. Five more lives snuffed out. Two couples, judging from the photos she could see in the bedrooms. One couple was in bed, the two men spooned together as if they'd held on to each other as the sickness became too much to bear. The male half of the other couple was slumped on the couch, his girlfriend on the floor, and to Elena, it looked as if the girl had fallen in a spasm and been unable to get back up. The second girl was in a tiny room at the back, the petite prettiness evident in the photos tucked under the edges of her vanity obliterated by the pox.

This victim's room might have been the smallest in the house, but it was well kept and made individual by the framed Broadway posters on the walls and the glittering masks hung around the same vanity mirror that held the photos. A dancer, Elena realized, seeing the costumes in the doorless cupboard. She recognized one of them from an off-Broadway show that had closed six months ago, after a respectable run.

Since the dead vampire was living in this part of town, she must've been a backup dancer and not yet a lead . . . had probably embraced the near-immortality of vampirism so as to have more time to pursue her dream of the stage. Elena understood why someone would sign on for a hundred years of slavery on the back of such overwhelming desire; dreams could be a commanding force.

Belle had been a dancer. Long legged and with a thousand dreams in her eyes as she practiced in the backyard. She'd laughed when Elena tried to copy her, but it had been the affectionate laughter of a big sister, and many times, she'd stopped her own practice to teach Elena how to do the moves.

"Like this, Ellie. You have to become the music, become the air."

Sadness weighing down her shoulders, Elena whispered, "I'm sorry," before leaving the bright little room, its color and flamboyance a painful foil for the small, rotting body that lay curled up on the bed.

As she went through the house more carefully, she noted another poster, this one from a Hollywood blockbuster that had a sticky note at the top proclaiming *Extras rule!* Then there was the marked-up television script on one bedside table, a musical score on another, next to a violin of glowing wood so beautiful, Elena didn't dare touch it.

"They were artists," she said to Keir, watching as he examined the body of the girl in the living room. "Dancers, actors, musicians. Must've banded together to rent this place so they could save on costs." It surprised her. "I always figured after a hundred years of service to an angel, vampires would come out with at least some savings."

"Not every angel is generous." Keir kept his eyes on the body, his hands gentle and respectful as he opened the girl's shirt to check the progression of the disease. "It's an unspoken rule that the blood kin who complete their Contracts should be given enough money on leaving to begin a new life, but that sum is open to interpretation."

He closed the sides of the shirt, doing up two buttons so it wouldn't gape. "Then," he said, shifting to look at the male, "there are the vampires who come out of their Contracts so used to being told what to do that they have no idea how to manage their money and end up going through it like water."

"The musician," Elena said, "I think he spent his money on his violin; the actor on drama classes, from the brochures I found in her room; so these five, at least, were working toward something." There was a vibrant sense of promise in every room of the house, the kind of energy that said all five had been on the same wavelength. "It seems so unfair. They were the good ones, the ones who did their hundred years, and this is their reward?"

"Life is rarely fair, Elena." Keir's voice held the echoes of thousands of years of existence. "But this, at least . . . no, it should not have happened."

Finding nothing in the living room that might provide a clue as to how all five roommates had apparently been infected simultaneously—a fact that seemed to negate their blood donor theory—Elena moved on. Ransom returned while she was in the kitchen. "Raphael is one scary motherfucker," was his greeting.

Elena's hand tightened around the edge of the fridge door,

the cold air seeping into her clothes to scrape over her skin. "Cici?"

"Sleeping like a baby. And yeah, your scary boyfriend's returned to the Tower to deal with something else." Lines of strain around his mouth, he blew out a harsh breath. "Part of me is glad Cici won't be haunted by this horror, won't wake up whimpering and screaming night after night, but we took a piece of her life, Ellie."

"I would rather die as Elena than live as a shadow."

She'd said that to Raphael once, and he'd kept her faith, hadn't messed with her memories. Maybe that was why she'd become complacent, forgetting he'd do so to others without blinking. Even to the people who were more her family than Jeffrey would ever be. "I'm sorry," she said again, door edge digging into her palm from the force of her grip.

Ransom shoulder-bumped her. "It's not your fault. I'd have had to report this to the Tower whether or not you were with Raphael. Only difference is, I'd have been wiped, too, and never known it, so thanks for having my back." Bending, he began to move things around in the fridge. "Hey"—utter motionlessness—"did you see this?"

Alerted by his response, she pushed the door wide and bent down beside him. "Blood." Bottles of it, tucked away in back of the second shelf. Most vampires preferred the vein, but bottled blood was like fast food—every city vamp had some within easy reach. "Supplier?"

If it was one of the major vamp-focused blood services, this could go nuclear very, very fast. Those services didn't test for disease, because *vampires weren't supposed to get sick.* Instead, they took in donors the human banks rejected, paying them enough that, for some, donating "food blood" was a steady source of income. And with New York being a Tower city, with a strong vampire population, demand was high. It would've been child's play for the carrier of this deadly pox to slip into the donor line.

"Blood-for-Less," Ransom read out. "That's a new outfit in the Vampire Quarter."

Known as Soho in the daytime, the area wasn't exactly a

cheap-rent part of the city, which meant, Elena thought, the business had to be at least moderately successful.

"Small-time blood café but with a growing fan base," Ransom continued, closing the fridge door. "Lower-quality blood, according to my vamp contacts."

"How can it be lower quality than diseased blood?"

"Word is they take anemics, people who overdonate, might even be watering the blood down a little, but it's cheap. There's a market for that—blood that's enough for a snack, not a meal. And since that's the Blood-for-Less motto, no one feels cheated."

Elena walked across to flip open the lid of the garbage bin. No bottles.

Then she spied a white plastic crate off to the side marked *Recycling* in sparkly purple pen that erased any distance she might've managed to keep from the victims. "Here we go," she said through a throat gone raw. "One large bottle."

"There was that half-eaten cake in the fridge."

"Yes." The remnants of the word *Congratulations* had still been readable, white icing over chocolate frosting. "A celebration, complete with cake and a shared bottle of blood to do the toast." God, it pissed her off that these people had died so an archangel already bloated with power could gain more.

"I can reach out to my contacts"—stress lines bracketed either side of Ransom's mouth as he spoke—"find out if there are any other budget operations like Blood-for-Less, if that information will help with whatever the hell is going on."

Elena could taste his frustration, but she wasn't about to risk his mind or his memories. "Yes," she said, and the responding flash of anger on his face cut like a knife; she had the sense of a wall going up between her and someone who'd been a part of her life since the day she'd first walked into the Academy. "I'll check out Blood-for-Less."

Less than a minute later, she said, "I have to fly out," to Illium, having grabbed the address from Ransom before he left, his expression tight. "I want you to stay here, keep a watch on Keir." No sane archangel would target a healer, but there was no guarantee they were dealing with anyone sane. And what better way to cripple New York than to eliminate the one person who had any real handle on the disease?

"You can't fly alone at night," Illium reminded her. "It's a blanket ban."

"Shit." She'd forgotten the precaution and it wasn't one it'd be smart to flout, given the current situation. "Who—" She broke off as the gleaming red motorcycle, which had disappeared in the time she'd been inside, purred to a stop in front of the house once more.

The tall male who slid off after removing his helmet had eyes of deep green and hair of chestnut, his face holding an inherent and lazy sensuality reinforced by his every movement. It would be a mistake, however, to trust that first impression—because while Janvier wasn't one of the Seven, he worked directly with them. No one held the respect of men that dangerous without being deadly himself.

"I return as per your command, dear Bluebell," the vampire now said, the cadence of his voice invoking images of bayous dark and mysterious.

Illium's order was to the point. "Make sure no one gets to Keir. Aodhan is arranging aerial backup—someone should be here within ten minutes." When Janvier flicked a salute, his motorcycle jacket shifting to reveal the gleaming black butt of a serious gun, Illium turned to Elena. "A lift?"

"Yes."

His hands around her waist, her own on his shoulders, Illium took off. Though he was whiplash-fast and could maneuver like nobody else she knew, he didn't have as much brute strength as Raphael, the lift taking longer than it did when it was her consort who held her. Eyes of gold looked into her own as they rose into the starlit sky, the lashes thick black tipped with blue in a natural echo of his hair. "You look angry, Ellie."

Oh, she was. It didn't matter that she understood she was being irrational—humans couldn't be permitted certain knowledge for the good of mortals and immortals alike. And if anyone leaked the news of this disease, it would not only incite panic, it might give Raphael's enemies the sign of weakness for which they no doubt waited.

Regardless of all that, she was angry at Raphael for being

so much an archangel. That, too, was in no way logical or rational, simply a sign that she'd lost sight of the truth of him because he'd become someone else to her. It was a bone-jarring shock to be so bluntly reminded that the man who was her lover was that man *only for her*. To the rest of the world he was— must be—the lethal, dangerous, and sometimes cruel Archangel of New York.

None of that was something she could share with Illium, this battle a very private one, so all she said was, "It's been a hard night."

His expression told her he knew that wasn't all of it, but he released her without further words as soon as they'd gained the correct altitude, and they flew in silence to the cute little warehouse that functioned as Blood-for-Less's current base of operations . . . and the heart of the infection.

14

Unsurprisingly, the blood café was open, the doorway glowing with a muted light that would be too dark for most humans, but perfect for its clientele. While the warehouse was technically in the Vampire Quarter, it was on the very fringe, no other vampiric businesses around it. As a result, the area was currently deserted, devoid of foot traffic.

Inside, the warehouse had been partitioned into two sides using heavy black drapes in lush velvet, one side acting as the store and office, while the other was set up with three sets of unexpectedly lovely seating arrangements featuring wine-red sofas accented with black rugs. There was even art on the walls, the black-and-white photographs carefully chosen to add to the darkly sensual ambience.

It was the kind of place that might tempt a group of friends to linger, drink a glass of blood together . . . maybe buy another more expensive one—because when Elena picked up a menu from a nearby side table lacquered in glossy black, she saw that Blood-for-Less also offered a premium service tailored to its market: rich blood flavored or spiced in a number of different ways, but at a price that wouldn't break the budget, as each serving was relatively small. Attractive enough pricewise that a couple on a date, for example, might buy several flavors to share, and fancy enough that it'd feel like a special occasion.

Smart business.

"Welcome—" The pretty Hispanic woman who'd walked out of the office cut off her spiel the instant she saw them. "Consort." Ruffles of white lace at her throat and cuffs, teamed with a tightly fitted vest and pants in black, she lowered her upper half in a deep bow. "How may I be of service?" Her gaze flicked to the door that Illium was closing as she rose back up, fear crawling into her eyes with a quickness that told Elena this vamp's angel hadn't been kind to her. "I assure you I've completed my hundred years. I have my discharge papers—"

Elena held up a hand to relieve the woman's panic. "I'm not here to take you in, but I need you to answer some questions. How much blood do you have in storage?"

Blinking, the vampire pulled herself together with commendable speed. "I just began this business three months ago, so it runs on a shoestring. My present stock is two hundred bottles."

A knock somewhere beyond the velvet curtains had the owner glancing over her shoulder, before she jerked her gaze back to Elena, perspiration glimmering on her skin. "That's the donor entrance. I get enough walk-ins to keep the stock relatively steady, but I haven't yet built up a strong network of regular donors. It can get hairy sometimes—last week I was down to twenty bottles before a group of college students dropped by." The explanation came out staccato-fast, as if she was attempting to hold back suspected bad news by drowning the air in words.

"I need to see the blood," Elena said, hating the fact that she now inspired so much fear in a legal, hardworking vampire.

A jerky nod. "Of course." The shorter, curvier woman led her inside the office and to three large fridges. "Is—is there a problem with my blood?" Her fingers trembled as she tugged at the lace of her cuffs.

"I can't tell you yet. If you could step out, stay with Illium."

Opening the nearest fridge once the vampire left, Elena picked up the first bottle, unscrewed it and took a sniff.

Cold iron, a hint of disease . . . but it was a disease she'd scented before.

"Cancer," she muttered and screwed the lid back on.

It took her a number of hours to go through the entire stock, and by the time she was halfway through, she'd found three that pulsed with the putrid stench she associated with the vampire pox. An angel dispatched earlier for courier duty took the infected blood to Keir as it was discovered, the healer having returned to the labs underneath the Tower.

No others set off her senses.

Regardless, none of the blood in this warehouse could be permitted into circulation. When she informed the owner, the vampire—who, Elena had learned, was named Marcia Blue— almost broke down in tears. "I put my entire payout into this business," she said, hugging her arms around her body. "I can't afford to rebuild my stock from scratch."

"Do you have insurance?"

A shake of the woman's head. "Premiums were too high, given my location and clientele." Trembling, she bit down on her lower lip and swallowed in a clear effort to hold back tears. "I made a profit for the first time last week."

Elena thought of the heartrending unfairness of so much of what had happened over the past three days, culminating in the broken dreams of this vampire who'd put in her time, done her hundred, and she made a decision. "I'll stake you for a percentage of future profits," she said, knowing she couldn't simply give Marcia the money.

Harsh as it might seem, that would make the Tower appear far too generous, the association between it and Elena automatic. And the Tower couldn't afford to be anything but ruthless . . . as Raphael couldn't afford to let her humanity alter the balance of power that kept the city stable.

Marcia's eyes went wide. "You?"

"Yes, I need to start investing my money, and I like your idea. But," she added when Marcia would've spoken, "you understand I'll have to go over your long-term business plan to make sure it's a sound investment?" That seemed like the kind of thing an investor would say.

"Of course." A shaky smile, Marcia's heart in her eyes. "I'll send it to the Tower at once." Bowing again, the other woman looked up, tears rolling down her cheeks. "You won't be sorry. I swear it."

Uncomfortable, Elena turned the conversation back to the hunt. "In the meantime, we'll advance you some clean blood—and you'll start operations again tomorrow at your normal time. Accept donors as usual but don't sell any of their blood. Sell only the blood you receive from us. Understood?"

A quick nod.

About to continue, Elena had a thought. "Did you put up a sign explaining tonight's closure?" If the carrier had returned during that time and become suspicious, he or she might not come back.

It was Illium who answered. "Front and donor door. Just said, *Family emergency, back tomorrow.*"

Since vampires often considered other vampires with whom they'd served, family, that was an excuse no one would question. "Do you have surveillance?" she asked Marcia.

"No. There was no money for that."

A quick glance at Illium, a nod in return, and she knew the cameras would be in place before the doors opened the next day. "I need you to keep strict data on who donates what blood," she said to Marcia. "Tag and label everything."

The vampire nodded, eyes shrewd. "Someone is selling tainted blood, and the taint's dangerous." Carrying on before Elena could interrupt, she said, "I won't speak a word of this, and I'll ensure none of the donated blood leaves the café."

"I hope so," Elena said softly. "Anything else would cost you."

Sweat broke out over the vampire's face once more, a slick sheen. "I do not lie, Consort."

Stomach tight at the renewed fear pulsing in the woman's eyes, Elena told the vampire to leave them the keys and return the following day an hour before she typically opened up.

"I just scared her on purpose," she told Illium. The act had been instinctive, the realization of what she'd done horrifying.

Illium shrugged. "The fear will keep her alive."

"Maybe, but I don't want to become that, become someone who controls others through fear." It sickened her to think she was being corrupted by the power now at her disposal. "What if a hundred years from now, I look into the mirror and see Michaela?" Cruel and capricious and nasty.

"Do you think we'd permit that?" Lips curving, he tapped a finger to her nose. "Raphael would be the first to warn you were you in danger of losing yourself."

Elena wasn't so certain. The man who owned her heart saw nothing wrong with acts that deeply troubled her. *She* was the human one in their relationship. Raphael had said more than once that she'd brought him back from the abyss of age and power—what would happen to the balance between them if she survived war only to break under the relentless pressure of an immortality textured by the power of being consort to an archangel?

Rubbing a fisted hand over her heart, she said, "Can I ask you something?"

"Ellie." His fingers brushing lightly over the back of her wing, careful to avoid the sensitive zones, but an intimacy nonetheless. "When have we ever been so formal? Ask."

"Why have you never resented me?" It was a question for which she'd needed an answer since the day she'd learned about his past. "Resented Raphael?"

Illium had been punished with the loss of his own mortal lover centuries ago, after he broke the greatest taboo of his race and spoke angelic secrets in her ear. Erasing the woman's memories of the blue-winged angel and all he'd told her, Raphael had also stripped Illium of his feathers, grounding him until the wounds healed. Even when he could fly again, there was no surcease; he'd had to keep his distance, eventually watch his former lover fall for someone else, live her life without him.

Golden eyes shadowed with old sorrow, Illium withdrew a small metal pendant from the pocket of his jeans, the surface worn smooth by centuries of handling. "When did Raphael tell you our secrets?" he said, not having to explain to her that his lover had given him the pendant.

Her heart ached at the sadness he ordinarily hid beneath a stunning joie de vivre. "As we fell," she whispered. "Raphael told me as we fell." Everything within her rebelled against the agony linked to that fragment of time—not of the flesh, for her broken body had been beyond that, but of the soul, because Raphael was dying with her.

"On the eve of what he believed would be your death and his." Putting away the pendant, Illium shook his head, the blue-tipped black strands of his hair kissing the sides of his face. "I had no such excuse. My lover was young and headstrong, and angry that I kept secrets from her. I couldn't bear her remoteness . . . so I told."

A sad, rueful smile that spoke of the besotted youth he'd been. "I'm certain other angels have told their mortal lovers over the centuries, the secrets going to the grave with those men and women, but I told a girl who could not keep her silence, who began to whisper hints to others in her village."

This time it was Elena who touched his wing, the silken silver-blue a living piece of art beneath her fingertips. "I'm so sorry."

"No angel can afford to break with such ease," Illium continued, "and though I loved her with all of my being, I also knew her down to the soul, knew she didn't have the will to hold secrets within. Raphael was right to punish me."

When he spread his wing and lifted his arm, she went, hugging him with the embrace of a friend, was hugged in turn, his grip so fierce she knew he fought not to splinter under the deluge of memory.

"The Sire," Illium said, his chest rising against her in a long, jagged breath, "was wounded at what he had to do. I could see it, feel it, and it is the greatest shame of my life that I drove him to the point where he had no other option."

Of everything he'd said, that was the least expected, but Illium wasn't done. "If only," he said, "I'd come to him as soon as I realized my mistake in telling, he would've quietly erased her memory of angelic secrets, warned me not to make the same mistake again, and I would've been free to love her. But I didn't and he could not help me once others learned of my transgression."

Elena's heart twisted as she understood at last. Ruthless he might be, but Raphael protected those who were his own. For him to not only be unable to do that, but to actually be forced to cause harm instead, would've exacted a terrible price.

Especially when it had been Illium, son of an angel who had both Raphael's respect and his love: the Hummingbird, someone he treated with heartbreaking gentleness.

"Whatever price I paid," Illium said into the quiet, "he paid it twice over."

Hurting for the loss that defined the blue-winged angel to this day, and the circumstances that had led to it, Elena leaned back, raised her hand to touch his face, and found herself hesitating.

"Be careful with Illium, Elena. He's vulnerable to the humanity you carry within."

The echo of Dmitri's voice, sin and seduction and violence, the vampire's expression unexpectedly serious as he cautioned her about Illium not long after her return to New York.

"It's all right, Ellie." A lopsided smile, Illium's body heat pressing against her own. "You are the Sire's and I would tear off my own wings before I would break that trust."

Dropping her hand, she took a step away, putting more distance between them. "I don't want to cause you pain," she said, affection intertwined with worry. Her worry wasn't only for how he reacted to her, but also the fact that he continued to mourn a woman who'd turned to dust centuries ago, having forgotten she'd ever been so unbearably loved.

When Elena had been human, she'd sometimes wondered how mortal-immortal couples handled the aging of one, while the other appeared as young as the day they'd first met. Never once had she considered that if the love was true, the pain would be endless for the one left behind. "You have enough hurt inside you already."

"The only thing that'll hurt is if you allow my mistakes to damage our friendship." A slow smile that painted over the sadness, eyes of liquid gold backlit with wickedness. "Shall I tell you about my lovers so you don't feel sorry for me?"

She cocked her head. "In the plural?"

"I wouldn't want to give anyone the wrong idea." Tugging playfully on her braid, he headed for the door. "The blood pickup team has arrived."

The vampiric team, gloved up and masked, made quick work of clearing the fridges. Locking up after them, Elena got a quick lift from Illium and angled her wings toward the Tower. Regardless of her personal anger with Raphael, they were and would always be a unit when it came to protecting their city, and she wanted to update him on the Blood-for-Less situation, as well as find out why he'd left the site of the five vampiric deaths so precipitously.

The light-filled column of the Tower a cold burn in front of her, she reached out to make certain he was inside. *Raphael?*

The answer came immediately, but it held the slight remoteness that denoted a certain amount of distance. *There is a situation, Elena. Michaela is here.*

15

Raphael didn't shift his eyes off Michaela as he instructed Illium to lead Elena to Gable House, the place the female archangel had taken in the short term. He'd left the house of disease as soon as one of his far advance scouts had spotted her flying into the territory, and made the long flight to escort her—a gesture she'd seen as welcome, but that he'd done to make certain she brought no army.

She hadn't, her escort consisting of a single angelic squadron and a vampire, the vampire catching a lift with the angels by way of a light carrier designed for that purpose. Had Michaela been in distress, or in fear of an imminent assault, he'd have waited to have this discussion, but dressed in a green catsuit that hugged her curves, she moved with opulent sensuality, her actions designed to remind him she was considered the most desirable woman in the world.

Raphael would rather sleep in a pit of venomous snakes than with Michaela.

He had, however, allowed her time to rest and have a meal after her journey, for he would not harm the babe in her womb.

"I'm glad you had the sense not to impinge on my home," he said now.

An insinuating smile. "It is an inconvenience not to use my own property, but I know you're protective of your little mortal—and Riker has a taste for her. It would've been impossible to stop him from crossing the woods to get to her had we been neighbors."

Riker, Raphael thought, wouldn't touch Elena. Last time he'd come close to her, Raphael had simply ripped out his heart and left him twitching on the earth. Should Michaela's pet vampire have forgotten that lesson, Raphael would be happy to teach it again—this time, with a permanent conclusion. "Do not bring Riker into my territory again unless you want him dead."

"Oh, Raphael, I didn't mean to make you angry." All but purring, she went as if to place her hand on his chest.

He gripped her wrist before she could, her bones slender under his hold, and, driven by instinct that said her every word was a honeyed lie, activated his healing ability. Knowledge poured into him, of Michaela's physical strength, of the sickening acid-green taint she carried within as a result of the day Uram had cracked her rib cage open to play with her blood-slick heart . . . of the emptiness in her womb.

Releasing her with enough force that she stumbled back a step, he said, "Do not cross more lines than you've already done by entering my lands without invitation. I am not yours to touch." Only a single stubborn, intelligent, and dangerous woman had that right.

A tightening of lush brown skin over the blades of her cheekbones, rejection anathema to a woman used to being worshipped by the male sex. "I thought to plead my case in person." Tilting her head to the side, the glossy black curls of her hair shining with bronze highlights, she placed her palms flat against the concave slope of her abdomen. "I thought you, of all the Cadre, would show kindness to a woman with child." Her tone altered, became huskier, her dawning smile painful in its apparent tenderness. "You watched over the angelic nurseries as a young man. I have ever respected that about you,

Raphael—your willingness to protect our most precious treasures."

Raphael wondered if Michaela was so used to manipulating men that she simply didn't understand he couldn't be molded to her requirements with sweet words buttressed by an undertone of sex. "I am no longer a young man," he said, seeing her eyes narrow at the continued ice in his tone, "and you have come perilously close to a fatal breach of the rules of Guesthood."

Dropping her hands, she turned in a dramatic sweep of shimmering bronze, her wings arcing gracefully over her back. "You are being cruel." Vivid green, her eyes were sheened wet when she turned to face him once more. "I ask you for sanctuary and you want me to play with formalities? You know I lost a child! I cannot lose another."

For an instant, he almost believed her, thought that perhaps she'd miscarried the embryo and "forgotten" the knowledge in her agony . . . but then she betrayed herself, her lips curving up the slightest fraction at his hesitation. The feline smugness of her answered his final questions, told him he had no need to be gentle. "Enough of the charade, Michaela."

"Charade? You mock me!" A thin ring of acidic green pulsing around the richer hue of her irises, an unmistakable physical sign of Uram's influence. "I am vulnerable; you are strong. I ask for your help! Where is the charade?"

Allowing his own power to rise, he felt his wings begin to glow. "You carry no babe."

Silence, her shock morphing rapidly into fury. "An accusation of deliberate falsehood! You incite a war!"

Golden light filled the wide mullioned windows of the graceful house where Illium indicated Elena should land.

"Pretty hunter, I've missed you."

She hissed out a breath, blades falling into both hands as she recognized the blond vampire who'd shaped the simple statement into a threat, the bones of his face refined to an unearthly beauty that made it clear he was far beyond a hundred years of age.

The last time she'd seen Riker, he'd been pinned to the wall of the house next to their own, a torn-off chair leg through his throat and blood dripping down his temples. Today, Michaela's favorite guard bared his teeth at her in a feral grin that was nothing natural, nothing sane, then waved his arm toward the front door in mocking welcome.

"My mistress flayed the skin off my back and made it into a purse."

Hairs rising on her nape at the memory of the way he'd made that admission with the same creepily fixed smile, Elena tightened her grip on the blades. "I see you've healed."

A lascivious stroke of his tongue along his upper lip. "I've been waiting a long time to be alone with you." His eyes flicked over her head just as she heard the cold whisper of sound that was Illium unsheathing the sword he always carried along his spine, the weapon hidden by a glamour that spoke to Illium's growing power.

"Go," he murmured, then raised his voice. "I'll watch Michaela's rabid dog, put him out of his misery if he proves troublesome."

Riker's eyes glowed bloodred, his fangs flashing, but he kept his distance when she walked past him and through the front door. *Raphael, how bad is it?*

Michaela is not with child, has likely never been with child.

I can't believe she used the memory of her own dead child in a scheme. Sickened by the callousness of such an act, she followed the sound of a raised voice to the large but otherwise unremarkable central core of the house. Raphael stood in the center, Michaela a few feet from him.

The female archangel's exquisite skin, the color of coffee swirled with milk and dusted with gold, was flushed, as if as a result of passionate argument; her body the epitome of female perfection in the emerald green catsuit that caressed every curve and valley.

Raphael answered whatever it was Michaela had said just as Elena took the first step toward him. "It's not a lie you can hope to maintain—so unless you do wish a war, cut your losses and leave."

Shooting Elena a dagger-sharp glare, Michaela said, "Look, your pet has arrived," the words saccharine-sweet. "Has she learned to sit and beg on command yet?"

Elena made her tone just as sweet as she played a throwing knife over her fingers. "No, but my aim's even better now." It might've been petty, but she enjoyed seeing the fury in Michaela's expression at the reminder that Elena had once buried a blade in her eyeball.

"Don't." It was a soft warning from Raphael as Michaela raised her hand, her fingertips crackling with dramatic green.

A ball of angelfire formed in Raphael's palm.

"I don't know why you're so amused by the creature." Michaela closed her fingers. "But I suggest you teach it manners."

Bristling, Elena nonetheless realized Michaela wanted an excuse to hurt her, and held her silence as Raphael spoke in a tone that could've drawn blood. "I judge it'll strain your squadron to make the return journey at once, so you may remain as a guest until midnight. Any later and I'll consider it an act of trespass."

Brushstrokes of violent red across Michaela's cheekbones, the sign of emotional intensity only serving to highlight her incredible beauty. "One day," she purred, "one day you'll understand what you reject this night, and then you will beg for my favors."

Can I stab her?

Only if she is still here after midnight.

Neither one of them spoke again until they landed on the lawn of their own home. In the short time that Elena had been inside Gable House, night had begun to give way to day, and across the river, Manhattan was wrapped in soft, swirling gray, the lights in the high-rises muted.

"I want you to keep a discreet watch on Michaela and her people," Raphael ordered Illium, the blue-winged angel having flown back with them. "It's almost dawn, so you can go alone, but check in with Aodhan every ten minutes."

"Sire." Illium lifted off with a bare rustle of sound, the

silver-blue of his wings swallowed up by the gray as he ascended above the cloud layer.

Wings brushing the dew-laden grass, Elena paced across the lawn. "Was it just me or was the Bitch Goddess 'off' tonight? She had this odd jerkiness to her movements."

"Uram's taint."

Elena's gorge rose at the thought of Michaela's former lover, the insane archangel who'd left a trail of mutilated and bloody bodies in his wake . . . including Jeffrey's mistress, that piti-able, pale copy of Marguerite. Ripped-off limbs thrust into screaming mouths, rib cages torn open to reveal glistening entrails, bodies hung and bled, Uram had committed atrocities Elena hadn't even imagined possible.

"Uram tore out her heart," she said, recalling her horror at the gaping wound, "left that glowing red fireball in her chest. Direct contact." The only other person to have such intimate contact with Uram, and survive, was Sorrow, and she'd undeni-ably come out of it altered on a fundamental level.

The young woman wasn't human any longer, but neither was she a vampire; she'd starve without blood as she'd starve without food. Then there was the would-be assailant twice her size whose neck she'd snapped in a self-defensive fugue. Now in training to learn how to consciously manage her strength and speed, Elena knew Sorrow was also under constant watch for signs of the same murderous insanity as her "blood sire," the term one she'd heard Dmitri use.

It infuriated Elena that the gutsy young woman couldn't escape Uram, but Sorrow wasn't the issue right this instant. "What if Michaela refuses to leave?"

"Then I'll force her out."

Guilt gripped her in its bony hands. If Michaela had gained an offensive power in the Cascade, any battle would be a treacherously uneven one for Raphael.

"I would wash off the night, Elena." Raphael turned toward the house.

Stomach in knots, her earlier anger at him buried under the chilling reminder that she might just have killed him, she went in silence.

Shutting the bedroom door behind them, Raphael walked

across to open the balcony doors, letting in the cold morning air. "Come here, Guild Hunter."

"What is it?"

"I would like to know"—his tone a serrated blade—"why my consort is keeping secrets that make her fly into herself."

She flinched, stepping past him to stand on the very edge of the balcony. "I'm angry at you, for what happened with Ransom."

"You might be angry, but you understand the decision." As ruthless an answer as the way he'd dealt with Cici. "That isn't what you're keeping from me."

"It's nothing."

"Now, you lie to me?" Cold, deadly, each word honed as bright as sword steel.

Spinning to face him, she fisted her hands. "Stop trying to intimidate me—I'm your *consort.*"

"I don't think you have the capacity to be intimidated," came the icy response, but his eyes, they were violent blue flames. "What are you hiding, Elena?"

Relentless and used to getting answers to his questions, he wouldn't drop this, she knew, but the thought of telling him the truth was a rock in her gut. "Leave it," she said, jaw clenched. "I'm asking you to just let it go."

"When it puts shadows under your eyes and makes you swallow your words?" He strode across to grip her jaw. "No. You're hurting and I will know why."

"But I didn't and he could not help me once others learned of my transgression."

Illium's words dashed cold water on the heat of her self-protective response. She couldn't do the same to Raphael, couldn't make him helpless in the face of her pain. Taking a shaky breath, she placed a fisted hand on his chest and knew it was time to stop hiding from the damage she'd done.

About to tell Elena that they wouldn't leave this balcony until she told him the truth, Raphael was silenced by the light weight of her fist against his chest.

"In the Refuge," she began, "I heard what they said: that

you were the most powerful youth anyone had ever seen." Her voice was raw emotion, her features bleak. "You became Cadre at the end of your first millennium—it makes you extraordinary. And now . . ."

He saw it then, the torture she'd been inflicting on herself, and had to willfully temper his anger that she'd do this, cause herself harm in such an insidious way. Releasing his grip on her chin so he wouldn't inadvertently hurt her, he ended the statement she'd begun, not bothering to conceal his fury. "Now others are gaining vicious powers, while I appear to have gained only a negative ability."

Stubborn as always, his consort held his gaze. "It's true and it's because of me." Visceral pain. "I'm your assassin—no one else!"

16

Elena could push him to the edge faster than any other, but Raphael fought his rising anger to say what she'd forgotten. "My ability is the only one that has had any impact on Lijuan." The Archangel of China had been stunned that he'd managed to cause her physical harm.

"Yes, but we both know it won't be enough." Skin pale from the way she held herself, all taut muscle and tendon, Elena dropped her hands to her sides. "Not against Lijuan's reborn and not against Neha's ability to create fire and ice, just to name two of the others. You said it yourself."

He'd never meant for her to take his words as an indictment. Even more, he'd never expected Elena, brash and honest, to hold such damaging thoughts within . . . but he should have. His hunter, after all, had held the horrific loss of her family inside herself for nearly two decades, keeping it even from her trusted best friend.

"I," he said, infuriated with her even as he wanted to bring Slater Patalis back to life so he could send him to a torturous death, "do not make a habit of hiding accusations behind the words I speak to my consort." That she may have believed such of him had rage lacing a film of red across his vision. "And I will not tolerate you concealing your thoughts from me in this way."

A glint in his consort's eye. "I told you—don't speak to me like I'm some soldier you're disciplining."

"I would break every bone in the body of any soldier who dared lie to me." Elena had never held her tongue around him, even when it might've been the smarter option, and he had no intention of allowing that to change.

Violence in those eyes of silver-gray. "You're making me want to go for a blade."

He raised an eyebrow, well aware she'd read it as a taunt.

Releasing a hissing breath, she thrust her hands into his hair and, tugging down his head, pressed her lips to his instead of slicing cold steel across his flesh.

He took the kiss, demanded more, demanded everything. Even angry and on edge, she was his, would always be his. Wrapping his arms around her as their tongues lashed against each other, their bodies primed for a furious intimate battle, he said, *Tighten your wings,* and took her into the air, spreading his glamour to cover her, until they were invisible to the world.

Chest heaving, Elena broke the kiss to see that Raphael was flying them across the river toward Manhattan. "Let me go. I have my own damn wings." And she was pissed with him for the way he'd spoken to her.

"Not yet." He kissed her this time, the hand he thrust into her hair unraveling her braid as he used the grip to hold her mouth to his own.

She could've escaped if she'd truly wanted to, her training as a hunter as well as that under Galen having given her more than one dirty trick, but she wanted to fight with him. So she bit at his lower lip and when he responded by deepening the kiss, his arms steel around her, his tongue licking at the roof of her mouth, had to battle her body's instinctive response, the place between her thighs slick.

Wrenching away her head, she glanced down . . . and saw he'd taken them high, high above Manhattan, to an altitude she couldn't yet reach on her own. Her eyes widened. "No." She glared at him. "I told you I will not dance with you above the—" Her words ended in a scream as he flipped them so their heads pointed toward the city . . . and closed his wings.

"Raphael!" The wind was a roar in her ears as they plummeted like a bullet shot from the sky. "I'm going to kill you if we survive this!"

His laughter dark and dangerous and sexy, he snapped out his wings to shoot them through the narrow space between two high-rises, the early morning skies almost empty. "Almost" being the operative word. "Home, now!" she ordered, but he took them back up into the sky, his body hard and muscled and flexing against her in ways that made her breasts swell, her entire body an erotic zone.

Baring her teeth, she gripped his hair once again and forced him to meet her gaze. "*Home*, or we're never, ever having sex again."

An arrogant smile as he shifted her so his rigid cock pushed against her soft slickness, the clothing between them no barrier to the sexual heat. "Could you resist me?"

"Push me and find out." She narrowed her eyes as they shot through the clouds and higher. Higher. And then—"God damn it!" Hair streaming down her back, she stared down at the skyscrapers getting closer at violent speed . . . and felt the adrenaline junkie in her take over, the dangerous pleasure a drug.

When she demanded another kiss, Raphael's response was hot and hard. But he broke the connection far too soon. "Hold on."

Elena had thought she'd seen Raphael fly. She hadn't.

Skimming down the side of a high-rise, he flipped them backward in a spiral that had her gritting her teeth to hold back a scream of exhilaration. Just when they would've kissed pavement, he snapped out his wings and swept back up, slicing through a gap so narrow that his wings brushed the edges of the buildings on either side, the early risers inside having no idea the Archangel of New York was giving his consort one hell of a ride.

That was nothing in comparison to the way he spiraled around the Tower, so fast she thought they'd smash through the glass more than once, then punched into the sky in a burst of incredible speed. "Raphael, watch out for the plane!" They were on a direct collision course with a commuter jet.

Raphael's smile was lethal. Shooting past the nose of the plane with inches to spare, he brought them down light as a feather until her feet touched one of the metal wings, the thin film of precipitation slippery. "Careful."

Wobbly for a second until her boots gained traction, she said, "Got it."

Releasing her, he flew over and across to the other wing, so the plane wouldn't unbalance. *The young ones sometimes do this—they call it jet surfing.*

Elena laughed, her arms spread to hold her balance against the roaring wind that caught at her wings. *I read a report once in a newspaper, but I figured someone had had a few too many margaritas on a flight.*

It's highly discouraged, but I look the other way every so often.

"Whoa!" She almost slid off when the plane banked, and Raphael was there, his arms locking around her as he lifted off before she could be sucked into the engines. Strong and protective against her, he was her everything and, all at once, she'd had enough playing. Kissing his throat, she whispered, "No more."

No response, but less than a minute of breathtaking speed later, they were in the privacy of their bedroom. Tugging off her clothes as he kissed her, Elena then pulled at his own until he got rid of the impediments to her touch, his body heat rough against her own. Hushed whispers and hungry caresses, their language that of lovers who know each other's every pleasure point, they moved together with raw intimacy.

Holding himself inside her toward the end, his thickness stretching her flesh, Raphael held her gaze. "Eternity would mean nothing without you. For no power on this earth would I trade my Elena."

Heart splintering at the piercing tenderness of his words, she touched trembling fingers to his lips and hoped his choice

wouldn't doom him, this man whom she loved until she couldn't
breathe.

With the donor blood coming into Blood-for-Less being
tested around the clock, they had a hit on the tainted donor at
three the following morning. Getting out of bed, Elena was
dressed and at the blood café within fifteen minutes, Raphael
by her side. He hadn't slept, having escorted a fuming but
compliant Michaela out of the territory, then returned to speak
to Galen and Venom via a visual link to the Refuge.

Landing at the back of Blood-for-Less so as not to alarm its
customers, they met Marcia in the shadows. When the woman
couldn't get a word out at the sight of Raphael, her fear so
potent that Elena saw Raphael's expression alter in subtle anger,
she took over the questioning.

*She's probably never been near an archangel. Cut her a
break.*

*It's not Ms. Blue who is the target of my anger. My angels
are instructed to be brutal if necessary to keep their vampires
under control, but this one's record is clean.*

Elena hadn't realized he'd checked Marcia's file. *You think
she was abused?* Given the violence and cruelty she'd seen in
the immortal world, she hadn't thought vamps doing their hundred had *any* rights.

*Damaging a useful tool until it's too fragile to function is
a waste,* was the coldly practical answer. *It seems I may need
to remind certain angels of that fact.*

Sensing that Marcia was failing in her attempt to force
words out through her terror, Elena motioned for Raphael to
disappear farther back into the shadows and caught his raised
eyebrow before he complied. *I've got a theory—if she can't
see you, she can pretend you're not here.*

It seemed to work.

"We've had only two other donors in the time since the
tainted donor, and the Tower is testing their blood now," Marcia
said in response to her question, the vampire's eyes turned
scrupulously away from the shadows that swathed Raphael.

"Surveillance images?"

Proving her intelligence and preparedness, Marcia held out a photograph of a thin young woman with stringy brown hair. "She has the blood that's been marked as bad by Tower personnel." The image shook as her fingers began to tremble.

Elena took it before it dropped to the ground. "You're certain?"

Immediately hiding her hands behind her back, Marcia nodded. "I marked the time of each donation and printed out a still from the surveillance footage as soon as the donor left."

"Anything else we need to know?"

Marcia swallowed, but got the words out. "I take sick donors all the time—they often need the money, and blood's blood. Usually." Sweat beading on her brow. "But she looked half-dead—much sicker than the last time I remember seeing her."

It was possible the carrier wasn't a true carrier, simply someone who could withstand the effects of the infection for longer. "Can you pinpoint the time of her previous donation?"

"I am truly sorry, Consort." Marcia's teeth began to chatter. "We a-allow anonymous donations so all I can say is that it was with-with-within the l-l-last week."

Elena sent the vampire back into her café before she had a fear-induced heart attack, then turned to Raphael. "I hope you terrify the fucker who did this to her, or I'll find him and personally cut off his balls after I beat him bloody."

"An excellent punishment. Be assured it'll be carried out."

Passing the stills to Raphael without any feelings of remorse at the sentence she'd just passed, she set aside her simmering anger and, after checking to make sure the area was clear, went over to the donor doorway. It was a carnival of scents, not unexpected given the number of vamps who no doubt moved in and around the building—the real problem was that the tainted donor was human and Elena was a bloodhound attuned to vampires.

On the other hand, she'd sensed the presence of the disease in the drawn blood, so perhaps the carrier's blood chemistry had altered enough to highlight her to Elena's nose.

This Marcia is indeed a valuable tool, came Raphael's voice into her mind. *She e-mailed the photo to the Tower as soon as the alarm was sounded and Aodhan is following up on it. Ransom Winterwolf, however, may have the better contacts when it comes to the humans and vampires who frequent this area.*

Elena stopped what she was doing to meet the painful blue of his eyes, extraordinarily pure, extraordinarily lethal. *If I bring Ransom into this,* she said, keeping the conversation on the mental level to avoid it being caught by the surveillance equipment, *and he ends up with information you can't permit a mortal to have, you'll wipe his mind.*

You know our laws, Elena.

Exactly. She thought of Illium's punishment and knew she couldn't ask special favors for Ransom. Raphael had already gone far beyond what could be expected of him when he'd permitted Sara into the Refuge. If Elena wanted to protect her friends, she was the one who had to put up the boundary walls . . . even if it meant they'd stop being a part of her life. Better that painful rupture than to watch them be treated as puppets by the immortals. *Knowing those laws is why I won't bring Ransom into this.*

You'd let innocent vampires die?

That isn't fair. Stepping up until they were toe to toe, she stood her ground. *Ransom's life is worth as much as that of any vampire—and I won't be involved in stealing any part of it from him.*

Some of the vampires who may yet die will be friends of his. The wild wind, the dark sea, crashing into her mind. *Do you believe he'd protect his own life at the cost of theirs?*

She knew Ransom, how loyal he was, how he'd bleed for others, but she was cut from the same cloth. *You wouldn't know about his connections if it wasn't for me, so this decision is mine. And I won't bring him in.*

Elena, my city is under a stealthy attack. Raphael's tone was a blade, his face coolly expressionless in a way that made her want to push at him until he dropped the mask. *I can't allow you to protect a friend at the cost of losing my territory.*

Is that a threat you'll go over my head? Aware her temper

had been hair-trigger of late, she tried to maintain her grip on it. *You'd make me an accomplice in the betrayal of a friend?* It was a breach of trust she'd never expected. *What if it was one of your Seven?*

    He isn't. He's a mere mortal.

17

The cold response was an emotional slap, another reminder that when push came to shove, mortals remained disposable to Raphael.

Fine, she said, conscious that something precious was about to break between them, a fracture that could never be repaired. *You do what you like, but you have to know I'll never again trust you the same way.*

A faint glow, his wings white fire in the darkness. *Emotional blackmail?*

No. No anger now, simply a spiraling sense of incipient loss that made her chest hurt, her jaw clenched so hard that pain shot up her temples. *I'm fighting to retain my sense of honor, of loyalty. If I can't trust you not to abuse the information I give you about my friends, how can you ask me to tell you anything?*

Our conversation isn't over. Hauling his consort bodily around when she turned back to the donor station, Raphael extended his glamour to cover her.

What else is there to say? A hardness in her eyes that he hadn't seen since the very beginning of their courtship. *A mere mortal, isn't that your final judgment?*

No one could push him to the edge faster than Elena, slamming right through centuries of unyielding control. *I allowed Sara into the Refuge.* It had been an act that went against their most deeply held laws, permitted only because he took full responsibility for Sara's silence. *The others believe I erased her memories. Only for you did I leave her mind untouched.*

That's supposed to make me grateful forever? A red flush high on her cheekbones, the ring of silver around her irises glittering against the paler gray. *Love doesn't work like that.*

Yet it allows you to turn your back after throwing such words at me? A memory of the question she'd asked that had sent him hunting Jeffrey, a reminder of the poison that continued to act on her, years after it had been introduced into her life.

He realized he couldn't allow her to remain blind to that toxic influence. *I'm not your father, Elena.*

Her breath coming fast and shallow, she shook her head. *Jeffrey has nothing to do with this.*

He has everything to do with it, Raphael countered, thrusting his hands into her unbound hair as she raised her own hands to grip at his arms, as if she would shove him away. *We will not go through eternity with you expecting the worst from me.*

A visible flinch, but his stubborn, furious consort refused to back down. *That's not what I'm doing.* Her body trembling from the force of her emotions, she said, *I know you, and I know how you see humans: as fireflies that live and die in a heartbeat, not worth anything.*

I fell in love with a mortal! Until she *was* his eternity. *Do you question that, too?*

Her eyes widened at the enraged question. "No," she whispered aloud, before returning to mental speech. *Your love is the one constant in my life, but I'm so afraid of what immortality will demand from us, what it'll steal.*

It can take nothing we do not give.

Then you need to listen to me. Stubbornness again, her expression that of the warrior she was, one who'd fight to the death to protect those who had earned her loyalty. *My friends, they're my family. I need to be able to protect them—if you take that away from me, you may as well cut out my heart.*

It had been an age since he'd seen mortals as she did, since he'd formed a friendship with a simple farmer who'd come to be a man he trusted not only with his life, but with Elena's. *I have forgotten, it seems, that I, too, once had a human friend I wished to protect.* He'd failed, Dmitri's life torn asunder—and the failing had marked Raphael, too, changed him in ways that could never be undone.

Then you understand. Elena's hair shone white in the harsh light that lit up the donor doorway. *It's not safe for my friends to be drawn deeper into the immortal world. Not unless you trust them to keep—*

No. Our laws exist for a reason. And it wasn't simply because angels thought humans beneath their notice. *The games immortals play would break mortals in a heartbeat.*

Silence from his consort, followed by a simple, resolute declaration. *Then he can't be here.*

He can't be here, Raphael agreed, his mind playing back the memory of the day he'd found Dmitri gripping a blood-drenched knife, his chest a ruin, the other man having attempted to carve out his heart in an attempt to join his murdered family.

Raphael would never forget Dmitri's grief and the horror that had preceded it . . . and he would not have Elena carry such memories for all eternity. *I will not force you to drag your friends into our world.*

Emotionally shaken as a result of an argument she knew had drawn a bright line in the sand of the life she was building with her archangel, their relationship coming out of it stronger rather than fatally damaged, Elena returned to the task of untangling the complicated murk of scents around the donor door.

Even so focused, she couldn't forget what Raphael had said: *We will not go through eternity with you expecting the worst from me.*

She'd argued against his perception, but now found herself considering if it was true. Had her father scarred her so badly as a child? No, it was far more complicated than that. "The greatest breach of trust," she found herself saying softly, having moved away from the area under surveillance, "was my mother's."

His eyes told her he knew her meaning. Understood the agony that had shredded her as she stood mute beside Marguerite's grave, Beth's tiny hand clasped in hers. Jeffrey had been behind them, his hands on their shoulders, his body their rock, strong and *there*.

"I was so angry at him for not stopping her." Catching a suspicious concentration of scent, she went down into a crouch, her wings on the cold asphalt. "After the funeral, I struck out at him, screaming that it was his fault when I knew it wasn't." Her mother hadn't survived Slater Patalis and what he'd done to her two oldest babies, no matter if her body had made it out alive.

"You were a child."

Elena shook her head at Raphael's response. "I was old enough to know better, but you know what? Jeffrey never, not once, argued against my irrational accusations. Because he blamed himself, too."

She hadn't thought about those first days after her mother's suicide for years, only what came after, when Jeffrey's broken heart had translated into a cold rage that had him erasing Marguerite from the house and their lives. "Every time I think I understand what we are—Jeffrey and I—I discover another facet and suddenly it's not so sim—"

Putrid rot, the miasma of death, an undertone of burnt flesh.

"There's something here." Her senses hummed. "It's faint, hard for me to sink my teeth into even though I can sense each of the notes." Ugly, fetid, unnatural. "Possibly because it's from a human."

"Can you follow it?"

"Yes, I think so."

"I'll keep watch from above." Walking a short distance away so as not to disturb the scents, he took off and was lost behind a veil of glamour.

It took painstaking patience to tug on that one faint thread among the dozens that blanketed the area. Blood-for-Less might be on the fringe of the Vampire Quarter, but it apparently got plenty of business—unlike on her previous visit, Elena had heard the heavy murmur of voices from within that indicated Marcia had a full house tonight.

The deeper she got into the Quarter, the more heavily trafficked it became, the central section a favorite among hip young vamps—and suburbanites who wanted to walk on the wild side without going into the more dangerous parts of town. Leggy models, mortal and immortal, were as ubiquitous a part of the landscape as slickly dressed vampires on the prowl, everyone congregating around the clubs that opened their doors after nightfall.

No one dared get in her way.

Keeping her wings folded tight to her back, she made sure her blades were in full view as she tracked. Not that she was afraid of being tackled by a fashionista vamp, she thought with an inward snort. Then again, stilettos were fucking lethal weapons as far as she was concerned.

Ten more minutes of meticulous tracking and she passed out of the central zone and into the Flesh Market. Most tourist guidebooks told visitors to "exercise extreme caution" in this part of the Quarter. Because while the vamps in this area were as stylishly dressed and as urbane, they were older, with darker appetites. Club Masque, up ahead, had a sign at the top of the mortal queue that said, *Fresh Meat.*

And still the young and nubile and stupid lined up.

Raphael, she said after another block, the stores here shut up for the night and empty of traffic except for a couple who crossed the street when they saw her and a drug dealer who suddenly had urgent business elsewhere. *I need to go down this passageway.* It wasn't quite an alley, but according to what she could see with her acute night vision, it was close enough for the homeless.

I have you in my sights.

Squeezing her wings as tight to her back as she could manage, she picked her way through the cardboard castles that housed the flotsam and jetsam of the city. They weren't exclusively human. Vampires could descend into this shadow life just like their mortal counterparts—all it took was an addiction to something. Certain enterprising bloodsuckers had created recreational drugs that worked on those of their kind, though apparently the high didn't last long enough for most to bother.

More in vogue were "honey" feeds, where a human donor would get high on certain drugs then allow the vamp to feed. Vampiric biology soon neutralized the drugs, but not fast enough to totally negate the pleasure—and sex, of course, was also often on the same menu. All for a price. Then there was gambling, and the sadder cases where an individual, vamp or human, lost the struggle with personal demons no one else could see.

"Hunter." The rasping whisper came from a shriveled-up old man tucked up inside a cardboard box fashioned into a home, the "curtains" open to reveal his reddened eyes and the brown-paper-bagged bottle in his hands.

Startled that he'd focused on what marked her as Guild, rather than the wings, Elena paused, a sick feeling in her stomach as her eyes adjusted enough to make out the knife scars on his hands. No hunter was ever left behind by his or her brethren . . . but some chose to walk out into the darkness and never return.

"Hunter," she replied, giving back the same respect he'd offered her. "The Guild is always open to you." All hunters paid a percentage of their income to the Guild; one of the reasons why was so the Guild could provide care should a hunter be physically or mentally incapacitated. "I can make the call."

"I like it out here."

Elena had no way of knowing what he'd survived, the reasons for his choices, so she made no judgment. "Are you here always?"

A nod.

"I'll ask one of the Guild patrols to come by with some food." They'd nudge him into better sleeping quarters, too, when the snow started to fall. "I can ask them to bring along a strong, basic tent for you." Nothing that would make him a target for thieves. "Is that all right?"

A long pause, his eyes seeming to judge her before he said, "Long as they bring enough for two." His gaze went to another cardboard enterprise a few feet over and across the narrow passageway. "Got to watch each other's backs. It's what we do."

Elena nodded. "Stay safe."

"Hunt well."

Continuing down into the pitch-blackness of the passage until it spit her out the other end, Elena found herself in an enclosed parking lot behind an Asian restaurant; she'd hit the edge of Chinatown. A single yellow streetlamp doused the area in an anemic glow, creating pools of shadow as thick as liquid, the dark green Dumpsters a silent menace.

"Get a grip, Ellie."

Following the suspicious scent to a broken part of the fence, she managed to get through the chain link without snagging her feathers. The scent was cleaner now, no longer overwhelmed by those of vampires, this area with its cheap and tasty restaurants a mortal haunt, though she knew a couple of angels who were regulars. The restaurants were closed up for the night, all except for a twenty-four-hour noodle place where a worker pushed a mop around while bopping to the music in his headphones.

A bedraggled mutt kept company with her for a block before being seduced by an overflowing Dumpster, though she saw the rotting carcass of more than one dead bird lying in the nooks and crannies. No one had bothered to clean them up here as they had in the restaurant area, and even the feral cats and dogs knew to steer clear of that festering meat.

When she looked around and saw the scaffolding, she realized the reason for the lack of care—no one was currently residing or doing business on this street, and from the looks of things, no construction workers had been by for a few days, either. Permit or money problems, probably.

A sudden end to the scent, there one second, gone the next.

Backing up, she realized the individual she was tracking had gone up the steps of one of the scaffolded buildings. *Looks like our carrier is squatting. No security, so it wouldn't be hard.*

Is she present within?

Unless there's a back entrance.

Wait. A pause before Raphael said, *The back entrance is inaccessible.*

Then she's inside. I found one recent scent trail, with an older one beneath, so my take is, she went out to sell her blood and came straight back.

A sudden wind was the only sign that Raphael had landed on the street. *Be careful on the steps,* she said, having returned to the door. *Looks like the target went through that window.* Pushed up, the glass missing, it would've been just within reach if someone climbed up onto part of the scaffolding. *We'll need your manly muscles to get in. If that's not beneath Your Archangelness.*

His kiss took her by surprise, her mind scrambling to understand the fact that she was being deliciously taken by a man she couldn't see. Releasing her before she'd gotten her head around it, he began to pry off the boards that barred the front door, doing so with an ease that made it appear the boards were just sitting there.

Thirty seconds later, the door was open.

18

Narrow, but we can get in if we angle our bodies. I'll enter first.

I'm the hunter, Elena reminded him. *I should go first.*

Of course you may go first. When I am dead.

Scowling at that statement delivered in an eminently reasonable tone that had fooled her into thinking he was going to agree, she pulled out her crossbow. *Go. We'll argue about your autocratic tendencies later.*

I look forward to it.

Since he'd dropped the glamour upon entering, his wings filled her vision until they came out into a more open area of what looked like a private residence, though it might well have been a combined business/home, the lower-floor open plan enough to have functioned as a retail shop.

Upstairs, she said, the scent trail a pulsing beacon.

You do not wish to clear this floor?

It's only the dead down here. More than a few days, from the degradation of the disease smell. The bodies hadn't rotted, likely because the house was as cold as a fridge, but it was no doubt the same vampire pox.

Her first victims?

Maybe her test subjects. Probably junkie vamps desperate for a honey feed—wouldn't take much to seduce one if she looked strung out herself. Perfect meal.

Again, Raphael went ahead and, though they tried to be quiet, the stairs were old, creaked and groaned no matter what. However, there was no sign their target had heard anything, even when Elena almost fell through a weakened board and Raphael jerked her to safety. There was, in fact, no sign of life at all.

You're certain she is here?

Yes. Her scent is rich and fresh. She met his eyes. *I can't tell if she's dead or just sick, but the scent of the disease is very strong to my senses, especially considering her mortality.*

Raphael stepped forward to look inside the doorway she indicated, while she swept quickly down to check the other room, make sure it was empty. His expression when she turned to face him told her all she needed to know.

"Damn it." Walking into the room, she halted beside an old bed that looked like it had been forgotten when the house was stripped. In it lay their prey, her eyes wide open and unseeing, the exposed parts of her pasty skin bubbled with small sores that echoed the more virulent ones on the bodies of the other victims.

"A carrier who can only last a short time," Raphael said, taking in the scene with a clinical eye. "Inefficient."

"If we're right and this is an attack against the city by one of the Cadre—"

"—then it could be he or she does not have the strength to immunize the carriers." Raphael nodded. "All the Cascade-born abilities appear to be limited in terms of strength as yet."

Elena eyeballed the body, but could find no signs that the woman had been a junkie who might herself have been somehow infected, perhaps by another individual who was the actual carrier. They'd have to wait till the autopsy to get a definitive answer. Certain that Raphael had already contacted Keir, she took a good look around the room.

"Nothing." She restrained the urge to kick at a mildewed wall, the mildew an improvement on the giant floral wallpaper. "There is absolutely nothing here that tells us who she was or where she came from."

"Unsurprising. Her archangel would not want her to give herself away."

Elena had to agree with Raphael's unspoken conclusion that the woman must've volunteered for her task, because, while she looked pitiful now, a broken doll, she'd carried and disseminated death, pumping poison from her body each time she sold her blood. The dead vampires Elena had sensed downstairs made it inarguable the woman had known exactly what it was she was selling.

Midday, and Keir confirmed the disease in the girl's body was identical to that found in the other victims. "But she had it far longer," the healer said, old eyes tired in that beautiful face that could've been of a boy on the brink of manhood. "At least two weeks—which makes her either the first victim or the carrier."

Elena kept her ear to the ground for any other reports of vampires dead of mysterious circumstances. Nothing. Not for the four days that followed their discovery of the girl it was becoming more and more certain had been the sole carrier. Finally, on the fifth day, they cleared Blood-for-Less for renewed use of donor blood, with continuing spot checks just to be certain.

"Is there any way we can wriggle out of this ball?" she said to Raphael on the eve of their journey to Amanat, the two of them in bed after an unexpectedly playful loving that had flowed on from a sparring session where they'd worked out the tension that had had them in its clawlike grip for days, as they waited for the other shoe to drop . . . only for the ordinary rhythm of life to descend upon the city.

It wasn't peace—it was New York—but it certainly wasn't a war. "I know you don't want to leave the city." Neither did she, an itch on the back of her neck that said, this odd lull aside, the Falling and the disease had only been the beginning.

"To not attend," Raphael said, his wing warm and strong under her body, his voice exquisitely familiar in the moonless dark, "would be seen as a sign of distrust in Illium, Aodhan, and the squadrons that guard the Tower."

Comforted by the steady beat of his heart, she drew lazy designs on the muscled heat of his chest. "Will that matter if the city is attacked by frothing-at-the-mouth reborn while we're eating bonbons in Amanat?"

"You have such a vivid way of putting things, *hbeebti*." His fingers stroking the sensitive inner edges of her wings, the act an absent one that made her deeply happy in a way she didn't consciously understand. "But no hordes will descend upon the city during the span of the ball."

Stretching out her wings in a silent request, she sighed as he stroked outward. "You sound confident."

"The one behind these attacks is no doubt Cadre. No other angel could've gained such abilities even in the Cascade."

Elena nodded, having seen Jessamy's research on the results of the last Cascade. Any information was fragmented at best, but the historian had been able to tentatively confirm Caliane's recollection that it was only the archangels who'd been fundamentally altered. "I get your point," she said. "Whoever it is, is caught in the same trap."

Raphael moved her hair aside to massage her nape, his other hand folded behind his head. "He or she must attend the ball or it'll not only be an insult to the sole Ancient awake in the world, but a sign the archangel in question does not trust those he would've otherwise left in charge. Then there is the other factor."

"Wait, don't tell me." Bones having melted as a result of the way he was touching her, she revved up her brain and struggled up onto her elbow so she could see his expression as she tested her understanding of how archangels saw the world. "It would be considered *extremely* bad manners," she said in the frigid tones of some of the stiffer old angels, "to attack a city while its archangel was at a ball thrown by an Ancient. Why, really, you might as well have been brought up by *mortals*, if you're going to act that way."

"Absurd, is it not?" Laughter in the intoxicating blue, his hand a possessive weight on her lower back. "Yet those rules of Guesthood are part of what keeps the world stable. Any archangel so ill-mannered as to step outside them in such an unspeakable fashion would find themselves ostracized. Eternity is a long time to be friendless."

"Put that way," Elena said, leaning down to steal a kiss just because she could, "it's not absurd but totally rational. How else would anyone ever have a party, with the way certain archangels are always trying to backstab others."

A smile curving his mouth, her archangel nodded. "Even Lijuan couldn't bear such a shunning. She might be able to compel obedience through brute force, but she'd lose the respect that is as much her lifeblood as power." Fingers idly caressing the lower curves of her body. "Can you guess the true irony of this particular situation?"

Screwing up her face, she was about to say no when it hit. Laughing so hard she had to wait until she could catch her breath enough to shape words, she said, "Lijuan isn't invited"— not after trying to murder Caliane and her son—"but she's such a stickler for the old ways, the others know they'll have her on their ass if they break the rules."

"Exactly."

"I wonder if there's an Angelic Etiquette handbook some—" Breaking off, she touched her fingers to Raphael's right temple.

"What is it?" Incisive intelligence in his gaze.

"Wait." She switched on the lamps that bathed the top half of the bed in a gentle light. Leaning back down, she went close to Raphael's face, rubbed her thumb over the spot, his hair brushing against her fingertips. "There's something on your skin." Unable to let it go, she got out of bed to grab a wet facecloth.

Raphael was in the bathroom doorway when she turned from the sink. Asking him to bend down so she could wipe at the tiny speck, she tried twice, the second time with a dab of soap on the cloth in case he'd somehow been touched by the tip of a permanent black marker . . . except even as the thought crossed her mind, she knew she would've noticed it earlier.

The speck hadn't been there before, and now—"It's not coming off." Her voice sounded even, despite the horrible feeling in the pit of her stomach.

Shifting into the bathroom, Raphael examined his face in the mirror. Elena came up beside him, wanting to believe it had been a trick of the light. It hadn't. So tiny, the speck would go unnoticed by most, but it shouldn't *be* there. "Maybe it's an insect bite," she began, trying not to think about dead vampires and disease.

"No, we heal too fast for a bite to have any impact." Expression grim, he turned to her. "Can you see it now?"

"No, it's gone." Crushing relief. "What did you do?"

"It is still there," he said, and the relief curdled. "I've concealed it using the barest hint of glamour."

"I wish Keir was still here." The healer had had to return to the Refuge to deal with other matters, would meet them again in Amanat. "What if . . ." She couldn't say it, couldn't even imagine it, her horror too violent.

"What if it is the harbinger of disease?" Raphael said for her. "If it is, Keir would be unable to do anything, so telling him is a moot point. I am an archangel, Elena. We may go mad with age and time, or because of the toxin, but we do not get sick."

His blunt words forced her to face the cold, hard fact that an archangel sick was a tear in the fabric of the world. That didn't mean she was about to give up. "Jessamy," she said. "She'd never betray you—we can ask her to search the Archives, see if there've been any similar cases in angelic history."

"There is nothing to tell her yet," Raphael answered with impossible calm. "It is but a single dark spot—if it's the sign of a disease created by a new archangelic power, my body should be able to fight it off."

"Of course, your healing ability." She turned to go throw some water onto her face in an effort to still her racing heart, her hands trembling, but Raphael tugged her into his arms and against his chest, his wings enclosing her in a silken prison.

"It is all right, *hbeebti*." His heartbeat strong and steady under her cheek as he spoke, his arms muscled steel. "I have no intention of leaving you to face immortality alone."

"If this is death, Guild Hunter, then I will see you on the other side."

He'd said that to her as she lay dying in his arms. Now, she whispered, "Wherever you go, I'll follow." She'd lost too many people she loved, survived too much death. "I can't keep going. I can't." As if she'd turned a nightmare key, she heard the sound that had haunted her since the day Slater Patalis walked into her childhood home.

Drip.
Drip.
Drip.

There'd been so much blood, her feet sliding in it to send her to the floor with bruising force.

"Come, Elena." Raphael's voice held a gentleness that told her he saw her terror, understood it. "Do you think I am so weak? Such a belief is a blow to my ego indeed."

Elena tried to smile, to not permit the fear to consume her, but it raged within, born of a childhood where everyone she loved had been taken from her. Jeffrey and Beth might have survived the massacre, but they'd been lost to Elena all the same. She couldn't lose Raphael, too. She *couldn't*.

The panicked thoughts ran in a loop inside her mind until it was all she was.

Then the rain-lashed sea was there, cutting through the dark clouds of memory. Reaching for Raphael with body and mind both, she drowned herself in the sheer powerful life force of the archangel who was the only man she would ever love.

Holding Elena when she finally fell into an exhausted sleep, his strong consort who had a ragged wound in her soul that had torn open with vicious force tonight, Raphael watched over her, standing sentinel against the darkness. And though he wasn't tired, he realized he slept when he began to dream.

Of that forgotten field where his blood had been glistening rubies scattered on the grass, the red liquid crystallizing into faceted gemstones that fascinated the birds who were his constant companions as the sun moved across the sky and the seasons changed from spring to summer. Flowers grew around him, over him, the grass shading his face, and still he lay there, waiting to heal enough that he could make it to the Refuge.

Archangel. Archangel. Archangel.

The voices around him continued to repeat that single word

until he said, "Silence!" in a tone no one except Elena had ever disobeyed.

The voices cut off.

Rising above the field once more, his body unbroken and of the adult he now was, that splintered, scared boy long gone, he gave a second order. "Show yourselves."

19

In answer came a sea of whispers, the actual words inaudible.

"Raphael."

It was unexpected, that feminine voice. And it was one so familiar, he'd know it even in death, the wing that brushed over his own warrior black and vivid indigo kissed with midnight blue and the haunting shade of the sky just before dawn.

When he turned toward the sound of her voice, he saw that Elena's body was translucent beside his, the colors of her like running water. Death rubies ringed her neck, cherry-dark gemstones created of his hardened blood.

That was wrong. Elena would never wear such.

"What the—" Reaching up, she tore off the necklace with a shudder, the blood gemstones falling soundlessly to the green, green grass. "Where are we?"

"The field where I fought my mother." He took her hand, and it was warm, alive, though she remained formed of glass.

"It's beautiful."

Looking through her eyes as the dawn sun played over the verdant grass, bathing the trees in a golden glow and highlighting the flowers he'd watched bud, then bloom, he saw the truth of her words, but for him it remained—would always remain—a place of pain and death and loss.

"My mother walked away, her feet crushing the flowers, as the insects licked at my blood." The tiny creatures had died, his blood too rich. Then had come the birds, curious about this winged being on the ground. "The birds sat with me for hours, brought me berries as if I were a fledgling fallen out of the nest." He'd forgotten that under the weight of the horror. "I couldn't eat for many days, my jaw and facial bones in splinters."

"This is a very sad place." A single tear rolling down his consort's cheek. "You should wake up now."

His lashes lifted to see the skylight above their bed, the moonless sky luminous with stars, but that wasn't what he wanted in his sight. Turning, he wiped away the tear that marked Elena's golden skin as she lay with her eyes open beside him, and he thought he should be surprised that so young an angel had managed to invade the dream of an archangel—but this was his hunter, who had never done what she should.

"You were in my dream."

She spread her wing so it covered him, her hand on his shoulder. As if she would protect him. "It was sad and terrible and beautiful, what I saw in you there."

"It was like that the day I fought my mother. Sad and terrible . . . and beautiful. She sang to me in the sky, did I tell you?"

A shake of his consort's head, her hair wild silk under his hand.

"Her voice is a gift and a weapon, a sound so pure it can break a heart or heal it." He'd seen angels fall to their knees, overcome with the wonder of Caliane's song, their eyes shining wet. "That day, she sang a song she used to sing to me in childhood and I wanted to forget the reason I had tracked her."

For that haunting fragment of time, he'd seen not the monster Caliane had become, but the mother who had kissed away his childhood hurts. "The sky fractured with wonder . . . then it fractured with power." It had been an uneven battle from the start, the child not yet full-grown against an Ancient.

Elena pressed her lips to his biceps, her body a warm kiss against his own. "The whispers in your dream, did you hear them as you fought your mother?"

"No, I was alone with Caliane." Then simply alone.

"I wonder who they are?"

He didn't remind her it had been but a dream, for that would've been a lie when he felt the strangeness of it in his blood. "Sleep, Elena. We have a long journey ahead."

She didn't speak, but he knew she didn't sleep, either, not until dawn touched the horizon. And he understood she continued to fence with the bone-chilling fear he'd seen in her eyes as she stood in the bathroom attempting to wipe away a spot of dirt that couldn't be erased. It was a fear sad and terrible in what it demanded from her . . . and beautiful in what it said of who he was to her.

The first thought in Elena's mind when she woke was of the speck on Raphael's temple, fear a dull gnawing in her heart. Shoving the ugly feeling into a tiny corner where it didn't threaten to paralyze her, she concentrated on making a mental list of Raphael's strengths. He'd executed an archangel millennia older and Made an angel, for Christ's sake—no disease would ever get the better of him.

"Damn straight," she muttered to herself as she sat in the luxurious cabin of Raphael's private jet, using her silent conclusion as a shield against the helplessness that had regressed her back to the ten-year-old she'd once been, scared and bloody and alone with a monster.

"Did you say something, *hbeebti*?"

It was a gentle question—he'd been careful with her all morning and, given the way she'd freaked out the night before, she couldn't exactly complain, but it was time to let her archangel know she'd patched up the wounds. "Every time I board this thing," she said, "I'm reminded of how filthy rich you are." Raphael could've completed the journey on the wing without problems, but her flight endurance was pitiful yet. "It's like a flying mini-Tower."

An amused look, no hint of the awful sadness she'd sensed in him as they hovered over the field where he'd lain broken and bloodied. "Would you like me to go through that?" He nodded at the folder in front of her that held Marcia Blue's financial statement and business plan.

Handing it over because she had no idea what half of it meant and wasn't too proud to admit it, she said, "I, too, am on the path to becoming filthy rich."

"With such a soft heart as yours"—he opened the file—"it'll be a challenge for me to ensure you do not end up penniless."

Elena squirmed in her deliciously comfortable seat. "Okay, okay, so I felt sorry for her. At least I asked for the business info—that should get me some credit."

"Hmm."

Leaving him to the documents, she hooked her phone into the jet's high-tech communications network and made a visual call to Sam, the sweet, funny little boy who'd become her friend and guide while she'd been in the Refuge. He told her about his recent adventures, made her promise to hold a position in her Guard for him until he was "growed up," and showed her the present he was secretly making for his mother.

"Sam," she said toward the end, "does Galen really teach you flights skills?"

"Uh-huh." A strong nod. "He's strict but not in a mean way. We like him." Smiling, he proceeded to regale her with the story of his last lesson with Raphael's weapons-master—where Galen had actually ended up laughing at the antics of his baby squadron.

By the time the call ended, Elena was conscious that she'd only ever glimpsed one narrow aspect of Galen's personality. "Your weapons-master appears to have an actual, beating heart," she said to Raphael. "Who knew?"

"Jessamy."

"I concede that point." Logging in to check her e-mails as Raphael continued to read over the file, she saw one from Sara asking her opinion on an antique weapon Sara was considering getting Deacon as an anniversary gift.

She'd just finished shooting her best friend a reply when a

new e-mail popped into her in-box. It was from Aodhan, the subject line making Elena's fingers clench convulsively around the phone and her mind hurtle two months into the past.

Elena swallowed, the paper crinkling in her hand the only sound as she stood in front of the elevator that would drop her down into the Cellars, the protected area under Guild HQ. She'd taken advantage of the underground safe house when she'd slit Dmitri's throat during the hunt that had forever altered the course of her life—though, in her defense, he had provoked the action.

It was Vivek, the hunter who ran the Cellars, who'd given her a gun meant to injure an angel long enough to give a mortal a chance to run, to escape. That gun had done far more, Raphael's blood pooling on the broken sheet of glass that had been the outer wall of her apartment.

"Do it, Ellie," she ordered, knowing the trip through memory lane was nothing but procrastination at its finest.

Reaching out, she stabbed the button to summon the elevator and, when the doors opened, input the special code on the hidden auxiliary touchpad so the cage would move downward, rather than up into Guild HQ. That code changed on a daily basis and since she'd contacted Vivek directly to get it, he was expecting her.

"I am so whupping your ass today," he'd predicted, in reference to their continuing Scrabble battle.

They'd always played a game or two anytime Elena was in town for more than twenty-four hours. Now that she was based in New York, she made it a point to come by at least once a week—because Vivek wouldn't come to her. He was capable of it, his wheelchair state-of-the-art, but hunter-born like her, Vivek found it difficult to be outside when he couldn't exercise his hunting abilities. The constant bombardment of vampiric scents scraped his senses raw, left him bleeding on the inside.

Exiting the elevator into the pitch-black area under the building, she navigated it without turning on the small flashlight she had in one of the pockets of her cargo pants. It had taken her some time to find a workable pathway after she'd returned to the city with wings, but she now moved through the darkness with confidence, easily avoiding the heavy pillars that were the foundations of the building.

Reaching the scarred and graffitied metal door meant to discourage any intruder who got this far, she coded herself in using another concealed keypad, then put her eye to the retinal scanner. The door slid open seconds later, inviting her into a solid metal cubicle where she was scanned three ways to Sunday in a new layer of security, her weapons noted.

"That way," Vivek had told her, the first time she'd visited after the upgrade, "if you turn out to be a bad guy, I can gas you, and bye-bye, Evil Elena."

"Funny," she'd said at the time, thinking about just how much trust they put in Vivek down here—all of them dead certain that trust would never be broken. He might be occasionally petty, but Vivek was nothing if not loyal to the Guild.

When the doors opened to release her from the steel cubicle, she knew it hadn't been an automatic action; Vivek personally cleared all incoming and outgoing traffic.

"Ohayō, Vivek," she said to the air.

"Gozaimasu, Elena." A pause. "Seriously? That one was so easy even Ransom would've got it."

"I'm going to tell him you said that." She waited patiently as she was scanned a second time, wondering what other tricks he had up his sleeve; she wouldn't put it past him to have had automatic gun ports built into the walls.

"Hey, I think I might have to double-check your identity." Vivek's voice came out strong and resonant through the speakers. "You usually start bitching about how long the scan takes the second after you walk in."

Fingers tightening on the piece of paper she'd crushed beyond any hope of repair, she rolled her eyes. "Next time you complain about the bitching, I'm going to remind you of this little conversation."

A chest-deep laugh, an unexpected sound when it came to the often moody hunter, before the final doors opened in front of her. She headed straight to the reinforced core from where Vivek held court, his steel hand controlling all aspects of the Cellars. That, however, was only a sideline—his true job was *keeping watch on anything and everything that might affect the Guild or its hunters.*

Today, he buzzed her into his inner sanctum without making her jump through any further hoops. "You're in a good mood," she said, when she entered to see him grinning from ear to ear.

"I just had dirty, dirty cybersex with a smoking-hot brunette from Italy. Let's hear it for intimate international relations."

"Too much information." Grabbing a chair, she swiveled it around to sit with her arms braced along the back. In front of her was the large wall-mounted screen where they most often played Scrabble, below it a sleek bank of computers, merely one set of the many that filled the core.

"I go to the trouble of getting a chair constructed to support wings," Vivek complained, "and you always do that."

"If you ever get rid of that chair, I'll never forgive you."

Pretending to think about it, he brought up a game. "I hope you have tissues—because I plan to make you cry like a widdle baby."

He was in such a good mood, she thought again. Vivek was often sarcastic, sometimes sulky, more than a few times curt, but truly happy? It was an uncommon thing. She didn't want to change the tone of this conversation, wanted to leave him as happy as she'd found him.

"You want the first move?" he asked, after the computer allocated their letters.

Shaking her head and knowing a delay would only make this more difficult, she reached out to put her hand over the one on the arm of his wheelchair, though she was conscious he couldn't feel the contact. He saw it, though, curiosity alive in those dark brown eyes. "What's the matter, Ellie?"

"I have a question to ask you." Shifting her hand from his, she used it to grip her chairback. "It's a question that might piss you off. If it does, I'm sorry—but know I'm only asking because I love you."

Smile fading, he turned his wheelchair around to face her. When he didn't say anything, just waited, she thought about simply showing him the crushed paper in her other hand, but that would be a cowardly act, not worthy of their friendship. "If you were a viable Candidate," she said into a silence underwritten with the quiet hum of Vivek's computers, "would you want to become a vampire?"

Blinking quickly, he swiveled back to the game. "Your move."

Elena made that move on autopilot, somehow ending up with a triple word score. Where her luck would've normally made Vivek scowl and promise retaliation, today, he made a three-letter word that wouldn't have challenged a seven-year-old. In return, she added four letters to the board to deliberately create a nonexistent word—and waited for Vivek to challenge her.

He didn't.

Five moves later, he said, "You'd never have asked me that question unless you already knew I was a viable Candidate."

20

Elena gave a jerky nod.

"How did you get my blood to do the test?" Vivek supplied his own answer before she could. "Guild physical, right?" Glancing at her, he turned the chair around again. "Do you think I need to be fixed?"

She heard the bitterness, knew she had to face it head-on if they were to go forward as friends. "I think you're unhappy deep inside." This wasn't the time to pull her punches. "You've built an extraordinary life." She waved her hand to encompass the room and everything that resulted from his skills with the machines that inhabited it, said, "Hell, you're the reason half of us are alive. I think you're brilliant and gifted, and gorgeous, too, while we're at it."

Clenched jaw, the tendons stark. "No need to go overboard."

"I don't lie to my friends." Vivek was classically handsome, the bones of his face clean and sharp against brown skin that would be warm if it was touched by the sun more often. It was true he was far too thin, but his shoulders were broad, his legs long. *"Put on some muscle, some weight, and you'll have women eating out of your hand."* She paused. *"If you don't scare them off with your attitude."*

A scowl, then narrowed eyes. *"You trying to get me mad?"*

"You're always more fun mad." Blowing out a breath, she locked her eyes with his. *"I asked for you to be tested because, amazing as you are, I know here"*—she slammed her fist against her heart—*"you hurt.*

"I'm hunter-born. I know exactly what it's like to attempt to cage that instinct." She'd tried so hard when she first realized how much her father hated anything to do with hunting. *"It feels like being clawed to pieces from the inside out. The fact that you've managed to stay sane? It makes you stronger than I could ever be."*

Vivek snorted. *"You slit a vampire's throat in broad daylight, shot an archangel, and lived to tell the tale. I don't think you have anything to worry about."* His eyes dropped. *"What's that in your hand?"*

"Confirmation of your Candidacy." Smoothing out the mangled piece of paper, she put it on a scanner. Two seconds later, it showed up on one of the screens. *"Because of the amount of damage to your spinal column and how long you've had the injury, it'll take years for you to get back full use of your body."* She wouldn't lie to him, wouldn't pretend it would be in any way an effortless transition. *"That tick on the right means you've been cleared to proceed to the next stage. If you decide you do want to be Made, the process can begin within twelve hours."*

Vivek released a shuddering breath. *"Jesus, Ellie."* Swallowing, he did something using the complex mouth controls on his chair to shift the form to the main screen, the Scrabble game minimized in a corner. *"It took me a long time to come to terms with the fact that I would never walk, never run, never fuck"*—a wry smile—*"never hunt."*

Elena said nothing, knowing he needed her to listen now.

"Once I did, I vowed not to look back, only forward." This time, his grin was self-mocking. *"I don't manage it all the time. You've seen me manfully brooding—not* sulking*—enough times*

to know that. But," he added, "I try to be conscious of any downward spiral, and I've found ways to enjoy my life outside of the job. Case in point: the hot brunette. Just because I can't fuck doesn't mean I don't understand pleasure."

"V, that never crossed my mind," she said honestly. "Especially after I walked into your Academy room to ask if I could borrow a pen and found Neve Pelletier screaming in orgasm."

A dazzling grin. "One of my proudest moments." Moving his chair away without warning, he rolled to another bank of computers and made a call before returning. "Sorry, saw something come in Sara might be interested in."

"You have eyes in the back of your head?"

"Exactly." Gaze flicking once more to the Candidate confirmation, he said, "If I become a vampire, I can't be Guild."

"Of course you can." Elena had already thought this through. "You won't be able to do what you do now—divided loyalties and all that—but you're hunter-born. We're rare and every one of us is needed."

"I've had no training—"

"You'll have all the time in the world for training," she reminded him. "Vamps are near-immortal."

"Who's going to take care of all this?" His glance took in the room. "You said it yourself. No one else can do what I do."

"No," Elena admitted. "But you think anyone in the Guild is going to begrudge you for making the choice to take your life in another direction?"

"That's not the point. That info I just passed on to Sara—it means she knows the situation might be hostile and that it should be assigned to a team. If I'm not here, that intel isn't picked up and people die."

Wincing, Elena admitted the truth. "I got confirmation you could be a Candidate a few weeks ago. The reason I'm only telling you now is because Sara had to work out how to cover your absence if you decided to go for it."

"Oh?" A dangerous glint in his eye.

"She realized she'd need six trained people to do what you do on your own."

The glint turned into a smug smile. "I told you I was indispensable."

"Yeah, yeah. Anyway, we were hoping that if you do decide to accept the Candidacy, you'd train your replacements before you go."

Vivek was silent for a long time, his eyes on the form. "A hundred years of slavery to have the use of my body." It was a whisper. "A hundred years at the mercy of some random immortal who might decide to treat me like a pet dog."

"The angels aren't stupid. You're highly gifted—no one is going to want to put you in any kind of a menial position."

"I won't be able to hunt straightaway, though, will I?" A frown. "Will I even be a hunter after I'm Made?"

"I have no idea." Elena wasn't going to lie to him about anything. "So far as anyone knows, none of the hunter-born have ever been Made—except me, and, well, I'm kind of a special case."

"So I might gain the use of my limbs, but lose my hunting abilities and the Guild."

"Yes, the risk is a big one." Only Vivek could decide whether or not it was worth it. "I can tell you one thing, though: you won't be under the command of some random angel—you'll be attached to the Tower, directly under the command of whichever of the Seven is in charge at the time."

"Pulling strings for me?"

"What did you think? I'd leave my friends to hang?" She glared at him until he had the grace to look sheepish. "Raphael understands loyalty as well as any one of us. So do the Seven. The fact that I'm taking care of my own isn't exactly a news flash." Stretching her wings, she resettled them. "But I'm not being unselfish here, so don't give me a halo."

"Friends," Vivek said slowly, "are important. Especially to an immortal in a place of power."

"I knew the hot brunette had left you with a few brain cells."

"If I do go through with this and come out with my hunting skills intact, then what?"

"Angels love hunters," Elena said. "Your skills will be used,

though not necessarily always as they would be by the Guild."
A blunt fact. *"You'll have to keep secrets from the Guild, and
your time will be the Tower's first, but I have a promise from
Raphael that you can remain on the Guild rolls."*

Vivek flicked off the screen. *"You've thought about
everything."*

"No, V, I haven't. I can't. Only you can do that." He was
the one who'd be stepping into the unknown, into what could
turn out to be a hundred years of hell regardless of her prom-
ises. *"I just wanted you to have every bit of information I could
give you."*

"Let's finish this game," he said at last.

Elena pointed to the board. *"You made 'cat' while I made
'zygote.' The game is so over it's prehistoric."*

Vivek laughed, his cheeks creased with lean male dimples
that were an unusual sight, his eyes brilliant. And she knew,
whatever his choice, their friendship would survive.

Raphael saw Elena glance at his temple as they took to the
clouds minutes after landing in Japan, their intent to ride the
winds for the final segment of the journey to the ancient city.
"There's been no change," he said to her, flying close enough
that they could speak.

"Good." She drew in long breaths of the cold winter air, the
mountainous forests of this part of Kagoshima spread out below
them. "I always forget how untamed it is here," she said, her
wings a dramatic splash of color against the dark green when
she dropped beneath the cloud layer.

Flying nearer to the forest giants, she skimmed the treetops
with a grace that would've been unexpected in one so young
in angelic terms had she not been a hunter, her body and mind
used to tough physicality. Her flight startled a herd of wild
horses, who went galloping off into the mists that hung over
the forests from a recent rainstorm. *Did you see?*

Sweeping down to join her, he said, *When I was a babe
growing up in Amanat, my friends and I would race the horses
kept in the city at that time.*

Laughter in the air, her hair afire in the mountain sunlight.
Did you always win?

No, that's why it was so much fun. It was the first time in
an eon that he'd recalled that memory, buried as it had been
under centuries of power and politics.

Look at the treetops, he told Elena, glimpsing movement.
Our curious friends are back.

Careful to maintain her height, Elena peered downward.
He knew the instant she spotted the monkeys that always
emerged somewhere along their flight path to Amanat—her
delight unhidden, she appeared the girl she'd never had the
chance to be, anointed in the blood of her sisters at an age when
she should've been making a pest of herself to those same
sisters.

There're some more to the left, she said, her mental voice
a whisper. *They're pointing at us.*

Staying at his current altitude as she dared go a little closer,
her white-gold primaries catching the light, he kept an eye out
for threats. A day before the ball, there were apt to be any
number of very dangerous people already in and around the
city. And they all knew Elena was Raphael's heart.

The strange shield of energy that usually protected Amanat
not in evidence today, they flew straight through to land at the
edge of it. Settling her wings, Elena followed the wild blue of
her archangel's eyes to a vampire running along the defensive
wall that surrounded the ancient city.

Elena's credentials from the Guild had always borne the
legend *Licensed to Hunt Vampires & Assorted Others.* The
historical licenses framed in the Guild library, yellowed and
crumbling, all noted the same—but the funny thing was, aside
from Elena's blue-moon hunt of Uram, the men and women of
the Guild didn't hunt anything except vampires.

She'd always figured the "Assorted Others" tag was to cover
them in case they had to go after a human in the course of a
Guild case, had been satisfied with that understanding.

Today, however, as she watched Naasir loping atop the wall

with a strange, liquid grace that made him appear boneless, she had the feeling she didn't know as much as she thought. "What," she said to Raphael, "*is* he?" Regardless of having visited Amanat more than once by now, she'd had very little direct contact with Naasir.

Raphael gave her a distinctly amused look. "Naasir is one of my Seven."

"Raphael."

"What do you think he is?"

"A tiger on the hunt, that's how I categorized his scent the first time I met him, and I haven't changed my mind," she said, as Naasir came down the wall with an ease that made it seem he walked on a flat surface. "His voice might be cultured, but there's something intensely feral about him. It's different from what I feel with Venom . . . or deeper, I don't know."

"I think," Raphael said at her frustrated growl, "I will leave Naasir a mystery for you to solve. I wouldn't want immortality to become boring for my consort."

Elena let out a snarl, but she was intrigued by the challenge.

The vampire reached them the next instant, inclining his head in a slight bow. "Sire." Eyes of pure metallic silver set against skin of a rich, strokable brown met Elena's. "Consort." The greeting was by-the-book formal, but as always, she had the feeling that in any other situation, he'd see her as prey.

Nodding in return and resisting the urge to go for a weapon, she realized the vampire had cut his hair. It had reached the bottom of his nape the last time she'd seen him. It now just brushed it, the jagged waves around his face still as choppy and as vividly silver.

It was hard to describe that silver—it wasn't anything like the gray of age. No, it was true silver, glittering and metallic, until she was certain that if you took strands of Naasir's hair and wove it into a bracelet, it would appear as if it was made of the precious metal. Yet when the wind lifted his hair away from the exotic lines of his face, she saw it was soft, each strand exquisitely fine. Then they settled back into place, and so did the metallic effect.

A tiger with silver eyes.

One she'd seen with his head bent over the neck of an angel

clearly in the throes of sexual bliss, his hand fisted in her hair and his fangs wet with her blood. Until that moment, she hadn't realized angels would allow vampires to feed from them, but then, Naasir was no ordinary vampire . . . if he was a vampire at all.

21

"No, Naasir," Raphael said, as if the other male had spoken. "You cannot make a meal of Elena."

"A pity," came the expressionless answer. "I've never eaten the flesh of such a young angel."

Eyes narrowed, Elena looked from one to the other. "Very funny."

Naasir's gaze lingered on her. "I did not realize there was a joke involved."

Okay, that raised the hairs on the back of her neck. *It was a joke, right? He doesn't actually eat angels?*

Raphael stretched out his wings. *Not usually, no. He prefers wilder game.*

Deciding she would definitely pay her far-too-amused consort back for this, she walked on ahead of the two of them, Raphael's presence beside Naasir the only reason she could accept the silver-eyed menace at her back.

As she walked, Elena took in the changes since their last visit. Amanat had been awakening in slow degrees, but was now literally in full bloom despite the cold. Recalling the temperate feeling in the city last time, she decided the shield must help maintain a constant pleasant temperature within.

Flowers tumbled from planters and window boxes, bright reds and lush pinks alongside unexpected blues and stunning yellows, the petals soft and the blooms ranging from tiny blossoms to roses the size of dinner plates. Their perfume was a rich tapestry that delighted her senses, lingered in the air, the colors vibrant against the stone gray of the buildings.

A passing woman dressed in a gauzy gown in a sweet shade of peach—pretty but no doubt chilly with the shield down—lowered her eyes the instant she glimpsed Elena.

Why is it every time we come here, she said, uncomfortable with the response, *everyone treats me like . . .*

Royalty? Because you are.

Her shoulders tightened. It was one thing to know she was consort to an archangel, another to be treated like a power when she knew full well that many of those who bowed their heads to her had far more power in their little fingers than she had in her whole "baby angel" body. *Caliane doesn't like me.* It made the formal respectfulness even more unsettling.

In fact, Elena added, turning right to follow an otherwise deserted pathway when Naasir indicated the Ancient waited in that direction, *she'd probably be delighted if Naasir indulged his carnivorous instincts.*

My mother is an archangel of old. Whatever her opinions of our relationship, she would never air the family's dirty laundry in public.

Have I told you how much I hate all these stupid polite rules? Scowling, she reached the end of the path . . . and the breath rushed out of her: In front of her was a small pond fed by a waterfall so elegant its sound was delicate music. Flowers grew riotously around the water, the area a carpet of bluebells that reminded her of Illium.

Only a single stone bench disturbed the blue-green of the natural carpet, and on it sat an archangel of breathtaking beauty, her hair as black as night and her wings a sweep of pure white. The crushed sapphires of her eyes seemed full of an aching sadness when she turned to see who disturbed her peace, but the dazzling joy that lit up her face at seeing Raphael soon eclipsed what had gone before.

"My son." Rising, she walked to him through the bluebells, her wings trailing along the grass . . . and though she stepped on the flowers, they sprang back unscathed. It was a potent display of power, all the more so because Elena was certain Caliane was unaware of it, all her attention on Raphael.

When he bent to kiss her cheek, Elena saw Caliane's eyes sheen wet. "Come." She took his arm. "Let me show you how my city has grown since last we met."

"Mother." Quiet steel. "You do not greet my consort."

"Guild Hunter."

Elena felt the urge to check the air for frost, the greeting was so icy. *I thought you said she was never rude,* she muttered on the mental plane, even as she made a graceful bow courtesy of Illium's tutoring skills.

It appears you are a special case.

Stifling a laugh at the cool response, Elena fell into step beside Naasir as Caliane drew Raphael ahead. She'd have to tell Sara about this—her best friend found her "mother-in-law problems" beyond hysterical. As a woman who'd never imagined she'd trust any male enough to tie her life to his, much less meet and deal with his mother, Elena found it cathartic to share the weirdness of this part of her life with Sara.

"Consort," Naasir said, in that smooth voice she had the sense could become a lethal growl without warning, "there's something the Sire has asked me to show you."

She couldn't read him. At all. It truly was like talking to a big, predatory beast that hadn't yet decided whether to eat her. Palm itching, she gave in and drew a knife, playing it desultorily through her fingers like a damn security blanket. "What is it?"

"This way." He waved to a narrower pathway to the left.

Raphael, I'm going off to parts unknown with this vampire who isn't a vampire.

He has promised not to bite without warning.

Imagining the fiendish revenge she was going to take on Raphael for teasing her so mercilessly, she followed the silver-eyed male who continued to make her senses itch and her primal hindbrain crouch in readiness for flight. "Can I ask a question?"

No response, no reaction.

Deciding that didn't mean no, she plowed on ahead. "Who Made you?" Venom, with his reptilian speed and the eyes of a viper, had been Made by the Queen of Snakes and Poisons; it could be that Naasir, too, carried the mark of the one who'd Made him . . . if he *had* been Made and wasn't a wholly unknown creature.

"A long-dead angel who thought to own me," was his enigmatic answer, the silver in his eyes almost liquid. "I tore out his throat. After that, I ate his liver and his heart. The remaining internal organs weren't as tasty so I gave them to his other creatures."

Elena's hand tightened on the handle of the knife, conscious Naasir carried gleaming blades of his own in the sheaths strapped to his arms. "I wouldn't think a vampire who killed an angel would be permitted to live."

A slow, feral smile. "I didn't say I killed him."

Every single hair in her body stood up, the same instinct that had probably saved her ancestors from saber-toothed tigers telling her to run the fuck away! Fast!

Except they'd reached an old temple that hadn't yet been repaired, parts of it tumbled and covered with creeping vines sprinkled with tiny star-shaped flowers of blue and white. The eerie vampire-maybe-not-vampire led her up the steps. His next words were pragmatic and so civilized, she could barely believe it was the same man who'd spoken about eating an angel's liver and heart.

"I made this discovery several hours ago," he said. "As it's on the edge of the city, easy to police, I decided to wait to act until the Sire's arrival."

An angel whispered out of the shadows on the heels of his words, her wings white with a kiss of delicate green at the primaries, from what Elena could see, and her clothing similar to Elena's own—except this woman's pants were of some kind of strong brown fabric instead of leather, and her white top a flowing thing rather than the more fitted styles Elena preferred. She wasn't yet expert enough at fighting with wings to risk tangling herself or her weapons up in froufrou clothes.

"Consort," the other woman said. "I am Isabel."

Naasir's partner, Elena realized, situated here to give the vampire winged backup. "Elena," she said and held out her hand, the other woman having been away from Amanat during Elena's previous visits.

Isabel shook it with a smile, her eyes an extraordinary dark brown, her black hair pulled back in an elegant knot at the nape of her neck, and her skin a tawny gold that reminded Elena of paintings she'd seen of Egyptian goddesses. "I've made certain nothing was disturbed," Isabel told her. "Those who ventured this way took little persuading to seek other pleasures."

A slight shift in the winds that traveled through the temple, Isabel's blouse shaped to her body for a fleeting second as Elena's senses jacked into high gear. *The scent of decay, putrefaction . . . and below it, of disease.*

Not needing Isabel or Naasir to show her the way, Elena walked into the damaged building, the roof a filigree that created delicate patterns of light and shadow beneath her feet. At any other time, she would've lingered, taken photographs of the effect to share with Eve, her youngest half sister utterly fascinated by the lost city come to life in a land far from its original homeland.

Today, however, she followed the scent trail in a near-straight line to halfway across the temple. The woman was sitting with her back against one of the intricately carved columns, one hand cradled in a basket of dead flowers, the basket positioned in a way that made Elena think the victim had set it down herself, her body too tired to go any farther. She wore a dress of deep red silk that flattered her femininity without being sexual, the fabric vibrant against the rich cream of her ravaged skin.

There smell was distinctive but faint, the current cold in the city having preserved the victim as she'd died.

Girding her stomach against the rush of pity and anger, Elena crouched down, her wings spreading on the icy smoothness of the stone floor. A single glance was enough to confirm that the unusually small number of sores that marked the woman were visually identical to those on the bodies of the New York victims. No other obvious injuries, but that could be deceptive.

Sadness overwhelmed her as she rose to her feet, the victim appearing a broken doll discarded by a careless child. Elena hoped she was now at peace, this lovely woman who'd spent a thousand years in Sleep, only to die before she'd ever explored the new world into which she'd awakened.

Leaving her sleeping against the stone, Elena walked out into the sunshine where Isabel awaited with Naasir. "How long was she missing?" she asked, walking down a few steps so she could spread her wings, needing to soak in the sunlight after the cold sadness within a temple clearly built to be a place of beautiful serenity.

"Eight hours at most." Isabel's tone was direct but it held the same heavy sadness that had seeped into Elena's bones. "Amanat is a small, tight-knit city," the angel continued, "and she shared a home with two cousins. They raised the alarm when she didn't arrive home for their nightly meal."

"Was she healthy before this?"

"It was taking her body longer to adjust to being out of Sleep than most." Isabel walked down to join Elena in the sunlight. "As a result, though she was mortal and not averse to sharing her life force with the blood kin, she hadn't fed anyone in many days."

The latter comment made it clear Isabel and Naasir had stayed up-to-date with the discoveries they'd made about the disease. "Since you've had no other infected"—a quick glance at Isabel to confirm—"it likely means the enemy intended to use her as a carrier. Except that she was too weak to handle the virus."

Isabel's jaw firmed, eyes flint-hard. "Had she been stronger, she may not have understood she was sick until it was too late, thus infecting those she fed in good faith."

Sad as the situation was, it did seem to confirm their theory that the disease could only be passed via a transfer of blood, and as Keir had stated, a certain amount of it. Otherwise, the archangel behind it wouldn't bother with such a slow method of infection—one that meant he or she had to make contact with the human chosen as the carrier.

Of course, an archangel could wipe a mind, so it wasn't that big a risk in the grand scheme of things, more an inconvenience. "Do Amanat's people go outside the city walls at any time?"

Isabel's nod was immediate. "Caliane has encouraged them to explore their new world, but they almost always go in groups and return together. Kahla, despite her relative weakness, was more intrepid—I can well imagine her going for a walk on her own."

Kahla. Having a name, a glimpse into her spirit, made it worse.

"The timing," Naasir said, speaking for the first time since Elena walked out of the temple, "cannot be a coincidence."

"No." Turning, she met both their gazes. "No one can know of this." The archangel behind it had to believe he or she had failed in the attempt to infiltrate the city. "We also need to keep Caliane's people within the walls for the time being." From the sly cowardice of the attacks, Elena didn't think the individual behind it would have the nerve to abduct and infect one of Caliane's people in so public a setting.

"No one will leave."

Elena didn't push the vampire for an explanation as to how he intended to achieve that—Naasir might make her instincts bristle in self-protective warning, but he was one of the Seven for a reason. If there was one thing Elena knew about Raphael's most trusted men, it was that they got the job done.

"And I," Isabel said, "will quietly examine anyone who has been outside the walls within the last three days, in case our enemy touched more than one." A glance back at the temple. "There is a volcano not far on the wing. I can carry Kahla to her final rest when night falls."

Touched by the gentleness in Isabel's tone, Elena nonetheless shook her head. "Keir will need to examine the body." Frowning, she considered the logistics of it. "He'll need to wait till after the ball to avoid arousing suspicion, but I'm guessing the shield's going to go up soon as the overnighting guests are all in"—Isabel nodded at her questioning look—"which means the temperature will rise." And Kahla would begin to rot.

"Amanat has no suitable refrigeration facility," Isabel told her, "but there is a fishing village two hours to the east. I'll have a local drive one of their refrigerated trucks into the forest where it'll be concealed from sight and out of earshot."

There in the cold, Elena thought, Kahla would sit alone while the city danced.

"I am sorry, Mother," Raphael said, as Caliane walked with him through her city, her people offering him shy smiles, their eyes drenched with love when they landed on Caliane. "Naasir told me of the loss of one of your own."

"Kahla was a sweet girl—lively as a small bird, inquisitive as one, too." Sorrow deep and true, followed by a whiplash of fury. "It is cowardice to take an innocent life in such a way, with no claim to the honor of open combat."

His mother, Raphael thought, would never believe she'd just echoed the words of the hunter who was Raphael's consort. "We will unearth the perpetrator and make his cowardice known." It was one thing to infect a volunteer from his or her own lands, another to attempt to use a maid who knew nothing of battle.

Caliane's expression softened as she tilted her head back to meet his gaze. "Yes, you will, my beautiful boy."

Again, they walked in silence for many minutes.

"In the last Cascade," he said, knowing she was the one living being old enough to know the answer, and someone who'd never betray him to another, "do you know of any archangel who heard whispers in his dreams?"

It was a strange thing to ask, but his mother simply looked thoughtful and he could feel her turning the pages of her eons-long existence. "No," she said at last, stopping beside a wall entirely covered with hot pink blooms, her expression searching when she turned it on him. "Do you?"

He heard the concern she couldn't hide . . . and he knew. "Father heard whispers, did he not?"

Sorrow darker and older than that caused by the loss of Kahla, a sadness that made his bones ache. "My beloved Nadiel would've been so proud to see who you've become. He always said you were the best of both of us."

In evading his question, she'd given him his answer. His father had heard voices in his madness and now Raphael heard them, too.

22

Twenty-four hours after she'd left the temple, Elena found herself in the surreal position of getting ready to dress for a formal ball while a refrigerated truck sat not far from the city, hidden from the sight of the angels who'd soon be flying into Amanat. A number were already here, the city in a flurry of excitement, the majority of the residents unaware of Kahla's death.

Caliane had made the decision to delay the announcement till after the ball—"for my people have worked so hard for this night"—the death to be explained as a tragic fall that broke Kahla's neck. The young woman would still be sent into the heart of a volcano, but as part of a full funeral service that gave her friends and family an opportunity to say good-bye.

"Won't people question the volcano?" Elena asked now, Raphael having just received the update about the funeral from Naasir.

He shook his head. "No, Amanat's people have never buried their dead, so it'll be seen as a fitting farewell."

"Caliane," she said, tightening the belt on her robe, "is she okay?" Raphael had spent time with his mother that morning, while Elena explored Amanat in Isabel's company.

"She mourns." His upper half shirtless, he stood at the open balcony doors of their third-level suite, looking out over the bustle of the city below. "My mother has ever treasured the people of Amanat."

Elena couldn't argue with that, not when she knew Caliane had taken her people into Sleep with her, she valued them so deeply. Those people, in turn, adored her with an openness and an affection so heartfelt, it gave them a rare sense of innocence and the city an unexpected warmth of heart.

"Kahla is the first she has lost since the Awakening." His hands closed over hers when she wrapped her arms around him from the back, her cheek on the living silk of one of his wings and her palms on the rippled muscle of his abdomen. "If she could call off this ball, she would, but it's too late."

Elena thought of the haunting sorrow she'd glimpsed on Caliane's face. "How does she not see anyone lesser as disposable, given how long she's lived?" Of all the archangels Elena knew, including Raphael, it was Caliane who appeared the most attached to her people, mortal and immortal.

"I asked her the same question once as a boy," Raphael answered. "It was after we'd been to the territories of two other archangels within a short period of time, neither of whom treated their people as I'd always seen my mother do.

"She told me there was a time when she, too, was utterly remote from the world. It was her love for my father that began the change . . . and my birth that completed it." Echoes of time, of memories from the dawn of his life. "In becoming a mother, she found an ability to love that transcended the change engendered by time and power."

Elena thought of the life Caliane had lived, tried to imagine the weight of so many years: To see an eon pass, then to fall in love and bear a child, only to watch your mate be consumed by a madness that forced you to execute him. And later, to be consumed by insanity yourself, cause harm to the child who was the last cherished reminder of your mate, to Sleep for over a thousand years and wake to find your son a man of incredible power . . . one who'd given wings to a mortal.

"If that happens to us," she whispered, unable to wrap her mind around the idea of a life so long and so full of tragedy, "if we feel ourselves, who we are together, becoming lost in time, I don't want to Sleep. I want to say good-bye when I'm still me and you're still you." A clean, sharp ending rather than a gradual unraveling.

Turning, Raphael cupped her face, his eyes incandescent. "Caliane and Nadiel never lost one another, Elena. My parents loved even in the madness." And so, Raphael thought, would he.

Elena's hands fell to his waistband, finger hooking slightly inside. "Together," she said, and he knew she was recalling what he'd told her about Caliane's inadvertent admission when it came to the whispers that plagued his dreams, his hunter's words a reminder of the promise they'd made to one another.

"We fall, we fall together."

Eyes going to his right temple now, she shook her head, jaw set. "If you dare go before me, I will haunt you in the afterlife."

"To be haunted by my heart is no threat." Tugging back her head, he claimed her lips. He'd meant only to initiate a kiss, needing to taste the fiery *life* of her, but they were by the bed seconds later, her robe falling to the carpet to leave her golden-skinned body open to his caresses. Passion a crash of sensation in his blood, he took her to the sheets, their limbs entangled and skin hot as they forged another memory that would hold through eternity.

H er body feeling deliciously used, Elena fixed the final straps of the gorgeous ankle-length gown that had magically appeared in the luggage one of Raphael's staff had driven to Amanat from the jet. She'd given up trying to figure out when or how formal clothes like these poofed into her wardrobe—or into her suitcase, for that matter—all she knew was that a tailor came by every couple of months, took her measurements, and things turned up when she needed them. She was good with that.

Today's gown was sea froth around her ankles, the color an evocative azure blue, the tiny buttons that anchored the straps designed to hug her body faceted diamonds, and the azure lace accent along one side unexpectedly striking. She didn't wear her workmanlike forearm sheaths but strapped on the jeweled upper-arm sheath and blade set Raphael had given her prior to the last ball they'd attended.

It had survived the ensuing carnage, and the blade, sweet and deadly, looked prettily decorative on her biceps. She slid a second blade into a thigh sheath, her dress created with a discreet slit that gave her quick access—the tailor knew who he was dressing, that was clear. Into the hair she'd put in a fancy twist, she slipped the blade pins given to her as a gift by Jason's princess, the spymaster currently on the other end of the call Raphael had received as he was buttoning up his severely formal black shirt.

"What did he say?" she asked when he ended the call.

Taking in the sight of his consort in her finery, Raphael walked across to run his finger along the curve of her bodice, the way she arched her neck in a responsive shiver enticing him to bend, press his lips to her throat. "You appear a pampered courtesan." The jeweled blade on her arm only added to that effect.

She smoothed her hands over the crisp fabric of his shirt. "Good"—her fingers slotting in the remaining buttons—"the better to fool people."

It would be a stupid individual indeed who'd miss the acute perceptiveness of Elena's eyes, the fluid hunting grace of her walk. "Jason," he said, in answer to her earlier question, "has heard not even a whisper of other vampiric deaths such as the ones in New York, and no incidents with mortals as in Amanat."

"Hmm." Slipping her hand into his, she led him to their balcony, which overlooked the cobblestoned square that was to be the center of the ball, the area lit with old-fashioned standing lamps of delicate iron, and accented with the natural blooms of the city. "Are all immortal balls outdoors?"

"For the most part—a ballroom big enough to comfortably handle so many wings would be an impersonal structure."

"Like a stadium." She made a face. "I get why angels would prefer an outdoor setting. It's much prettier this way. The carpet over the cobblestones—it must've taken the weavers a human lifetime to complete."

Raphael nodded, making a mental note to take her to visit

the master weavers in the Refuge on their next visit. Elena would appreciate both their skill and their artistry. "Do you see how the buildings are built in a staggered pattern around the square?" Sliding one arm around her waist, he pointed out the design with his other. "It's so each rooftop has an uninterrupted view of the festivities."

Elena's face glowed as she took in the informal seating areas that had appeared on those rooftops, each warm with candlelight. "It was built this way on purpose!"

"Yes. Should we ever have a ball in Manhattan," he said, laughing when she pretended to stab herself in the eye, "it will require us to get creative. I was not thinking of angelic balls when I built my city."

"Thank God or I'd have had to divorce you." Leaning against him, their wings sliding intimately against one another, she returned to the darkness beneath the sparkle and the gilt. "If Jason's right and Amanat was the only other target aside from New York, then it reduces the short list of possible enemies down to one."

"Yes, Lijuan seems the perfect candidate, yet Jason is dead certain Lijuan has not left her stronghold for the past month."

Elena frowned. "Not that I doubt him, but she has that whole other noncorporeal form."

"I had the same question, but your favorite archangel has apparently been highly visible attending celebrations thrown in her honor in her territory." He watched a tiny bird come to sip at one of the large blooms that climbed up the side of the house, its wings a splash of red and green. "Lijuan was at a winter festival during the entire span Kahla was missing from the city."

"Damn, that takes us back to square one."

"Not quite, for we now know Lijuan is not the diseasemonger." Yet his instincts said she had a hand in this nonetheless. "The others, bar Neha"—who had a legitimate reason for excusing herself from the gathering—"will be here tonight."

His consort smiled as the jewel-toned bird hopped onto a small table to one side of the balcony. "I'll see if I can get close enough to pick up a scent," she said, her eyes on the tiny creature. "Maybe since this is a bloodborne disease, the angel will carry some hint of it in his own blood and it'll speak to my hunter senses."

Raphael had no disagreement with her idea, but, gripping her chin gently, he held the silver-gray of her gaze. "Do not permit yourself to be separated from me this night." The situation was too volatile, the risks deadly. "I would declare war should anyone do you harm, and the entire immortal world knows that fact."

Two hours into it and the ball was extremely . . . civilized. Elena, her senses hyperalert, was almost disappointed that everyone proved to be on their best behavior—even Michaela. The archangel had chosen a dress in dazzling crimson, the cut caressing her every curve, her curls glossy and lush down her back, her eyes made up with sweeps of bronze and gold; it was impossible to deny her sheer, painful beauty.

Of course, that beauty didn't make her any less of a bitch.

"Raphael," she said with a sensual smile. "We parted badly and I was at fault. You must not be angry with me"—a pout—"we have always been meant to be intimate friends."

Pointedly ignored by the female archangel and happy about that fact, Elena focused on drawing in Michaela's scent. All she picked up was the complex notes of a lush perfume . . . then there it was, that bright splash of acid hidden deep.

I can definitely sense Uram in her.

Can you judge the depth of the infection?

No. Her angel-sense was nascent at best; the fact that she could pick up anything at all from Michaela was likely due to the fact that Uram had been a bloodborn angel. Bloated with the toxin that turned humans into vampires and was meant to be purged at regular intervals through the Making process, he'd gone truly insane, becoming a monster more vicious than any vampire, his thirst for blood and death unquenchable.

After Michaela, they ran into Elijah and Hannah, followed by Titus, then Favashi. Neither Elena nor Raphael had any suspicions about Elijah, but she took a scent reading nonetheless. Nothing. The other two archangels didn't register on Elena's senses, either, but that might not mean anything. When

Astaad, with his dark eyes and neatly trimmed goatee, lifted her hand to his mouth, her mind flashed to what his own hands must've done mere months ago, when he'd beaten one of his concubines to a pulp.

That brutal act would've made Elena want to cut off the hands in question, but according to Raphael's own experience in Astaad's territory, while the other male was a harsh and often cruel ruler, he adored his women, spoiling them to outrageous levels. No one had ever before seen him raise so much as his voice to any one of them, and the general belief was the aberration had been connected either to the Cascade or to the disruption caused by Caliane's Awakening. So while it wasn't easy, Elena tried to keep an open mind when it came to the male archangel.

As soon as the formalities were complete, she turned her attention to the vampire by his side. The woman's eyes were a haunting darkness, her rich brown skin and striking features placing her ancestry in the Pacific Islands that were Astaad's domain, her beauty so refined as to be unearthly. An old vampire, her exquisiteness the result of centuries of subtle change.

Smiling, she said, "I'm Elena."

The other woman's eyes widened. "I am Mele," she responded after a quick glance at Astaad that put Elena's instincts on alert—except that Mele didn't look again in the archangel's direction.

They ended up speaking for over a half hour, discovering common ground between Mele's long-term study of vampiric soldiers and Elena's experience as a hunter. At one point, Elena confessed, "I feel like an idiot."

"If I have said a—"

"No." Elena shook her head. "I had this mental image of a 'concubine' "—she'd asked Raphael if it was polite to use that term, been told yes—"and you just smashed it to smithereens." The other woman was a scholar who spoke languages Elena hadn't even known existed until Mele mentioned them.

"Ah." An open smile that made her more stunning than Michaela would ever be. "You'll no doubt meet others who are the ornamental pieces you expected, but my archangel has always valued intelligence and spirit. All his women are thus."

Comfortable with the other woman, Elena whispered, "Do you ever get jealous of one another?"

A laugh. "They are my sisters of the heart. I cannot be jealous of myself."

Raphael, in case you're getting ideas—I won't be this civilized if you decide you need a concubine. In fact, it's a good bet I'll turn homicidal.

He didn't look up from his conversation with Astaad as he said, *A pity,* in that cool "Archangel" tone of his. *I will now have to ask the pilot to empty the hold of my chosen females.*

We're going to have to talk about this new sense of humor of yours. Smiling in spite of her private warning, she continued chatting to Mele, while Raphael and Astaad subtly tried to extract each other's secrets while giving away none of their own.

After they parted ways, Raphael placed his hand possessively on her lower back, her wing below his arm. "I think you have made a friend of Astaad."

"Astaad? I spent the whole time talking to Mele."

"You are consort to an archangel, and yet you treated his most favored concubine with true respect. Even many mere angels consider concubines beneath their notice."

So many layers to angelic society, she thought, so much that made no sense to her. "Astaad and Mele are obviously attached to one another." Love existed there, perhaps not love as she and Raphael understood it, but love nonetheless. "I'm guessing they have a healthier relationship than Neha had with her consort."

"No doubt." His eyes focusing on someone up ahead, his lips curving in a way that went well beyond simple politeness. "Tasha."

23

"Raphael." The angel in front of them had slanted eyes of vivid green and wings of silken copper against hair of darkest scarlet, her nearly translucent skin showcasing her otherwise vivid coloring to dramatic effect. Reaching up as Raphael bent down, the act appearing familiar to them both, the stranger pressed her lips to Raphael's cheek in a soft caress.

"And this," she said, turning to Elena with a deep smile, "must be your consort. I am honored to meet you."

"Tasha is a friend from long ago," Raphael explained, a warmth to him she hadn't seen with any other female angel. "We played in Amanat as children."

"Do you remember when we decided to raid every fig tree in the city?" Musical laughter, sparkling eyes. "Your mother was so cross, she made us plant ten fig trees each. I can still see you with the shovel, your face streaked with dirt and leaves stuck in your hair."

The gorgeous image of Raphael as a mischievous boy made Elena smile, even as her instincts cautioned her to be wary. Unlike Michaela, who made no effort to hide her desire for Raphael and contempt for Elena, Tasha was all warmth and laughter . . . while subtly reminding Raphael they had a history together that Elena couldn't match.

The depth of her sudden dislike made Elena pause, wonder if she was being fair . . . but then Tasha put her fingers on Raphael's forearm as she brought up another shared memory. Elena didn't play games like this, and in any other situation, she would've called the woman on it, but there were far more important things in play tonight. Still, she wasn't sorry to see the back of Tasha when the other angel was called away by a friend.

Raphael's head jerked up without warning a second later. "Lijuan is here."

Looking up, Elena saw nothing but starlight. "You can sense her?"

It appears my ability has another aspect.

An instant later, the sky kind of . . . rolled overhead, akin to a heat wave in a desert. Then an angel with wings of flawless dove gray and hair of pure white, her dress an ethereal black, was landing in the center of the courtyard in a graceful descent. The crowd gasped, tension crawling across the large space like the blood Lijuan so often brought with her.

Stay with me, Elena. Raphael cut through the frozen mass of guests, his target not Lijuan but Caliane.

The blade from her thigh sheath already discreetly in hand, Elena made sure to keep Lijuan in her line of sight as they moved through the gathering. *Will your mother take this as a hostile act?* Elena wouldn't blame her if she did.

It's a possibility. She may, however, decide upon chill politeness.

Here's hoping for a win for angelic etiquette. Two seconds later and they were there.

Caliane's face a mask of icy fury, she acknowledged Raphael with a glance before stepping out into the now empty—but for the single uninvited guest—center of the courtyard.

"You do not observe the rules of Guesthood." Caliane's words were coated in frost and when Elena's breath misted in front of her, she realized the drop in temperature wasn't only metaphorical.

Lijuan smiled, her hair flying back from her face in a wind

that affected nothing else. "On the contrary." She raised a hand. "I bring you a gift."

Ten winged warriors landed behind her with military precision, all dressed in dark gray with Lijuan's red symbol on their chests.

Raphael stepped toward his mother. *Elena.*

Understanding the message, she came to a stop slightly behind and to the left of Caliane, while Raphael flanked the Ancient on her right. As if they'd been waiting for exactly that, a squadron of fighters in the midnight blue of Caliane's forces landed behind them.

"The gift," Caliane said, actual frost beginning to coat the hem of Elena's dress and the tips of her wings, "is unsuitable and must be declined." It sounded like a rote response, except that Caliane's razored voice had come a hairsbreadth from slicing flesh.

"A pity. They are a well-trained unit." Smile deepening against skin so thin Elena could see her skull beneath, Lijuan didn't break eye contact with Caliane.

Elena wondered if Raphael's mother heard the screams she always did when looking into those pearlescent eyes, as if Lijuan held within her a thousand trapped souls.

"I," Lijuan continued, "also bring reparation for the damage I did your city on my previous visit."

Two of her men carried forward a chest, opening it to reveal a pirate's ransom in gold and gemstones. "A sign of my goodwill."

"The damage done cannot be so easily repaired," was Caliane's frigid response. "The breach is final."

Audible gasps, the guests closest to the confrontation flinching as if in anticipation of violence.

Elena tightened her grip on her blade, her fingers chilled but functional. *Raphael?*

My mother has just told Lijuan that no matter how long they live, there can never be anything but enmity between them.

Not a surprise, and nothing that explained the panic she could see on the faces of those who stood nearby. *It's not done to say it so bluntly?*

Not unless one side is anticipating another betrayal.

Oh. Caliane, she realized, had just called Lijuan a liar in front of a crowd of the most powerful angels and vampires in the world.

Lijuan's smile didn't fade, but Elena saw a slick of black begin to crawl across the eerie paleness of her irises. "It disappoints me to hear that."

"It disappoints me to have to say it, but your welcome was also a steep disappointment."

Another round of flinches, but this time Elena had caught the insult buried in what seemed, at first, an incomprehensible statement. *She's talking about the fact Lijuan attacked her right after she rose from her thousand-year Sleep.*

The crashing sea of Raphael touching her mind, clean and strong and wild. *It's a shadowy line, so not all may agree, but it was a questionable act at best.*

You might want to warn your mother that Lijuan is batshit, won't play by the rules.

I did so this morning. Do you have other weapons aside from the blade on your arm?

Another knife, but I can easily take a sword from the vampires strutting around with them as fashion statements. Long swords weren't her weapon of choice, but Galen had drilled her until she could fight with them in a pinch. *For future reference, I am never, ever going to a ball again without a crossbow and a flamethrower.*

I do not think there will be any further such events until the Cascade is over.

Spreading her feet a fraction farther apart under the skirts of her dress, Elena positioned herself to spin out and grab the sword of the poppycock to her left at the first sign of trouble. But then Lijuan unfolded her wings in a whispering sweep. "I welcome you to my territory. I am certain the breach can be mended." Her liftoff was silent, as was that of her squadron, the silence so thick, Elena knew it for another blatant display of power.

Raphael lifted off at the same instant, Caliane's squadron at his back as they tracked Lijuan out of the territory. *Naasir is close to you, Elena. Do not stray too far from him.*

Recalling his words from before the ball and recognizing

the worry behind the autocratic order, she said, *I won't. Be careful.*

The air warmed around her, the frost melting away to nothing as Caliane turned, her eyes liquid blue flame. And although Elena knew she was beyond outclassed in the power stakes, she continued to flank Caliane when Raphael's mother moved through the crowd with elegant grace. Tasha fell in on Caliane's other side, and in her hand was a gleaming sword—held in a grip that said she knew how to use it and use it well.

"My lovers have always been warrior women."

The realization slammed into her with the force of a hammer blow, just as Caliane met Elena's gaze for a fleeting second . . . and inclined her head in the slightest nod of acknowledgment.

R aphael returned deep into the ball, having escorted Lijuan to the sea border.

The rest of the gathering was drama free, the revelry going on till the early hours of the morning. To Elena, the celebrating had the feel of desperation, as if the ordinary angels and the vampires knew war hovered on the horizon and were aware that in a fight between behemoths, it was the weaker who'd become cannon fodder.

Caliane bid them good night sometime after three a.m. and retired to her bed, accepting the escort of a man with the same green eyes as Tasha. Elena and Raphael stayed an hour longer as she'd asked them to act as hosts in her stead, the pain of Kahla's loss clearly weighing heavily on her once more.

"Keir?" Elena asked, once they'd left the courtyard and the final revelers to their play.

"He has just reached the body. I have Naasir and Isabel standing watch while he examines Kahla."

Around them, Amanat didn't slumber, but instead settled into a romantic quietness as couples and small groups strolled through its softly lit beauty, leaving one another alone for the most part. Running her fingers along the carvings that decorated the wall to her left, Elena thought of the body that lay so close to the city, the death that had almost engulfed Caliane's people, and breathed a sigh of relief.

"I've also advised my mother to reinitiate the energy shield for the time being."

Lijuan, Elena remembered, could get through that shield, but it was impermeable to an ordinary angel, which would leave Lijuan fighting alone against Caliane and her forces. Not something the Archangel of China would risk. "How does your mother do that? The shield, I mean."

"Alexander could also create such a thing, so perhaps it's a gift that comes with age. He, too, is an Ancient and now Sleeps." He spread his wing across hers in a silent signal that he wanted her closer.

The familiar intimacy unlocked the questions twisting her up. "Tell me about Tasha."

"Her parents were warriors who served my mother. They have once more returned to Amanat—you saw her father offer Caliane his arm as she left tonight."

Surprised, Elena met his eyes, the heartbreaking blue intense even in the soft shadows of night-not-yet-become-morning. "She didn't take them into Sleep?"

"No. It was their task to watch over me should my mother ever disappear or die." His wings glittered in the lamplight that fell from an open window. "Even in her escalating madness, she thought to leave guardians I could trust. Avi and Jelena were—are—to her what my Seven are to me, and though it was the Hummingbird to whom I chose to give my trust, that does not say anything of my deep respect for Avi and Jelena."

The tie between Raphael and Tasha, Elena realized, went far deeper than a simple physical love affair. "You grew up with Tasha." Was connected to the other woman by thousands of fragments of time.

"We played through Amanat like wild creatures." Turning left, he led her to the field of bluebells beside the pond where they'd first seen Caliane. "She remained my friend as we grew, but childhood's end took us on different paths."

The area in front of Elena had become a wonderland of shimmering night plants hidden by the bluebells during the day, a silver oasis undiscovered by the others who walked in the city, but she couldn't concentrate on the wonder of it. "You met again as adults, though, didn't you? You were lovers."

"Hundreds of years ago."

Walking to the edge of the pond, she fought her habit of pretending things didn't matter when they did, and admitted the truth. "I knew I'd run into one of your lovers sooner or later. I just never expected the first one to be so impressive."

Raphael thought of the centuries he'd lived growing increasingly remote from the world, the power at his command eating away at the boy he'd once been, and knew Elena didn't understand the piercing depths of who and what she was to him. Tasha, scholar and warrior, was a friend, but she'd seen the surface of him and been content with that.

In all his existence, Elena alone had torn at that surface, heedless of the risk, until she revealed the man beneath the archangel. And Elena alone had challenged his decisions and his views, forcing him to look at the world in a way he'd never before considered. "There is no comparison," he said to the only woman he'd ever claimed for his own. "You know me in ways no one else ever has or ever will again."

The ring of silver molten around her irises, the bones of her face strong and exquisitely unique, she parted her lips on his name just as another message touched his mind. So quickly, the moonlit night was no longer a place of beauty but a reminder of the putrid darkness that slithered on the outskirts, waiting to ravage and violate.

24

"Keir has returned."

An immediate change in Elena's expression, his consort shelving their personal discussion for one that affected their people.

Gathering her into his arms, he flew them directly to their suite, having made sure Keir was assigned the suite next door. When they walked through to Keir's living area, it was to find the healer staring into the cold fire, his eyes grim.

His report was deadly in its familiarity.

"The disease destroyed the victim's internal organs." Keir's jaw strained white with the force of his emotions. "As with the others, the sores were a secondary effect. It is categorically the same infection, and, given the lack of further victims and the fact of her humanity, I agree she was meant to be the carrier."

Keir rose to pace across the room, his anger vicious in a way Raphael had never before seen, his wings held so tight to his back it had to be painful. "The only good news is that while the infection was identical to that found in New York," the other man continued, "it was appreciably weaker to the senses that make me a healer. Had Kahla not already been compromised, I believe she and any of those who fed from her may well have made a full recovery."

"Even Lijuan," Raphael said slowly, "cannot create reborn after reborn with no rest in between. Doing so causes their infectiousness to decline."

Keir paused in his pacing. "Jason has been spending time in interesting places."

It was what his spymaster did best.

"If we're right," Elena said, from the armchair into which she'd curled, "and the disease maker's run out of juice, that means New York and Amanat are both safe, at least for the short term."

"We cannot predict how long it'll take for the architect of the disease to recharge," Keir murmured, "but I think it will not be soon. He or she has done too much too quickly." Pausing, he stared at the carpet before raising his head. "I cannot say this without any doubt, but I believe the Falling was caused by an attempt to seed the sky with a disease targeted at angelkind, as this bloodborne disease is targeted at vampires."

Raphael had thought as much, the risk to his people one he had to find a way to negate. "The energy expended in that attempt would also explain why the disease maker is exhausted after creating only two carriers that we know of." Seeing the healer sway slightly on his feet, he said, "Rest now, Keir." *Do not let the rage eat away at you.*

Keir glanced up. *Now you quote my own words back at me.*

They were wise ones. Said to the angry, broken youth he'd been. "We'll leave you in peace."

The healer's expression remained tense, but he was no longer pacing when they walked out the door. Leaving Elena getting changed in their suite, Isabel on watch outside, Raphael flew to his mother. He knew she wouldn't be asleep—angels so old as Caliane slept but rarely and the two of them needed to talk; not only as mother and son, but as archangels who might soon be drawn into a global war.

"I'm not ready for war," she said, as they walked through the quiet corridors of her home, her arm tucked through his, her wing a warm weight against his own. "My power has returned, my people are strong again, but my spirit? It wants only peace." She smiled and it was a creation of sadness. "I've fought too many battles. Now I feel only the driving need to enshield Amanat and wait this out."

Raphael couldn't blame her for that choice. "You should protect your people. They are yet babes in this new world."

Eyes so similar to his own, yet with such age, such pain, such loss in them, met his. "You are the babe of my body, Raphael. I will not abandon you as I once did." Steel in the blue. "My resources are yours. I will not permit your city to fall."

"Mother." He held her against him, continually surprised at how small she was, for she had always loomed larger than life in his memories. "I'm no child, and if you divert your resources to New York, you know Lijuan will attack and destroy Amanat."

Drawing back, she took his arm again and led him toward the wide stairs to the roof, her voice unyielding. "What use is my city if my son is dead?"

Realizing he wouldn't win this battle if he spoke as a son to his mother, he spoke as one archangel to another. "Victory in New York will be meaningless if Lijuan gains a stronger foothold in this part of the world." Amanat's simple existence was a symbol that Lijuan was not as all-powerful as she would have the world believe.

"And if you move your people to protect them," he added, "thus abandoning your city, it'll be viewed as a capitulation." In wars between immortals, perception could often be everything. "Those who might now be undecided on a side will begin to see her as the true power, once it becomes known she drove you from your city."

The elegant lines of her face exposed by the way she'd pinned her hair into a loose knot, Caliane pulled away to walk to the edge of the roof. "I'll be making a choice, not being driven anywhere by that repugnance who styles herself an archangel."

"That isn't the story she'll tell, nor the one people will believe." When there was only silence from Caliane, her feathers limned with power against the starlit night, he reminded her of the one fact against which she couldn't argue. "We cannot know how long the coming wars will last, and we cannot coexist in the same territory, Mother, not for anything beyond a short term." It was the reason the members of the Cadre were separated from one another by water and land, their powers too violent to permit long-term proximity.

There were two known exceptions to that rule. The first was pregnancy—had Michaela truly been with child, he could've offered her sanctuary, for the vulnerability that came with carrying a child would've dampened the effect. The second was love of the kind shared by Caliane and Nadiel, their deep emotional bond somehow ameliorating the effect. Michaela and Uram, by contrast, had never lived together, their love affair conducted over short periods of intense intimacy, followed by weeks of distance.

An adult child fell into neither exception. "I would end up viewing you as a threat, and you would feel the same about me, our instincts driving us mad as we fought the urge not to kill." It was a prediction borne out by angelic history. "You need to maintain and hold this territory."

"I could cross over and obliterate Lijuan's stronghold while she is gone, take her territory."

"Her stronghold is deep in the heart of her territory and you went into Sleep with two squadrons alone." Strong and skilled men and women, but a tiny number nonetheless. "While you fly into her territory, her commanders will send squadrons to destroy Amanat. You must think of all the permutations of any action you take."

Wings rustling, Caliane turned to face him, her expression softer . . . bleaker. "When did you stop being a boy and become a man so used to the ways of politics and power?"

"I was always going to end up here." The child of two archangels, one an Ancient, could have little choice in the matter, power fused into every cell of his body.

Poignant emotion in her eyes, she flared out her wings and, stepping off the edge of the roof, made a silent descent to the street below. "Walk with me through my city," she said to him when he followed, "and tell me of your foolish but brave consort."

It was the first time she'd ever acknowledged Elena as his consort without his prompting. "You must first tell me your decision on matters of war."

"You are right in all you say, and I cannot permit my love

for my son to blind me to that." Fingers brushing his cheek. "Do not fail, Raphael. I have outlived my consort. I cannot outlive my son."

"Should I fail," he said, instead of making a promise that might prove false, "you'll be the only one who remains who might defeat Lijuan. You cannot abrogate that responsibility."

"Can I not?" Cool arrogance. "I see you believe you can make decisions for another archangel."

He laughed as the night winds played with the wintery white of his mother's simple gown. "I learned how to be a ruler by watching you."

A scowling maternal look. "Always, you were able to get your own way by giving me that smile." Sighing, she led him to an enclosed private garden he knew she'd created for her maidens, the air perfumed by the riot of flowers that fell from the temple balconies that surrounded the space. "Your Elena, she has no sense of her own mortality."

"She is a warrior." One with a human heart. "As with all warriors, fear is a tool she uses to her advantage."

"Tasha is a scholar and a gifted warrior, yet Avi and Jelena tell me you didn't pursue one another beyond a single summer. She would've made you a perfect consort."

"Would you have your son in a polite political alliance?"

Taking a seat on a stone bench overhung with yellow roses turned silver by the moonlight, Caliane shot him an exasperated look he well remembered from boyhood scrapes. "Stubborn child." Sighing again, she said, "Come, then. Tell me why you love this once-mortal enough to defy the world. I would hear the story of your courtship."

Coming to sit with her below the roses, he braced his forearms on his thighs and said, "It began with a bloodborn angel and ended in ambrosia."

Too wired to sleep in spite of the late hour, Elena talked Isabel into a sparring session in the private courtyard of the house occupied by only Raphael, Elena, Keir, Naasir, and Isabel. The other angel was good, but Elena more than held her own.

"I think I've become soft in this position." Isabel wiped the sweat off her brow. "Galen will have my head when I rotate back to the Refuge."

"He's a tough bastard," Elena agreed. "But since I'd be dead without the lessons he beat into me on a daily basis, I can't curse him too loudly."

Isabel stifled a laugh, and the two of them separated to shower, with Naasir taking over the watch. Conscious Caliane would want to spend as much time with Raphael as possible, Elena didn't wait for him before going to bed, her body happily tired. She expected a total knockout . . . but it was as if the nightmare visions knew she was alone, vulnerable.

Drip.

Drip.

Drip.

Elena's wings kept dragging through the congealed blood no matter how hard she tried to keep them raised off the slippery tile, the white-gold tips turning a muddy rust. "Belle? Belle, where are you?"

Her oldest sister crawled to her from behind the counter, her blood-soaked fingers leaving darker streaks on Elena's wings as she tried to grab on. "Ellie, my legs hurt."

"Wait, I'll help you get up." She slipped in the liquid that smelled so wet and metallic even as she spoke, landing hard on her back, her wings crushed between her body and the tile in a tangle that wrenched at her tendons.

Gritting her teeth, she managed to get onto her hands and knees, but her body kept sliding backward, the kitchen floor suddenly a slope. "I can't reach you." Her voice was that of the child she'd been, the girl used to having two older sisters who told her what to do when she wasn't sure. "Belle! What should I do?"

But Belle couldn't speak anymore, her head separated from her body, her beautiful long legs in pieces. Sobbing, Elena tried to find Ariel. Ari would know what to do; Ari always knew.

Heart pulsing in her mouth, she glimpsed her sister's slender fingertips behind the chair, began to claw her way forward. She knew it was Ari, because Ari had just painted her finger-

*nails a shade she called "nude"—the color wasn't her favorite,
but it was one that didn't get her in trouble at school. "Ari?"
She reached out to touch Ari's hand. "Belle's hurt. She's really
hurt. We have to help her. Ari?"*

*She was holding her sister's hand. It had been torn off at
the wrist.*

Raphael walked into the suite at dawn to find his consort
in bed, her body rigid and her hands fisted. Immediately putting
his hands on her shoulders, he shook, knowing she needed to
be wrenched out of the vicious grasp of nightmare. "Elena,
wake!" *Elena!*

A jerk of her head, but she didn't wake. Tugging her toward
him with a grip in her hair, he kissed her, kept kissing her until
he felt her nails dig into his arms, her body losing that ugly
nightmare tension. The sob that tore from her when he broke
the kiss had him crushing her close.

"I hate this," she said, after the storm had passed and they
sat on the edge of the bed staring out at the approaching dawn.
Her voice was flat, near defeated, unlike the woman he knew.

Not closing the distance she'd put between them because
he sensed she wasn't ready, her hands white-knuckled on the
edge of the bed, he kept his eyes on the clean line of her profile.
"You're having far fewer nightmares than you did when we
first met."

Jaw clenched, she stared down at the carpet. "And I still
wake up like that, terrified out of my skin." A throb of anger
beneath the defeat, his Elena rising through the battered and
bruised places in her soul. "When does it stop? When do I get
over it?"

Judging she wasn't willing to listen to reason—she might
not even hear him in her current self-punishing mood—he rose.
"We're not scheduled to leave for two hours." He could not be
seen to be racing back to New York. "We have time for a sparring session."

She didn't get up. "I had one with Isabel last night."

This, Raphael realized, was even more serious than he'd
believed. Elena never turned down a chance to spar with

him—he was one of the few people who pushed her to her absolute limit, uncaring of the risk attendant in causing even unintentional harm to the consort of an archangel. To him, the inevitable bruises were acceptable if the lesson would help her stay alive.

Picking up her favorite blades, he threw them at her. Hands snapping up, she caught both. "I *said*"—spoken through gritted teeth—"I don't want to."

"And I say you've sulked long enough." He stripped off his formal wear and pulled on a pair of pants suitable for sparring.

Eyes of silver-gray slitted in frigid outrage. "I just dreamed I had my sister's severed hand in my own. Sorry if that inconveniences you."

Raphael shrugged and very deliberately used the one thing he knew would infuriate her enough to cut through the apathy. "I'll see if Tasha is up for a session, then," he said and reached for the doorknob. "Be ready to leave in two hours."

The knife quivered to a stop on the doorjamb an inch from his face.

25

Not saying a word, and aware of Elena swearing behind him as she rushed to pull on clothes, he walked out and down the steps into the courtyard. When she emerged a couple of minutes later, it was in khaki cargo pants and a specially designed black tank that took her wings into account. Like his, her feet were bare, but she had knives while he was unarmed.

A fair balance, given his extreme strength and speed.

When he made a "come on" gesture with both hands, Elena narrowed her eyes and threw one of those blades at his face. He was distracted just enough by the unexpected act that she almost swiped him with the second blade as she came in low. Grinning, he avoided the strike with a twist that slapped her with his wing.

It wasn't meant to hurt, only to distract in turn, but Elena had learned from their past sessions, and turned with him, going for his wing with the blade in her grip. His consort had a tendency to make mistakes when angry, but not today—he'd succeeded in angering her to the point where she fought with icy fury.

Barely avoiding the sharp bite of metal, he used his wings

to lift himself a foot off the ground in order to avoid a kick. "A little slow, *hbeebti*."

She smiled at the taunt . . . and threw the second blade directly at his wing. Positioned as he was, he couldn't avoid it in time and it pinned his wing to the wall of the house. But he was an archangel, had it out a split second after it went in, his body ready to handle her secondary attack.

"You now have no knives," he said, exhilaration in his blood as he parried her fists and kicks. Elena couldn't truly hurt him, not yet, but her fighting style was unique, one she'd created as she reworked her hunter training and adapted Galen's teachings to take her personal strengths and vulnerabilities into account. And because she hadn't been an angel all her life, she didn't know she wasn't supposed to be able to do certain things, so she just went ahead and did them.

That element of surprise made each session as fun for him as it usually was for her.

Now she came in close . . . and suddenly had two more knives headed straight for his neck. Blocking them using a maneuver he'd learned from Alexander before the other archangel started to view him as a threat, he bared his teeth. "That's cheating."

"Oh?" A saccharine-sweet smile. "Didn't realize we were playing fair." Another fury of blades, their bodies moving with a speed and a ferocity that had drawn an intrigued audience of three—Keir, Isabel, and Naasir. All watched from the balconies that ringed the courtyard and someone clapped when Elena managed to swipe his forearm, drawing blood.

Ignoring the cut, he touched the tip of the knife he'd pulled out of his wing to her cheek to register a hit. He made sure it didn't break skin, for his passionate, beautiful lover didn't heal as fast as he did, but she made no effort to hide her fury that he'd gotten so close. Twisting out of reach before she could take advantage of his proximity, he moved to come at her from behind.

She threw the knives over her shoulders without turning.

Startled by the unexpected tactic, he almost took one in the chest, only his agility saving him from a wound that would've taken at least ten minutes to repair. Turning the instant the blades left her hands, Elena swept out with a kick to capitalize on his shaky balance, but she'd forgotten her wings.

Grabbing one, he hauled her close, his blade at her throat. "I win," he said, both their chests heaving.

A sharp prick against his heart. "Wanna bet?"

Grinning, he bent his head and kissed her, half expecting her to slide the blade in, she was so pissed. But she returned his kiss, hot, wild, and wet, her tongue rubbing against his own. "You ever taunt me with Tasha again," she said in a harsh whisper when they broke the kiss to gasp in air, "and I will geld you."

Raphael winced. "That would take at least a day to repair. Are you sure you want to lose my . . . attributes for that long?"

A twitch of her lips, eyes bright. He could see her struggling to hold in the laughter, but it was a losing battle and she was soon doubled over with her hands on her knees, her laugher wild color in the air.

For the first time, I envy you, Raphael.

Glancing up, he caught Keir's gaze. *It's not every man who has his lover out for his blood.*

Keir's laugh was quiet, as, waving good-bye, he disappeared into his suite. It was Naasir who jumped down onto the courtyard with feral grace. Picking up the discarded knives, he held them out to an Elena who was now upright and wiping tears of laughter from her face.

"Thanks," she managed to say, before secreting away the knives with such speed, Raphael couldn't follow her movements or tell where exactly she'd hidden the sleek weapons.

"Why did you cheat?" the vampire asked, head cocked. "With the knives?"

"Er, I was fighting an archangel who can crush me like a bug. Of course I was going to cheat—especially since we had a score to settle."

Naasir stared at her, then grinned. "We'll spar when I'm in New York."

Twenty-five minutes later, they'd showered and dressed in preparation for the trip home, and Elena still wasn't sure quite what had happened. "Does he like me now?" she asked, as they ate a light breakfast in readiness for heading out on the wing.

"Naasir likes very few people, but I think he finds you interesting."

"Hmm." She bit into her honey toast. "I'm not sure I want to be found 'interesting' by a tiger creature. He probably finds other fresh meat interesting, too."

"Tiger creature?"

"Stop laughing." Scowling, she poured him a glass of orange juice and pushed it across. "Sorry about the funk when I woke up."

He took the juice, the humor fading from eyes the breathtaking hue of a high mountain lake. "Why today?" he asked gently. "You've never been so defeated by the nightmare memories."

"I don't know. I really don't." It had simply felt as if she'd been beaten to a bloody pulp, every one of her achievements erased by the crushing ugliness of horror. "I just"—she blew out a breath—"I wish I could be fixed, so I could remember my sisters, my mother, without the pain."

Raphael didn't offer her platitudes, just grim pragmatism. "You're young. The memories will never disappear, but they'll lose their power to cause such harm over time."

"No offense, but I don't want to be screaming myself awake for the next hundred years." The immortal concept of "time," she'd learned, was far different from a mortal's.

"You're far too stubborn for such a possibility to come into being." Reaching across, he rubbed his thumb over her cheek. "There's a reason the nightmares are getting worse, and you know why."

Startled, she frowned. "What reason? It's not close to the anniversary."

"Sometimes, *hbeebti*, you surprise me." Dropping his hand, he said a single word—"Eve"—and all the pieces fell into place.

Her half sister, only a little older than Elena had been when Slater Patalis destroyed her world, was just coming into her power as a hunter. As Elena had been that fateful year. "Wow," she whispered, her fingers motionless on the white tablecloth. "How did I not see that?"

"It is too close a hurt."

"Maybe." Picking up her juice, she finished the glass before speaking again. "I guess some part of my subconscious is terrified it'll happen again."

"Yes—especially as you've now formed a true bond with Eve."

Where before, they'd been strangers with half the same blood. "Do you think Jeffrey's scared, too?" she asked, thinking of the vicious wounds it must score on a man's soul to bury first his children, then his wife.

"His emotional state is irrelevant." Raphael's face was brutal in its repudiation. "It's because of him that you didn't have what you needed to heal as a child."

She knew he was right, but it was strange, how now that she'd finally begun to look at Jeffrey through the eyes of an adult and not a child, it was so much harder to despise him. "I don't know if I can ever forgive him for what he did to me, but I might not hate him if he gets it right with Eve." Except she was terribly afraid that was a futile hope.

A half hour later and they were on their way out of the city when who should flag them down onto a rooftop but Tasha. "I'm so glad I caught you," she said, her hair tied back to showcase the blade she wore diagonally across her back. "I did so wish to say good-bye."

Trying not to gag at the oh-so-sincere comments that came her way in the next few minutes, Elena smiled. "I'm sorry we can't stay longer, but it looks like rain." She put on her best frown as she tilted back her head to stare at the clouds.

"Elena is right," Raphael said to Tasha. "We cannot risk a delay."

"Of course." Tasha was all elegance and charm when they said their good-byes. "I hope we'll meet again soon."

That was very bad of you, Elena, Raphael said once they were in the air. *You know the coming sun shower will pass in but a moment.*

I also know Tasha McHotpants is regretting she didn't scoop you up when you were young and single. Altering her mental tone, she said, *Oh, Raphael, what luck I caught you. And me dressed up like a warrior with a sword and everything.* She snorted. *Luck my ass.*

McHotpants?

Shut up. I'm mad. Especially after that stunt you pulled this morning.

Then you know I'm more partial to knives than swords anyway.

Teasing me right now could be bad for your health.

To her surprise, he did go silent. It wasn't until he pointed out the volcano some distance to their left that she understood why, her own blood heavy with turbulent emotion. Later that day, a young woman who'd done nothing but go for a walk in the woods would be laid to rest in the heart of that volcano.

As soon as the rites were completed, Amanat would once again become a closed city, according to what Raphael had told her as they showered. Caliane had agreed to stand sentinel against the darkness on this side of the world, while they fought it on the other. Much as Elena wanted all their preparation to be for nothing, she knew that was a wasted hope.

The drums of war pounded closer with every heartbeat.

Winging into Manhattan after the jet landed on a private airfield nearby, Elena breathed deep of the biting cold air of home. It had promised snow for a couple of weeks without delivering, but she felt sure that'd change very soon. "Anything from Aodhan?" she said, when Raphael came alongside.

"No, the city has been quiet since we—" He paused, his eyes locked on the Hudson.

"What is it?" It appeared as it always did to her, but she knew he had the piercing eyesight of a bird of prey.

"Watch."

The water began to crash and froth even as he spoke. Managing to hover beside Raphael as he halted at the river's edge, Elena glanced to the right . . . and that was when she saw it, the wave of red. Rich and dark, it rolled down the river in an eerie tide that made the hairs rise on the back of her neck, the scent of living iron pungent in the air. "Is that blood?"

"There's only one way to find out." He swept down to the water, hovering lower than she could manage with her current wing strength, until his fingertips skimmed the red stain.

Bringing his fingers to his nose, he shook off the wet and rose to her side. "Blood," he confirmed. "But it's weakening."

As they watched, the water turned rose red, then pink, then blush, until it was the murky brown of a churned-up Hudson again, the unmistakable scent gone as if it had never existed. That was when the snow began to fall, airy flakes that whispered over her wings and face to settle on the city, a caress of whiteness to erase the blood.

"What we just saw"—she stared at the water—"should've been impossible."

"Did Jessamy not say something about blood raining from the skies during the Cascade? This would seem to fall along the same continuum."

"And the archangels were not who they should be, and bodies rotted in the streets and blood rained from the skies as empires burned."

"Jesus, Raphael," Elena said, as the historian's words rang in her mind, "this is really happening." And it wasn't just going to be a war. "It's going to be an event that changes the face of our world." Her brain could barely comprehend the scale of what was coming.

Raphael's eyes met hers, the snow continuing to drift from a crystalline sky. "In the hours I spent with Caliane, she told me more of the last Cascade." Shadows of terrible darkness in the intense, impossible blue of his eyes.

"I almost don't want to know," she whispered, all the while aware this was a truth that couldn't be avoided.

Her archangel angled his wings toward the Tower, and she did a wider sweep to follow. "You are consort to an archangel. You no longer have a choice."

26

Aodhan was waiting for them on the Tower balcony outside Raphael's office. "Sire, I've sent out people to keep watch for any signs of unrest caused by the event."

The event.

Elena guessed there really was no other way to describe a river turning to blood.

"Panic has been stifled before it could take root." Aodhan's eyes reflected splinters of Manhattan as he looked toward the water. "However, members of the public no doubt captured live footage of the event and the Tower will need to issue an explanation."

"No." Raphael's tone was autocratic, his face stripped of all traces of "humanity." "There are to be no explanations. Say only that it is Cadre business and if anyone insists on further information, tell them to contact me directly."

Anyone stupid enough to take him up on that offer, Elena thought, deserved what they got. Most mortals never came near an archangel for a reason—the power differential was so vast it created a gulf that couldn't be crossed from either side except in the most extraordinary of circumstances. The longer she spent in the immortal world, the more she understood that that gulf was a safety net; anything else would lead only to death for countless humans.

Still—"People will be scared." She had to speak for the humans and the ordinary vampires, because Raphael simply didn't understand that kind of helplessness. He'd never been weak, not even as a child. "If we don't do something to reduce their fear, the morale of the city could dip to dangerous levels, and it's already shaky after the Falling."

"Illium is of the same opinion," Raphael said, his skin glowing with a fine undertone of power she'd never before seen. It defined his bones even more sharply, his eyes such violent flames it was difficult to look at them. "He requests your assistance in creating a diversion."

Elena hesitated. *Raphael, you're doing the scary archangel thing. The really scary one.*

Resettling his wings to shrug off the snow, he touched his fingers to her jaw as Aodhan disappeared into the Tower. The touch made her skin tingle, her heart thud against her ribs, because the power of him was a pulse in her blood. "You've become stronger," she whispered, her relief intermingled with worry, because while this was good news, she didn't like the sudden cold remoteness of him.

This man, she thought, would never taunt her in a fight or take her dancing through the skyscrapers. He was too distant, too inhuman. He was also hers and she wouldn't surrender him to anything or anyone. Raising her own hand on that fierce vow, she placed her palm against his cheek, the power seeping into her potent enough to steal her breath. *"Raphael."*

"It's a storm inside my skin." His voice echoed with the same whispers she'd heard in their shared dream.

Her mind shuddered, reminded of the screams she'd heard in Lijuan's voice . . . but this, it was different. It made her skin chill in a way that had nothing to do with the falling snow, yet there was no instinctive revulsion, no horror, no sense of evil. No, all she sensed was *power*, of a kind she'd never touched, even after coming in contact with the Cadre. "The storm came with the blood river?"

"Yes. I felt it form as the tide rolled in, grow stronger when my fingers touched the water." The whispers still there, he kissed her and she felt the ice of his newfound power seep into her bones, the cold bitterly painful. But she held on, her hands spread on his chest and her love for him a passionate fire.

"Such fear I feel in you, Elena," he murmured, his eyes on her mouth before he kissed her again, the cold blade of him searing her flesh. "Do you think I'll cause you harm?"

"No." Breath harsh from the bands of ice that crushed her rib cage, she wrapped her arms around his neck and spoke against his lips. "I'm worried about you."

"There is no need."

"No offense," she said with a scowl, "but it's hard to accept that when your skin is glowing and I'm about to turn into a freaking icicle!"

He laughed, the breeze playing through his hair and the snow caught on his eyelashes. "I'm digesting the power, for lack of a better word." Another kiss, this one rawly sexual. "Is that better, *hbeebti*?" It was a private whisper, his hand on her breast in the cocoon created by his wings.

She shuddered, her breast seeming to swell to fill his palm. "One way to heat a woman up." The ice of his new strength remained, but she could feel his cock against her abdomen, sense her Raphael beneath the power-laced skin of the archangel. "I want to take you home and lock us in our bedroom until you're no longer so cold."

A squeeze of her breast, another demanding kiss before he dropped his hand and folded back his wings. "Later. For now you must go and help Illium calm the populace."

Not wanting to leave him when he was still not quite right, but conscious they had to get the mood of the city under control, she kissed him again before flying off. *If you get the sudden urge to raise flesh-eating dead,* she said from the air, *let me know so I can come snap you out of it.*

You have my promise.

Still not sure she was happy about the whole river-of-blood/ strange-influx-of-power situation, she landed on a rooftop not far from the river's edge just as the snow stopped falling, the sun's rays refracted off a city covered in a fine, featherlight blanket of white. The rooftop had a direct line of sight to the river, and she could see swarms of people on the piers, gesticulating wildly as they gathered around camera phones that had no doubt caught the weirdness.

Blue feathers with glittering silver filaments filled her vision a second later, followed by the wings of an angel with eyes of gold abundant in their mischief. "Come on, Ellie." He threw her a baseball mitt, his own left hand already gloved, a ball in his right. "Let's go play catch above the Hudson."

Elena stared. "That's your grand plan for managing people's fear?"

"You ever seen angels playing catch?" A raised eyebrow. "Exactly."

Figuring what the hell, she followed him to the river, where they were joined by three other angels from the Tower, all of whom grinned and saluted her before calling out to Illium to stop delaying and prepare to get his ass kicked. Illium shot back a colorful insult . . . and then they played catch, angel-style.

"Holy hell!" She dived and rose as the ball went in every possible direction, the players attempting to beat one another to it and/or stop it from hitting the water. Elena wasn't anywhere near as fast as Illium or the others, but she held her own by using her brain to calculate angles, even making a couple of surprise intercepts that put her on the points table.

Less than two minutes after they began, the people on the bank stopped staring at the Hudson and started cheering for their favorite player. Factions formed, an enterprising group finding a blue scarf to wave for Illium. The idea quickly picked up steam, and soon there were five different scarves for the five players, Elena's a distinctive hunter gold.

Had to be someone from the Guild down there, she thought with a grin.

Elena wasn't the least surprised when a media chopper appeared in the sky, a harness-bound cameraman hanging out the side, though the crew stayed at a respectful distance. Funny how they'd been doing that since Illium made it clear that in a chopper-versus-angel fight, the chopper would come out worse. Much worse.

"Got it!" Managing to catch a throw that would've otherwise

hit the center of the cheering crowd, she fired it high and to the left . . . where it was intercepted by an angel with eyes of splintered green and wings of icy sunlight. When he rocketed the ball toward Illium using his left hand, the blue-winged angel tumbled head over feet from the force of the powerful missile before thrusting up his hand with a grin, ball firmly in his grasp.

Elena and the other three players exchanged looks and silently retired from the game, their chests heaving as they took a seat on the edge of the nearest roof, happy to watch Aodhan and Illium showcase their extraordinary skills in the air. "Have you seen them do anything like this before?" she said to the angel beside her, an older squadron commander she'd never seen laugh before today.

"Not for two centuries." The solemnity of his response was erased by his roar of approval when Aodhan scooped up the ball as it actually hit the water and fired it back over his shoulder without looking, his body and wings turning him into a living diamond under the piercing winter sunlight.

Stunning, Elena thought, just as her phone vibrated with an incoming message from Sara. Illium caught the ball before it would've hit the roof of a car crossing a nearby bridge, but his body appeared to be on a collision course with a bus. Someone screamed, but the blue-winged angel executed a perfect turn through the girders of the bridge to launch a throw that sent Aodhan flying backward with the might of it.

Ransom is taking bets on which of the two "pretty boys" loses the ball first.

Elena grinned and messaged back: *Put me down as backing Illium to win. Aodhan's too well behaved to expect Bluebell's more sneaky moves.*

Turned out she was wrong. Aodhan seemed to know Illium's tricks inside out and vice versa. By the time it ended in a draw caused by the recall of both players to the Tower, the city had well and truly awakened to the fact that there was an extraordinary new angel in their midst. The horrifying news of a bloodred Hudson had been relegated to a secondary news item, the entire city—heck, the entire country—in fascinated discussion about Aodhan and, of course, the game.

Every single channel had roped in a baseball commentator to discuss the angels' technique, and speculation was rife about a possible rematch, with the Manhattan-based reporters smug as cats in the cream as they said, "Watch this space for further news about *our* angels."

"I'd say Illium's ploy was a success," she said to Raphael later that night, in the privacy of the large bath in their Tower suite. "Aodhan's appearance topped it off."

"He surprised all of us." Raphael no longer looked as "other" as he had after the river ran red, but every so often she'd hear a hint of those strange whispers in his voice. "Why are you sitting so far?" he asked now, his arms spread along the tiled edge of the tub the size of a small pool. "I assure you, I haven't been overcome by the urge to make the dead walk."

Floating across to him, she rested her hands on his thighs below the waterline. "The power, it's holding?" No matter if it freaked her out, he needed to grow stronger if he was to stand against the others.

A darkness in the cerulean blue, shadows shifting under the sea. "No. It filled me to overflowing, but it has drained away ever since. I will return to myself by dawn."

"Damn."

He raised an eyebrow. "Yes, quite. If I need to wait for another extraordinary event to taste such strength, we may, as you put it, be screwed. Especially given the other factor."

Eyes going to his right temple, she said, "Show me," having kept her silence in Amanat for fear his enemies would get wind of what might be a sign of fatal weakness.

Raphael removed the mask of glamour to reveal the speck, except it was no longer a speck. It had spread in a fine line over the bone, become about an inch long. And—"Raphael." Heart stuttering, she touched her finger to his skin. "It's turned a deep, deep red."

Terror sought to squeeze the breath out of her chest. Fighting it, she found her voice again. "It doesn't look swollen or infected, though, more like ink beneath your skin." Except, unlike his spymaster, Raphael didn't have a facial tattoo. "Do you feel anything?"

"There is no weakness, no sense of sickness." He ran the

back of his hand over her breast, his knuckle touching her nipple. "It's done no harm thus far." Both hands sliding down her rib cage to her waist, he brought her over his thighs, his erection rubbing against her, the blunt steel making her nails dig into his shoulders.

Molten heat in her navel. "God, how can I be so ready for you so quickly?"

"Because you're mine." With those stark words of possession, he lifted her, then brought her down so the head of his cock pushed at the slick heat of her opening. "Fuck me, Elena."

Even as she took him with a moan of exquisite pleasure, part of her scrabbled to fight the rising passion, to *think*. That was near impossible when Raphael hauled her lips to his, one hand fisted in her hair, the other molding her breast in a caress both bold and possessive as his tongue thrust deep into her mouth.

It wasn't the roughness that had her brain scrambling. Raphael was often raw, and she loved it, loved that he didn't hold back, but this, today . . . That was when she felt it, the "cold" in his kiss, the ice that penetrated her own blood through their intimate physical link. Even at his most sexually demanding, Raphael always made her feel unbearably cherished. Tonight his touch felt remote, for lack of a better word, and when she opened her eyes, she saw he watched her even as he played her body.

No way in hell.

She bit down hard on his lower lip, and when his hands dug into her flesh, his wings beginning to glow, she licked her tongue over the hurt and ran her lips down his throat, squeezing him with her internal muscles at the same time. His body went taut, his cock pulsing inside her.

Oh yeah, she knew exactly which buttons to press, too.

The instant she felt his hand fisting in her hair again in preparation for taking back the reins, she gripped the tendons along his neck between her teeth. A growl, the glow off his wings intensifying, but he let her control their next kiss, his tongue dueling with hers as she pressed her breasts to his chest, well aware he loved the feel of her aroused nipples rubbing against his flesh.

Flexing his hips, he urged her to go faster, harder. When she resisted, he tipped her back over his arm without warning and sucked one of her nipples into his mouth, rolling the taut little nub over his tongue like a succulent berry. The stab of sensation went straight to her womb. Pulling at his hair, she tried to stop the erotic torment, take back control.

The touch of teeth on her sensitive flesh.

She tightened around the thickness of him and was rewarded by a lavish lick, his mouth releasing her nipple only to brand the other with the scalding heat of his kiss. It was near impossible to think now, but she needed to know this was her Raphael. Clamping down hard on his cock, she held him possessively as he released her nipple to throw back his head, his jaw a brutal line.

Dangerous man. Gorgeous man. Her man.

Easing her sexual hold on him, she used her internal muscles to caress him again as she leaned in to kiss his throat, one hand on his chest, the fingers of the other rubbing at the highly sensitive inner edge of his wing. It was the final straw. Raphael gripped her jaw, bringing her in for a kiss that might as well have been sex, it was so untamed, so deep, so fucking hot.

Then there was no more strategy, no more battling for the reins, only a passionate engagement that had her screaming soundlessly as she orgasmed around the heated steel of his possession, her eyes locked with those of heartbreaking, unshadowed blue.

27

Raphael patted Elena's wings dry, his consort having wrapped her body in a fluffy blue towel as she stood in the bathroom glaring at him via the mirror. "You were weird," she said, succinct and to the point. "Like that time when you went Quiet."

Raphael didn't like who he became in the Quiet, that state of being where he acted with a cruelty driven by cold reason untempered by emotion. In the last and what he'd decided would be his final period of Quiet, he, who had once watched over angelic nurseries, had threatened a babe in pursuit of his goal. "Did I cause you harm?" he asked, dropping the towel to clasp his hand around her nape.

"Of course not." An irritated scowl that to him was a kiss. "You did fuck my brains out, but since I did the same to you, I'm not complaining."

Her temper the ultimate reassurance, he released her. As she walked out into the bedroom and found a robe, he followed to pull on a pair of black pants. He wouldn't sleep this night; there was too much to do—the reason they were at the Tower, not the house—but he'd work from the bedroom until she was past the first problematic hours of sleep.

"I go into the Quiet when I expend a certain level and kind of power," he said, "but this felt like something outside myself." As if he stood in the deepest ocean, insulated from the world.

"An assault?" Curling tendrils of near white around her face where the strands had escaped the knot at the back of her head, Elena closed the short distance between them.

"One that drenched me with power? No." He had a feeling it had been something far more dangerous. "If I am coming into my power, it appears it has the potential to fundamentally change me."

"Never going to happen." A stubborn glint in his hunter's eye. "I'm not gonna lose my man."

"I know." Even in the strange cold, he'd tasted her fury, her passion, the searing depth of her love, and it had wrenched him back into her arms, all distance erased. "Now it's time for my woman to go to bed." She had circles under her eyes from the string of tension-filled days and interrupted sleep. "If you do not argue, I shall send you into slumber with bedtime tales of blood and death and annihilation from the last Cascade."

"Yippee." Slipping off the robe to reveal a body lithe and golden, she snuggled under the blankets.

He lay on his side atop those same blankets, tugging her hair from its knot to play with the wild silk of it. "Have you heard of the lost city of Atlantis?"

"Of course." Her eyes widened, soft wonder in the silver-gray. "It was real?"

"My mother says the legend springs from a water city that existed millennia upon millennia ago—a city of remarkable artistry created by an archangel who had abilities such as those we now believe Astaad to have, except this archangel's powers were at their height at the time."

Bleak realization stole the wonder. "It was destroyed, wasn't it?"

"Caliane is uncertain if some part of it does in truth lie below the ocean, protected by its archangel, but it fell victim to the last Cascade wars, as did many other great civilizations."

"Such wonders lost forever, Raphael. Things that eclipse the creations of this modern world, until the boastfulness of today is that of children who have never seen true grace."

Repeating Caliane's judgment for Elena, he told her the rest, how the wars had circled the globe, soaking the earth in mortal and immortal blood both. "By the time they came to an end, a century after they began, half the world was gone and civilization had regressed by millennia."

Elena shook her head, as if the knowledge was too terrible to bear. "These Cascades, there's no way of telling how many have come and gone, how many times civilization has been all but erased only to start again."

"Yes." Shifting so his body covered her own, his hand in her hair, he told her the prelude to the final brutal fact. "Caliane has survived more than one Cascade." That, he was certain, no one knew. "She says not all are equal, and that from the changes apparent in the Cadre so soon into the Cascade, this may be the strongest in all her eons of existence."

Unhidden horror, his hunter's arms holding him close. "If the last Cascade ended in the destruction of half the world . . ."

"Yes."

Given Raphael's ominous bedtime story, it was a miracle Elena slept as soundly as she did. When she woke, however, to a haunting quiet that told her more snow had fallen overnight, it was with a blinding need to escape the madness of the immortal world for a fragment of time.

Sara had the morning off—as much as a Guild Director could ever have time off—so Elena hooked up with her best friend and Zoe at a small neighborhood eatery for brunch. The owner and most of the regulars knew Elena from before her transformation and, while there were a few people who snuck photos, no one bothered them.

An hour and a half later, they stood in Central Park, watching a giggling Zoe try to catch the pigeons. Bundled up like a little polar bear in an orange snowsuit, the tiny girl would sit down in the snow every so often to rest, then be off again after the birds. Elena's breath frosted the air as she laughed in delight at Zoe's antics, the temperature freezing enough that Elena, too, was dressed for the weather, wearing a long-sleeved top underneath her black hunting leathers. Her immortal body might be tougher than a mortal's, but it had become clear she was too young to shrug off this kind of cold—especially in flight, where she had to deal with wind chill as well.

"How's Vivek?" Sara said, after sending Deacon a photo of Zoe sitting in the snow.

"Aodhan is supervising his transformation." Elena had made certain Vivek was in hands she trusted. "I haven't been to visit him—he asked me not to. I don't think he wants any of us to see him while he's so vulnerable." Paralyzed he might've been, but Vivek had never been helpless as long as Elena had known him. "You know how much he likes to be in control."

"I get it, but he's still a proud idiot," Sara said, her tone deeply affectionate.

"Keir's personally monitoring his progress." Sara had met the healer during her visit to the Refuge, knew the deep respect with which he was held in the immortal world. "It's been a long time since the Making of a mortal with such a significant long-term injury."

"Mommy!" Zoe ran back to them in that wild, almost-falling-over-at-any-instant way. "Isses!"

Crouching down to snuggle her little girl in her arms, Sara smothered her adorable face in the requested kisses. The two looked so gorgeous together that Elena snapped a photo with her own phone, Sara's deep purple coat vibrant against Zoe's orange outfit, their faces creased in identical smiles. Zoe giggled when Sara pretended to tickle her, then gave her mom a smacking kiss on the cheek before holding up her arms to Elena, dark eyes bright. "Nantie Ellie!"

Laughing, "Nantie" Ellie lifted Zoe into her arms and, after sneaking a cuddle, threw her into the air, catching her in a firm grip on the downward flight. Zoe squealed happily, her hood falling off to reveal gorgeous curls of bronze threaded black tied in two neat pigtails. "Zoe fly, Nantie Ellie!"

"Yes," she said, utterly besotted with Sara's baby. "You're flying, Zoe."

Five goes later, the little girl was seduced by the sight of an angelic feather drifting to the snow from a passing squadron and raced off to snag it for her collection.

"I swear," Sara muttered, "I have a heart attack every time you and Deacon decide to treat my tiny, tiny baby like she's a damn basketball."

Elena grinned. "She's your kid—you're the one who jumped off a building in pursuit of a vampire." Leaving Elena swearing a blue streak as she stared down at the alley, fully expecting to see her friend's broken body. "And you caught him, too." Sara had calculated her jump to take her into a Dumpster full of food waste. Nasty, but safe.

Now, her best friend pointed a finger at her. "You do not tell stories like that within earshot of Zoe."

"Give it up, Mama Bear. She has the ex-Slayer for a father and the kick-ass Guild Director for a mother, plus a totally awesome hunter-born for an aunt." Patting Sara's shoulder, she said, "Kid's never going to be satisfied sitting at home doing jigsaw puzzles."

"Deacon made her a miniature crossbow." The look on Sara's face was an odd mix between horrified and proud as she said, "Zoe's a crack shot already. Thank God her 'bolts' have sponge heads or we'd all be dead several times over."

"You know she'll have every hunter in the Guild, and if I have my way, every angel and vampire in the Tower, looking out for her."

Sara brightened. "There is that . . . though it'll probably drive her to rebellion. We must fine-tune our cunning plans to insulate her from danger."

The subject of their machinations raced back right then, breathless with excitement. In her little fist was a feather of deep brown edged with black. "Angel," the little girl said, stroking her finger gently over the filaments she'd taken care not to crush.

"Well done, baby." Beaming, Sara crouched down again. "Do you want me to keep it safe for you?"

Sara didn't speak again until Zoe had returned to her play, and when she did, her words were heavy with concern, her face solemn. "Vivek's going to need us after he wakes up. I can't bear to think he might have to keep his distance."

Neither could Elena. "I've got an idea on how we can make sure he has that support without him violating his oath to Raphael and the Tower."

Two hours later, she tracked Aodhan to the top of one of the massive towers of the George Washington Bridge, his legs hanging over the side as he sat atop the metal frame, and his eyes on the traffic below. He'd have been a hazardous distraction had it been a sunny day, but the overcast sky kept the sunlight from refracting off him, the drivers unaware they were being watched.

She thought about how to bring herself down safely on the relatively narrow surface, and managed it on her second attempt. "Not bad." Grinning, she didn't draw attention to the fact that Aodhan's hand had shot out to grab her when it appeared she might slip and fall. Automatic though it had no doubt been, it was a sign the angel's dislike for touch wasn't so deeply rooted as to trump his instinct to protect.

"Your balance is excellent," Aodhan said, his expression thoughtful, "but you need to strengthen the muscles used to hold a low hover."

"Any specific exercises?" she asked, happy to learn anything that would make her more efficient in the air.

"Yes." Attention returning to the passing traffic, he added, "I can teach you."

Curious as to what had him so captivated, she took a seat beside him, careful to ensure their wings didn't brush. "Are you looking for someone?"

A shake of his head. "I find myself fascinated by the fact that even though the river was full of blood less than a day past, it appears to be business as usual for those who call this land home."

Elena laughed. "New Yorkers are a tough breed, Aodhan." Reaching back, she tightened her ponytail. "Kick us and we might go down, but we'll come back up with fury in our eye and grit in our souls." She loved the bloody-minded strength of her city. "No outsider will ever see us cry."

Eyes of shattered glass met her own, her face reflected back at her in startlingly beautiful splinters. "I haven't forgotten our talk of fear and aloneness," he said, before shifting his gaze toward Manhattan. "You and this city teach me much about coming back after pain and fear. You're right—I've licked my wounds long enough."

Stunned at the openness with which he'd referred to his emotional scars, she went with her gut. "We're all allowed time to curl up and recover from shock or hurt. But if it goes on too long, it begins to eat away at you." Elena knew that from experience, her angry pain where Jeffrey was concerned having left her with indelible scars of her own. "It's better to face the pain, neutralize the acid of the memories."

"And if that fails? If I fall again?"

"You will," she said, because the truth was a far better weapon against the darkness than any false hope. "Over and over. Sometimes, it'll get so brutal that curling up and hiding again will seem the better choice." She thought of the way she'd wanted to shut down in the aftermath of the nightmare in Amanat, of the exhilarating, hot-blooded knife fight that had followed. "Don't give in, Aodhan, because you can't imagine the glory that waits on the other side. Fight to see it; fight to own it."

His responding words held an undertone of heart-piercing joy she'd never before heard from him. "It was worth the risk to play a game with my friend again," he said, the diamond-coated strands of his hair brushing against his cheekbone in the gentle wind. "Until I threw that ball at Illium over the river, I didn't understand I hadn't felt alive for over two hundred years."

A companionable silence fell between them for the next few minutes, until Aodhan said, "You searched me out on purpose?"

"Yes. I wanted to ask you something." Her eyes on his profile, his skin—alabaster lovingly caressed with fine gold—flawless. "Does Vivek belong to you? Since you Made him?"

Shaking his head, he said, "All vampires belong to the archangel in the territory where the vampire is Made. Supervisors are chosen from among the senior angels."

Damn. "So I'm too young to supervise a vampire?"

"In ordinary circumstances, yes; a new-Made vampire can sometimes be violent, difficult to control, and you are weak in angelic terms. Vivek Kapur, however," he said, making it clear he understood why they were having this discussion, "won't come into his full physical strength for some time and you have Raphael's resources at your command."

"So it's doable?"

"It is done." He held her gaze. "You understand you'll be responsible for the hundred years he has Contracted to serve—and that service must be completed."

"I know. It'll breed resentment otherwise." As far as Elena knew, Dmitri's wife, Honor, was the sole exception to the Contract rule in Raphael's territory, and it was an exception not a single immortal would ever question. Dmitri had, after all, been Raphael's loyal second for a thousand years and counting, had spilled his own blood countless times in defense of his archangel.

"What are your plans for the term of his Contract?" Aodhan asked.

"He'll be with Tower communications as discussed, but as soon as he regains use of his limbs, I plan to put him in training at Guild Academy." It was what Vivek had decided on when they'd discussed things prior to his Making; a man didn't need to be physically strong to become a lethal shot. Vivek planned to practice his shooting skills while building up muscle. "In the meantime, he'll be attending intensive lessons at the Academy to bone up on areas of practical knowledge he didn't need in his previous position."

"That won't be enough," Aodhan said, just as she glimpsed wings of distinctive silver-blue changing course to head toward them. "He must be seen to be in your service."

"The training will be to ready him for a position in my Guard." That wasn't something she'd known to offer Vivek before, but it seemed the perfect solution. Still, Elena had no intention of forcing the decision on her fellow hunter; Vivek had already had too many choices taken from him. "I trust him down to the bone and he's already saved my life more times than I can count."

"Good," Aodhan said slowly. "Once your intent becomes known, it'll be assumed he was Made to serve in your Guard, explaining the extraordinary effort expended on his behalf."

Illium arrived before she could respond, landing to grab a seat beside Aodhan. "Why are we sitting on a bridge presenting postcard shots to the tourists on that boat?" he asked, waving at said tourists, who jumped up and down, their squeals carrying on the winds.

"No one noticed us until you deliberately did a low flyby over that same boat," Aodhan pointed out.

"Wave to the nice tourists, Sparkle. I promise it won't cause pestilence and firestorms."

Elena bit the inside of her cheek at Aodhan's glare—she'd never seen anyone crack his reserved shell. "Sparkle and Blue-bell, nice."

"Never," Aodhan said, hands stubbornly on the girder, "ever repeat that. Illium seems to have forgotten I promised to sepa-rate his tongue from his mouth should he utter it again in his immortal lifetime."

"You have to catch me first," Illium taunted . . . and fell backward over the edge of the bridge tower.

"Illium!" Elena cried out as he tumbled toward the heavy traffic, his wings tangled.

"He's playing a trick," Aodhan said calmly. "He used to do that to his mother all the time, until one day, she did it back to him. I do not think I have ever seen Illium so chastised and white."

"No, Aodhan, he's falling too fast." Heart in her throat, Elena twisted in desperate readiness to take off, try to help . . . except it was too late: Illium was about to be crushed between two trucks. "No!"

Silver-blue wings snapping out at unbelievable speed, his nimbleness on astonishing display. "Ellie"—wicked laughter in the gold when he flew back up—"you look like you've seen a ghost."

"I am not talking to you." Breathless from the fright, she spoke to Aodhan instead. "I'm going to tell the Hummingbird he's been up to his old tricks."

Aodhan's lips kicked up in the slightest, slightest smile.

"Hey! Wait!" Illium tried to get into her line of sight. "Don't tell Mother. I promise I—"

Elena's phone rang right in the middle of Illium's plea for

mercy. "Sara, I—" she began, wanting to share the good news about Vivek.

Her best friend cut in, tone stark. "Ashwini spotted a sick vampire in the Port Jersey container terminal. She thinks she can corral him, but she'll need the Tower to take him off her hands."

Elena's blood turned to ice. "We're on our way."

28

Ashwini was bleeding badly from cuts on her arms and scratches on her face when Elena arrived with Aodhan and Illium. "Sick vamp didn't touch me," she said, before Elena could ask. "Cuts are from before—the retrieval I have immobilized in the car. Idiot male had nails like fucking knives and I was stupid enough to get too close." She nodded down the row of shipping containers. "Your vamp is in there. I managed to herd him into a dead end."

Elena went in with Illium and Aodhan, while Ash watched their backs, in case there was more than a single infected vampire in the area.

"Don't touch him," she said to the others when they spotted the vamp, who was indeed mobile. "One thing to believe we can't be infected, another to know."

The vamp had seen them, too, was trying to shuffle-run across the wide space, his fingers in a rigid clawed position and his eyes red. The pustules on his face had burst, the ones on his arms infected.

"Stop!" she called out.

No response, the vampire continuing to close the distance between them.

Taking her lightweight crossbow from where she'd strapped it to her thigh, she took aim at the vampire's left leg. He didn't even hesitate, leaving her no choice but to fire.

The shot was clean, the vampire going down with a high-pitched scream that just sounded *wrong*. Her gut roiled at his agony, though she knew the wound would heal within hours. "Keir said a live victim might help him better understand the disease."

"I'll arrange a retrieval team in suitable biohazard gear, then contact the healer." Aodhan lifted off in a whisper of sound.

The vampire continued to scream as if hot pokers were being driven into his flesh. "This isn't right." The fact that his suffering might help save the lives of others didn't make it seem any less like torture. And that was a line she would never cross. "We have to end—"

"No." Illium retrieved his sword, Lightning, from the sheath on his back. "He is not in such pain. The location of the injury means it hurts going in, but it's only a dull pulse once the bolt is embedded." Striding forward, he put the tip of his sword on the vampire's chest while staying out of reach of the creature's torn, bloodied fingernails. "Quiet."

The vampire froze.

Crossbow raised to cover Illium, Elena walked close enough to look into the vampire's face, and what she saw made pity rain in her veins. "You want to die." Those bloody eyes held a glimmer of true consciousness, enough that this vampire understood what was happening to him even though he couldn't stop it.

"Can't kill," the vampire said, a tear rolling down his face, the liquid pinky red. "Can't kill."

Can't kill?

"Did you try to kill yourself?" she asked, but he was gone, febrile madness crawling over his eyes to leave him clawing out chunks of his own face.

"I can't watch this." Not wanting to end the vampire's life when Keir might be able to help him, she took a gun and flipped it, intending to knock him out with a tap to the head.

"Wait." Illium stared at the vampire, his eyes burning true

gold . . . and the sick male stopped writhing, his hands falling to the sides and absolute peace in his expression as his lashes closed.

Elena looked at Illium with new eyes. He was, she realized, not just powerful. He was becoming a *power*.

"Why are you looking at me like that, Ellie?" Sliding away his sword, darkness in the gold. "You're afraid."

"Not of you. I just realized you might one day leave the Seven." No one as powerful as she suspected Illium would eventually become would want to be in service to another—if that was even a choice. "I can't imagine you not being a part of this city, of my life."

"It's not going to happen anytime soon." A dazzling smile that erased the shadows, his wings spreading to brush her own before he folded them back in. "Forget the coming war, the Tower would fall down without me."

"So modest." Her smile faded as her eyes landed on the vampire, who slept so peacefully and who she knew would probably never wake, though she hoped Keir could save him. "What does it say about the archangel behind this, that he has the ability to create disease?"

"You know the answer to that."

Yes, unfortunately, she did. Power corrupted, and often the corruption was absolute and ugly.

Glancing at the angel, beautiful and gifted, who crouched down to more closely examine the victim, his wings a carpet of exquisite blue and silver on the concrete, she hoped that when the time came, when his power matured to its full strength, he'd have someone who'd act as his anchor, as she and Raphael did for one another. She couldn't bear to think of Illium corrupted. Not Illium.

The vampire died twelve hours later, having never wakened from his sleep. "It was a blessing," Keir said, before he left the city—the healer had arrived in time to examine the victim while he lived. "The disease had eaten its way into his internal organs, would've caused him excruciating pain had he been conscious."

Keir's tests had also shown the male had had a genetic abnormality that made him less susceptible to the virus, though, as they'd seen, not immune. As to how he'd been infected, that was unknown. However, interestingly, he'd just returned to the country after a business trip to China.

"If we're wrong and it is Lijuan," Raphael said to Illium as they flew back after escorting Keir to the jet, "then she's gaining strength at a pace far beyond that of anyone else in the Cadre." It could well make her invincible.

Illium held position, wing to wing. "It's possible she could simply have facilitated the infection by offering safe passage through her lands to her coconspirator."

"Not a great scenario, death and disease acting in concert, but better than Lijuan being the sole holder of such vicious 'gifts.'"

Snow started to fall again around them, the world below dusted in innocence and peace, but the illusion didn't last. Early the next day, a plane bound for New York, its point of origin Shanghai, made an emergency medical landing in San Francisco, the human pilot sending a request for Tower assistance through air traffic control.

To the mortal pilot's credit, he refused to permit anyone else aboard the plane until the arrival of the Tower team, his actions containing the disease within the steel belly of the aircraft. All seventeen vampires on board proved to be sick, their bodies grotesquely contorted, sores on their faces.

The humans were placed in isolation for forty-eight hours, then released after a thorough check showed no signs of infection, while the vampires went into strict medical quarantine.

Five days later, they began to recover—and according to Keir, all now had an immunity to the disease. It was the first good news they'd had. "Our enemy became impatient and over-reached," Raphael said to Elena that morning, the two of them going through different martial arts routines on the lawn of the Enclave house. "Keir now believes we may have the ability to create a vaccine, though it'll take considerable time."

"That's some good news, at least." Elena completed her kata and picked up a small towel to wipe the sweat off her face, the sun shining this morning, though the snow hadn't melted. "What about vampiric travel?"

"Highly restricted." Raphael's expression was that of the archangel he was—cold and resolute. "News has begun to spread of the disease and most vampires are voluntarily restricting themselves. Anyone who attempts to defy the order will be dealt with."

"Good." She knew it had to frustrate those vampires who needed to travel for business or other professional commitments, but it wasn't only their lives at stake. "If that vamp pilot hadn't been hit by a car and replaced an hour before takeoff, this could've been a far bigger disaster." Going to stand in front of her archangel as he finished his own exercises, she placed her hands on the warmth of his skin, his upper body bare.

"At any other time," Raphael said, eyes furious, "I would launch a preemptive strike to halt any further sneak assaults, but with my forces decimated, the only option is to intensify our defensive position. We simply do not have enough people to protect the city and launch an attack at the same time."

Wrapping her arms around him, Elena leaned into his body, the heat of his fury far more welcome to her than the strange cold after the river ran with blood. "I'm going to see the injured angels after breakfast." She held on tighter. "Being around you and the Seven, I'd begun to get a distorted idea of how quickly angels healed—and I didn't understand just how bad the side effects of that drug could be." The men and women in the infirmary were growing back their torn-off limbs and ravaged organs a literal inch at a time, their pain so excruciating, it drove many to tears.

Her own eyes burned as she said, "Izak was sobbing when I arrived yesterday, and he was so ashamed I'd seen him like that." A knot in her throat she had to swallow repeatedly to speak around. "I told him there's no shame in acknowledging pain, that I've cried when I've been hurt and been no less strong for it, but I don't know if he believed me."

Raphael ran his hand over her hair. "He's a young boy at heart still and he adores you." A kiss against her temple. "Speak to him about what he'll have to do to prepare to be in your Guard. It'll give him the reassurance he needs."

"Should I tell him he's about to be thrown into training with Dmitri and Illium? It might scare him." Izak was a baby in comparison to the lethal men in the Seven.

"He may feel fear, but if my judgment of him is correct, it'll also give him the impetus to fight through the agony to come so he can prove his claim to the position."

Raphael's prediction turned out to be right on the money. Izak went sheet white when she told him exactly how tough he'd have to become now that he was part of her Guard . . . then he took a deep breath and gave her an unexpectedly solemn, adult look. "Thank you. I thought perhaps you'd only agreed to offer me the position because you felt sorry for me."

"I'm saving up the pity for when Galen arrives to take over your training."

He winced. "I was hoping he'd remain at the Refuge."

"If he does, you'll be shipped there." Forcing herself not to look at the raw red of his wounds, she kissed him on the forehead. "I'm sure he won't beat you black-and-blue *every* day."

"Ellie, I didn't know you were so mean."

Leaving him with a scowl on his face and a smile in his eyes, she visited with the others, all of whom she'd begun to know on a personal basis. It was hard, seeing so much hurt done to people who now belonged to her, but if they could bear the unfathomable pain, she could bear to stand with them through the journey.

When she finished speaking to the final conscious angel, she had an informal visit with an active squadron, then checked to see if her sister, Beth, had canceled their appointment. No. Taking a deep breath and aware there were no more excuses, she swept off the Tower to fly to a storage locker in Brooklyn. She hadn't been there in weeks, not given everything that had been happening in the city . . . No, that had nothing to do with it; the truth was, she'd been avoiding it even before the Falling.

As she landed, she didn't understand the reason for her resistance when she'd been so painfully happy to find Jeffrey hadn't thrown out her mother's belongings after all. She didn't even know why she continued to keep everything in storage when there was plenty of space at the house for it. She hadn't even taken the precious quilt her mother had stitched by hand.

"Ellie?" It was a wobbly sound.

Turning, Elena saw a sweetly curved strawberry blonde with eyes of translucent turquoise, her body covered in a flirty cherry-pink dress coat belted at the waist. She'd paired the flared coat with knee-high black boots that matched the jaunty beret on her unbound hair, the whole outfit topped off with a gorgeous handmade fabric rose pinned to the top left of her coat.

Her baby sister had always liked to dress up, even when they'd been kids. Belle had often treated her like a living doll, to Beth's great delight, adorning her in necklaces and lace as they put on a fashion show for the rest of the family. "Calling me Ellie now?" she teased with a smile, those memories untainted by blood and death. "Don't let Jeffrey catch you. It's Elieanora."

Beth stuck out her tongue, but the moment was fleeting, her face falling as she looked at the door of the storage space. "Mama's stuff is really in there?"

"Yes." Jeffrey had signed over everything to Elena.

Beth had been so young when Marguerite died that Elena didn't blame her father for his decision—the items would have little meaning to Beth. But Elena knew the stories attached to each treasured piece and those stories were part of Beth's legacy, too.

"Hey," she said, cupping her sister's wet-eyed face. "You don't have to do this, Bethie, not if it makes you too sad."

"I want to." Hot tears running over Elena's hands. "I want to remember . . . s-so I can tell the baby."

Elena froze for several seconds. "Harrison?" she got out at last.

A shamefaced nod. "I know I threw him out and I meant it, too, but I love him, Ellie." The tears kept coming. "Even though he didn't wait for me to be accepted, too, before being Made, I still love him." She swallowed, twisting her hands together. "I think he's sorry for what he did now that he understands he'll have to bury me one day, bury our baby, too."

Elena didn't like Harrison because, no matter his love for Beth, he'd demonstrably wanted immortality more. He *hadn't* waited until Beth's tests were completed, tests that had shown her sister wasn't a viable Candidate; Beth would die horribly if she attempted to become a vampire. Elena wished she could alter that, but she couldn't. It was a biological fact written in stone. As it appeared Harrison was now beginning to comprehend.

Still, Elena admitted begrudgingly, he wasn't a total asshole; he had always treated Beth like a princess, including after she asked for a separation. Elena could almost believe he truly was sorry now that the consequences of his selfishness had begun to dawn.

"Are you mad?"

Drawing Beth into her arms at that trembling question, Elena kissed the top of her baby sister's head—because Beth would always be that to her, Elena's relationship with Eve independent of the one she had with the sister who'd toddled after her as a baby. "No, I'm not mad, sweetheart." She squeezed her tight, Beth tucking her head against Elena's chest as she'd done since childhood. "I'm happy for you."

Beth's shaky smile was as sweet as her heart when she drew back. "I'll love this baby so much, Ellie. No one will ever hurt my kid's feelings."

In that instant, Elena knew Beth had been far more sensitive to the tensions in the Big House than she'd ever realized. "Come on." Heart aching, she took her sister's hand and unlocked the storage space.

Once inside, they shut the door, the temperature-controlled room lit up by a cool white bulb, and began to go through the boxes. "This was yours." Laughing, Elena passed Beth a battered fire engine. "You wanted to be a fireman when you were little."

"Me?" Squeaking with laughter, Beth ran her fingers over the wooden toy. "Can I keep it? For the baby?"

"Everything here belongs to both of us, Bethie." She touched her sister gently on the cheek, unable to believe the family's baby was going to have a baby of her own. "You don't have to ask."

They spent over two hours in the room and it wasn't until the end that Elena took out the quilt her mother had given her on her fifth birthday. Seated on one of the crates, she tried to breathe past the sorrow in her heart as she smoothed her hands over the pretty, printed cotton. "Mama used to sit in her sewing room working on her quilts while we played in the corner, designing clothes for your dolls."

Beth squeezed onto the same crate, cuddling close as she'd

always done. "Suzy and Janey." Soft words, her fingers reverent on the flowered panels. "Those were the names of my dolls."

"Yes." It surprised her that Beth remembered—her sister had locked her dolls permanently away in an act of childish grief and rage the day after Ari and Belle's funeral. When Elena asked why, she'd said Suzy and Janey had been "mean," that they'd said Ari and Belle wouldn't ever come back.

"Mama used to sing to us as she cut out the pieces," Beth said, pulling the quilt across both their knees. *"Frère Jacques, frère Jacques, Dormez-vous? Dormez-vous?"* Her voice was soft, husky as she sang the nursery rhyme. *"Sonnez . . ."*

"Sonnez les matines," Elena continued when her sister faltered. *"Sonnez les—"*

Then they were both crying, Beth curled up in Elena's arms, her body shaking, Elena's own eyes blinded as their teardrops fell to the quilt in a silent symphony. She'd held Beth the day of Marguerite's funeral, too, her sister's body shivering in her arms, her eyes glazed with shock.

"I want Mama," she'd kept saying. "Why did Papa put her in the ground, Ellie? She doesn't like the cold. You have to tell him to bring her back. I want Mama. Please, Ellie."

Today, Beth said nothing, but her heartbroken sobs told Elena her wish hadn't changed. About to become a mother herself, Beth wanted her own by her side.

29

Raphael watched Elena sleep, not the least surprised when she began to twist restlessly, a thin sheen of perspiration on her skin. She'd come to him with pain in her eyes, what little she'd told him of her time with Beth enough that he hadn't left her even after she fell asleep.

Wake up, Guild Hunter. He used what she called his "Archangel" tone, the words a command. It hadn't worked when she lay silent for a year after they fell together the day Manhattan went dark, but today, her eyes opened in a flicker of silver-gray.

"Raphael." A whisper, her fingers weaving into his hair. "I need you."

"I am here." Covering her body with his own, her skin clammy, he cupped the side of her face as he initiated a tender kiss that told her what she was to him. When she shivered and wrapped her arms around him, he moved his hand down to caress her breast and the line of her hip.

It was only skin he touched on her top half, his consort having come to bed without her sleep T-shirt after discovering one of the wing-slit buttons had fallen off, but she wore panties from her lusciously impractical collection. Soft peach satin edged in white lace, this pair cupped her with exquisite perfection. Breaking the kiss to run his lips along her throat, he continued to stroke her breast to hip until her skin warmed, her breath no longer unsteady.

When he raised his head from her throat, it was to find her sensual eyed and lazy limbed, but she pushed at his chest, nudging him onto his back. He went, his hands on her hips as she straddled him, her wings draped behind her and her breasts lush temptation. "Would you lead the dance this night, Guild Hunter?"

Shadows yet in her eyes, she leaned forward and, bracing her arms on either side of his head, dipped her head for a wetly sexual kiss, all tongue and teeth. "Yes," she whispered in the aftermath. "So lie back and take it."

Raphael laughed, the masculine sound a rough caress over Elena's skin. Shivering, she said, "Stop that," knowing full well he'd pitched his voice to arouse.

"Stop what?" It was a purr, a thousand strands of exquisite fur.

Moaning, she kissed her way down his throat and chest, her panties having gone from damp to wet in the space of a heartbeat. "So not fair, but"—she licked her way along the fine line of hair on his navel—"this should even the stakes."

No warning, no buildup, she took his cock into her mouth.

He jerked, his hand fisting in her hair as a groan left his chest. Whimpering at the way that sound rubbed across her intimate flesh, she swallowed deeper, pressing her tongue along the underside as she laved him with affection, the pleasure as much hers as his. Her scalp smarted when he tugged . . . so she grazed him with her teeth.

"You are playing dangerous games with your consort," came the rough warning from the magnificent man who was her own.

Sucking hard, she drew her mouth oh-so-slowly off the long, thick length of him. "You mean you didn't like it?" she asked as innocently as she could.

He flipped her off him and onto her front so fast, she had

no idea how he'd managed it without tangling their wings. "Now"—a dark warning—"it is your turn to be good and take it."

"Oh, God." Hands fisted in the pillows, she bit her lower lip in anticipation of his touch and shivered when he slipped his fingers under the sides of her panties.

Hot breath, his mouth on the dip at her spine, his tongue flicking out to taste her skin before he drew her panties down over her butt and lower. Halting with them tangled around her thighs, he turned his attention to kissing her inner thighs, the panties trapping her when she tried to widen her stance.

"Raphael."

Nipping at her thigh in retaliation for that sensual complaint, he tugged off the panties and rose up over her again, his cock rigid against her back and his weight delicious as he leaned down to murmur in her ear. As he spoke, describing the erotic pleasures to which he'd like to introduce her, his hand slipped under her body to squeeze her breast, tug at her nipple. When he asked her to let him into her mind, she didn't hesitate, the trust between them such that she knew he'd never take advantage.

Pleasure flooded her body in slow waves, ripple after ripple, as if he'd turned a switch in her mind. "I can," he said against her throat, "do this to you at any time." His body shifting, the blunt head of his cock nudging at her hypersensitive entrance, her flesh creamy with welcome. "So long as I can touch your mind, I can bring you pleasure . . . even in the midst of a crowd."

"Don't. You. Dare," she managed to get out between gasps as he thrust in with exquisite slowness, the hard steel of his cock relentless against her swollen flesh.

Masculine laughter, his hand continuing to squeeze and pet her breasts; his mouth shifting to the inner curve of her wings. The instant he licked directly along the edge where her wings emerged from her back, she went off like dynamite, clenching around him until he gripped her hip, pinned her down, and began to ride her, hard and deep.

Bucking up against him, her body out of control, she cried

out his name as the orgasm peaked with a fury and felt him fall with her in a final, powerful thrust.

Later, as they lay tangled in bed, the near white of Elena's hair tumbling across his skin and her head on his shoulder, he gently squeezed her nape. "What did you dream?"

She went motionless, her hand folding into a fist against his chest. "You woke me up before anything really happened."

"You're getting into a bad habit, Elena." His voice was hard, the echoes of pleasure fading rapidly under a wave of anger.

Rising off his chest, his consort shoved her hair out of the way. "Don't use that tone on me." It was a furious command, her eyes angry and alive and beautiful. "We're more than that."

"If we're more than that," he said, his own anger honed to a deadly edge, "then why do you keep lying to me?"

White lines around her mouth, she swung away without replying. When she got out and began to dress, he did the same. His consort, he'd begun to realize, did not do well in contained areas when driven by anger and nightmare, so he'd give her the sky. The one thing he would not give her was distance.

They flew out three minutes later, heading seaward. The waves were high tonight, the sky dark once they left the lights of Manhattan behind. Elena flew and flew and he knew that, once again, she was pushing herself well beyond her limits when it came to the physical strength needed for endurance flights.

It had nothing to do with determination and everything to do with physiological fact.

Elena's body simply hadn't developed the necessary musculature, immortality yet growing into her cells, but he didn't stop her headlong flight. Words would mean nothing, not when she was like this; no, she had to come face-to-face with the perilous risk she took without thought to the consequences.

And worse, this was the second time she'd done the same thing. A third could well be lethal.

If she fell from this height? It was doubtful she'd survive. Even if her luck held, she'd break every bone in her body, her organs collapsing from the impact. Young as she was, that would kill her—either the actual injuries or the inevitable drowning. Unlike him, she couldn't yet survive without air.

Flying above her, high enough that she wouldn't feel hunted, he knew the exact instant she realized the danger. Immediately sweeping left and around, she headed homeward, but her wings had begun to falter, her body dipping lower to the water in erratic drops before she stabilized herself. Only for the pattern to repeat, her body dropping faster and longer each time.

Still she didn't ask for help.

Teeth gritted, he dropped close enough to assist, unable to allow her to cause herself harm, even to teach her a lesson. *Are you planning to let your pride drag you to the bottom of the ocean?*

Silence, her right wing so strained, he knew it could collapse at any instant. Winging his way in front of her in a burst of speed only another archangel could match, he turned and flew directly at her, grabbing her in his hold. He was careful to ensure his arms slid under her wings to avoid any further damage. "Close your wings."

"No, let me go." Jaw set, she shoved at his shoulders, her open wings causing significant drag. "I didn't ask for your help."

"The tendons on your right wing are about to go. Just like last time. Do you wish to cripple yourself?" He wanted to shake her. "Injure the same area over and over, and you'll be grounded for years!"

"I'm fine." Slamming fisted hands against his chest, she twisted, almost freeing herself because he hadn't expected such an irrational move.

"Let me go or I swear to God I'll—"

"Use one of your blades on me?" he asked, his arms steel around her. "Would you draw my blood in earnest, Guild Hunter?"

Fisted hands going still, she looked away, but folded in her wings at last. Her silence rasping against his senses, he gripped her chin with one hand, intending to tug her face toward him, force her to acknowledge his presence. She resisted . . . and then he felt a single hot droplet splash onto his hand.

"Elena."

Her tears shocked him; he'd seen his consort cry, but never during a fight between them. Such emotional manipulation was beyond her, and even now she dashed the wetness away, as if to refute their existence. "Are you in pain?" he asked, concerned she'd snapped a tendon before he caught her.

"No, I'm fine."

Her answer infuriated him anew. "You're clearly not fine." His tone ice, he jerked up her chin. "Tell me—"

This time, it was Elena who interrupted. "Or what? You'll take it from my mind?"

"You question my honor now? Is this the trust you have in me?"

Instead of looking shamefaced, she responded with unmasked fury. "I trust you more than anyone else in the universe! That's the problem."

"You find it a burden to give me your trust?" Fingers tightening on her chin, he spoke through white-hot anger. "You are mine, Elena. Your trust is my right."

"Something is happening to you!" It was a scream, her fisted hands raining blows onto his shoulders and her eyes locked on the spreading line of darkest red along his temple.

"I am going nowhere," he said, realizing the shape of the fear that had stalked her dreams.

"You can't know that! We don't know what's happening." Her fingers on his temple. "Every time you drop the glamour, I see how much further it's spread, how much more of your skin it's begun to cover."

"I'm not dying." It took conscious control to keep his rage at those who'd done this to her, seeded such a grave fear into her heart, out of his voice. Marguerite Deveraux, after all, was forever out of his reach. "I am an archangel."

Chest heaving and cheeks red, she gritted out her reply. "I don't need you to placate me with arrogance."

"It's not arrogance. It's reality," he said, holding her gaze so she'd hear him through the roar of her anger. "There are very, *very* few things on this earth that can kill an archangel, and disease is not one of them. Never in our history has an archangel succumbed to illness."

"Vampires aren't meant to die of disease, either," she

snapped back, but her fingers were gentle as she touched the
blemish on his face again. "Every time I look at this, I get so
scared. I thought I had a handle on it, but it's like this constant
icy fist around my heart. I can't breathe, I can't think."

A thought and the mark was gone, erased with the illusion
of glamour.

"Don't! Don't hide things from me!" Elena realized what
she'd said as soon as the words left her mouth, her eyes locking
with those of a hue so pure, it had no true parallel on this earth.

He was still angry at her, that much was clear, that heartbreaking blue kissed by an icily metallic edge. Yet even in his
anger he held her safe, when she'd done her best to break every
bone in her body with her reckless flight.

Not once. Twice.

"Shit," she muttered, and when he raised an imperious eyebrow, said, "I'm sorry." Her Guild trainers would've kicked her
ass if she'd dared do something this lamebrained as a cadet. "I
can't believe I almost fucked things up so badly a second time."

"Will there be a third?" The question snapped like a whip.

"No. Even a hardheaded hunter like me learns her lessons
after two near-lethal mistakes." If she didn't, she'd have been
long dead by now. "Thank you for the assist."

"I'm glad to know I have some use." A voice so cold, it was
a wonder she didn't have hypothermia.

"That's not fair." She might've been an idiot with the flight,
but that didn't mean he could walk all over her. "I've never
been more intertwined with anyone my entire adult life!"

"And it makes you afraid."

Her breath caught, and she wanted to say no, to remind him
she was a blooded hunter, fear nothing but a tool. But what she
said was, "Yes," because this fear threatened to strangle the life
out of her. "I haven't been this afraid since I realized the monster
was in our house."

"Do you think I don't understand?" Every muscle in his
body went taut, his voice so rigidly controlled, she knew he
battled brutal emotion. "Have you forgotten what I said?"

"I didn't know fear until you, Elena. Use the power wisely."

Shaking her head, she wrapped her arms tight around his
neck. "I haven't forgotten." Lips against his, she reminded him

of something, too. "I cut you some slack when you went all caveman. Cut me some here."

"I didn't almost kill myself when I went 'caveman,'" he said, his kiss hard and hot and possessive, all of it spiced with molten anger. "I didn't make you watch as I did my best to cause myself mortal harm."

30

Her seriously pissed-off consort flew Elena almost the entire way home.

Now that the madness of the fear-laced anger had passed, she was damn well embarrassed. Not only that, but her wings felt like jelly where they weren't threatening to (painfully) detach from her flesh. Still—"I can't have you carrying me into Manhattan. If Ransom spots me on his high-powered telescope, he won't stop teasing me until I'm at least eighty-seven." The truth was, her returning home in Raphael's arms might be seen as a sign of possible weakness by their enemies, should any be watching.

Raphael's responding glance told her he knew the real reason for her request. "No lies, no half-truths. Can you deal with any flight?"

Elena took her time assessing her body. "Yes, as long as we keep it lazy, like we're out for a stroll." It would hurt like a bitch later if her archangel decided she should suffer for her sins and refuse to heal her—and she'd deserve it if he did—but a few extra minutes of gentle flight wouldn't alter that for the worse.

"Be ready to open your wings." Releasing her with care, Raphael positioned himself above her.

She knew it was so he could grab her if her wing snapped. *Archangel?*

Yes, Consort?

Yup, he was definitely still supremely pissed. *I just wanted to tell you something I probably don't say enough,* she said, as they flew over the George Washington Bridge, her altitude low enough that she could see the late-night commuters. *I love you.*

That has never been in question.

His icy answer made her grin. Yes, the love had never been in question—on either side. *I wonder if Montgomery has cake in the kitchen.* Back when she'd been mortal, she'd sometimes wondered why no one ever saw an overweight angel. Now she knew exactly how much muscle strength it took to fly, energy burning off with each wingbeat. She was eating five times what she'd done as a hunter, and just barely managing to keep her weight at a healthy level. *Do immortal bodies run at a higher metabolic rate?*

No one has ever tested that to my knowledge, but yours is undoubtedly doing so as immortality grows deeper into your cells.

That made sense, she thought, just as the sky in the distance began to boil black and thunderous. "Raphael."

Land on the closest surface. Now!

Looking down, she saw a passing barge and was down three seconds later, Raphael landing beside her. The crew stared slack jawed, but didn't approach. "I have my cell phone," she said, having stuffed it into a pocket from force of habit. "I can call Aodhan—"

"It's done." Raphael's eyes remained on the roiling blackness as he spoke. "All of the angels in the air have received the instruction to land."

Skin crawling at the phenomenon, Elena made a different call. "There might be another incident," she told Sara, knowing that as Guild Director, her best friend had access to an automated warning system that could send out a text message to every hunter in the vicinity. "Tell everyone to watch for—shit, tell them to watch for anything."

"Got it."

Hanging up, Elena stood with her body aligned to Raphael's, their eyes skyward as the barge continued to move along the river. The crew had their heads tilted back now, voices pitched high and words tumbling one over the other as they spoke rapidly in an unfamiliar language.

Elena's faint hope that the unnatural clouds would just disperse or float out to sea died a quick death when the boiling patch settled right over the barge, following it as the watercraft traversed the river. Then the cloud began to fall at high speed, causing the crew to scream, duck, but Elena and Raphael kept their eyes on the sky.

So they saw the "cloud" wasn't a cloud at all.

"They're not falling." That alone distinguished this phenomenon from the one that had begun the strange events.

As they watched, hundreds—thousands—of birds landed all around them, until the tiny winged beings completely covered the barge, their combined weight making it sink deeper into the water. The truly eerie thing was their absolute silence. No chirping, no fighting even where they sat on top of one another, nothing . . . but for the fact that every single set of tiny bird eyes was locked on them.

No, not on them. On Raphael.

Okay, creepy. They're staring at you.

Or something is.

The birds rose into the air in a mass of wings the next instant, dispersing so fast it was difficult to imagine they'd been there as a cohesive force—until she looked at Raphael. His skin burned with cold power, as if a cool blue light glowed beneath the surface of his skin.

Come, Consort.

Heart thumping against her ribs at the piercing ice of his mental tone, she ignored the cringing crew to turn into his arms for the liftoff. He released her as soon as they'd gained the correct altitude, both of them angling toward the Tower in silence. Aodhan was waiting on the balcony outside Raphael's office, his eyes reflecting the glittering night of Manhattan in jagged shards.

"No casualties or injuries," the angel said, "no reports of

anything except for garbled messages originating from a barge on the Hudson."

"Thank you, Aodhan."

Waiting until the angel left, she walked to stand beside Raphael on the very edge of the railingless balcony that looked out over the nightscape of their city. "Archangel."

"Yes." He turned, and on his face, the red blemish pulsed.

Again, he was distant. But this time, she didn't wait. Shifting to stand toe to toe with him, she drew him into a kiss that tasted of the sea and of darkness, cold, silence. Heavy and old, so *old*, as if the silence had grown for thousands upon thousands of years, until it was an entity that lived and breathed.

Shivering, she pressed closer, her breasts crushed against his chest, his hand fisted in her hair. It wasn't until she broke the passionate ice of the kiss, her chest spiderwebbed with frost, that she saw. "Your irises"—that incredible, unearthly blue—"they're black."

"A temporary effect." Raphael could feel the darkness as it crawled through him, chill and drenched with a strange, potent power. It sank into his cells, an intruder the angelfire inside him attempted to eliminate.

He fought his instincts, knowing he needed to own this power, hold it—except it threatened to own him. Even now, his blood felt as if it crystallized into frost, his view of the world filtered through a layer of chilling remoteness, until only Elena was drenched in color. Vibrant and alive and with the wings of a warrior, she burned against a backdrop of gray, the rest of the world meaning nothing to him.

If he needed to obliterate this city to win the war, it would be an inconvenience that could later be remedied. Millions would die, but he was an immortal, knew others would replace them given enough time. All that mattered was the power, holding on to it, shaping it, becoming it.

Fingers on his cheeks, the silver ring around Elena's irises liquid fire in the night. "No." It was a deadly quiet word. "It can't have you. You're mine."

And he knew. Shoving Elena behind him so she wouldn't unbalance and fall, he rose into the sky, high above the clouds, past where even Illium or Aodhan could fly. *Land!* It was an order blasted out to every single angel in the vicinity.

Then, and with only the slightest hesitation at the loss of the profound violence of power, he released the dark matter of it in a lightning storm that cracked the sky.

Elena fought the screaming urge to go to Raphael, the need a raw compulsion in her chest as she tried to use the sense of reason she hadn't used earlier. Not only were her wings in bad shape, she'd be struck down by a lightning strike within seconds of takeoff. There was too much of it in the air to avoid.

She could see angels landing wherever they could all over the city, many who'd been up high simply folding their wings so they'd plummet closer to the ground in an attempt to outrace the lightning, before snapping out their wings at the last minute. She witnessed a few close calls but no injuries, Raphael's warning having come in just enough time, but her archangel, he burned in the center of a cold white storm.

"Ellie." Illium's hand on her nape, Aodhan on her other side. "The Sire has gained another ability."

No, she thought, he'd just rejected one, but kept her silence.

An hour, an eon later, there was no more lightning in the sky and Raphael winged down to hold out a hand toward her. Taking it, she stepped off the edge, their hands parting as she swept around to fly side by side with him, heading homeward— though she was dead certain he had her in his sights the entire time, ready to catch her if her injured wing threatened to collapse. But she made it home, where Raphael used his healing ability to ameliorate the damage.

She wouldn't have been surprised if the reminder of her injury, and how it had come about, reignited his temper, but he sent his power into her in silence, the warmth of it an embrace. "You'll be fine now, Guild Hunter." A kiss on the back of her neck.

Skin heating in response, she turned in his arms, the glow from the library fireplace gilding them both in gold. "Talk to me, Archangel." If she had a tendency to shut down, pretend things didn't matter, then Raphael had the habit of handling everything himself. Not surprising, given his status as an arch-angel, but he had her now.

Walking to the square crystal decanter on a side table, he poured a splash of amber liquid into a tumbler and threw the liquor back in a single hit. Alcohol didn't affect angels as it did humans, and it had *no* effect on Raphael, but he'd told her he liked the kick of heat, the taste. "If this is the emergence of a new power," he said, the fire reflecting off the faceted tumbler, "then it's one I cannot control."

Taking the tumbler from him when his fingers tightened, threatening to turn the crystal to dust, she put it down. "You've only had two chances to—"

"It changes me," he said, cutting through her words. "You sensed it attempting to take control. You were right." His fingers clenched on the mantelpiece, his wings arcing to the floor in a display of white fire. "I could murder millions in the grip of it and not blink."

Her stomach lurched, her eyes rising from the stunning beauty of his wings to his face. "Drop the glamour." The instant he did, she swore.

Striding over, she traced the dark red with a fingertip. "It's grown." Not only that but it had curved with a jagged edge, the line thicker, darker. "This can't be coincidence—it's linked to the power fluctuations in some way."

Raphael shoved away from the mantel. "It matters nothing, not when to utilize the power, I must allow it to erase my per-sonality. I may as well give the city to Lijuan if the Raphael who rules it is one forever in the Quiet."

Elena tried to think past her instinctive repudiation of the idea of him permanently in that place of malevolent calm where he was no longer the man she loved, the man who loved her. "The birds," she said suddenly, something niggling at her. "The first time they fell, is it possible it wasn't one event but two?"

Raphael's eyes, no trace of that cold liquid black in their depths, locked with hers. "You believe it was mischance they got caught up in the wave of disease that took down the angels?"

"The sky boiled just like tonight," she said, trying to put her instinctive realization into words. "Could be they were coming

to you and were simply in the wrong place at the wrong time—
remember, they were moving from Manhattan to the Enclave."

Wings continuing to flicker with that illusion of luminous
white fire until he moved out of range of the firelight, he pushed
open the doors to the lawn. "You may be right."

"But it doesn't give us any answers, does it?"

Standing in the doorway, his eyes on the pristine snow
beyond, he said, "The power, it seduced, whispering to me to
weave it into my own cells." A glance over his shoulder. "Before
you, I would've no doubt accepted it and it would've destroyed
me from the inside out."

She followed him when he stepped out onto the stretch of
unbroken white, a snowflake falling to dust her cheek, her
wings kissed by the soft, whimsical rain. It wasn't heavy, just
enough to be pretty, covering up their tracks from the house in
a glittering veil, the unexpected stars above making the ice
crystals sparkle.

It seemed wrong to talk about the horrors of war and power
in such a magical moment, but they had no choice. "Before
you," she whispered, "I was shut up inside my heart, protecting
it from harm, and never knowing the glory I missed." She
linked her hand to his. "You and I, we're a unit. I dare any evil
on this earth to tear us apart."

Spreading his wings, Raphael drew his warrior into his
arms, and as he closed those wings around them both, he knew
that while war was inevitable, the loss of his soul was not. The
chill price of immortality was one Elena would never allow
him to pay.

"I would rather die as Elena than live as a shadow."

His consort's words from their courtship—though perhaps
she would not call it that—whispered into his mind. Raphael
had no intention of dying or of surrendering his territory to
anyone, but should he ever be forced to make that choice, he
would rather go into the last goodnight as Raphael, the archangel who fell in love with a mortal, than Raphael the archangel
so bloated with power that he no longer understood such an
emotion.

"One thing good came out of tonight, though," Elena said,
leaning back so their eyes met, her hair wildfire against the

backdrop of white. "The lightning storm will give anyone getting ready to attack second thoughts about exactly what you've gained in the Cascade."

"Possibly, but what troubles me is why they haven't already launched a direct assault." Even with everything he and his people had done to hide the extent of the harm done to the city's defensive force, their enemy had to suspect he or she had struck a vicious blow. "It makes me believe they wait for something, something with enough chance of so fundamentally changing the balance of power in any war that they willingly risk giving New York extra time to prepare, rather than capitalizing on the damage already done."

"I really need that cake now."

Startled laughter in his blood, unexpected light in the shadows, the taste of snow in her kiss. And he knew that come what may, they'd stand together. In the light and in the terrible darkness.

31

Jason's report at noon the next day made it deadly clear what they would face when the hostilities did begin. "Lijuan is openly consolidating her troops," Raphael told Elena after scanning the report.

"How bad?"

"Her numbers have always been greater than mine—a consequence of her age."

Elena didn't need Raphael to spell it out to realize that Lijuan had been kept in check previously only because every member of the Cadre was more or less equal in power, thus Lijuan risked death in a fight. That clearly no longer applied. "Is there any chance New York isn't the target?"

"No." He showed her a piece of heavy paper, the texture rough silk, as if it had been handmade. "A courier brought this in just before you came up from the infirmary."

Elena couldn't read the message, but recognized the language as an ancient angelic one she'd seen in one of Jessamy's history books. "It's a declaration of war," she guessed.

"Lijuan is 'civilized' to the end." Expression harsh, he glanced back down at his spymaster's report. "Jason also confirms there is no indication whatsoever that she has gained the ability to cause disease, and the fact she wasn't in the vicinity of Amanat at the time of Kahla's infection bears out the theory she has a conspirator."

"So we might be about to face not one but two enemy arch-angels." Meanwhile, the Tower infirmary remained full, only three of the injured fighters having recovered enough to rejoin their squadrons. The good news, however, was that with the transfers from outside the main city, they weren't as badly disadvantaged as Lijuan might believe.

"We'll also have the benefit of fighting on home soil," Raphael pointed out when she shared her thoughts, "while her fighters must arrive on the wing. I'll speak to Elijah, test the strength of our alliance—the odds change dramatically if we and our people stand together."

Leaving Raphael to speak to the other archangel, she flew out with the intention of sneaking a visit with Eve during her break at school. Her sister's recent e-mails had held an undertone of anxiousness she didn't like and she planned to get to the bottom of it—just because the world was going to hell didn't mean Elena was about to abandon the little girl who needed her.

However, she'd barely flown a block when the dull throbbing at her temples suddenly increased in volume and duration. "Damn it." The pulsing headache was her own fault; she hadn't gone back to bed the night before and, regardless of Raphael's healing, she'd given her body a shock with her unforgiving flight over the sea. It was now telling her she either rested or exhaustion would kick her in the ass without warning.

The throbbing turned into stabbing.

Wincing, she realized she'd be of no use to Eve if she was distracted by a migraine. And, if she timed it right, she could catch her sister after school and before Jeffrey returned home—Eve's mother, Gwendolyn, knew Eve needed the guidance of a fellow hunter, wouldn't block Elena from talking to her daughter.

Decision made, Elena detoured to the Enclave house and, waving off Montgomery's offer of lunch, went upstairs. "Soon as I get up," she reassured him, when the butler frowned and reminded her Keir had ordered she eat regular, high-protein meals to fuel her growing immortality.

Ten minutes later, stripped of her weapons and boots, but still in her combat leathers, she lay down on top of the comforter for a power nap that'd keep her going for the rest of the day.

She dreamed again, but this dream, it was different from the one that had nearly broken her in Amanat. There was no blood. No death. No screams.

"There you are." Marguerite looked up from the cake she mixed at the counter, streaks of flour on her cheeks from where she'd no doubt pushed back recalcitrant tendrils of hair as pale as Elena's.

Her father called it "captured sunlight."

"Sit, *chérie*. Talk to your mama."

"Mama?" Hope incandescent in her blood, she crossed the gleaming kitchen floor to take a seat on the counter across from the beautiful butterfly who was her mother. "What are you doing here?"

"My silly Elena." Marguerite laughed, the long dangles at her ears tinkling with the faint, familiar music that was a part of so many of Elena's memories of her mother. "You know it's your sister's birthday tomorrow. This cake must set overnight. Why don't you chop the black cherries?"

Picking up the small knife that was the only one with which Marguerite would trust her, Elena began to cut up the cherries into smaller pieces, looking every so often to her mother for encouragement. She'd been here, in this instant before, her fingers smaller, her legs hanging off the stool on which she perched, and her sister Belle at the kitchen table behind her.

"Shush, short stuff," Belle had said when Elena tried to talk to her about a television show. "I have to write a tome about *Romeo and Juliet* for English homework."

"Can I dance with you later?"

"Only if you sneak me some cherries."

Today, Marguerite and Elena were alone in the kitchen, though Belle's writing pad and pen sat on the table, as if she'd stepped out for a second. "Mama, can I ask you a question?" she said, continuing to use the little knife, though she had longer, sharper blades in her arm sheaths.

"My pretty baby, you can ask your mama anything." Her eyes sparkling, her smile radiant. "Not so big, Elena. Little pieces."

"Yes, Mama." Concentrating, she cut some more and showed her mother. "Like this?"

"Perfect." A caress of loving fingertips on her cheek before Marguerite returned to her mixing. "What was your question?"

Elena kept her head down, unable to look at her mother as she asked the question that had haunted her for more than a decade. "Why?" It was a whisper. "Why did you leave me and Beth?" Her lower lip quivered, her eyes burned. "Papa was broken. You know he was broken."

"Give me those cherries." Accepting the glass bowl when Elena handed it over, her vision blurred, Marguerite tipped them into the mix. "You and your sister are living pieces of my heart, Elena, cut out of my chest at the moment of birth."

"But you left." Jerking up her head, she yelled the accusation. "You left us!"

"I loved your elder sisters, too, *bébé*. I couldn't bear to think of my Ariel and my Mirabelle alone in the dark."

Sobbing, Elena wiped the backs of her hands over her eyes, her chest hurting with the force of her childish sobs. "I miss Ari and Belle so much. I miss you. You left Beth and me all alone, too, and now there's no one to teach Beth how to be a mom."

"I know, oh, I know." Walking around the counter, Marguerite took Elena's tearstained face in her soft, flour-dusted hands. "But I have told you, Elena, you were always the strongest of my babies. Even my wild Belle, she had a heart that carried bruises always, but my Elena, my Elena is strong. Like my mama. Did you know her name was Elena?"

"Really?"

A smile that lit up her face to such beauty, she was the prettiest woman Elena had ever seen. "Yes, it was her, how you say?" One of those unexpected but familiar pauses in her otherwise fluent English. "Her home name. Only her best friends used it."

"I didn't know that."

"Yes, you did. I told you stories about her during the time my little Beth used my womb as a football pitch." Laughter that was melted honey against Elena's skin, sweet and a little wild. "Tales of my strong mama to my strong baby."

Elena jutted out her chin, her anger intermingled with a bleak happiness at being able to feel her mother's touch again. "I thought you didn't remember much about Grandmama."

"I remember enough." The scent of gardenias lush and fragrant in the air, her dark gold skin silken, her hands fine boned when Elena lifted her own to hold her mother's to her cheeks.

"I left you the day that beast came into our house," Marguerite whispered. "You know that."

Elena thought of the bloody streaks on the carpet that told of her mother's brutal fight to get to her daughters, the broken look in her eyes when she understood her two firstborn would be forever silent, and knew Marguerite told no lies. She'd died that day along with Ari and Belle, leaving behind an empty shell. "I still needed you," Elena insisted, ignoring the truth because it hurt too much. "You would've been okay."

"I wish that was so, *azeeztee.*" A word of gentle affection from a sun-drenched desert land Marguerite had never known. "I wasn't strong, not like you, not like my mama." Kissing Elena on both cheeks as she'd always done, her mother looked into her eyes. "Look after Beth. And look after my husband. A part of him died with me."

Elena shook her head, gripping her mother's wrists in a futile effort to hold her to the world. "He hates me."

"No, Elena. He loves you too much."

Elena woke with the echo of her mother's words in her mind and the delicate notes of Marguerite's favorite perfume in the air. Unwilling to lose the fragile link to the woman who had borne her, she lay prone on the bed, her wings painted by the early afternoon sunlight slanting in from the balcony and the idea of her father loving her as strange a thing as the Hudson turning to blood.

Oh, Jeffrey had once loved her as he'd loved all his daughters. She remembered the way he'd held her hand in the warm strength of his as he took her to see the bodies of her dead sisters, fighting against other family members in order to give Elena what she needed, the peace of knowing Ari and Belle were safe, that the monster hadn't made them like him.

Jeffrey's eyes had been wet when she looked up from saying good-bye, his strong face struggling against what she now knew must've been unbearable grief. It couldn't have been easy for him to face the broken bodies of his two eldest girls, but he'd done it for a daughter who lived, paying the painful price and never making Elena feel wrong for her need.

"Don't cry," Elena had said, wiping away his tears when he bent down. "They're not hurting anymore."

That "Papa," strong and loving and kind, had been lost to her long ago.

Touching her hands to her face, she imagined she could feel the imprint of her mother's gentle kisses, a bittersweet ache inside. "I love you, Mama," she whispered, and it was as true as her anger at the choice Marguerite had ultimately made.

It was hard to leave the moment and the final vestiges of memory, but a glance at the clock told her it was already past two. Staring into the mirror in the bathroom, she tried to see the shadow of her mother's fingers, but the imprint was gone, faded into time. It hurt. Breath jagged, she washed off the tears she'd cried in sleep, dried off, then forced herself to keep her word to Montgomery.

The food choked down, she was strapping on her crossbow when her phone rang with a boy band ringtone her younger half sister had programmed in for herself. "Eve? I was just coming to see you."

"It's Amy," was the surprising answer.

Elena's fingers froze on the strap she'd been about to tug into place. Gwendolyn's older daughter didn't speak to Elena, likely out of loyalty to her mother—unlike Eve, Amy was old enough to understand that there was something wrong in her parents' relationship, that her father didn't love her mother as he should.

And yet, Amy loved her father, which left her with no one to blame. Elena didn't mind giving the teenager a focus for her anger, not when she understood what it was to be that girl, confused and angry and sad at the same time. "What is it?" She knew it had to be bad for Amy to break her silence. "Has something happened to Eve?"

"We had a half day at school so we came home at lunch. After we ate, Father locked Eve in her room." A rush of words, as if Amy had been holding them inside too long. "He says he's shipping her off to boarding school in Europe in a few hours."

"Where's your mother?" Gwendolyn had fought for Eve's right to stay in Manhattan and attend Guild Academy.

"Visiting Grandma." Amy's voice trembled. "I can't get through—I've been trying and trying. Sometimes reception isn't good where Grandma lives and it's been raining there."

Elena knew exactly what it was like to feel helpless to protect a sibling, and it enraged her that Jeffrey had put Amy in the same position. "I'll take care of it." She was already at the balcony doors, the snow below glinting under sunlight. "I'm on my way."

"My windows aren't big enough for you."

"That's okay." Elena wasn't planning to skulk into the Deveraux home; she was planning to slam headfirst through Jeffrey.

She shoved open the French doors to her father's study less than ten minutes later, the glass vibrating as the doors slammed into the stops on either side. "You're imprisoning children now?"

Jeffrey's head jerked up from the papers on his desk. Pushing back his black leather executive chair, he rose to his feet, the sunlight glinting off his wire-framed spectacles. "Elieanora!"

"What? You want to lock me up, too?" So angry she could barely see straight, she braced herself with her hand on the right doorjamb. "What is *wrong* with you?" Fury and a plea combined. "Do you really want her to hate you like I do?"

"I want her to live!" he yelled, his voice stripped bare of the urbane sophistication he used so effectively as a weapon. "She came home with a black eye yesterday. Combat training. Combat training! For a child!"

"She needs that training!" Elena screamed back. "We've had this conversation! She'll go mad without an outlet for her hunting abilities."

"I've lost two daughters already! I won't lose another!"

Stunned by the raw declaration, her mother's words still fresh in her mind, she squeezed the doorjamb in an effort to find her lost sense of reason. "You're doing this to protect her?"

Ripping off his glasses, Jeffrey dropped them on the desk, meeting her gaze with unshielded eyes of the same distinctive gray that marked her and Eve as blood. "Do you know what happened when you were sixteen?" he asked, his hands fisted to bloodlessness. "You went to the Academy in the holidays and returned to your boarding school with broken ribs. Three months later, it was a dislocated collarbone, six months after that a black eye and a fractured jaw."

Elena hadn't realized the boarding school had reported the injuries, much less that her father had kept track of them, he'd done such a good job of freezing out anything to do with the fact his daughter was hunter-born. "It was necessary," she said through her shock.

The only reason she'd even been able to attend those intensive holiday classes was that the Guild had gone to bat for her, getting a judge to sign an order that did away with the need for Jeffrey's consent. Like Eve, Elena would've gone mad without the outlet of those practice sessions where she could give her ability free rein; a hunter-born *had* to hunt, the need a compulsion.

But when she'd communicated with her father, it had been with her hunter skin locked away; a child hungry for his approval, she'd pretended to be the nice, normal, obedient daughter he wanted her to be. The fraught peace created by her silence, and his, had lasted until she turned eighteen and enrolled at the Academy full-time over his objections. Their bitter fight that night had left her emotionally bloodied, the resulting estrangement lasting a decade. "I had to become more skilled than the va—"

"Yes, because the monsters are so strong, they could tear

off your head with their bare hands!" Stalking around the desk, he grabbed her by the upper arms and shook so hard that her teeth clattered. "Do you know what it's like to watch a woman get her head torn off? The blood spurts hot and dark and it gets in your mouth, in your eyes, in your nose, until it's the only thing you can see, all you can smell!"

32

Elena couldn't move, even to break the bruising tightness of Jeffrey's hold. She didn't understand what he was saying, the words making no sense in the context of who he was: Jeffrey Parker *Deveraux*, his blood so blue, it was created from the foundations of the city. History, family, tradition, that was the Deveraux way. The blood and the death had come with Elena, Jeffrey's "abomination" of a daughter.

"I was four," he said, his breath hot on her face. "Playing under the covered bench where she cleaned her tools. She was agreeing how I'd make a great policeman, while I played with my trucks and she sharpened her blades"—eyes falling to the blades on her forearms, his fingers digging deeper into her flesh—"and that's when they came for her. Three vampires who wanted vengeance for having been returned to their masters to face punishment."

Elena started to tremble, her heart stuttering in her chest. As far as she knew, Jeffrey's mother was alive and well and active on the boards of several major charitable organizations. Cecilia Deveraux was also not, and had never been, a hunter.

"When I tried to help her," Jeffrey said, "they laughed and

tossed me aside as if I weighed nothing." Jagged words. "The fall broke my legs, one of my arms. I *tried* but couldn't get to her. Instead I had to watch while they kicked my mother, beat her, breaking every bone in her body before they ripped off her head."

"Papa." It was the first time she'd called him that in an eon. "Papa, I'm sorry." Sliding her arms around his chest, she held him, his body an icy rock. "I'm sorry. I'm sorry."

Her father's arms came around her, crushing her so tightly, she could barely draw breath. One hand cupping her head, the other around her upper back over her wings, he held her close to his heart, his breath choppy. When his body shuddered against her own, she thought he might be crying, but it was a thought her mind couldn't accept.

Her father didn't cry. The child in her confused and shaky, she just held on until his breathing evened out, his hand stroking over her hair with a gentleness she'd never again expected to experience from her father.

"I will always be your father . . . and I wish to God I wasn't."

The hateful words no longer hurt, not when she heard the fear she'd been too angry to hear the first time. Her father, this man who held her with such fierce tenderness, was afraid to watch his daughter die the same horrific death as his mother. It altered the bedrock of their relationship, left her without a mooring.

Dead certain the brittle moment would end the instant she stepped back, the wall of pain and loss that divided them once more in place, she held on for just a little while longer. So did he. In silence, their words locked down where they couldn't hurt and cut and make the other bleed.

The world, however, continued to spin, the sound of a chopper passing overhead breaking the fragment out of time in two. They drew apart without a word, her father turning to walk to his desk, pick up his spectacles, while Elena backed out of the doorway. Heading around the side of the house, she gritted her teeth and made a vertical takeoff into the cold air, bringing herself to a hover in front of Eve's window.

Her sister, the skin around her left eye purplish black, was waiting for her, came into her arms without hesitation. Elena saw Amy's forlorn face in the window next door as they left, her hand pressed to the glass. *It's all right,* Elena wanted to say. *I'll bring her back.* Gwendolyn would accept nothing else. All Elena had to do was keep Eve away from Jeffrey until Gwendolyn returned. Her father, she'd realized at last, would never be rational when it came to hunters and hunting, the brutal wounds inflicted too young, the scars too aged.

Chest aching, she concentrated only on flying slow and steady toward the Enclave, the flash of blue that appeared in her vision an unexpected brilliance. "Ellie? Which beautiful maiden do you have there?" A wink directed at her youngest sister. "Hello, Evenstar."

Eve poked out her tongue at Illium, having met the other angel on visits to the Tower to see Elena, but shifted into his hold when he offered. "I'm heavy," she said, before Elena could protest.

"You're a feather." Illium held Eve's sturdy little body as if it weighed nothing. "But Elena isn't yet strong enough to carry another more than a short distance. I, on the other hand, can do this." With that, he shot up into the sky, Eve's delighted scream rippling through the air.

Hearing it, Elena shut the door on the questions roiling in her mind, because her first priority had to be the emotional health of her sister, and continued on toward the Enclave. Illium would make sure Eve got home safe, and the excitement of the blue-winged angel's daredevil tricks would help ameliorate the stress of Eve's last few hours.

Landing at the house, she tracked Montgomery to the kitchens, where he was discussing the dinner menu with Sivya. "I'm sorry to interrupt," she said, rubbing a hand over her face. "But Eve will be staying with us tonight, possibly tomorrow, too. Could you have a room made up for her?"

"Of course, Guild Hunter." The vampire's eyes searched hers. "Is she well?"

Elena knew the question was meant for her, too, but she wasn't ready to go there yet, wasn't ready to think about how she felt. "Cookies or some cake wouldn't go amiss," she said instead.

"I'll make certain Miss Evelyn has everything she needs."

"Thank you." Leaving the butler to organize things, she made an important call and returned outside just in time to see Illium land. The sunlight at his back made the blue of his wings glow, his hair wind-wild and his grin as open as the gold of his gaze.

It was a sight gorgeous and infrequent.

As she'd seen so clearly that night at the blood café, behind Illium's playful personality lay a terrible sadness that cast shadows on his soul. As behind her father's anger lay a horrific loss.

Had Marguerite known?

Yes. She'd been Jeffrey's heartbeat, his lover in every way, the trust between them absolute. For Marguerite to then do what she had, to leave him when he had to have been grappling with the nightmare repeat of his childhood . . .

Elena rubbed a fisted hand over her heart, forcing another smile as Eve ran over, cheeks flushed and hair as wild as Illium's. At eleven years of age, her sister had a child's spirit, but her face could turn as solemn as an adult's without warning. As it did now.

"Thanks for coming." Big gray eyes holding her own. "I knew you would."

"You need to thank Amy when you see her," Elena said, bending to hug her close. "She called me."

"Amy always takes care of me." Stepping back from the hug after squeezing her tight, Eve said, "This is going to make Mom and Father fight, isn't it?"

Elena wanted to lie, tell Eve it would be all right, but her sister was too smart and oddly wise for that. "Yes. I think this is going to cause a very big fight."

"Could you get Amy?" Eve looked at Illium, not Elena. "It wouldn't be hard for you to carry her. She's—"

Elena touched Eve's shoulder to get her attention. "I rang her. Amy wants to stay at home."

Unhidden distress. "But Father will punish her for calling you."

"No, I don't think he will." Jeffrey's mind was on the distant blood-soaked past, not the petty infringements of today. "Here."

She handed Eve her phone. "Why don't you talk to Amy yourself?"

Walking a small distance away, Eve made the call. When Illium went as if to speak, Elena shook her head. She couldn't talk about what was wrong. Not now. But when he raised an arm, she allowed herself to lean against him, to accept the undemanding warmth of his friendship, his wing heavy against her own.

"Amy's being dumb," was Eve's blunt appraisal when she walked back to them, her face set in pugnacious lines. "She says Father shouldn't be alone, even after he was so mean to me. I hate him." Arms folded, jaw set, she glared at the grass.

"I hate you!"

"Don't say that." Elena crouched down in front of her sister even as her skull rang with the words she'd spoken the day she walked out of the Big House, never to return. "He might have crossed a line today, but whatever Jeffrey's done, he's done it out of love for you." It was a love twisted by tragedy until it threatened to become a stifling cage, but it was love nonetheless. "I think it's too late for me and him, but not for you."

Eve's glare didn't fade, but her response held an uncertainty that made her youth and innocence clear. "I thought you hated him, too. Don't you?"

"I'm not sure what I feel for Jeffrey. I do know that you love him."

Scuffing at the ground, Eve bit down on her lower lip. "He's a good father except about the Guild."

"Everyone has blind spots."

"I guess."

A half hour later, Elena left Eve in Montgomery's capable hands, knowing the elegant vampire was lethal, would protect her with his life, as would the rest of the staff. She wouldn't have made the same decision had Eve appeared the least scared or intimidated, but her youngest sister had settled in without a hitch. Having borrowed Elena's laptop, she'd set herself up at the kitchen table and logged into her school account to do homework, was chatting to Sivya about her science problems when Elena left after receiving a hunt order from the Guild.

She could've asked to be replaced, but she needed some way to release the tension coiled up inside her, get her brain clear again. Checking the hunt details on her phone one more time, she took off at a run over the snow-dusted cliffs, the water glittering under the afternoon sunlight, as if a dip wouldn't give you hypothermia within seconds. The hunt order was relatively simple: she was to retrieve a thirty-year-old vamp who thought he was too good to bow and scrape to the angel who was his master.

Nothing unusual about that. Seduced by the idea of immortality and the beauty it so often bestowed, people lined up to be Made, but found the reality of a hundred years of service to the angels hard to swallow. What made Sidney Geisman different was that he'd written a booklet denouncing the "slavery" into which he'd been "tricked," a booklet that had gone viral among other young vampires.

Needless to say, his angel was beyond pissed. Elena knew Sidney's punishment would be harsh, an example to others who might seek to follow his seditious path, but while she pitied him, it wouldn't keep her from doing her job as a hunter. Because Sidney hadn't been tricked, not in any way, shape, or form.

The angels made zero attempt to hide the consequences of being Made, of what was required of those who served them. Even forgetting general public knowledge, all Candidates who passed the first part of the selection process were given the euphemistically termed "Intake and Orientation" file and told they were free to walk out the door should the contents of the file not be to their liking.

As consort, Elena had seen a copy of that file firsthand: it went into extreme detail and included graphic images of the punishments that might be meted out to a vampire should he or she fail to please the angel who held his or her service. Smack bang in the center of the file was a four-page article detailing the vicious public sentence handed to one vampire, whom Raphael had left in Times Square after breaking every bone in his body.

Below the article were the words: *Betrayal will not be tolerated.*

Sidney Geisman, Elena thought as she landed on the roof of a skyscraper to the south of the Tower, appeared to be suffering from a case of buyer's remorse. Too bad. You couldn't return the gift of near-immortality, so you were stuck paying the price for it. Not that she thought Sidney would be rushing to return that particular gift, even if it was possible. Cynical, perhaps, but she bet every hunter in the Guild would say the same. Too many people wanted to do the whole "have your cake and eat it, too" thing.

A single knock on the glass door to the roof atrium and it slid aside to leave her face-to-face with a slim vampire dressed in a brown tunic with a mandarin collar and gold detailing, his pants the same brown shade. "Guild Hunter," he said, then hesitated. "My humble apologies. I should've used 'Consort.'"

"No, 'Guild Hunter' is fine." All this polite deference made her skin itch, but it was part and parcel of being with Raphael and since she had no plans of ever changing that, she'd have to learn to deal. "Do you have what I need?"

"Yes." Walking to the table just inside the atrium, he opened a flat black box to retrieve a neatly folded shirt. "Will this do?"

Elena took the item of clothing and tried to hone in on the scents trapped within the fabric.

Raspberry and ginger, with a hint of mint.

A pretty, refreshing scent but it wasn't from the shirt. "If you'd step back past the doors."

"Of course."

Waiting until the wind swept away the raspberry and ginger, she took another deep breath.

An astringent chemical . . . disinfectant, softened by a delicate caress of lilies.

"I need the secondary sample," she said. "You made sure to take it from a different location?"

"Yes, the shirt was from his washing basket, and this T-shirt is from his gym bag."

The second test returned the same reading, the disinfectant not a taint but part of Sidney's scent, as interpreted by her hunting abilities.

"Thank you." Returning the T-shirt, she walked off the edge of the roof, snapping out her wings before she could even begin to fall. Her next destination was the home of Sidney's mortal family, the address part of the background report attached to the hunt order. All vampires with living relatives eventually went home, the smart for a clandestine visit, the stupid to stay.

Sidney, it turned out, fell into neither group.

"I haven't seen him since he took up that filthy habit." Words spit out by the elderly woman who answered the door, her hazel eyes watery with age but her cheeks hot spots of color. "Drinking blood is the devil's work." She slammed the door in Elena's face.

Not taking the woman at her word, Elena circled the small, neat house without picking up even a sliver of Sidney's scent. "I guess home isn't sweet for you, Sid," she muttered, hauling herself up the fire escape ladder to the second floor. She'd become expert at low-height takeoffs in an effort to balance out her inability to do regular and easy vertical takeoffs; and having done the latter once today already, she wasn't going to risk another unless it was a life-or-death situation.

Now, she gritted her teeth and got herself airborne before she kissed pavement. Once in the air, she ignored the other addresses in the prehunt report and headed instead to a particular section of Central Park: the Blood Theater.

33

Sidney was a man proud enough of his opus that he'd put his name on it—someone like that wouldn't be satisfied with disappearing into the mist, bereft of an audience. No, every instinct she had told her he'd have hit the Theater as soon as he could.

"Do you know what it's like to watch a woman get her head torn off?"

Shutting down the resurgence of memory before it could incapacitate, she winged her way across the green space at the core of Manhattan. About to land in the correct section, her brain suddenly poked at her to consider the situation . . . and maybe part of that poke came from the echo of her father's words, though she couldn't think about that now.

As soon as she landed, she would become vulnerable in a way that—ironically—she'd never been as a human. Her wings would make it hard for her to run at speed, dodging between the trees near impossible. A vertical takeoff would also not be a viable option if the hunt went bad, since she couldn't get aloft fast enough. Added to that, the Theater was in an isolated section of the park and, while night hadn't yet fallen, winter darkness was starting to edge the light in the sky.

It'd be nice to think no vampire or angel in the territory would dare lay a hand on her, but there were always the outliers—and the mortals. If a group of hopped-up junkies took out her heart or injured her internal organs badly enough, she'd die, her immortality tenuous yet. Then there was the risk Raphael's enemies had agents in the city just waiting for Elena to make herself a target.

"Yep," she said to herself. "Landing right now would not be the most intelligent thing you've ever done, Elieanora P. Deveraux."

Holding a hover—she was definitely getting better at that, thanks to the exercises Aodhan had taught her—she considered her options. It'd have to be the Guild, the Tower already stretched. "You have anyone who can back me up?" she asked Sara. "I'm at Central Park."

"Gimme a sec." A rustling, the phone going silent, then, "Deacon's in the area with Slayer, and he has a crossbow. Why take a crossbow on the dog's walk, I hear you ask? Because my beloved does not know how to leave home without being armed to the teeth."

Elena laughed, Sara's affectionate words giving her the respite she needed from the horrific images Jeffrey's revelation had burned into her brain. "You know I'd never turn down Deacon." Sara's husband might no longer be an official member of the Guild, but they all knew he was one of them. "Wait, what about Zoe?"

"With my parents—they're in town and spoiling her like only they can." Elena could hear Sara's smile. "Deacon's yours long as you need him."

"Thanks. I'll call him to arrange a meeting spot."

Less than two minutes later, she landed beside Deacon's tall, heavily muscled form a short walk from her target location. "I appreciate this," she said, after lavishing affection on Slayer, the huge black dog who was Zoe's adored best friend.

"No problem." Quiet green eyes that Elena was certain missed nothing, even though his stance was relaxed, Slayer leaning against his leg. "Where are we headed?"

"Blood Theater." Nothing special during daylight hours, that particular part of Central Park transformed into a decadent, sex-laced vampire haven at night, one mortals were advised to avoid unless they intended to become well-fucked dinner.

Deacon retrieved the crossbow he'd slung over his back. "Hardware has a good deterrent effect." The instant the crossbow was in Deacon's hands, Slayer turned from playful, tail-wagging pet to a silent menace.

"Yep." Retrieving the longer blades from her thigh sheaths, she made certain the gleaming edges showed beneath her fists. "I don't want to draw blood, but some of the younger ones are morons."

A faint smile on Deacon's lips as they set out along the narrow path to the Theater, the snow packed down as far as Elena could see. Given, however, that it hadn't snowed since close to dawn, the crushed snow was probably evidence of the previous night's debauchery, not a more recent event. The Theater was apt to be empty at this time of day and if she was right, and Sidney had made an appearance there, she might be able to pick up a trail.

Despite the high possibility she and Deacon were alone in this part of the park, she didn't drop her guard, aware of every rustle, every tiny sound, then the distinct lack of it. "No birds," she murmured sotto voce.

"Yes." Deacon went back-to-back with her without any further discussion, her wings pressed against the dark green of his trench coat, while Slayer padded silent and dangerous in front of them.

Weapons held with open aggression, they turned right off the main access path and onto another that spilled them into the small clearing with a natural dip that turned it into a miniature amphitheater. Elena's nape itched with the certainty of the eyes on them, instinct verified by the fresh lines of scent in the air, but no one appeared out of the deep pools of shadow between the trees.

Watery blood. A lot of it.

"Ellie."

"I smell it." If someone was dead inside the Theater, he or she hadn't been dead long enough for the carrion birds to have become aware of the feast, the area devoid of the sounds of their feeding. Either that, or the birds had been held off on purpose, because beneath the snow-diluted blood, she caught the scent of disinfectant softened by lilies.

Shit.

"Deacon?"

"I have you covered."

Shifting position, she made her way into the dip and to the gruesome sight that awaited. Sidney Geisman had lost his head. Literally. It was currently spitted on a crude wooden spear carved from a hacked-off branch, the vampire's eyes orbs of bulging red and his tongue a grotesquely swollen black where it hung out of his mouth.

It was too cold for flies, the bloody snow below the head pounded into ice. The rest of the vampire's body lay discarded a short distance away. She could see indications of arterial spray on the nearby trees, the blood having turned a putrid brown that nonetheless stood out to her enhanced vision. What interested her more were the multiple gaps in the pattern, as if this execution had had an audience that would've been sprayed with Sidney's blood.

Breathing through clenched teeth, the cold paradoxically intensifying the miasma of scents for her, she stepped close enough to the head to read the note stabbed into Sidney's forehead with what appeared to be a metal nail file. Inventive. The note consisted of a single word written in blood: *DISEASED.*

Oh, fuck. Fuckety fuck fuck!

Continuing to breathe through her mouth, she crossed to the body and began to check Sidney for any visual signs of disease. It didn't take long to find the sores on his hands. They were small, barely formed, so the infection had only just dug into his cells when he'd been killed. Which meant either there was now another carrier in the city or—best-case scenario—Sidney had been hoarding bottled blood in anticipation of his escape.

Raphael?

When she heard only silence in response, she remembered he'd mentioned he might be leaving the city to meet one of his senior angels. Digging out her phone from the pocket where she'd stuffed it, she called Tower operations, using the direct line that meant she'd get either Aodhan or Illium.

It was Aodhan who answered. Not wanting to say too much over an unsecure line, she simply told him she needed him in the Blood Theater. He didn't ask any questions, saying that he'd be there within minutes.

That done, she began to walk the scene to see how many useful scents she could identify.

Aodhan arrived with the encroaching darkness, his wings glittering brighter than the snow. She saw immediate comprehension on his face when she pointed out the note. The vampires in the city were turning on one another—if this continued, it could spiral out into indiscriminate paranoia, painting the city bloodred.

But that wasn't the most immediate problem.

"Could the infection have passed in the arterial spray?"Aodhan said, softly enough that his words wouldn't travel to the vampires who continued to watch from the shadows; those vamps would soon find themselves with nowhere to go, Aodhan having instructed a squadron to surround the area.

Elena looked again at the rusty brown that marked the trees. "Depends if enough of it got into the mouth, as well as through the mucus membranes of the eye. Low risk, since a drop won't do it, but a risk nonetheless—the spectators and the execution-ers were standing damn close." More than one had likely had an open mouth as they no doubt screamed at Sidney and cheered one another on. "I can track at least some of the people here in the last few hours, but given the way he was beaten"— she pointed out the vicious marks on the body—"it looks like it might've been a mob attack."

A hardness to Aodhan's expression she'd never before seen, splintered irises hauntingly white with reflected snow. "Find as many as you can as fast as you can."

Having already isolated the strongest scent trail, Elena started the track, Deacon at her back. The intensity of the scent told her the vampire in question had run from the Theater probably at daybreak, his body and face covered with Sidney's blood, a strange mélange of disinfectant and lilies entangled with the vampire's own natural scent.

The odd thing was, he hadn't run out onto the street, but scrambled deeper into Central Park. Where she found him ten minutes later. Covered in patches of dried, flaking blood the color of dirt, he sat rocking to and fro under the shade of an oak devoid of its leaves, its arms skeletal against the incongruously stunning starlit night.

"They killed him. They killed him. They killed him."

Crouching beside the male, far enough away that he couldn't lunge for her throat, Elena said, "Who killed him?" her tone nonconfrontational.

"They killed him. They killed him. They killed him."

Elena tried again, even chancing a touch, but the vampire was trapped in some personal mental hellhole he couldn't escape.

She and Deacon stayed with him only until he was picked up for transport to the Tower. Returning to the main site, now busy with Tower staff, Elena chose the next most promising trail. Thirty minutes later, she received a message from Illium stating a friend of Sidney's had confessed to supplying him with food blood out of her own frozen supply. *He drank a bottle from Blood-for-Less. Bottle dated within the period of the original donor-carrier.*

Five hours after that, she'd tracked down three other vampires who'd watched and/or participated in Sidney's bloody execution, but who hadn't stuck around to experience the aftermath. One was terrified, one defiant, but it was the third who was the most problematic: he'd started to show advanced signs of the disease.

Stepping outside the bedroom where the vampire shivered so hard his teeth clattered, his mind lost in a febrile haze, she met Deacon's eyes. "You should get back home. Sara will be waiting." She would not risk his mind, his memories.

A piercing look. "I already know what Sara knows."

"You have to leave before you know more," she said, then brought up the one thing she knew would get him to back off. "Zoe needs you. Don't get involved in immortal bullshit that could bleed onto your family."

"You change your mind, Ellie," he said after a long minute of silence, "just call."

That done, she contacted Illium. "None of the idiots I've found are talking and we need the names of the others who were there and might be infected. Can you do your mental voodoo?" Raphael was on his way back, but still at least an hour out.

"My mental voodoo is nowhere as well developed as the Sire's, but I have a better idea."

Arriving at the guarded warehouse where Elena had quarantined the two apparently uninfected vampires, the infected one in another warehouse, Illium asked the vampires for the names and, when there was no answer, withdrew his sword and sliced off the left leg of the brown-haired male.

The gleam of red on steel was not what she'd been expecting, her heart slamming into her throat, but the brutal tactic delivered: the uninjured vampire broke down even as her friend clamped his hand over his stump in an attempt to stanch the pumping blood. "I'm sorry! We made a pact not to nark!" Sobbing, she began to give them names, the maimed vampire joining in when she faltered in her recollection.

It took less than an hour to track down the nine other vampires who'd scattered, including—ironically—a number who'd been fans of Sidney's work. One more was discovered curled up in bed, the disease ravaging her cells, the other eight terrified out of their minds.

"We need to find out where each one, but especially the two infected, went after the murder," Elena said, furious at the stupidity that might've done more damage than the other attacks combined. "The *only* bright point in this situation is that the disease needs a blood transfer to infect."

The interviews went fast—courtesy of the amputated leg sitting in the middle of the warehouse; none of these vampires was old enough to heal such an injury in anything less than twelve excruciating months.

Most of the murderous idiots had run home, but two had gone to a club. Where they'd fed on and been fed by fellow vampires. One of those two was the sick woman. Beautiful, sexy, and an unmistakable magnet for male vamps who wanted to sink their fangs into sweet, hot flesh.

"God damn it!"

Had the club been a high-class place like Erotique, where

blood sharing was considered a seduction, a pair often spending hours together, there was a good chance they could've quickly halted any further spread. Unfortunately, Bezel was on the opposite end of the spectrum, catering to young vampires who were all about sex, blood, and more sex, multiple partners the norm in both categories.

The first indication Elena had of how bad this was going to be was when she landed in the club parking lot just as a tall, skinny vampire staggered out on four-inch heels, only to collapse to the concrete screaming that it hurt, it *hurt*!

34

Nine grueling hours later, Raphael looked down at the report Aodhan had just pushed across his desk and said, "How bad?" The disease had finally been contained, but not until it cut a swath through a particular segment of the city's vampiric population.

"Three hundred and eight dead or sick," Aodhan told him. "Two hundred under observation for the next day."

It wasn't the total disaster it had been shaping up to be, especially as none of Raphael's vampire soldiers patronized Bezel, but given the already downed angels, added to the fear that now permeated the city's vampire population, it was a brutal blow to the beating heart of his territory. "Continue to monitor the situation and alert me if there are any signs the disease has escaped containment."

Montgomery, he said after Aodhan left, *is Elena home?* She'd been working side by side with him until an hour before, when he'd ordered her home, able to see her exhaustion after two tumultuous nights.

Yes, Sire.

Make sure she rests.

The slightest pause. *I do not believe I could make the Guild Hunter do anything.*

Despite knowing New York was on the brink of a catastrophic final assault, he almost felt the urge to laugh at the tentative response from the centuries-old vampire. *True enough,* he said, and touched his mind to Elena's in a quiet question. When he heard only peaceful silence in response, he knew she slept.

Her sister? In all the chaos, he and Elena had had little time to speak, but she'd told him about her biological grandmother right before she left the Tower, the continuing shock of the revelation a strain in her expression. But trumping that had been her concern for what this might all mean for Eve.

Miss Evelyn is sleeping peacefully.

Thank you, Montgomery. With that, Raphael turned to input a number into the large communications screen on one wall of his office.

Titus's face appeared on it a minute later. "Raphael, my second tells me you wish to speak to me," the warrior archangel said, the mahogany of his skin gleaming in the light in the room from where he spoke.

"I hear you're encountering the same vampire disease in your territory that almost brought down an aircraft in mine." There'd been no way to suppress that information, their enemies no doubt aware the strike had found a target. Yet still they waited.

"I will trust you with this information, Raphael." Titus's eyes bored into his. "Do not betray me."

Raphael inclined his head. "You are one archangel whose word I know is his bond. We are united in battling this scourge, and I'll share all I know of it if you'll do the same."

Apparently mollified, Titus nodded. "The disease has at times threatened to decimate my ground forces. We tracked down and eliminated the carriers, but Charisemnon keeps sending more of the infected over our border, their only aim to disseminate their blood in the hours before the disease begins to show."

Since the instant he'd received Jason's message about the problems in Titus's territory the day before, Raphael had had his suspicions about the archangel who was neighbor to Titus. "So. It is Charisemnon who is the architect of the disease? Is there any indication of Lijuan's hand in its creation?"

"No," Titus said. "The men I have in his court confirm this. Charisemnon's power is now apparently much faded from overuse, but he has a stable of infected from whom he takes blood to infect more, continuing the cycle—he has somehow convinced his ground troops they die in the cause of protecting their territory." Titus rubbed his face in a rare gesture of fatigue. "I ask you now if he initiated the Falling, for if so, we are even more vulnerable than I believed."

"We have no proof, but believe the indications are there."

A deep groove formed on either side of Titus's mouth. "That he strikes so viciously at you, while only harassing me, means he must've thrown his lot in with Lijuan. I would stand with you in the war against her, Raphael, were Charisemnon not sitting on my border waiting for me to blink."

"The information you've shared is worth as much." It gave him the name of his secondary enemy, Lijuan still the most dangerous. "I tell you now that we've begun to develop a vaccine—it'll take time, but my healers say it can be done. Do you wish me to send the information to your own healers so they can join in the work?"

Titus nodded. "Your honor is strong that you share such. I'll instruct my healers to work with yours in every way."

Not wasting time, Raphael sent a mental command to the team in the Tower that was working on the vaccine under Keir's remote guidance, the healer unable to abandon his duties at the Refuge.

"We must stop Charisemnon and the deathmonger, Lijuan." Scowling, Titus slammed his ceremonial spear to the ground, the lethally sharp tip painted with pure gold. "We are archangels, protectors of the world, and they seek to defile it in their delusion of godhood." A roar that no doubt shook the walls of his stronghold before he pinned Raphael with his eyes. "I hope you do not fall prey to the same pride."

"I have no desire to rule the world—but neither will I allow anyone to threaten my territory." Warrior to warrior, he held the other man's gaze. "I would call you ally, Titus, and accept your word and any information you pass my way as truth, if you'll do the same." To no other angel, even Elijah, would he speak so bluntly, but Titus had no time for double-talk and political subtlety. He would, Raphael thought suddenly, be someone Elena would like, and he had a feeling the admiration would be returned.

Now, Titus made his decision with his customary lack of delay. "The alliance is forged."

As he ended the call, he thought of a time when Titus had called him a "stripling" and slapped him on the back in congratulations for a bout well played. Now they were allies standing firm against the same deadly threat. Another change, another sign that the world would be forever altered before this was over.

Eve was lying flat on her back in the middle of the central core of the house when Elena came downstairs at nine in the morning, having caught approximately four hours of deep, uninterrupted sleep. Body and mind both felt refreshed, the emotional stress of the previous day no longer threatening to scrape her raw.

Good morning, Archangel, she said, connecting with Raphael's mind across the water, the link effortless.

The cool kiss of the rain, the turbulent sea in her mind. *Good morning,* hbeebti.

Heart warm and a smile tugging at her lips, she walked across the silk carpet to look down at her sister's sprawled body. "Eve?" she said, noting that the bruise around Eve's left eye had faded to a sickly yellow-black that denoted healing.

"Hi, Ellie." The greeting was breathy. "Sorry, ate too many cakes."

"Did you scam Montgomery?" She didn't think the vampire had much experience with children, especially smart children—and Eve was very, very smart.

"I didn't think he'd actually give me cake for breakfast if I said I was feeling sad." Astonishment on her face. "Or that he'd give me *more* when I said I was still hungry. I couldn't not eat it after that. It wouldn't have been polite after I asked for it."

Elena's shoulders shook as she tried to contain her laughter. "Is that why you're lying on the floor? Because you can't breathe?"

"Uh-huh." Eve patted her stomach. "It's a nice view."

No doubt she should return to the Tower, find out if the disease situation had deteriorated in the past few hours, but Elena went down to the carpet and said, "Rise up just a little."

When Eve did so—with a groan—Elena slid her wing beneath her sister's body, her arm under Eve's head, and they lay side by side. The skylight above *was* beautiful, a sparkling shatter of light.

"Does it hurt if I lie on your wing? I'm kinda heavy."

"It doesn't hurt, and you're not heavy." Eve had her mother's petite bone structure paired with a gutsy strength, would no doubt grow up to be a sleek little dynamo.

"I have a layer of puppy fat—that's what I heard one of my friend's moms say." Stated with equanimity. "I don't think I'm going to become a swan like Amy or Mom or you." A ferocious scowl. "I just want to be a bit less fat, but I really like cake."

Elena felt an overwhelming wave of affection. "Would you like to hear a story?"

"Okay."

"Beth and I, we had two older sisters, did you know that?" She was unsurprised at the shake of Eve's head, but it hurt to be reminded how thoroughly her father had buried the long-legged dancer he'd once waltzed across the kitchen floor, as thoroughly as the serious second-born with whom he'd discussed stocks and bonds at the breakfast table. "Their names were Mirabelle and Ariel."

"Did they die?" A quiet question, Eve weaving her fingers with Elena's.

"Yes. They died." The words were still so hard to say. "Ari wanted to take care of everyone, and she was kind of bossy."

"Amy is bossy, too. But I know it's because she loves me."

"Yes." Elena felt the scars of loss stretch painfully as she thought of the time Ari had told her off for running down the stairs, only to cuddle her when her lower lip quivered. "Belle had more of a temper, but she wouldn't let anyone be mean to me."

"She sounds like a good sister."

"She was." Elena concentrated on the happy memories, fighting against the blood-splattered shadows that threatened to taint the joy. "And she was a dancer. The way Belle could move, it was like watching the wind."

"I bet she studied a lot."

"Yep." Hours and hours, determined to grow up to be part of a prestigious ballet company. "But you know the best part?"

"No, what?"

"Belle used to look just like you when she was younger." That same appearance of sturdiness created by stubborn baby fat. "I saw the photos. But her dancing soon created lean muscle—just like your hunt training will do for you."

"I like going to the Academy, even if I get bruises sometimes." Patting her free hand gently over the inner surface of Elena's wing, she said, "Ellie?"

"Yes?"

"I'm scared."

Elena drew her sister into her arms. "I know, baby. I know."

Having settled Eve in the kitchen with the laptop after her sister told her she'd e-mailed her teacher the previous night and received the day's lessons to do at home, Elena had just taken off when Montgomery caught her attention from the clifftop. "Miss Evelyn's mother is at the gates," he told her.

"Open them." Elena folded back her wings, thinking Gwendolyn must've driven through the night after receiving the message Elena had used the hunter network in the area to personally deliver.

"Eve?" the other woman asked the instant she stepped out of the mud-splattered black SUV, deep shadows under the dark blue of her eyes.

"Doing her lessons inside," Elena said. "I didn't think it was a good idea to send her back to school until you'd returned."

Gwendolyn ran a trembling hand through her raven black hair. "I've just come from the house. Jeffrey—" A sudden break, walls of polite reserve slamming down, as if the other woman had remembered she was talking about her husband to his estranged daughter.

"Would you like a cup of coffee?" Elena asked, stifling her impatience to get to the Tower—Eve's future welfare could depend on what Gwendolyn chose to do next.

"No, I've already had too much caffeine." Gwendolyn's confession was a fracture in the reserve. "I appreciate you helping Eve."

"This is serious, Gwendolyn," Elena said, struggling with the ethics of whether or not she had the right to share the truth about her biological grandmother. "Jeffrey really scared her. I don't think he's ever going to come to terms with the fact she's hunter-born."

The other woman's cheekbones pushed white against her skin. "I'll make sure he doesn't pull anything like this ever again."

Elena had total faith in Gwendolyn's love for her daughters, but she understood her father far better today than she'd ever before done. "You can't watch her all the time."

"No, but even though Jeffrey and I might not have the relationship he had with your mother"—a bleak reference to a painful earlier conversation where Gwendolyn had admitted she'd known of Jeffrey's former mistress, and that the woman bore a faded resemblance to Marguerite—"your father needs me in a way I doubt you'd understand." A sad smile. "He'll keep his end of our bargain."

"Mom!" Eve tumbled out the front door at that instant, racing to Gwendolyn.

As the other woman's slender arms hugged her daughter tight, Elena hoped Gwendolyn was right in her judgment of Jeffrey. Because Elena would not stand by and watch him hurt Eve as he'd hurt her.

"I'll do whatever I have to, to protect her," she said to Raphael later that day, outside the warehouse being used as an observation facility.

Raphael had expected nothing less from his consort. "I've ordered our communications team to monitor Eve's name, as well as the flight plans of the Deveraux family jet. You'll know within minutes should there be anything that throws up a red flag."

The chain-link fence at Elena's back was a harsh reminder of the grim reason why they stood here, but her radiant smile threw that into the shade. "Thank you, Archangel." A distinct and very Elena glint in her eye. "It's extremely awesome to be consort to a man who is lord of all he surveys."

"That, Consort," he said, having already told her of his discussion with Titus, "is a fact Charisemnon and Lijuan would like to change."

"You know, that Charisemnon guy always wigged me out. Now I know why." Folding her arms, she met his gaze. "I've asked Sara to make me inactive on the Guild roster for the time being. Tell me what you need me to do to help you ready the city for an assault."

35

He cupped her jaw, proud of the woman who was his own, who didn't flinch from standing by his side, come what may. "Talk to the vampire leaders, have them contain the panic within the groups to which they have access. We can't afford any more impromptu executions."

Elena scowled. "Talk? I figured you'd want me working with the ground troops or something."

"Talk—not as a hunter, but as my consort." Dropping his hand from her jaw, he wrapped his arm around her waist in readiness for takeoff. "Your presence will make the seriousness of the request apparent without further orders on my part."

"I suppose I can dig up some civilized-but-scary manners." A kiss on the mouth as they rose into the air, the taste of her lush intoxication. "I don't know absolutely all of the vamp leaders. Does the Tower have a list?"

"Illium'll go with you. He knows each by name."

"Wouldn't he be the better option to talk to them?"

"Before I had a consort, yes. Now, you speak with my voice."

That ring of silver bright under the winter sunlight, her expression suddenly solemn. "I won't let you down."

"I know."

Ten minutes later, he watched her take to the skies with Illium. *Do not allow her to come to harm.*

I'll protect her with my blade and my life.

Shifting his attention from the midnight and dawn of Elena's wings on the strength of Illium's promise, he picked up the phone. It was time for his second to return to New York.

Raphael spent the rest of the day finalizing the transfer of his senior vampires and angels into the city, while Aodhan handled daily Tower operations and Dmitri—linking in from the jet Raphael had sent for him and Honor—worked with his trusted people to ensure their permitted weapons reserves were at maximum. The next step would be to place anti-wing guns on a number of rooftops.

"We'll do it in the short lull after the late revelers head home and the early risers are yet asleep," Illium told him, the lights of a night-cloaked Manhattan glittering at his back as the two of them stood at the apex of the Tower. "Better the guns appear overnight than to have the curious watching and broadcasting our efforts in the daytime."

"Agreed." Raphael's city never truly slept, but it was quietest in those twilight hours. "Do you have enough people to get it done within that time frame?"

"Yes. Aodhan can also assist now that Dmitri has returned to take over Tower operations." A steady glance from golden eyes shadowed by thick black lashes dipped in blue. "Sire, you can't be here."

When Raphael raised an eyebrow, Illium stood his ground. "Forget the enemy, the morale of our own troops will take a severe hit if you're seen to be assisting in such a 'mundane' task."

Raphael knew the angel was right. "The task is yours," he said, and spent the next hour drilling a specialized night-maneuvers squadron before heading home.

His consort was in her solar, cleaning her weapons with a single-minded focus that told him she wasn't seeing the lethal items at all. Taking a seat across from her, he picked up a cut-glass tumbler and poured himself a drink from the decanter she kept for him, a silent invitation into her inner sanctum. "Illium tells me you charmed the vampire leaders." Whatever she'd done, the effect had been immediate, the city calmer, vampires on their best behavior.

She snorted. "Illium did the charming. I talked business—vamp leaders are all about that—and rampaging vampires are bad for it. We came to an understanding." Lashes flicking up, humor in the gray. "I may have channeled you at your politest and scariest, to drive home the point that you'd be very, very disappointed should they fail in their task."

Lips curving, he took another sip. "You are proving to be a most efficient consort, Guild Hunter."

"Don't you forget it." A dagger pointed at him to underscore her command, before she went back to her cleaning.

"Is it your father's revelation that occupies your mind?"

A nod. "I had a bit of time before you got home, so I logged into the Tower's information network from here."

"Did you find her?"

"Yes—the facts weren't hidden. I just didn't know to look for them before." Fingers clenching on the dagger, Elena met eyes of pitiless blue that watched her with an intense patience that told her she mattered. "Her name was Elizabeth Parker." Her heart pounded in sympathetic memory of the stunned shock she'd felt at the discovery. "Belle and Ari were his first-born, but he didn't give them her names, just me and Beth."

Elieanora Parker Deveraux and *Elizabeth Marguerite Deveraux.*

Releasing and setting the dagger aside when her fingers began going numb, she dropped her head in her hands. "It's almost as if it took him that long to trust in the happiness he'd found, have enough faith to open the door a fraction to his past." Only for the horror to be repeated. "God, Raphael, no wonder he's so damn fucked up."

"Tell me about her."

It was exactly the question she needed to hear. Somehow, she had to find a way to come to terms with a fundamental change in the fabric of her history, her vision of her father altered in a way she was having difficulty comprehending. And even though she knew Raphael had no sympathy for Jeffrey after what her father had done to her, he listened as she released the torrent of words and questions and confusion.

Hours later, when she'd emptied it all from inside her head and could think again, he took her to bed and held her safe from the nightmares, his wing spread over her body in a heaviness of silken warmth that made her feel safer than any weapon.

Raphael decided to rest in truth this night, his hunter's skin warm against his own. She'd talked herself out and, in so doing, come to a kind of peace with the ghost of a woman she'd never met, but who'd thrown a shadow across her entire existence.

"Elizabeth Parker," she'd said quietly at the end. "She's a part of me and I'm glad I know that."

Now, she lay tucked trustingly against him, her wings tangled around his body in the way of angelic lovers, his own acting as her blanket. Only when he was certain she'd fallen into a deep, nightmare-free sleep did he press a kiss to the warm curve of her neck and close his eyes.

He dreamed again of that forgotten field, and of a woman's bare feet as light as air on the ruby-flecked grass, his mother walking away from him after he fell to the earth, his body bloodied and bones broken.

Except . . .

He stood able-bodied on that field—and it was the same field, on the same day. He'd never forget the breathtaking clarity of the sky; the way the dew sparkled as if a careless hand had spilled a thousand translucent gemstones on the lush green blades; the distinctive patterns of light and shadow formed by the blossoming tree to the right; the tiny insect that crawled painstakingly across the grass, food held in its pincers.

He'd watched that insect for what felt like hours as it made its way across the field. When the food slipped out of its pincers, it would stop, pick it up again, and restart its journey. Lying broken on the grass Raphael had thought of himself as an insect, too, an insignificant, discarded piece of angelic flotsam beneath an endless sky.

Today, he could step on that insect without thought, ending its existence and struggle, but he took care to walk around it, the clear morning sunlight a cool brightness on his face, the slight wind adding to the sense that dawn had just broken. Tilting back his head, he saw nothing in the sheet of blue above . . . no, there was his mother. Though he stood in the wrong place, his view was the same as on that fateful day—when he'd watched her from a hidden vantage point, needing to see her free and beautiful just once more before he sought to bring her down, end her life.

She'd caused the death of every adult in two thriving cities, creating a silence painful and eternal. The survivors had all been children, little ones so bruised in the heart that they'd curled up and died of terrible sorrow, hundreds upon hundreds of tiny lives snuffed out without ever being given the chance to truly burn.

He'd known all that, understood she needed to be stopped, but she'd still been the mother who'd once sung him such lullabies that the Refuge stood silent to hear her. So he'd taken that single moment to watch her, to remember who she'd been before the madness sucked her under.

Graceful and strong, her wings backlit by the sun, she flew above him . . . but now there was a cloud across the sun. That wasn't right. There had been no clouds that day, the sun a burning orb that baked his spilled blood to crystalline hardness and threatened to boil him alive from the inside out.

The clouds grew darker and darker, until they blotted out the sun. And his mother, she was gone. All he could see was a thick blanket of featureless gray. Beneath his feet, the verdant grass had turned brown, the insect a carcass. And the wind, it blew cool across his face, but it wasn't fresh.

It tasted *old*.

There was no scent of putrefaction or of death, simply a sense of unfathomable age, of dark, hidden places full of secrets and whispers. Breathing it in, he continued to walk across the field, for someone was waiting for him. He was halfway across the dried-up landscape—so *old*, this place—when he saw that dawn had come . . . no, that was Elena's wing arcing over him as she folded it away to reveal the skylight above their bed, the world outside the hazy formless gray of the time just before true daybreak.

The rim of silver around her irises glowed in the muted darkness as she leaned closer. "I didn't mean to wake you."

"It was time." He knew he'd never have reached the end of that field without . . . something, something he was meant to have in order to complete the journey. "Why do you watch me in such a way?"

"Occasionally I wake," she whispered, as if it were a secret, "and I have this instant where I don't believe the happiness inside me, can't imagine you could ever belong to me, but you do." A smile that pierced the lingering grayness. "You're mine."

"I had another dream," he told his hunter, for she belonged to him as much as he belonged to her.

Elena cocked her head, listening as he described the forgotten field and the weight of age, the scent of old, old things. "There was no sense of threat," he said, "but I felt I'd lose something indefinable if I did not do an act of which I had no knowledge."

A thoughtful silence. "It might simply be your subconscious's way of working out everything that's been going on, but after that shared dream, I have my doubts."

As did he. "And you, Elena," he said, deciding to let matters lie for now, for the intrigues of the dream world had to take second place to the harshness of reality, "what did you dream?"

"Not a damn thing." Her beaming relief segued into concern all too soon. "Did Jason send through another report last night?"

"The reborn component of Lijuan's gathering forces appears to be suspiciously small, especially given how many villagers have disappeared from the areas closest to her stronghold."

Elena sucked in a breath. "You think they might already be on the way?"

"Or have arrived, been stashed away until needed." It wasn't impossible that they could've been smuggled in on shipping containers. A container would provide a perfect cage, and, once released, the starving and infectious creatures would decimate the population. "Jason also has information that Lijuan has 'improved' on her design so these reborn are not sentient in any way, simply creatures designed to kill and feed."

"Infectious, mobile weapons."

He nodded, agreeing with her assessment. "Charisemnon's forces are also strong, but Titus has stepped up the aggression on their border to ensure Charisemnon cannot risk seconding any squadrons to Lijuan."

"That's good news, isn't it?" Elena said. "I know Lijuan has more fighters, but she can't move all her forces against us or she risks leaving her territory vulnerable."

"She has also been an archangel for millennia, and as such, has many, many more older angels and vampires at her command." Harder to kill or disable, the senior fighters could endure far longer than younger ones.

"Hell, I didn't even think about that." Elena spread her hand over his heart, the look in her eyes telling him she was calculating every angle. "Home field advantage remains our best weapon."

"Yes, and we must utilize it in every way possible."

When they flew into the city a half hour later, it was to see its rooftops bristling with weaponry inimical to winged fighters.

"Even the old angels," Elena said, satisfaction in her tone, "will take time to heal if we blow the bastards to smithereens."

So bloodthirsty, hbeebti.

A grin. "You know you love me that way."

"Which is why I wish you to join the squadron practicing with crossbows in the air." He knew his consort would never sit in safety while her city burned, so he'd make certain she was prepared.

"Good. I'm not fast in flight, but I'm a crack shot." A tender kiss, a fleeting memory of the short, passionate minutes they'd taken for themselves earlier in the morning. "You're meeting with Dmitri?"

"Yes."

That discussion took over two hours. Leaving the other man to organize an extended sentry line, Raphael was about to take off from the Tower to meet Nazarach—the senior angel having relocated to the city overnight—when he felt the wind turn violent, whipping his hair off his face. Along with its fury came a scent of age and old, *old* things. Buried things.

The sky turned as red as the Hudson had done in a pulsing wave, the birds swirling a constellation above the Tower. Fighting the wind, Raphael lifted off, heading directly to those birds, called by an ancient power that licked over his skin. The tiny winged creatures parted to let him in, and so he became the center of the constellation as the bloodred sky pushed down on him and the warm rain was drops of blood on his skin, his face, his hair.

36

Elena looked up from the roof of the building where she'd landed when the wind turned murderous, her crossbow gripped in one hand and her heart kicking against her ribs. *Raphael!* she cried out with her mind, able to see him in the center of the fury of birds that circled black against a crimson sky.

He didn't answer, and the rain, it was blood that tasted of the sea and the wind and of Raphael, but below that was a chill old and inhuman. *No, no, no! The cold power can't have him!* Jaw clenched, she strapped on the crossbow and ran over the edge of the roof, intending to ride the wind up to Raphael, but the force of it threatened to throw her against a building, smashing her to pieces.

Gritting her teeth, she fought against the violence, but her wings had begun to crumple when a flash of blue appeared under her, holding position with a strength that made his growing power clear. Realizing what Illium was trying to do, she allowed herself to drop. He twisted at the last second to catch her, spiraling down to another rooftop in a controlled descent.

As soon as they landed, Elena looked up again and saw that Raphael remained in the center of the bloodstorm, his mind distant from hers. "Can you reach him?" she said, screaming to be heard over the rising wind.

His own hair whipping off his face, arms tight around her, and eyes glowing gold, Illium shook his head. "Something is blocking me, blocking all of us!"

No, she thought again, this time not in panic but in resolute fury. No one was ever going to separate her from Raphael. He was hers. Focusing through the bloody rain that slashed at her face and turned the world crimson, she looked only for the archangel who was her own, her mind reaching for his, powered by a connection that was the sum of both of them.

It was as if a great wall stood between them, but Elena wasn't about to give in. Hacking at it until it felt as if her mind was as bloody as the rain, she smashed a hole big enough to thrust her hand through. *Raphael!*

He heard Elena's voice in his mind, cutting through the whispers that surrounded him, whispers that weren't words but that he understood all the same. This was a test, the voices said, as had been the others. But who would dare test an archangel? That was a question to which he had no answer, but he knew one thing: no power in the universe could separate him from his hunter.

Smashing through the gray wall of whispers, he grabbed hold of her hand. *I am here, Elena,* he said, the connection between them pure and unhindered. *Fly to me.*

The wind—

It won't stop you. Nothing had the right to touch his consort without his permission. *Illium,* he said to the member of his Seven who held her safe, *release her.*

Parting the wind with a blade of agonizing power, he watched her take off, her wings a spread of midnight and dawn streaked with indigo and twilight blue, resplendent against the bloody rain that soaked the city. That rain parted for her as the wind had done—as the birds now did. Until her body aligned with his, her hands on his shoulders, her wings folding in silent trust, his arm around her waist.

Bright eyes of silver-gray searching his own. "You're here."

"Yes." The power, cold and beautiful and dangerous, had threatened to swallow him, but in his refusal to be cut off from Elena, he'd found the clarity to understand once more that he couldn't hope to control the vicious strength of it . . . but even a mere taste had been potent. If he could just find a way to hold a fraction of it, no other immortal would dare turn his or her eyes to his territory.

Elena's fingers digging into his shoulders. "Hey, hey, your eyes are going black again."

"So much power, Elena," he said, burying his face against her hair as the cold fingers of it snaked through his veins. The whispers urged him to accept what he was given, as the scent of age, of time, filled his senses, as if this power had slept an eon and woke only for him. "I would be the most powerful archangel in the world."

Shivering at the ice in that whisper, in her awareness that his heart no longer beat, his breath frigid, Elena tugged back his head to look into those inhuman eyes. "You would be a monster," she reminded him. "I'd be nothing to you, my life one you'd snuff out without thought."

"You are everything." His kiss was so cold it threatened to shock her own heart into halting its beat. Unlike him, she wouldn't survive.

Raphael, my . . . she managed to get out through the searing cold, her breath frozen in her chest when he broke their kiss. *I'm dying, Archangel.* It took all her strength to force that out past the ice in her brain.

A blink, incandescent blue flaring outward from his irises as one of his hands flattened over her breastbone. *"NO!"*

A punch of violent white-hot power that made her scream, her back bowing and her heart stuttering back to life. Somehow finding the will to think, to get her frozen hands to his cheeks to cup his face, she said, "Let it go," through chattering teeth. "The power isn't worth the price."

Both arms crushing her close, his breath still frigid but his eyes that incredible, astonishing blue, he said, "Hold on, *hbeebti.*"

The sky exploded in an ear-piercing lightning storm of blue electric with piercing white fire that sheared away the ruby red to expose patches of the sky as it should be. With the blood went the abnormal cold and Elena found herself gulping in air that didn't feel as if it was frozen crystals in her throat, in her lungs, her heart kicking into a normal rhythm.

She jerked when the first icy droplet hit her cheek . . . but this was only water, the air scented with the clean, fresh ozone of the rain that crashed down from a storm-darkened sky, washing away the stain of blood. Leaning back as much as she could given the tightness of Raphael's hold, she tugged down his head with a hand on his nape and kissed him again—this time, the raw heat of him made her body burn, her breasts swelling against the heavy wetness of her combat gear.

"Glad to have you back, Archangel." Another soft, suckling kiss of his lips, warm and alive, the rain turning to steam where they touched.

His forehead dropped to her own, his breath harsh and chest heaving. "I want no power that makes me cause you harm." One hand rising between them, he rubbed it over her bruised heart, the curls of heat telling her he was fixing the damage.

"All good," she murmured when he dropped his hand, her skin prickling with the need to reinitiate their bond in a more primal way.

"I also," he said, his body pushing hard and ready against her abdomen, "do not want any power that turns my cock to ice."

Oh yeah, he was back, she thought with a grin. "You have no idea how fervently I second that." And though they hung in the midst of icy winter rain, she took the time to press her mouth to his, to indulge in a kiss so sexual, he might as well have been inside her body. No ice, no distance, only a molten heat between male and female, between an archangel and his consort.

Landing at the Tower, Raphael discovered from Aodhan that people were scared, believing he'd made the sky rain blood.

That, Raphael thought, could work to their advantage.

When he said as much to Elena while they dried themselves off in their Tower suite, she paused with the towel over her breasts, a gleam in her eye. "You should make sure Charisemnon and Lijuan hear about your new 'power.'"

"I'm certain they've already heard." Dry, he took the towel and bade her turn so he could pat the last of the moisture off her wings, her feathers designed to sleek off wet. "Dmitri says recordings of the event are already trending on media sites worldwide."

"Right, what was I thinking?" Elena threw up her hands. "That New Yorkers would actually, I don't know, hide or something else sane when the sky was raining freaking blood?"

"Our people are not so timid." Dropping the towel, he drew her close and touched his lips to the side of her throat.

She shivered, leaned back into him, and they simply stood skin to skin for a stolen moment.

The memory of her warmth was still with him when he met with Nazarach minutes later. The dangerous midlevel angel with wings of burnished amber and skin of gleaming black had bad news. "I've had a confirmed report that reborn have been spotted on the outskirts of Atlanta. It's believed the initial group was brought in on a long-haul truck, possibly after being smuggled in through shipping containers."

Raphael hadn't expected such sneak tactics from Lijuan on the eve of true battle. He'd believed she'd unleash her reborn during the actual battle, to go up against his ground soldiers. No doubt this was Charisemnon's influence. "Take your squadron and go stamp out the menace before it spreads." He couldn't leave the task to younger, weaker angels, not given the danger.

"If New York falls—"

"We can't afford for the reborn to infect any part of the territory. They're too virulent." Holding the Tower remained critical, but that didn't mean he'd permit the rest of his territory to fall into ruin.

Nazarach left with a promise to return as soon as possible. When Nimra came to Raphael with the same reports about her territory a few minutes later, followed by Andreas, Raphael had had enough. Anger simmering under his skin, he put through a call to Lijuan's second. The old archangel eschewed modern conveniences, but her people had recently convinced her to upgrade.

Xi, with his black eyes and striking wings of red-streaked gray, answered within moments. "Archangel." A polite incline of his head. "How may I be of service?"

"I have a message for your mistress," Raphael said, too furious to temper his words. "Tell her I did not expect such cowardice from her." He ended the call as anger flushed red across Xi's sharp cheekbones, and was unsurprised when Lijuan's face appeared in the glass wall of his office moments later, in a show of her power.

"You *dare* call me a coward?" Unhidden rage, her face skeletal as her physical form faded in and out.

Raphael held her gaze, his own rage as potent. "What is it if not cowardice to release your reborn on the edges of my territory, forcing me to scatter my forces?" He gave away nothing by admitting that, since news of the fighting against the reborn would soon spread across the world. "You must believe your forces weak indeed that you use such contemptible tactics."

Curling black in her irises. "You should take care in making such accusations."

"Ask Xi to turn on a television set. I'm sure the pictures will be available within minutes." Continuing to face that inhuman visage with its gaping eye sockets and mouth full of silent screams, he said, "Perhaps you should choose your allies more wisely," certain Lijuan had put Charisemnon in charge of her reborn forces.

No response, her face disappearing from view . . . but there were no more reports of new infestations in the hours that followed. That still left them dealing with the creatures already loose in the territory—and that proved no easy task for his people, even though Jason's warning meant they were prepared for Lijuan's "improved" design.

These new reborn didn't shuffle; they ran in a fast crablike walk. And they weren't sad or broken at being trapped in their dead bodies; they were mindless creatures that wanted only to feed on living flesh.

Then they discovered Charisemnon hadn't forgotten the port city of New York.

"Jesus Christ," Elena said, watching the reborn scrambling down the sides of the cruise ship that had apparently berthed early evening, soon after the steady rain had tapered off at last. Under guard because it had stopped in Charisemnon's territory some weeks earlier, before the start of hostilities, it had been scheduled to be searched and processed in the next half hour.

Then one of the dockside workers noticed the blood-soaked "guests" on deck.

"How the hell did people not know they had those creatures on board?" She shot a crossbow bolt at one particularly fast one that had made it onto the pier, taking out its heart and immobilizing it for the moment.

At least the pier blazed with floodlights, making the task easier.

Beside her, Illium unsheathed Lightning, the sword a gleaming piece of death. "No one to ask, but if I had to guess, I'd say Charisemnon's staff booked out an entire deck for their party and either bribed or threatened someone into permitting them to board at night, before the other passengers. These reborn don't look human enough to pass otherwise."

He used Lightning to point out another snarling creature about to hit the pier, so she could shoot it. "The initial group of reborn was most probably a small, manageable number, kept alive and sated with the flesh of living victims brought on board at the same time."

"With the plan to unleash them on the other passengers once they'd docked in New York," Elena completed, seeing the gruesome logic of what he was saying. "Each person they feed off, but leave relatively whole, then rises to become another weapon."

Illium nodded. "I assume their handler was alive until an hour ago, since he kept them from rampaging till the ship docked, but either he's dead now or he didn't get the order not to attack."

Down!

Dropping at Raphael's order, Elena covered her ears as he blasted the cruise ship with a bolt of power from above. The massive piece of machinery simply disintegrated, taking the majority of those inside with it—Elena knew the friends and relatives who'd come to meet the ship were distraught, believing their loved ones might somehow have survived the monsters, but Elena knew that was a false hope.

The reborn scrambling off the ship had had mouths rimmed with blood.

No way would they seek to abandon a buffet of trapped humans unless that buffet was now empty. Especially given the report that had come in from Nimra's territory stating the creatures could scent living prey from meters away and would gang up to break through any impediment to that prey, their focus so absolute, it could be utilized to set up an ambush.

Today, however, it wasn't about drawing the creatures to a certain point but making sure none left the pier alive.

"Go! Go! Go!" she yelled to the ground fighters around her as the dust cleared to show some of the reborn had managed to jump free of the ship before it blew and were now swimming to shore.

Raphael dropped down to join her, unsheathing dual swords rather than expending more power on creatures that could be killed by being beheaded. And so began the grim task of cleaning up the mess Charisemnon had dumped on their doorstep. The absolute worst moment of the entire operation came when Elena found herself face-to-face with a twelve-year-old girl in a drenched sundress, her exposed skin bearing vicious scratches . . . and her teeth stained with blood.

Claws out, the girl screamed and ran at Elena, feral hunger in her face.

37

Hot blood splashing against Elena's combat gear, that small, blonde head rolling off into the water, Raphael's hand cupping the side of her jaw. "Elena." It was a snapped command.

"I'm okay, I'm okay." She'd just frozen there for a second, unable to raise her hand against a child. "I forgot there must've been kids on board."

Ten minutes later and the mobile reborn were all dead. "How many in the water?" she asked Illium, who'd been talking to the teams of vampires in watercraft on the river, their spotlights sweeping the water.

"Two or three dozen at most. The Sire's strike incinerated the majority, but we need to make certain none of the drowned are given the chance to rise." Wiping the back of his hand over his mouth, he walked over to the drowned bodies laid out on the pier and began to behead them one after the other.

He hesitated at the tiny body of another child, this one a boy of barely four or five.

"Illium?" she asked when he went down on one knee beside the body, not knowing what answer would be worse—evidence that the child *had* been alive when Raphael blew up the ship or that he'd joined the monsters.

The blue-winged angel's eyes were bleak as he rose and brought down his sword across that fragile neck. "There was flesh caught between his teeth, under his fingernails."

Rage and sadness burning in her gut, she got a lift from Raphael into the sky and began to sweep the river to make certain none of the bodies had washed downstream. All it would take to spark a deadly infestation was for one reborn to come back to the mockery of "life" that was Lijuan's gift to her people.

After the unrelenting horror of the past few hours, Elena was in no mood to see stunning wings of silken copper in Raphael's office. Needing to deal with an urgent situation in another part of the territory, he'd returned to the Tower thirty minutes earlier, while she'd remained behind with the team doing the final checks to make absolutely certain the reborn threat had been neutralized.

Tired and dirty, she wanted a shower, the arms of her consort, food, then sleep, in that order. Instead, she saw Tasha of the warrior's blade and faux friendliness put her hand on Raphael's arm as she leaned in close to Elena's man, who was still in his bloodied combat leathers. Face uptilted and that glorious scarlet hair tumbling down her back, the other woman hung on Raphael's every word.

Elena didn't realize she had a throwing knife in her hand until the scent of the sea and the rain crashed into her mind. *Getting blood out of white carpet is extremely difficult,* hbeebti.

Fuck the carpet. *Why are you allowing another woman to touch you?*

I was attempting to be polite to an old friend, but clearly, that approach has failed. Lifting Tasha's hand off his arm, he placed it by her side. "I'm afraid we won't be able to accommodate you at the Enclave. There are, however, guest quarters in a skyscraper nearby."

"Oh? I am disappointed, Raphael." Tasha's voice was

musical even in her regret. "I truly believe I can offer assistance with what is happening in your territory." A smile Elena could hear in her tone. "A sounding board as well as my sword."

It was the last sentence that threw the switch on Elena's temper from hot to cold. *Bitch knows I'm here and she's trying to provoke me. Why? So she can show herself to be the more cultured, civilized one? Does she think you'll love me less if I lose my temper and act like an idiot?* The absurdity of such an idea astounded her. *Or that I'd turn tail and run, even if she humiliated me?* Pride mattered nothing when it came to her love for Raphael—she'd crawl naked and bloodied over hot coals to get to him.

She has no comprehension of what we are to one another. A single, searing instant of eye contact that made her heart ache. *Tasha thinks as many immortals do—in terms of political alliances.*

"Tasha." She waited for the other woman to turn, ersatz surprise in those slanted eyes of emerald green. "The old days might have been 'saturated with joy,'" she said, quoting something Tasha had just been saying, "but time has moved on."

"You are young, Elena." If Tasha's smile had had any more sugar in it, it'd need to come with a warning label from the dentist. "You cannot understand the bonds that tie together those of us who've known one another for a millennium and more."

Oh, I'm soooo terribly, terribly wounded by that velvet arrow.

Laughter in her mind, the kiss of the sea. *Velvet arrow? Your use of language is getting more creative by the day.*

I can't take credit for that one. It's all Bluebell. Now be quiet so I can concentrate on not stabbing Ms. McHotpants through the heart to put her out of her misery.

"I may not understand the bonds of such a long shared past"—Elena relaxed against the doorjamb—"but I understand the present. And in the present, you're attempting to seduce my consort. It cheapens you, Tasha."

No smile now, tension in that flawless jawline. "You have no right to make judgments of me."

"You gave me that right when you flew into my city and

attempted to fly into the arms of my consort." She folded her own arms, having secreted away her knife before first speaking to Tasha. "You should know the latter is an impossibility."

"You're very certain of yourself for a mortal."

Elena didn't correct her on the whole mortal issue. As far as she was concerned, it wasn't an insult. "If I'm certain of one thing, it's that I love Raphael and he loves me," she said simply, that truth the very foundation of her life.

"Yes, there is that, isn't there." A dazzling smile. "I'm sorry if I've caused any discomfort. I'll remain in the city to assist in any way I can in the coming battle."

"One of my people will escort you to the guest quarters," Raphael said.

"Thank you." Stepping out with those quiet words, the other woman made a flawless takeoff into the midnight sky, a younger angel falling into flight with her.

"She thinks I'm ridiculous," Elena said, eyes narrowed, "and that you'll fall for her soon enough."

"Do you believe the same, Guild Hunter?"

"I believe if Tasha continues sniffing around, I may get annoyed enough to slice off her wings—while smiling sweetly, of course."

"Of course." He opened his arms, and she walked into them without hesitation. "My beautiful, fierce, bloodthirsty Elena," he murmured into her hair, a smile in his voice. "Tell me about these velvet arrows. I am quite fascinated."

Laughter bubbling out of her, she rose on tiptoe to kiss that smiling mouth and knew that, as with the bloodstorm, Tasha and her ilk had no weapons that could ever sever the connection between her and her archangel.

The world was swathed in the heavy dark of early morning when Raphael went up to the Tower suite he shared with Elena, not tired, but wanting the touch of his consort, their kiss earlier the only contact they'd had. He needed more, needed to drench himself in the life and warmth of Elena, parts of him yet raw from the icy power that had sought to infiltrate his body.

He'd have fought the urge had his senior angels not all

reported in to say they believed they'd contained the reborn threat in their regions, though they'd do further sweeps to make certain. Manhattan, too, was calm, and with three of his Seven at the Tower, he could be assured nothing would slip through the cracks should he step away for an hour or two. Right now, it was Aodhan who stood lead in the operations center–turned–war room, with Illium as backup.

Elena was asleep facing the center of the bed when he arrived. Stripping, he slid in and tucked her close. She sighed, threw her leg over him in an unconscious possessiveness that made his tension melt away, and didn't stir again. Stroking the fluid muscle of her thigh, he was considering how most pleasurably to rouse her when there was a knock on the doorway of his mind.

Sire.

Sliding out without disturbing his hunter, he pulled on a pair of black pants before walking out onto the balcony off the bedroom. His spymaster whispered out of the shadows, midnight wings folded tight to his back.

"I didn't expect you until tomorrow." He slid the mirrored door quietly shut behind him to block the cold from getting in, Elena's body yet sensitive to the bitter temperatures.

"I find I am eager to return home."

"Mahiya is now at the Tower." Part of Raphael's power came from his Seven, and Charisemnon was underhanded enough to attack that which each male held most dear in order to break them down. In Jason's case, that position was occupied by the princess he'd brought home from Neha's land. "I did it for her protection, but it'll be more dangerous here very soon," he pointed out. "I give you leave should you wish to move her to a safer location."

"Our place is here," Jason said without hesitation. "My Mahiya wouldn't wish to be stowed out of harm's way while her friends and family fought."

Elena, Raphael remembered, had said exactly the same about Jason's princess, his consort and the other woman having formed a budding friendship. "What news do you bring?" he asked, accepting his spymaster's decision without question, for his Seven knew their own minds—and he was dead sure Jason spoke Mahiya's true opinion. His spymaster and the princess had quickly become an impregnable unit.

"While Lijuan has always been treated as a demigoddess by her people," Jason said, the swirls and curves of his facial tattoo barely visible in the dim light, "she now truly believes herself a god. Furthermore, she has begun to regard the others in the Cadre as lesser."

"Caliane?"

"Her position on the Ancient remains unknown, but my instinct is that she plans to ignore your mother until she believes her power has developed to the point where she can kill Caliane in a single engagement. Though," Jason added, "I have no doubt that you are right in your request of your mother—should Caliane leave Amanat vulnerable, Lijuan would strike at once and with vicious fury."

Raphael nodded. "My ability to harm Lijuan threatens her delusion of godhood." That understanding eliminated any hope of a peaceful resolution. "Her offensive forces?"

"On the verge of leaving her territory. If she uses both modern means and winged flight to get them here, she'll be ready to strike within the next four to five days."

"I think it's time to recall Naasir." His mother wouldn't need the vampire while Amanat was safe under her shield, and Naasir was a berserker fighter on the ground. Then there were his more subtle talents, every one of which would be needed with so many of their winged fighters out of commission. "The question is, do I recall Galen and the Refuge squadron?" His weapons-master would be a lethal asset in combat, but it would leave Venom alone to protect Raphael's Refuge stronghold.

"With her delusions of being a deity," Jason pointed out, "Lijuan may not feel she needs to obey the rule that places the Refuge out of bounds of war. We can't risk her viewing your stronghold as a weak target."

"You're right." Especially since Lijuan and Charisemnon might not be the only threats. Every archangel had forces in the Refuge—pulling Galen and the squadron could well make Raphael's stronghold too tempting a target for one of the others. Not only that, but the people who looked to him in the Refuge would see any such move as an abandonment, while still others would interpret it as a sign of weakness. And the fall of the stronghold would demoralize his Tower troops, for many had family within those walls.

No, Galen, Venom, and the squadron must remain to guard against a possible Refuge strike. Raphael would have access to Galen's warrior mind, and Venom's slyly inventive one, through the constant communications link between the Tower and the Refuge stronghold.

Jason, Naasir, Illium, Dmitri, and Aodhan, they were a formidable force. He knew each would fight with the fury of a thousand ordinary fighters. But as he'd pointed out to Elena, Lijuan, too, had men and women of power by her side. Even with the assistance Elijah had pledged, Raphael's troops would have to fight with cunning and intelligence to balance the enemy's greater numbers and strength.

That, however, was a conversation that didn't have to take place right this instant.

"Go to your princess, Jason," he told his spymaster. "We'll talk of the rest come dawn."

He felt the door open at his back even as Jason took off in silence, a winged piece of the night, and turned to hold out his arm. A sleepy-eyed Elena came into his embrace, the satin of her robe cool against his skin. "Jason?"

Enclosing her in his wings to protect her from the cold, he said, "He brought the news we expected."

The sleep faded from her expression as he told her what Jason had shared. "I know this is a fight between immortals," she said, "but I think you'd be remiss not to accept those from the Guild who want to join in the defense. This is a Guild city, too, home of our HQ."

Raphael had, in truth, not thought of the hunters, dismissing the mortals from the field of battle as too weak, too easily broken. As Elena had once been broken . . . but before that, she'd fought with such heart as even an archangel couldn't fault.

"Ask Sara to join us in the war room tomorrow morning— she can disseminate the news to her hunters." He paused. "Ask Deacon, too." The mortal male was a genius with weaponry, could well come up with innovative strategies on how they could best utilize the weapons at their disposal.

"Can we go out, meet Lijuan's forces midway?" Elena asked, thinking like the warrior she was. "Rather than letting them hit the city, I mean."

"Dmitri, Galen, and I gave the option serious consideration, but with our forces weakened, we're already in a compromised position. Should our people fall in battle over the sea, we may not be able to retrieve them in time." Meaning loss after loss. "Inside Manhattan, in comparison, we can set up a defensive perimeter, giving us a secure base from which to launch our attacks."

"What about the rest of the city?"

"I don't think this is about sacking New York or causing carnage. Lijuan wishes to display her power—to do that, she needs to take the Tower and either kill or subjugate me to her will." Soft, heavy snowflakes hitting his wings. "Inside."

Not arguing, Elena walked in and, dropping the robe, jumped under the comforter.

He kicked off his pants and slid in beside her, running his knuckles from her breastbone to her navel. "To reduce the number of possible casualties, I'll be ordering the evacuation of all humans except Guild personnel who wish to stay."

Her eyes widened. "All of Manhattan? How can that be done?"

"Illium has taken the lead in the planning and tells me he foresees no problems."

"Some people won't want to leave."

"They won't have a choice." Cupping her between the legs without warning, he caught her gasp with his kiss. "Enough talk of battle. Right now, I need my consort."

The stark statement melted Elena's bones. Closing her fingers over his nape as her flesh grew warm and damp against his fingers, she tugged him down for a slow, sipping kiss, as if they were two people on a first date . . . but for the fact that he had his hand between her legs, and his thumb was brushing across her clit in a slow, erotic tease.

Wrapping her leg over his hip, she played her fingers through his hair and continued to kiss him soft and sweet. "Come inside me," she whispered, needing the intoxicating physical connection.

He removed his hand to shift over her, his wings spread in

magnificent display. "You are wet for me, *hbeebti*." It was an intimate murmur in the dark, the blunt head of his cock pressing against her sensitive entrance.

"So wet for you." She shivered as he began to push inside her, thick and hard and insistent, her hands splaying on the tensile muscle of his back.

One arm braced beside her head, the hand of his other possessive on her breast, he molded her flesh with erotic confidence and continued to push inside. The intense slide of heated steel across her delicate tissues made her moan, her back arching.

He paused the inexorable pressure to claim a kiss, his tongue tasting her deep, before holding her gaze and thrusting the final thick inch into the tight clasp of her body. They both shuddered, locked together as close as two bodies could get—then his mouth touched her throat and her lips his shoulder, as his hand slid off her breast to caress her thigh.

It was a slow, tender dance, their bodies rocking together as they kissed and touched and murmured to one another in the dark. "*Knhebek*, Archangel," she said at the end, pleasure a languorous ripple in her blood and her lover's skin rough heat over her own.

"*Elena.*" The masculine groan made her clench around his cock, the hot pulse of his seed marking her in a primal claim.

Wanting to watch his pleasure, she lifted her lashes . . . and felt her breath leave her lungs in a rush, Raphael's wings edged by an intensely beautiful flicker of haunting white fire.

38

The next day, after a three-hour warning to permit people to gather what they needed, angels hovered over every major route out of Manhattan as an army of cops made sure residents left in an orderly fashion. Normally, the Tower didn't mess with the civilian force made up of mortals and vampires, but, as with everything else in this territory, the organization fell ultimately under Raphael's authority, and he'd exercised his power.

Not that the police officers were averse to what they were being asked to do. One of Elena's cop friends had put it best: "After our briefing this morning about the hurt Lijuan's planning to bring down on the Tower, and seeing those fucking nasty reborn things scuttling on the pier, I wouldn't want my family in Manhattan."

The cops' next task would be to maintain order in the surrounding boroughs and make certain no one crossed back into Manhattan.

Fear lingered an acrid taint in the air during the evacuation, but the sight of grim-faced angels overhead and equally lethal vampires on watch in the evacuated parts of the city meant no one stepped out of line—especially after Illium picked up a pair who had thought to burglarize an empty building and dumped them into the freezing waters of the Hudson. He left them there for the maximum survivable time, their eyes panicked and lips blue.

"Next time," the message went out, "we will not retrieve those consigned to the water."

There were no further incidents.

Jeffrey, Elena was glad to see, moved his family—including Beth—out by helicopter the first day. Beth, by contrast, was hysterical when she called Elena that afternoon. "What if Harrison dies?" her sister sobbed.

Elena didn't lie; she didn't say any one of them would make it out of this alive. Instead, she reassured Beth that the city's defenses were strong, the evacuation a precaution. After hanging up, her sister marginally calmer, she returned to the young angelic squadron to which she'd been attached, their task to assist in the evacuation of the city's most vulnerable.

Not strong enough to carry sick adults or older children across to hospitals outside Manhattan, she carried bundled-up babies and toddlers. The latter, despite their illnesses, grinned throughout each flight, not a lick of fear in their expressions. "Can we do that again?" a four-year-old asked when they landed, his cheeks bright red because he'd wanted to face the wind the entire time, despite her attempts to shelter him.

Bending down to hug his thin body, the IV port on his left hand appearing far too harsh for his delicate skin, she said, "Yes," and hoped it was a promise she'd be alive to keep. "After we fight the bad people, I'll come back and see you again."

Then she passed him to the care of the nurse who waited, and she returned to carry across another child, the ambulances—road and air—reserved for those who needed the support of medical machinery. Tower, Guild, police, and corporate choppers were all pooled into the effort, while hunters drove the elderly, and those others who required special assistance, from point to point.

Most evacuees had friends and family with whom they could stay, and still others were invited in by kind neighbors in surrounding areas. However, for those who found themselves homeless, emergency services—acting in concert with the

Tower—had set up temporary but snug housing facilities on Tower-owned land in nearby areas. The latter had been done well before the evacuation was announced, which spoke to the precision planning behind the entire operation.

Elena had never seen any evacuation proceed with such speed and lack of trouble—but then again, this was the evacuation of a healthy city into equally healthy areas. No natural disaster had blocked supply lines, damaged roads, or hit the workforce.

Forty-eight hours after it began, Manhattan was a ghost city.

Flying above the empty streets, the odd bit of paper fluttering on the pavement and a lone dog looking up at her, Elena felt a shiver crawl down her spine. The heart of her city was meant to be loud and noisy and full of people. Not that she believed they'd evacuated every single mortal—it was a sure bet some enterprising souls had managed to avoid the mass departure, but they were hidden ghosts, the landscape desolate.

Unable to bear passing over the deserted silence of Times Square, she angled to land at one of the air defense stations, the anti-wing guns primed and ready. Not far from her stood Dmitri, his attention on whatever was being said by a pair of vampires who were experts in using the weapon.

Raphael's second looked no different from before he'd left the city, his presence darkly sexual with an undertone of deadly violence. But he'd come back with a hunter wife now at work as part of the combined Guild-Tower operations team—Honor wasn't yet at full strength, but neither was she an ordinary new-Made vampire, her skin brushed with a shimmer of gold, her eyes a luminous jewel green, her mortal beauty honed as sharp as a blade.

The other hunter had laughed at Elena's flabbergasted expression when they first came face-to-face. "I know, I know. It was a bit of a shock to me, too." A deep smile, Honor still Honor. "But hey, I was Made by an archangel and feed solely from a dangerously sexy thousand-year-old vampire."

"Is it weird?" The question was one Elena had only felt

comfortable asking because Honor was a friend. "The blood drinking?"

Honor's honey gold skin had turned a fascinating shade of pink. "Oh, um, no."

"Oh, um, no?" Elena had teased, delighted to see Honor so happy after the horror the other woman had survived. "Dmitri clearly gives good . . . blood."

"My husband," a still pink but laughing Honor had said, her words holding an adorable possessiveness, "gives phenomenal . . . blood."

Now, the husband in question finished his conversation with the two gunners and strode over. Even dressed in scuffed black boots, jeans of the same black, and a black T-shirt, his attention totally focused on the city's defenses, no time for the insidious scent games he usually liked to play, there was something about Dmitri that whispered of sex—the bloody, painful kind.

"Are you free?"

She nodded at the curt question, having just finished her duties with the team assigned to make absolutely sure all the hospitals had been evacuated. "You have a job for me?" Dmitri would never be her friend, and she'd never see in him whatever it was that Honor saw, but when it came to protecting their city, they had no arguments.

"The Guild teams need a winged consult." He pointed out another high-rise. "The two team leaders are up there."

Demarco and Ransom looked up at the wash of wind generated by her wings. "I hear you guys asked for a consult," she said, meeting Demarco's light brown eyes first, because she didn't want to see the coolness in Ransom's.

"Ellie." The rangy hunter grinned, streaky blond hair ruffled by the wind and long legs folded in a crouch in front of what appeared to be a chalk outline of the defensive perimeter. "Our own personal hunter angel." Shifting, he showed her the front of his oatmeal-colored T-shirt. "Didjya know they're selling these in Times Square?"

Groaning at the solid black silhouette of a gun and crossbow-toting female with wings, the name *Elena* emblazoned above the figure, and the words *Hunter Angel* below, she rubbed at her eyes. "God damn it, get rid of that monstrosity before I go blind."

Demarco just grinned as she dropped her hands from her face to walk over and crouch between the two men. Then, when she couldn't avoid it any longer, she dared look up at Ransom.

His expression as tentative as she felt, he gave her a lopsided smile. "Hey."

"Hey," she said, painfully relieved he wasn't holding a grudge.

"Why are you two acting like moobs on a first date?" Demarco asked in open confusion. "Did you dump the librarian and the archangel and rub your naughty bits together? Man, it must've really sucked eggs if you're avoiding eye contact."

"Demarco," Elena and Ransom growled together.

"And awkward moment over." Demarco winked, his usual laid-back grin on his face. "Let's talk angels, crossbows, and bullets."

They spent the next ten minutes in a discussion of optimal positioning, after which the focus shifted on how the shooters—crossbow wielders and those with specialized anti-angel guns—could do the most damage with the least effort.

Elena's advice was simple. "Aim for the wings." It was highly unlikely either weapon could kill immortals of the age and strength as those in Lijuan's army, but if the Guild team could keep wounding the enemy fighters long enough, the immortals on their side might be able to finish the task.

"We have crossbow users like you who have precision aim," Demarco countered, his careless charm discarded to reveal hard-eyed intensity. "You can get bolts through the neck. It'll disable the enemy fighters for longer."

"It'll take longer to get off a shot." Elena thought of the intricate timing that'd be required and shook her head. "We can take out more with the wing hits."

"Yeah, but the ones with injured wings will rise faster, too."

They both looked to Ransom. Frowning, the other hunter said, "We have approximately twenty-five precision bowmen. We can embed them with the ones aiming for the wings, so the enemy doesn't know who to take out and the shooters have time to aim under the cover provided by the others."

"Works for me." Demarco glanced at Elena, and when she nodded in agreement, said, "Okay, positions."

They spent the next few hours making sure all the shooters knew where they were supposed to be once the shit hit the fan. When Ransom and Demarco were satisfied with that aspect of things, Elena rounded up a crew of junior angels and did fly-overs so the hunters could practice aiming at a moving, winged target. The gunmen used blanks, the crossbow users blunted bolts.

When they called the exercise to a halt, Elena spent a quarter of an hour discussing possible refinements with Demarco and Ransom, before taking off again, her intent to head to Raphael. He was at a higher elevation, working out something with Illium and Jason that periodically cracked black lightning across the sky.

She'd just swept around to begin the climb when it happened.

The Hudson altered color in a rolling wave. This time it wasn't the shade of blood, but a deep, vibrant blue electric with a luminous white fire. Angels who'd been nearby hovered above the water, but Elena saw the gulls dive in and out with no ill effects, the shimmering blue glittering on their feathers until it drained off.

"An interesting development," Raphael said, having dropped down to hover beside her. "Astaad is rumored to have a certain control over the sea—but it may well extend to domination over water in general."

"Maybe, but those are your colors." That heartbreaking blue, more pure than any gemstone on this earth, existed only in the eyes of her archangel and the woman who'd given birth to him; never had she seen it in any other circumstance. Until now.

"The day I ascended to the Cadre," Raphael murmured, "the skies rained such a hue and the waters of the world became my eyes. I did not have you in my heart then; there was no dawnlight."

Elena glanced at the purity of his profile, the deep red mark on his temple hidden behind glamour. "Could it be a sign? Of further evolution?" She couldn't help but remember the astonishing beauty of the white fire on his wings that he'd said must've been an illusion created by a pulse of power that ignited a glow.

It sounded right . . . except her gut insisted that what she'd seen had been real, that if she'd reached up and touched his primaries at that instant, she'd have caught a flame on her fingertip.

"If this is a sign of evolution," Raphael said, "it's not one I can sense, as I sensed my ascension from angel to archangel." Angling his wings, he swept down to the water.

Elena followed as close as she could get, close enough to see him run his fingers through it. *The water,* he said, *tastes of the same power that attempted to push its way into me.*

Get away from it, she ordered, her heart stuttering at the sensory memory of the terrible cold that had come with the bloody rain.

There is no chill beyond that of a winter river today, he said, but flicked off the water and rose to her side.

The color began to retreat at almost the same instant.

"Regardless of what this portends," he said, expression brutally pragmatic, "we can't permit it to distract us, not when Lijuan's winged fleet has been spotted less than two days' flight from making landfall." His hand closed over hers. "Omens and signs are worthless when we're about to go into battle against a flesh-and-blood army."

Some mysteries, Elena thought, as the masculine heat of him reassured her the water had had no ill effects, would have to remain unsolved. The lives of millions were at stake. Because if Lijuan defeated Raphael in battle, it'd mean the death of the only being in the world with a proven ability to cause the Archangel of China any significant harm. Left unchecked, Elena had no doubt Lijuan would soon turn the planet into a festering graveyard peopled by her reborn.

A court of rotting corpses to worship at the feet of the Goddess of Death.

39

The Tower's satellites got clear eyes on Lijuan's forces the next day, the heavy clouds that had been blocking their view dissipating under piercing sunlight.

"Impossible," Jason said at the sight of the incredible mass. "That army is at least three times the size of the one that left her region. Even if she brought all her winged fighters, leaving only her vampire troops to defend her territory, she has too many squadrons."

Raphael had always known they were going into this war at a disadvantage, but if all those men and women were experienced fighters, the scales had tipped so severely in Lijuan's favor that every one of their plans would have to be reevaluated. "We need to know exactly what we face." He turned to the fastest flyer in his squadrons, some said the fastest flyer in all of angelkind. "Go."

Illium left at once, taking a small recording device with him.

It was a bare hour after that that their battle plans suffered another blow.

"We are overrun with reborn," Elijah told him, his cheekbones cutting sharply against his skin. "I don't know how

Lijuan got them in, or even if she did it with more than a single creature—we both know it would've taken only one to start the process." An indictment of the creatures' sheer infectiousness. "It appears to have been a plan put in place over months, the infected seeded throughout my territory and kept chained up behind locked gates. Evidently, she predicted we'd ally and stand against her, for those gates have now been opened."

The Archangel of South America shoved a hand through the gold of his hair, his eyes backlit by a furious amber glow. "I'm shamed to break my promise of aid," he said, the words clearly hard for him to shape, "but I need to use every weapon at my command to hit hard and fast before the reborn riddle every part of my territory. Already, they've killed or infected thousands, savaging entire villages and townships."

"The risk is ours," Raphael said, reminding Elijah they shared a land border. "No shame comes of your decision. Should you contain them, you more than uphold your part of our pact." He considered who he had near that border, if they could provide any assistance.

"My strongest people are here, others on watch in areas where we had small reborn infestations of our own, but I'll order every able individual near the border, mortal and immortal, to mobilize with flamethrowers and fuel to set up fire lines. They can at least clean up any reborn that attempt to escape your forces." The reborn couldn't survive fire as they couldn't survive beheadings. "I wish you luck, Eli."

"And I, you, Raphael."

When Illium returned in the twilight hours beyond midnight, Lijuan's forces still at least twelve hours away, for they had to move at the speed of their slowest member, he brought worse news than anyone could've imagined.

"Your people didn't fail," Raphael said to a quietly infuriated Jason, pointing out a commander to Lijuan's left. "She was part of Uram's troops."

Dmitri pinpointed three more of the dead archangel's people, all commander level, just in the first row. "Uram's territory was parceled out after his execution," the vampire said, "his troops divided. If all the extra fighters prove to be Uram's, she has over half his squadrons. She shouldn't."

Aodhan was the one who answered, voice quiet but words potent. "If Raphael were to perish, the Seven divided, would we not come together should we have a chance to avenge his death?"

"I didn't think the guy inspired that kind of loyalty," Elena said, staring at the photographs of the massive force that would soon hit Manhattan. "I mean, he murdered hundreds of his own people."

"He was a good archangel once." An archangel Raphael had called friend an eon past. "That is who his loyal soldiers remember, who they seek to avenge."

"Sire," Galen said from the screen on the wall, where he and Venom had joined in the discussion, "the enemy outnumbers us five to one. We need to pull our forces inward and compel the enemy to mount a siege. So long as the Tower does not fall, Lijuan doesn't win."

Raphael knew what it must've cost his weapons-master to make that recommendation, for Galen was a warrior who lived by the blade. And though he knew the other man's counsel was sound, the idea of abandoning any part of his city made his blood rage.

It was Elena who gave him perspective. "With the entire area evacuated," she said, "we'd only be protecting buildings anyway. Buildings can be rebuilt." Bleak acceptance in the silver-gray, his hunter who loved every tiny pocket and corner of her city.

"Go," he said to Dmitri. "Do what needs to be done, commandeer the people you need." All the anti-wing guns would have to be moved, for a start. "I'll rework the troop placements."

Dmitri left with a curt nod, taking Jason with him and ordering Illium to rest after his long flight. Aodhan went in a separate direction, having assumed the task of ensuring there'd be enough food stock inside the Tower for the hunters and the wounded, should the siege continue beyond a few days. Water, at least, was no problem, the Tower having a secret independent line that had been put in place at the time of its construction.

Raphael turned to the last member of his Seven who remained, Galen and Venom having signed off to return to their task of holding the Refuge stronghold secure. "How many more do you need in your team?" he asked Naasir. The vampire had arrived forty-eight hours before, fed well, and was at full strength.

"The team is complete," was the response, Naasir's silver eyes intelligent as only a predator's could be. "Janvier and his hunter."

"I wouldn't call Ash that to her face," Elena pointed out, wondering what it was Naasir planned to do. If she had to guess, given the team members and their abilities, she'd say it was about causing sabotage and disorder among the enemy camp.

A feral grin that said Naasir still found her interesting, and then he was gone.

Alone with Raphael for the first time in hours, Elena touched her fingers to his face and he lifted the glamour to expose the mark on his temple. It had grown at an accelerated rate since the river altered color . . . to the point where it was now clear it had nothing to do with disease—no, it was a symbol both savage and dangerously elegant. Created of complex but jagged lines, it curved down his temple to the top of his cheekbone on one end, the other end curling in on itself.

"Raphael, it's not red anymore," she whispered, astonished at the primal beauty of a finished design that reminded her of a stylized dragon. "It's the color of us." An incredible violent blue lit with searing white fire, so drenched with light and color that it appeared alive.

Reinitiating the glamour until they were in the bathroom of their suite, Raphael dropped it to examine the mark in the mirror. "I've seen this design before," he said, to her surprise. "In old places in the Refuge, from times so long gone, no one has any memory of when the carvings were created."

She hitched herself up on the counter so she could continue looking at the mark that no longer terrified, but compelled. "Any hint as to its meaning?"

"No. I asked Jessamy once, and she said she'd looked in the texts herself and found no mention of them. 'Perhaps they are an enigma left behind by our ancestors to inspire us to search for knowledge,' was what she said to me." Shifting into the space between Elena's legs, he was patient as she traced the vibrant, living mark with her fingertips.

"It's truly beautiful."

Raphael raised an eyebrow. "Many would say it's savage."

"Savage can be beautiful." It suited him, her archangel whom she'd seen fight the reborn with raw ferocity, his twin blades moving so fast, she'd wanted only to watch him. "I don't think there's any longer any question that you're evolving."

That hard, pragmatic look back on his face. "Not fast enough. The mark may be complete, but in power, I'm no different than I was yesterday. We must focus on the factors we can control." He stepped back, the glamour going up. "I need to reconfigure squadron placements. You should wake the leaders of the Guild and vampire shooting teams and do the same."

Elena nodded. "One thing, Archangel." She drew him to a stop with a touch on his wing. "I don't think you should hide the mark come morning."

"Fool the enemy into believing I've gained more power than is true?"

"And give our own forces heart," Elena said, pushed by the same instinct that told her his wings were changing in more ways than in surface appearance. "There's nothing to lose."

Hours later, with the sky shifting from darkness to gray, Raphael left Aodhan on watch and walked up to the suite, having sensed a disturbance in Elena's sleep patterns. He'd kept an eye on her since she'd finally gone to bed two hours past, knowing her tiredness and the tension-filled day made for optimal conditions when it came to the horrors that stalked her dreams.

When he reached the bedroom, he found her restless but not yet in distress. Lying down beside her, he spread his wing over her body in a protective wave and murmured words of love from an archangel to his consort until she sighed and sank into a deep, peaceful sleep. "Sleep well, *hbeebti*," he said softly, brushing a kiss to her temple.

Not needing to rest, he had every intention of leaving the bed in the next few moments . . . but then he was dreaming, with no awareness of having closed his eyes. This time, he wasn't on that lonely, forgotten field, but in a place so dark, it was beyond the rich black of night. He could hear nothing, see nothing, feel nothing, the blackness pressing down until it felt as if it would suffocate the life out of him.

More games.

His anger ignited, his wings glowing to fill the dark with light. The blackness swallowed the glow, pushing down harder on his body. Furious, he struck out with his power, and it parted the black, only to reveal more blackness, a world of nothingness. About to strike again, he thought suddenly that he needed Elena, needed the passionate *life* of her, born of the brilliant firefly existence that was a mortal's.

"Raphael." A touch, fingers rough from weapons-work sliding into his to curl around his hand.

"How did you find me?"

The rim of silver around her irises luminous in the blackness, she said, "I heard you call my name." Screwing up her nose, she glanced around. "I'm not sure I like this new dreaming habit of yours."

Sliding his wing over hers, he said, "I have to agree with you," as around them, what had been impenetrable black became a soft gray. "Your heart drives away the dark." She'd seen terrible things, been bathed in blood, yet in her lived an innocence of soul of which she seemed unaware.

"No," she murmured, her hair flying backward in a gentle breeze. "I don't think it's me. It's us." Wing shifting under his in a soft susurration of sound, she said, "The white fire, Archangel. Ignite the white fire."

He reached within him for that wild, near-uncontrollable flame, coaxing it onto his hand. Where it had once manifested a radiant white-gold with iridescent edges of midnight and dawn, today the white-gold bore swirls of violent blue, the flame just as volatile, as passionately alive. "Us," he whispered and threw the wildfire up into the gray.

"Wildfire," Elena whispered, as if he'd spoken aloud. "Yes, that describes it so much better."

The wildfire arced out into the gray in every direction,

eliminating the fog to leave them encased in sun-shot water of a pale, haunting green.

Elena ran her fingers through the water, the ripples disturbing the flawless serenity of the place, but there was no sense that the disturbance was unwelcome. "Oh, I like it here." She danced her hand gracefully in the water, her delight without affectation.

It made his lips curve, his heart remember what it was to be a child. "We're deep inside the ocean," he said, understanding the sunlight wasn't sunlight at all but the lingering burn of the wildfire.

"I've never been anywhere so beautiful." Wonder in her eyes, their handclasp unbroken, Elena pointed out a tiny jellyfish-like creature that floated by, its body a translucent coral . . . but the wildfire, it was fading, the water caressed by gray, then enclosed by darkness.

"I understand," he said, as his consort came into his arms, her hands on his shoulders and her kiss one that branded, drawing him out of the dream and into the warmth of their bed. She was strong and lithe underneath him, his warrior with her mortal heart, eyes of silver-gray open in the murky light that told him he hadn't slept long.

"The risk," he said, when their lips parted, "is being consumed by it."

"The darkness?"

"Without you, I might one day have become another Lijuan." Scowling, she would've shaken her head, but he stopped her with a grip on her jaw. "No, Elena. This truth I must confront—in me lives more power than any other angel my age has ever had. That much power changes a man, and it changed me."

"Okay, that's a fair point, but what's also true is that you're not the archangel I first met." Elena's expression stubborn, the hands she'd thrust into his hair fisting tight. "You're still *becoming*—and, unlike Lijuan, you're not afraid to take risks. She's a coward who killed the mortal who made her feel; you claimed me as yours." Tugging him down, she nipped hard at his lower lip in sensual rebuke. "Don't ever think to compare yourself to her."

"As my consort decrees," he said, speaking with his lips on hers, his body cradled in the silken prison of her legs. "I know you'd never permit me to turn into a megalomaniacal tyrant with delusions of godhood."

"Glad we got that straightened out." Rubbing her nose against his in an open affection he knew he'd never tire of, should he live to be a hundred thousand years old, she said, "Where we were, it was a place of power, wasn't it?"

"Yes." That power had saturated the water, the darkness, the living creatures that swam in those deep waters. "Not malevolent, and attuned to me, but out of my reach." The final bitter seal on the revelation he'd had in the bloodstorm.

"That sucks."

His lips kicked up at the succinct description of his own angry frustration. "It does." Kissing her one more time, he rose to sit on the edge of the bed, his hand cupping the side of her face. "Sleep. It is early yet and you must rest—I will need my hunter more than ever in the days to come."

Elena closed her fingers over his wrist to stop him from leaving. "How bad is it, Archangel?" It was the question of a consort, and the answer he gave her was one Elena knew he'd give no one else in the Tower, not even his Seven.

"My men and women are loyal and will fight to the bloody end," he said, his broad shoulders holding the weight of a staggering number of lives, "but I'm afraid I am about to lead them into certain death."

Getting up onto her knees, she wrapped her arms around him from behind, their faces side by side. "Not one of those men and women would ever want to serve Lijuan, you know that." She pressed her lips to his marked temple, her understanding born of the hours she'd spent in the infirmary with the injured, and with the able-bodied soldiers who came to visit their fallen comrades. "Our people would rather go honorably in a fight against evil than cower under its hand."

Raphael took a long, deep breath, his shoulders straightening and his head rising. "No one," he vowed, "will ever subjugate those who are our own. Never will we surrender."

40

Five hours into the new day, Raphael's spymaster flew back to tell him Lijuan's troops had crossed the early-warning border. A single command and Raphael's offensive squadrons formed around him, the defensive perimeter tight and in place as he led the squadrons out across the city and over the water.

"Hold this position," he told his commanders when they reached a location where his people could see the approaching army but remained within a hard, fast flight distance to their perimeter.

Leaving them hovering in precision formation, he flew out to meet Lijuan midway between the two armies. His move was a risk, given her increasing madness, but he believed part of her remained an archangel of old as yet, and seconds after he began his flight, his belief proved true. Cleaving to the rules of battle laid down at the dawn of angelkind, the Archangel of China flew alone to meet him in neutral space.

"Raphael." Her pale, pale gaze turned to flint as she took in the mark on his temple. "You've been keeping secrets."

"It appears we've all been doing that of late," he said. "You must've worked long and quiet indeed to gain the trust of

Uram's scattered forces." Until the ordinarily loyal men and women had abandoned their assigned posts and territories to swell her ranks.

"A goddess," she said, her physical form fading to turn her skin translucent, "thinks not only for today, but for many tomorrows." The eerie shift revealed the skeletal structure of her face, the sight merging with the crawling sense of screams beneath the surface of her voice, the trapped souls of those Lijuan had murdered.

"Your men wear only swords and crossbows." Guns, at least, were a familiar weapon to most angelic fighters and wouldn't have weighed down a winged fleet. "Do you foresee an easy victory?"

"I have been gathering my forces for ten thousand years, while you are a boy. We outnumber you until it will be no battle but an annihilation."

Her arrogance, Raphael thought, might just be the Achilles' heel that'd give his people victory in this unbalanced war. "Such is your belief, Lijuan. That doesn't make it the truth."

"It soon will be, but before the inevitable, I give you one more chance and invite you to surrender," she said in that voice full of horror. "I cannot leave you or your consort alive, of course"—utmost civility as she spoke of his and Elena's executions—"but I will treat your people as I would my own. Your Seven are extraordinary and will serve me well."

His Seven, Raphael thought, would spend their existence attempting to erase Lijuan from the planet rather than lift a finger in her service. "There is a better way," he said, extending the talk to give Naasir a final few minutes to put his plans in place. "You do not have to start a war."

"I am not starting a war. I am stopping one before it begins." She smiled at him, her eyes pale orbs with fetid shadows hidden within—as if to look too deep would be to fall into an inescapable hell. "You have never respected me as you should. I cannot allow that to continue. You understand."

"Yes, I understand." That Lijuan was a being of perfect madness, so mad she believed herself sane. Raphael recognized the signs; he'd seen them first in his father. But the powerful man who'd once played tag with him above the Refuge had never become the ugliness that was Lijuan. She was something new, a nightmare born of the rot at the core of her soul. "In turn," he said, "you must understand that I cannot allow you to take my Tower and my city."

"Then I'm afraid we are at an impasse." Her smile never faltered, her teeth and jaw visible through skin turned to smoke. "We will be civilized about this. I will not attack you until you are with your troops, and you will not attempt the same."

Accepting the stipulation, he said, "If you wish to cease hostilities at any stage, you need only remove your forces from my territory."

"And should you wish to surrender, your fighters need only lay down their arms. Mine will not attack once your people are no longer a threat—unlike Charisemnon, I have no wish to degrade. My aim is only to conquer." A pause. "It was not well done of him to so dishonorably use the reborn I gave him as a gift. I have told him I will not tolerate any further acts that bring disgrace upon my name."

Raphael inclined his head. "I will see you in battle, Lijuan."

"Good-bye, Raphael. You would've made a great Ancient one day, if only you had learned to respect your betters."

Flying back to his troops at high speed, Raphael reached out to Elena. He needed her touch to erase the ugliness that permeated his bones, Lijuan's presence a seeping wrongness in the fabric of the world. *Elena, battle is imminent.*

We're ready. A kiss of untamed wildness that could be no one but his consort. *I'm watching for you.*

Ordering his troops to retreat inside the siege zone, Illium leading them in, he took the rear with Jason and Aodhan at his flanks. It was a wise move, Lijuan sending a blast in his direction the instant he hit the edge of Manhattan. Her power manifested as a hail of black daggers, gleaming and deadly.

The other archangel, however, was too far away to do much damage, her aim no doubt to send his troops into disarray. Brushing the daggers aside with a minimal use of power, he turned to see that none of his people had dropped even an inch out of formation. There was no second attempt, Lijuan obviously realizing she couldn't do any real harm from that distance, and a few minutes later, his squadrons crossed the line of their defensive perimeter.

Wings filled the sky in every direction, each and every fighter dressed in a distinctive black uniform to distinguish them from the dark gray and red of Lijuan's forces. To further avoid confusion, every single pair of wings—including Raphael's—was marked above and below with streaks of a shimmering blue paint developed exactly for this purpose. Designed not to clog or otherwise harm their feathers, it meant the shooters could see if an angel was friend or foe at a glance.

Those shooters lay concealed in protective hides on the rooftops and in the now windowless top floors of several high-rises, as well as on the perimeter line alongside vampires expert in anti-wing weaponry, the guns pointed skyward. More vampires stood on the ground armed with flamethrowers and swords, their task to attempt to eliminate or so disable downed enemy fighters that they couldn't heal and rise again. A third group of vampires prowled the city, on alert for any reborn threat.

Rising above the squadrons, so he was visible to all, he raised his arm and his sword. "This is our land," he said, augmenting his voice so it'd reach every man and woman, mortal and immortal, who'd fight this day. "We will not be intimidated, and we will not surrender. We did not begin this war, but we will end it!"

A roar shook the world, arms and voices raised in solidarity.

Pride rocked Elena's heart where she lay on her front on a rooftop, crossbow notched and eyes alert. Protected by a hide that meant flying troops wouldn't immediately spot her, the shell also one that'd protect her from shots from above, she had a perfect line of sight to the man who was her own.

You should be proud, Archangel. Your people fight not because of fear or arrogance, but because it's the right thing to do.

A caress of the sea and of the crashing storm of him. *Be safe, Guild Hunter.*

You, too. Heart a hard knot inside her chest, she took a deep breath and wiped her mind clear of all thought, the word having just gone out that Lijuan's troops were about to hit.

The enemy was heralded by a hail of black daggers and the staccato sound of gunfire as the anti-wing weapons went into action. But they'd calculated correctly—there were too many enemy fighters for the guns to catch and the first wave of unmarked wings came into view and into range within thirty seconds . . . as Raphael's troops dropped toward the earth in a sudden, planned plummet, leaving the sky full of the enemy.

Elena's first bolt hit the neck of an angel with wings of dappled brown; she was already slotting in a second bolt before the angel registered the hit and began to spiral down, one hand clasped over his bloody throat. At the same time, black and blue collided in the sky above as two archangels went head-to-head. Knowing she'd be of no use to Raphael if she couldn't hold it together, Elena shook off her fear for him and focused on the enemy, trusting her consort and lover not to break her heart while she did her part.

Bolt after bolt she shot, until the sky was suddenly empty of wings unmarked by shimmering blue. Elena waited for a message through the communications devices everyone had tucked over their ears. It came within seconds, the voice Dmitri's.

"Lijuan's troops have retreated beyond our defensive perimeter, but we've lost a quarter of the anti-wing guns. Stand down but do not leave your positions."

Elena used the opportunity to check her supply of bolts. Seeing that she was nearly out, she switched channels to send a request to the senior Guild trainees running supplies, flicking back in time to catch an updated report from the Tower.

"Enemy troops have settled on buildings outside the reach of our weapons. We injured a large number, but they're recovering and are likely to strike again within the hour. Alternate breaks authorized."

With Lijuan falling back with her troops, Raphael had time to return to the Tower, get a report from Dmitri. His second was coordinating their entire force, making the split-second decisions so necessary in a fight, and which Raphael couldn't make so long as he was battling Lijuan. He knew Dmitri would rather be out in the field, fighting like the honed blade he'd always been, but the other man was the best commander he had. Even Galen deferred to Dmitri when it came to matters of strategy.

"No fatalities," the vampire said, bearing out Raphael's judgment and faith. "A number of serious injuries among the aerial defense gunners, but the angelic fighters nearby acted quickly to cover the injured, while other shooters dragged them to safety." He pointed out several black Xs on the map laid out on a large table in the war room. "Here's where we lost the aerial defense weaponry, but that loss was expected and is already factored into our plans."

"Did Lijuan suffer any fatalities?"

A nod. "Significant in the first wave, when the shooters sent near to half a squadron to the ground for the vampires to clean up, but the enemy learned from that loss. When one fighter falls, two more land with him to fight off the ground teams and lift the injured to safety."

It was more or less what Raphael had expected of this first engagement. "The true test will come with the next clash, now that we no longer have the element of surprise."

Jaw a harsh line, Dmitri nodded. "Elijah called not long ago, wished to speak to you."

"I'm sending you two of my elite fighter squadrons," the other archangel said, when Raphael returned the call. "They're already halfway to your Tower."

"The reborn?"

Elijah's smile held blood fury. "My animals have learned the hunt now, and their sense of sight and smell is beyond anything the reborn have the capacity to avoid. While I continue to need most of my forces to ensure we get each and every one of the creatures, the two elite units will be of far more use to you."

"I'll have Dmitri send through a clear flight path," Raphael said, his trust in Elijah such as he'd never expected to have in another one of the Cadre. "Lijuan's people haven't yet managed to surround us, so your squadrons can come in without encountering enemy fire."

The good news was rapidly followed by bad. Satellite

images showed several aircraft flying low over the ocean perhaps an hour's flight from the city, then ejecting what appeared to be large pods from their holds that floated rather than sank.

"Looks like a quarter of Lijuan's fleet is taking off toward the pods, likely to tug them in," Dmitri said, having eyes on the enemy through the city's network of surveillance cameras as well as the special spy cameras Naasir's team had put in place. "They have to contain ground troops."

Raphael agreed. Which meant Lijuan would soon have vampires to battle his own, leaving her angels free to remain in the sky rather than go to the aid of downed winged fighters. Even with the addition of Elijah's squadrons, Raphael's forces would've remained badly outnumbered. This simply tipped the scale further in Lijuan's favor.

Three minutes later, one of Jason's people called in a report: cargo planes had just left Lijuan's territory, loaded with rocket launchers and guns, as well as further ground forces. It seemed the "goddess" had changed her mind on certain points. Raphael's people had both types of weapons, but the rockets, they'd decided, would only be used in a last-case scenario; no matter how well aimed, the resulting damage would leave not only Manhattan but the entire city a ruin.

And the fact was, they weren't particularly useful in a sky filled with friends and enemies locked together in such close combat. Not unless you didn't care about murdering your own people in order to destroy the enemy.

Lijuan annihilated her own city, he said to his consort, after he'd assimilated the information, images of the smoking crater that was Beijing at the forefront of his mind. *She won't worry about obliterating ours to win this war.*

It was as well that no large-scale technological weapons of any kind were acceptable in an archangelic war, be they tanks on the ground or bombers in the air. It was the reason why the mortals who'd come up with the ideas for such items of warfare had abandoned the research decades ago—there was no market.

Even the rocket launchers and anti-wing guns were short-range, line-of-sight weapons. For a win to count in the immortal world, for an archangel to keep the respect of his or her own people, it had to be intimate, face-to-face. An odd stipulation perhaps, until you remembered that an archangel couldn't be killed by any weapon, no matter how destructive—it was only the lesser angels, vampires, and mortals who'd be among the maimed and the dead.

"Sire." Dmitri walked to where he stood in front of the glass wall that looked out over the field of battle. "Jason's man just sent another report confirming the number of cargo planes heading our way."

Raphael knew it was further bad news from the brutal lines of his second's face. "How many?"

"Ten."

The word reverberated between them. With that many ground fighters and short-range weapons, Lijuan's people would swarm his own, coming up from below while the angels kept the winged squadrons occupied. "I must take the planes out before or directly after they land," he said, knowing he spoke of the death of hundreds. "It's the only option."

"You can get past her using glamour," Dmitri said with coolheaded strategy, "but the instant she hears of their destruction, she'll know you're not in Manhattan and unleash all her power on the Tower."

And if the Tower fell, the battle would be over in the eyes of the world, New York and the entire territory Lijuan's. Raphael would fight to take it back, of course, but he knew the loss of the Tower would crush the morale of his people, for it wasn't simply a place, it was the symbol of their strength.

Seeing movement from the enemy side at the same instant as his second, he dropped the discussion for the moment and left to take to the skies, the second wave of attack far more vicious than the first. Blood splattered the snow everywhere he looked, innocence forever tainted.

41

A day of punishing fighting later, Elena lay in her hide again after a short break, protected from the light snow falling out of a sky patchy with cloud. It was a pretty night, peaceful with occasional starlight that glinted through the clouds and devoid of the sounds of battle, but her heart thundered in her ears because Raphael had left the city almost twenty-five minutes earlier.

Lijuan had managed to wound him in their last skirmish, his chest raw and burned down one side, but he'd shrugged off the injury—one that made Elena want to stab out the eyes of the murderous bitch who'd hurt him—to focus on how to stop the cargo planes that carried such a deadly payload. His plan, if it succeeded, would provide a much-needed boost to the spirits of their battered people, but it could also go spectacularly wrong.

"Naasir, you crazy bastard," she muttered under her breath, "I hope to hell you come through." The cargo planes would be landing around about now, and somehow, their side had to keep Lijuan distracted long enough for Raphael to make it back after destroying the planes.

"I'll take many lives this night," Raphael had said to her in the single private moment they'd had in the midst of the fighting. "Hundreds of vampires who've done nothing but be loyal to their archangel. I know it must be done to protect my own people, but that doesn't change the fact that their blood will stain my soul."

The bleak acceptance in his eyes had broken her heart. And she'd known that even two years past, he wouldn't have said the same thing, the remoteness of over a thousand years of violent power hardening him to the lives of others. "That their deaths matter to you," she'd whispered, "it's your salvation." Unlike Lijuan, he didn't see either his own *or* the enemy fighters as disposable.

Now, she waited for him to return, wanting only to hold him after the brutal ugliness of what he'd been forced to do, all because an archangel believed herself a goddess. More like a fucking specter of pure evil, Elena thought, knowing that if there was any way on this earth she could kill Lijuan, she wouldn't even blink before raising the blade.

"Bees, Ellie," came Sara's voice in her earpiece less than a minute after the scheduled arrival of the planes, her friend in the control room, tasked with handling the Guild teams. *"It's the weirdest thing—there are gazillions of bees around Lijuan's people and from what we can see they're mad and stinging like crazy.*

"And even weirder, the ones not squirming and slapping off bees are grinning like lunatics because they're coated in butterflies. I've never seen so many in one place. I didn't even know butterflies flew around at night."

Grinning, Elena pressed the reply button on the comm device. "Naasir apparently has some tricks up his sleeve." Hell, if he kept this up, she might have to risk being eaten and kiss him on that gorgeous and freaky mouth the next time she saw him.

"I'll say." Sara logged off.

Two minutes later, Elena got a confirmation that Raphael had destroyed the planes. *"On alert,"* came the order in her earpiece seven minutes after that, the ongoing distractions having apparently bought them that much time. *"Enemy forces preparing to launch major offensive."*

Breathing calm and heart rate steady, Elena kept her eyes
on the night sky . . . so she saw the flares that lit it up, dazzling
the senses. An enraged scream sounded from Lijuan's side of
the line with the second flare, bolts of archangelic power going
completely wide of the Tower by several blocks. Glass smashed,
bricks fell, but the Tower remained unscathed.

Was the crazy old bitch sensitive to light?

It made sense, given the paleness of her eyes. But since she
appeared fine in daylight, it wasn't a debilitating weakness,
simply one that could be aggravated by the right conditions.
Elena decided she really *would* have to kiss Naasir for figuring
that out with his sly tiger-creature brain.

Flares continued to light up the sky over the next few minutes, exacerbating Lijuan's screams of fury and keeping her
own forces down because her bolts were going so awry, she
could as easily hit them. Then the fireworks started.

Elena couldn't help it; she began to giggle. They were fighting a battle for their lives and it was going to be fireworks that
saved them?

Giggles passing when a glance at her watch showed Raphael
would only be halfway home at this point, she kept her eyes
on the brilliant display—and suddenly became aware of midnight blades slicing through the storm of color to hit the Tower
and surrounding buildings. "Shit. Lijuan's figured out a way
to adapt to the light." Trying to spot Lijuan's people among
their own as wings filled the air, she found herself blinded by
the fireworks. "Dmitri! Get Naasir to shut it off!"

"Three seconds."

The last firework went out as Lijuan's second blow hit the
Tower, leaving a significant dent and destroying an entire row
of windows. Scanning the sky, she spotted the Archangel of
China's distinctive white hair above the sea of wings. There
was no way to hit her that far up. "Fuck."

Teeth gritted, she started aiming at the enemy angels as
they swarmed, their objective clearly to land on the buildings
that housed the aerial defense systems and the shooting teams.
Precision aim was near impossible with the lack of light and
the enemy's sheer numbers, so she switched approach to go for
the wings.

All they had to do was hold on until Raphael's return.

Angel after angel went down with torn and badly damaged wings, but there was a constant wave of reinforcements, giving the wounded angels time to heal and arise anew. Meanwhile, Elena knew their own forces were being worn down by the constant barrage, above and below, the vampires on the ground no doubt locked in violent combat against vampires and wounded angels both.

Black lightning splintered the sky the next instant, taking down a number of Lijuan's people. The lightning didn't stop Lijuan, but it irritated her enough that she tried to aim for the source, only to find her way blocked by a rain of glittering stone so sharp it threatened to shred her wings. On its heels came a pulse of golden power that smacked into the enemy fighters and Lijuan both, cutting the ordinary angels down like bowling pins and making Lijuan fight to hold her position in the sky.

Stabilizing, the Archangel of China raised her arm to unleash her power, and the black lightning struck a second time.

Jason, Illium, and Aodhan, Elena realized, were working together to keep Lijuan annoyed and distracted. It worked, at least for a while. Then Lijuan decided to leave them to her generals, while she flew above the fighting, her focus on the Tower. Her first blast blew out another row of windows to shower the streets in glass; a second one to the same spot would do serious structural damage.

"Archangel," Elena whispered, taking aim at one of the enemy generals, "if you're planning to do something, now would be the time."

Her bolt ripped through the red-winged angel's right wing, just as another hunter hit his left . . . and a spear of incandescent blue kissed with wildfire slammed straight into Lijuan—or it would have, if one of her troops hadn't angled across her in a suicide intercept.

Screaming an eerie high-pitched scream, Lijuan retaliated with a hail of black knife blades. Raphael had told Elena the glamour was near impossible to hold at this level of combat, and now she saw him come into view, dodging Lijuan's power while attempting to find a hole in her defenses. That was all

Elena had time to see, enemy fighters continuing to fill the air, Aodhan, Illium, and Jason locked in combat with Lijuan's generals.

Notching in bolt after bolt, she continued to shoot, her concentration absolute.

When blood splattered her face as an angel crash-landed in front of her, her eyes went immediately to his wings. "He's one of ours!" she yelled to the trainees by the rooftop door, covering them in concert with another shooter as they dragged the angel to safety. Wiping the blood off using her sleeve, she returned to her task, but it was as if the enemy was multiplying.

An entire squadron flew right at Elena's roof, not flinching when five of their team went down with bolts through their wings and necks, every shooter on the roof switching focus as they understood this was a full-on assault designed to take them out. But there were too many of the enemy, the roof overrun in seconds.

Rising up out of her hide, Elena dodged the bolts of two enemy fighters and kept shooting, aiming for the vulnerable eyes and necks now that they were so close. Several headed right for her, swords drawn, while their brethren engaged the other defenders on the roof. Out of bolts, she dropped the crossbow and, with the same movement, reached for the machine guns she had strapped to her thighs. "Fire in the hole!"

Her people dropped at the warning and she sprayed the rooftop with gunfire, the bodies of the enemy jerking, limbs twitching where they fell as the strong ones struggled immediately to heal from the assault. Blood and brain matter splattered the concrete, and still they kept coming, an endless wave. That was when she realized she was being driven to the edge of the building. They *wanted* her to fall, to fly off.

"Fuck!" It was a trap, one they were willing to sacrifice their people to set. "Ransom!"

Gunfire erupted from her left, the other hunter careful not to hit her as he took over. Screaming a battle cry, she shot out a heavy spray of her own, then, instead of going over where they wanted her to go over, ran right through the enemy. "Keep shooting!" she said, her own guns pumping fire.

Her boots pounded over crushed and bloodied feathers as

she shot her way past the startled angels still standing, the air full of bullets she couldn't totally avoid. One caught her a glancing blow on her arm, the other dug a fiery groove across her cheek, but she reached her target without any real injury, going over the opposite side of the building from where she'd been herded. The enemy turned to follow her en masse, which hopefully meant the others on the roof would be all right.

"This is my city, you bastards." Managing to get her guns strapped down in midair as a result of hours of practice doing the same, she swept down a wide avenue, the wind whipping off the blood trickling down her cheek. "Let's play hide-and-seek."

As the battle raged overhead and buildings shuddered after being hit by stray bolts of power, the city as a whole began to go progressively darker. She'd seen this before, during the fight with Uram, and knew it was because Raphael and Lijuan were both sucking power from the electricity grid, batteries, anything that could supply them with the energy they used to supercharge their strikes.

The darkness was her friend. Teeth bared, she led the enemy angels in and out of streets, through buildings she knew had accessways wide enough for flight, under the High Line and between certain widely spaced trees in Central Park. They were fast, the ones on her trail, but they didn't know Manhattan.

Of course, she couldn't keep this up forever. *Naasir, you fucking smart predator,* she thought as her wings began to tire, *it's showtime.* She'd managed to make a short cell phone call halfway through her darting flight, and, as instructed, now led her pursuers into a narrow gap between two high-rises.

It dead-ended at the back of another building.

Reaching the end, she spun around, wings spread. The leader of the pack, his left eye a pulpy mess where a bullet had hit him, grinned . . . and ran right into the steel net that snapped into place in front of the speeding squadron. The ones at the back tried to fly up to avoid the net, but it fell from above, too—courtesy of a certain blue-winged angel—before a net sprung up behind them.

Trapped, the enemy fighters tried to land, but their wings were too fouled up in the net and with each other. Falling hard to the asphalt, they dragged the nets down with them—nets that, she saw with a wince, had cut lines into their flesh and wings, the edges razored. "I love you right now, Naasir, but you have a scary, scary mind."

She flew up and out before the enemy figured out how to escape the trap. "I need to get to the Tower!" she yelled to Illium—since it was obvious Lijuan had put a target on her back, she was now a liability to the shooting teams.

"I'll take you in!"

"What about Lijuan's generals?" If he'd broken off that engagement to help her, he had to get back to it—those generals had serious firepower.

Illium's grin was satisfied. "I and my brothers in arms earned our power! Lijuan trusts no one with real power! Her generals are puppets—and right now, the Sire is holding all her attention!"

"As long as Lijuan lives, Xi will continue to gain power. Without her, his body wouldn't be able to hold what it does."

Illium had told her that at the Refuge, in reference to one of Lijuan's generals, but she hadn't realized the male was this closely linked to his archangel. But there was no more time to think about that—the two of them had reached the battle zone.

They had to go in shooting, Illium faster with a crossbow than she'd realized, given his preference for using a sword. Halfway through, Tasha appeared out of the mass of wings to flank her other side as Lijuan's men and women deliberately blocked Elena's path to the Tower. Much as Elena would've liked to nurture her dislike for Tasha, the other woman had fought with brilliant fury in the battles, as she did now.

Grabbing her guns, Elena took aim at the enemy. "Get the fuck out of my way!"

Their wings shredded, Lijuan's fighters crashed to the streets and buildings. Illium and Tasha rejoined the fight as soon as Elena landed safely on the Tower roof. Frustrated at having been grounded, she ran inside and to the Tower "aerie," a small nest directly above the war room and connected to it by an internal staircase. It had a three-hundred-sixty-degree view, as well as windows that could be shoved up.

Dmitri stood in the center of the aerie, running everything from his supreme vantage point.

Elena didn't bother to exchange pleasantries with the vampire. Having grabbed ammunition from the stash just outside, she slammed herself into place in front of one of the windows, pushed it up, and started pulverizing any enemy fighter who came too close. There weren't too many, the defenders managing to hold them from the Tower, while Raphael kept Lijuan occupied above.

As Elena watched, Raphael's wildfire just scraped the side of Lijuan's face, ripping off a chunk of her cheek. Screaming that awful scream that made Elena grit her teeth, the older archangel retaliated with a fury of jagged black that Raphael couldn't completely avoid. Horrified, Elena watched as he took a bad hit on one wing, the ugliness of Lijuan's power an oily black that began to crawl over the white-gold as it had done during the battle in Amanat, the blackness infiltrating his very cells.

It shouldn't have affected him that badly—not with the wildfire awake inside him, its ferocity an antidote to Lijuan's ugliness. But he was tired, had just fought nonstop with Lijuan for God knew how long after the trip to destroy the weapons carriers, *and* he'd been using the wildfire against the other archangel since the fighting began. In Amanat, he'd only been able to create it for a tiny period of time, the power new. It might have developed in the interim, but it was still new.

Skin chilling, she realized he had no more in him.

42

Already moving, Elena didn't stop to question the instinct that drove her to put down her gun, leave the aerie, and run to take off from a nearby balcony as Raphael spiraled down from above, his wing mutilated by the black.

Archangel!

Get inside, Elena!

Hell, no. Having instinctively calculated the speed of his descent, she slammed into him, wrapping her arms around his torso. "Use it!" she said, her left arm beginning to pulse with stabbing pains, though nothing touched her skin. "Use me!"

One of Raphael's arms clamped around her, the other shooting a bolt of angelfire toward Lijuan. That arm, his left, she saw, was scored with wounds.

"You need to get back in the Tower!" It was a furious order as they began to fall faster and faster, his "infected" wing pitch-black and useless. "I can't protect you and fight at the same time."

"You're not listening to me! Don't you sense it, the connection?" Her own wing felt as if it were being eaten alive by the black, the pain excruciating. *"Us, Raphael! Us!"*

The dream word hung between them as a laughing Lijuan created a rain of lethal black needles. "Fitting you should die with your mortal!"

Slamming up a hand, Raphael deflected the black with his own power, but the shield began to buckle almost at once, his injuries having apparently depleted his ability to draw power from outside sources.

Elena grabbed his jaw, slamming a kiss on his lips. "Batshit Lijuan will get us anyway so forget about protecting me and *reach*!"

A hard glance out of eyes of wild blue yet free from the oily black, and then she felt a wrenching inside her that made her scream . . . as Raphael's shield turned electric with wildfire. *Yes!* Throat raw and chest aching, she looked at his wing to see the black eaten away to leave only luminous white-gold in its wake.

Another chilling scream, Raphael having deflected Lijuan's needles right back at her. *Stay close.*

Snapping out her wings when he released her, she grabbed the handguns at her hips, mourning her custom-built crossbow, as well as the absence of the machine guns. As it turned out, she only had to shoot a couple of enemy fighters. Clipped by one of Raphael's bolts, which destroyed the bottom half of her right wing, Lijuan called a retreat, and her entire force fell back behind the defensive perimeter.

Elena didn't fly to the Tower but to her shooting team, dreading what she'd find. But somehow, the entire group had made it through, injured but alive. Walking over to her, a bloodied but whole Ransom said, "You owe me a big, wet kiss," the wound on his thigh bleeding through the field bandage.

When she scowled and told him to get himself to a medic, he rolled his eyes and withdrew his hand from behind his back. "Your crossbow, Consort."

She did kiss him then, to the wolf whistles of the rest of the team.

That, however, was the sole point of light in the darkness. As night turned to dawn, the city drained of power, the Tower running on massive generators stored below ground and turned on only when Raphael and Lijuan weren't in the air, they cataloged their losses while watching for any movement from the opposing camp. The news was bad.

"Half of the injured," Dmitri said, after sharing the pitiless numbers, "will be able to fight again in a few hours, but the rest are either dead"—a grim look—"or so badly injured they'll be out for days at least." Black T-shirt wrinkled and bloodied from where he'd fought a squadron that had landed on a Tower balcony, he shoved a hand through his hair. "Jason, did you manage to get any reliable numbers on Lijuan's casualties?"

The spymaster nodded. "Double ours."

Everyone in the room understood that even with the impressive abilities of the Seven in the mix, that still left Lijuan at a huge advantage, and the remainder of the time was spent discussing what they could do to lessen the near-impossible odds. It was grueling, because there weren't many more rabbits they could pull out of hats. Especially given the fact that while Lijuan hadn't begun any hostilities in the Refuge, Galen reported that her stronghold was bristling with aggression.

"The instant they see any sign that we may head your way," Raphael's weapons-master had said, "there's no question they'll attack." A tic in his jaw, he'd shaken his head. "If Lijuan survives this war, she'll do so with more enemies than she knows. Every man, woman, and child in the Refuge understands the threat originates from her."

An hour after Galen's message, Jason received another report—more cargo planes were being stocked with weapons in Lijuan's territory, and this time, instead of vampires, there would be reborn in the holds.

"It appears," Raphael said, rage a cold burn in his blood, "the goddess has decided there is no dishonor in using her 'servants' to win this war."

"You know," Illium said with a smile that held no humor, "it's a compliment. She's starting to worry you might actually hurt her and win."

Too bad the compliment could well lead to hell on earth.

Having forced herself to grab a couple of hours of down-time while she could, Elena was still grappling with the horrific possibility of a New York overrun with reborn when she walked into the refueling station to grab a cup of coffee just before dawn. "Sara."

Face drawn, her best friend shared a photo her parents had sent of Zoe peacefully sleeping somewhere in a commune in Nebraska. "We'll beat Lijuan, Ellie, whatever it takes." An unyielding vow. "I will not have my baby growing up in a world ruled by a monster."

Deacon came in just as they finished their coffee, and Elena left to give them a few minutes' privacy, Deacon's wide shoulders blocking Sara from view as he drew her into his arms. Elena couldn't imagine how hard it must be for the two of them to be so far from Zoe. As far as she knew, their little girl had never before gone to bed without a kiss from Mommy or Daddy.

She hoped with everything in her heart that Sara's words would prove prophetic, that they'd win this terrible fight so Zoe could play in the snow again, safe and happy and with wonder in her heart at the shadow of an angel's wings. Picking up a feather of dappled black and gray that looked like it came from a squadron commander she knew well, she put it carefully into a pocket to save for Zoe.

Her aim was to find Raphael, maybe steal a few seconds in his arms, but when she reached the war room, she saw that he was in intense discussion with Jason. Not wanting to interrupt and needing some fresh air, she went to the balcony doors. She'd pushed the door to one side when she looked up and froze, her eye caught by the unexpected tableau outside.

Aodhan and Illium stood near the edge, weapons in hand, both bearing wounds that said they'd been in one of the ongoing light skirmishes along the perimeter. Aodhan had a cut on his cheek and what looked like a couple of shallow slices on his upper arms, while Illium's right wing was notched as if by a blade. Not a disabling injury, Elena judged, and one that was healing before her eyes.

That, however, wasn't what held her attention. It was the fact that they stood side by side, their wings overlapping the slightest fraction. Aodhan never made the mistake of putting himself in a situation where he could be touched, which meant this wasn't a mistake. Fingers clenching on the doorjamb, her heart full at this sign of healing amid the hurt and the horror, she was about to turn away, leave them in peace, when Illium turned toward Aodhan.

The two angels were both tall, but Aodhan was perhaps an inch taller, and now his eyes locked with Illium's for a long, quiet moment before he lowered his head very slightly. Illium raised his hand, the movement slow, hesitant . . . and then his fingers brushed Aodhan's cheek just below the cut that had almost sealed. The first ray of dawn kissed the tear that rolled down Illium's face, caressed the painful wonder on Aodhan's as he lifted his hand to clasp the wrist of his friend's hand.

That instant of contact, the power of it, stole her breath.

Then Illium smiled, said something that made Aodhan's lips curve—Elena thought it might've been "Welcome back, Sparkle"—and they were separating to sweep off the Tower in a symphony of wild silver blue and heartbreaking light.

"Raphael," she whispered, having felt him come up behind her. "Did you see?"

"Yes." His hand on her nape, his thumb brushing over her pulse. "Of course it would be Illium who reached him," he murmured. "They've been friends since Illium first talked Aodhan into flying to the bottom of the gorge—he was younger than Sam is now, Aodhan even younger."

Elena hadn't realized Illium was older, Aodhan was always so solemn. "Did they get in trouble?" she asked, turning sideways to his body.

"Yes. It's a forbidden flight for such young babes—the gorge floor is far from the city and, though coasting down is not so hard, young angels don't have the wing strength to get back up.

"When they were found," he added, tucking her against him, "everyone knew it was Illium who must've been the instigator, and he took the blame without pretending otherwise." A laugh. "He has never lied, your Bluebell, even as a child, and that's why no one could ever be angry with him. 'I did it' is apt to be the most frequent thing he said as a child."

Elena could just imagine. "And Aodhan? What was he like?"

"Always quiet, shy, gentle of heart. But that day, he was intractable, insisting Illium alone wasn't to blame, that they'd come up with the plan together. He wouldn't listen when Illium told him to shush, and the next thing the Refuge knew, they were close as two birds of the same nest, each as often at the other's home as his own."

Pressing his lips to her hair, he said, "Two hundred years, Elena, that is how long we have waited for our Aodhan to return."

The solemn words made her eyes burn. Wrapping her arms around him, she stood in silence with her consort, their eyes on the squadrons that patrolled the uneasy border. Each time she glimpsed wings of silver blue, she looked for those of broken light.

Heavy fighting began again with true sunrise.

The Tower forces, Elijah's two elite squadrons included, did considerable damage, but it wasn't enough, not with Lijuan's generals recharged by their mistress. Having learned from their previous skirmishes, they ganged up on the Tower's most powerful fighters while an overwhelming number of ordinary fighters engaged anyone who might come to assist. Their tactic worked, bringing down five of Raphael's experienced commanders one after the other.

Of the Seven, it was Aodhan who took the worst damage.

The angel, with his unearthly beauty, was almost decapitated when he left his flank unprotected in order to save the life of an injured commander. Aside from the gruesome neck wound, one of his wings had been hacked half off, his left arm gone. Crash-landing on a roof, he broke a number of bones and it was only the relentless fire of the shooters around him that kept the enemy angels from landing to finish the job.

Yet even close to death, he eschewed anyone's touch but Illium's.

Racing to the infirmary as soon as he forced Lijuan to retreat once more, Raphael saw that the other angel was conscious. "I must touch you, Aodhan."

Throat destroyed, Aodhan spoke mind to mind. *I will heal. Help the others.*

Shaking his head, Raphael placed his hand very gently across the neck wound, and when Aodhan went white and stiff, knew he was throwing the angel back into the hell from where Raphael had carried him in his arms. *I'm sorry,* he said, adding yet another reason to the list of why he needed to kill Lijuan. *I cannot lose one of my Seven.*

He wasn't certain Aodhan breathed until he lifted his hand, the neck wound sealed, though the other injuries would take weeks of painful healing. "I would not have done this unless I needed you."

It is all right, Sire. Aodhan's splintered eyes held forgiveness for the unutterable pain caused. *Get me in front of a window. I can use my offensive abilities as long as I have a line of sight.*

After personally moving Aodhan's bed to a windowed area and smashing out the glass so the other man wouldn't do it himself the first time he used his abilities, Raphael returned to the field of battle. Every time he rose, Lijuan did, too, meaning he couldn't help his own forces, and sometime after midnight, she scored a hit almost directly to his heart.

The wildfire seared at the oily black of her power, but it was stuttering, almost overwhelmed. Knowing he couldn't fight Lijuan and heal at the same time, Raphael blasted out with angelfire and managed to wing Lijuan, just as Jason sent his black lightning slamming into the other archangel. Neither hit was serious and Lijuan could have kept coming after him, but for some reason, she retreated—possibly, he realized, because her own power was starting to fade.

Her hair and eyes had both changed to oily black during the battles, but now he realized they were back to their usual shade. Lijuan, it seemed, wasn't as all-powerful as she liked to make people believe and that was something they could use. Landing on a Tower balcony, he kept his feet by sheer strength of will as the battle raged within his body, Lijuan's black poison attempting to shut him down, while the wildfire fought back.

He couldn't fall, couldn't allow his troops to see how badly he was injured.

Managing to make it inside, he caught Dmitri's eye, saw his second understood what was happening, but Dmitri didn't betray it by so much as a flicker of an eyelash. "Lijuan's forces are pulling back," he said. "I expect intermittent fighting throughout the night, but we should rest our troops in groups."

Raphael spoke through a haze of red. "Numbers."

Walking over so their words wouldn't be overheard, his second said, "More than half our forces are dead or too severely injured to recover anytime soon. The others are exhausted, even our strongest. I predict Lijuan's forces will launch an all-out offensive with the dawn—we have no other surprises to throw in their path and they know it."

"Authorize the use of the rocket launchers come dawn," Raphael said, but they both knew it wouldn't be enough. "The cargo planes with the reborn?"

"Lifted off two hours ago," Dmitri said, then lowered his voice. "Go. Heal. We'll finish this discussion later."

"Watch over my city, Dmitri." He left the war room with agony searing up his spine, making it to his and Elena's private Tower suite with teeth gritted. Collapsing on the living room floor on his front, he clenched his jaw to stifle the violent scream that wanted to erupt from his throat. A single sound and his entire fleet would realize how close they were to losing the city.

43

"*Elena,*" came Dmitri's voice in her ear, "*the fighting has lessened in intensity. You can stand down for now.*"

Frowning, she tapped the reply button. "I'm fine, Dmitri. Pull some of the others." Her mortal friends were showing worse signs of exhaustion—while she might be a baby immortal, she *was* still an immortal and it had an impact.

"*You need to get back to the Tower.*"

Ice trickled down her spine. "Understood."

Flying directly to her and Raphael's Tower suite after timing her flight to avoid the sporadic bursts of continued fighting, she entered through the locked balcony doors by using her palm print. "Raphael!"

She shoved the door closed because she knew he wouldn't want anyone to see him like this and ran to go down on her knees by his side. For a second, she was afraid he was dead, but then she saw the rigid muscles of his arms, his hands fisted tight and his spine locked, and knew he fought a battle against Lijuan's poison.

Not knowing what to do, she just stroked her hand through

his hair over and over. "I'm here, my love. If you can hear me, reach for what you need inside me."

She felt nothing, Raphael's body locked in combat against a vicious enemy. The feeling of helplessness was terrifying, but she refused to surrender. Instead, she kept stroking his hair, her other hand closing over one of his fists, and swallowed the tears of rage at the pain of her mate.

Time passed at the pace of a snail's crawl. Elena was barely aware of what was happening outside, but she felt the shudder as either Lijuan or one of her generals managed to hit the Tower. When it wasn't repeated, she guessed it had been a general and that either Jason or Illium had managed to head him off. A while later, who knew how long, she heard Dmitri's voice in her ear.

"If you can speak to the Sire, tell him Naasir and his team just successfully decapitated one of Lijuan's strongest generals by stringing a wire across two buildings on their side of the line. He might not die, given his strength, but he's out of the fight."

Elena shared the news with Raphael, not knowing if he could hear her. "Those three lunatics are in the heart of enemy territory and they're doing damage," she said. "God, I bet Ash will have some stories to tell after this is over." Leaning down, she pressed a kiss to his sweat-soaked temple, the dragon mark pulsing with a glow.

As if, she thought, it, too, fought the poison.

Another blow made the Tower shudder some time later. "Dmitri?" she asked, touching the communications device.

"A general we took down yesterday appears to have recovered. Aodhan has managed to shove him back and is keeping him busy for the time being."

Elena frowned, thinking of the casualty lists she'd seen. "The general with the white wings, yellow primaries?"

"Yes. He shouldn't have recovered after Illium's blade cut him almost in half, but he is whole."

Skin chilling at what that might mean, Elena decided to keep her silence on that piece of news until Raphael had fought this battle. "Come on, Archangel. The bitch can't beat you—you've sent her scuttling off to lick her wounds time and time again."

His body shuddered under her touch, his muscles going lax.

"Raphael?" she said, scared by the sudden change. "Archangel?"

Fists opening, he pressed his palms down on the carpet and turned over onto his back. His face was sharper, the bones of his face more prominent. His body, she thought, had burned itself up in an effort to fight the poison. "I'm here," he said, chest rising and falling in harsh breaths, one of his hands reaching to intertwine with hers.

Bringing their clasped hands to her mouth, she pressed a kiss to the hot burn of his skin. "It's gone?" she asked, seeing no obvious signs of the poison.

"Yes, but the wildfire is almost completely depleted." He squeezed her hand. "In you, too, Elena. There are mere flickers in both of us now."

"What about your capacity to create angelfire?"

"The sources from which I can draw are now farther and farther away—I could take it from the generators but it would mean the Tower going dead for a relatively small boost. My ability to generate power within myself is being hobbled by the fact my energy is constantly being redirected to heal." His eyes held her own. "Lijuan retreats because she doesn't like to be hurt, but there's a good chance I won't be able to cause her any real harm in our next engagement if I fight as I have been doing."

A strange calm descended over Elena. They hadn't spoken about this, but she'd always known it was on the table. "You have to get closer," she said, even as, below the calm, horror clawed its way across her soul.

A nod. "If I can get close enough to grip any part of her, I can release every last flicker of angelfire and wildfire inside me. If a single fragment reaches her heart, I don't think even Lijuan could survive it."

All those words, but he was talking about blowing himself up. "I'm coming with you." She pressed her fingers to his lips.

"I have some wildfire left inside me, you said—we have to give it our best shot."

His expression was gentle, the arms he held out to her strong. Going into them, her head on his shoulder, and his wing below her body, she lay in quiet with her archangel and she wasn't afraid of the darkness that awaited. Whatever death held for her, she'd go into it with Raphael by her side.

Something slammed into the Tower moments later, blowing out the windows of their suite and covering them in a coat of splinters.

An hour later, and with dawn at least another sixty minutes away, Raphael knew they had to move. The Tower had taken heavy structural damage despite their deflective efforts. Lijuan hadn't risen, but her generals were *all* recovered and at full strength, while his strongest aerial fighters—Illium, Aodhan, Jason—were battling through crushing fatigue to repel the blasts.

Once more, Raphael had to fight his instincts to go out there, join in the effort. If he did, he'd lose what little strength he'd regained, and Lijuan would have no impediment to her next attack. As it was—"Naasir." He jerked up his head as the vampire ran into the war room, bleeding from a massive wound on his face.

Elena ripped open a sterile packet from the first aid supplies and pressed the heavy cotton dressing to the vampire's face to soak up the blood. Not pushing her away, which told Raphael how badly he was hurt, Naasir went to his knees, Elena beside him, but the vampire's silver eyes were locked on Raphael. "Lijuan is absorbing power," he said. "All her injuries are healed and she now works to bloat herself with energy. Come dawn, she'll be as powerful as when she began the battle."

"How?" Raphael asked, as Elena pulled the dressing off to expose a raw gash, a flap of skin hanging down over Naasir's cheekbone, bone and muscle exposed.

As she grabbed the small butterfly bandages that would keep the flesh in place while Naasir healed, the vampire spoke of horror. "She has truly become an Archangel of Death. I saw her slit the throat of one of her fighters herself, to the point of near decapitation—she then thrust her face into the bleeding gash and seemed to feed."

"Because she couldn't get any more creepy." Elena continued to pin Naasir's flesh together, and it was only when she nudged the vampire forward a little that Raphael realized Naasir's spine had almost been cleaved in two. The fact the vampire had been able to run, much less stand, spoke of his strength.

Now, he gave a feral grin, clearly amused by Elena's words. "It takes her twenty minutes at least to drain the life out of one of her people. The fighter I saw was a mummified husk when she was done; that was when she moved on to the next volunteer, her face a mask of blood." He growled without warning, eyes flashing.

"I'm sorry." Elena continued to work at his back. "I need to pull the flesh together or your spine will be exposed to the air and it'll take longer to heal." Not stopping in her task despite the constant low-level growl, Naasir's fingers claws, she said, "That's how she's been fixing her generals."

Raphael nodded, considering why Lijuan hadn't done this earlier. Likely because it, too, was a limited power, something she could only do once within a certain period. Not that it mattered—because the fact was, he couldn't hope to defeat a full-strength Lijuan in ordinary combat, not after she'd worn him down to a threadbare edge.

Rising to his feet, his back held together by larger bandages that worked the same as the butterfly ones on his face, Naasir turned to offer Elena a hand. She took it and he hauled her up. Then, grabbing her around the waist, he lifted her up and brought her startled face close to his own.

Raphael?

He won't hurt you.

Elena made a squeaking sound as Naasir nipped her sharply on the chin. "I've decided I won't eat you," he said, putting her down on her feet before turning to Raphael. "Lijuan's forces have harried ours over the night hours, but most have rested. They will launch a major offensive with the dawn."

"Thank you, Naasir. Go and feed—we'll move very soon against the enemy." He couldn't afford to give Lijuan any more time to glut herself with power.

The vampire left with a curt nod for him and a grinning and unexpected snap of his teeth for Elena. Seeing the expression on her face, Raphael almost smiled. Naasir would've no doubt fascinated and confused her for some time to come, but his consort wouldn't see the end of this day if they were to stop a monster. "It's time, Elena."

Should they succeed in their final act, Lijuan's forces would still outnumber the Tower's, but Raphael's people were smart and they thought for themselves, while Lijuan's were tied to her. If Raphael and Elena took her out of the equation, not only would her generals lose their power, the enemy's entire command structure would collapse. He had every faith the members of his Seven would utilize that fracture to hold on and claim victory. "We can wait no longer." And it wasn't only New York at stake—fighting had broken out in the Refuge an hour past, and Raphael knew whatever happened in his city would end the battle in the Refuge, one way or another.

A frown, Elena's eyes going to his temple. "You're rubbing the mark."

Dropping his hand, Raphael stared at it. "I did not realize."

"Does it hurt?" She brushed her fingers delicately over it.

"No, but it pulses." Like a heartbeat. "That pulsing has increased in strength over the past hours." Shaking his head, he cupped Elena's face, a cut under her eye and across one cheek, her arms bearing countless nicks from the exploding windows and earlier skirmishes. Her body, too, was nearly at its limit, its ability to heal sluggish.

"I do not like that your colors are hidden." She'd found some brown dye, used it on her hair and wings in a bid to keep Lijuan from immediately realizing who it was that flew beside Raphael.

"It'll wash off with a couple of soapings. I'll do it after we take care of Lijuan." Nothing less than total confidence in her tone, though they both knew they might soon share their final kiss. "*Knhebek*, Raphael."

"You are my heart." The amber in the ring she'd given him

glowed pure and beautiful as he took her mouth, passionate and with as brilliant a heart as his warrior.

Twenty minutes later, he stood on the cracked but still holding balcony outside the war room and met Illium's and Jason's eyes, Elena by his side. The two angels would run interference in the hope Lijuan didn't realize Raphael's intent until it was too late—both could well lose their lives.

"Whatever price we pay this day," he said, "whatever the outcome, know that I am proud to have had your loyalty." On the mental plane, he made sure his message reached Aodhan and Dmitri, who even now watched their backs, and Naasir, who fought on the ground. The others would make sure his words were passed on to Galen and Venom, the two locked in battle as the peace of the Refuge was splintered with violence. "It is a point of great honor in my life."

Both bowed their heads, but it was Jason who spoke. "The honor is, and will always be, ours," he said, as Aodhan deflected another fury of blows aimed at the Tower. One got through, the balcony shuddering.

All four of them instinctively adjusted their stance to keep their feet.

"Did you manage to see Mahiya?" Elena asked his spymaster, and it was the question of a consort.

Jason's face betrayed none of his emotions as he inclined his head, whatever had been shared between him and his princess, who'd worked in the infirmary throughout the fighting, a private matter. Raphael hoped it wouldn't be the final conversation the two would ever have, for Jason had earned his happiness. To have it stolen from him, a bare heartbeat after he'd found it, would be a great unfairness—but as they had all learned in the preceding days, sometimes good did not prevail, evil triumphant.

Today, they'd do one final thing to change that, turn the tide. The ordinary fighters were ready to start the attack the instant they took off, forcing Lijuan's forces to move before they were ready. Rocket launchers would be used to take out groups of enemy angels, his remaining winged fighters instructed to do everything in their power to create those groups by pushing the enemy together.

Those fighters understood that it was likely they, too, would die in the blasts. "If I take five of them with me," one of his commanders had said, "it will be a sacrifice well made."

Turning to Elena, his pride in his people absolute and the mark on his temple pulsing so hard that it seemed impossible no one else could see the movement, he said, "Ready, *hbeebti*?"

Elena notched a bolt into her crossbow. "Let's go kill that murderous bitch."

Snapping out their wings on her vow, Raphael, Elena, and his men were about to fly out through the bombardment that continued to shake the Tower when a bloodied angel came to a crash landing in front of Raphael, his blood splattering on the thin layer of snow. A crossbow bolt was embedded in his stomach.

"Azar." Raphael knelt beside the advance scout, Jason beside him, while Illium took off to assist Aodhan in deflecting the blows now aimed at the balcony on which they stood.

"What are you doing here?" Jason asked the fallen angel. "You were stationed on the edge of the city."

Gripping Jason's hand as Elena called for the medics, Azar's mouth bubbled with blood, the fluid crimson against his gleaming black skin in the dull light of the time before dawn. "I couldn't get through on the communication lines, Sire. And you had to know."

Raphael connected with the scout's mind to make communication easier. While Raphael was always open to his Seven, Azar wouldn't have been able to initiate such contact, especially from a distance. *What do you have to report?*

Another assault force, the slim angel said, green eyes dark with pain, for while angels could heal many wounds, those wounds did not hurt any less. *On the horizon, perhaps five minutes behind me. I left as soon as I spotted them, but they are so fast*—a dangerous assessment from a scout known for his extraordinary speed—*they gained on me with every wingbeat.*

Raphael looked at the devastated city around them, the

Tower's smashed walls and splintered windows, considered the number of fighters injured or dead, and knew his people simply could not survive against another fresh force, no matter how huge their hearts. *Estimated numbers?*

Hundreds, Sire. They flew in the most perfect fighting formation I've ever seen.

44

Handing Azar over to the healers, Raphael shared the information the scout had flown through enemy fire to deliver. "We go now and we do as much damage as possible to give our people a chance," he said, as realization formed a layer of grim ice in Dmitri's expression, his second having stepped out onto the balcony.

Illium, back with them, swore under his breath, next to a quietly stoic Jason.

Elena's expression was a study in fury, and it made him want to smile even in this moment, for she was a woman any man would be proud to have by his side on the eve of the greatest battle of his life. "Warn our people," he said to Dmitri, "and tell them that if there comes a time when there is no hope of victory, they do not dishonor me by choosing to retreat or surrender. With Lijuan gone from the world, they will not have to serve under evil."

Dmitri's eyes held his. *I'll make it known, but I'll never serve anyone except you.*

I know, old friend. Were it my choice, I would leave my city and my territory to no other angel, but to my second.

Fly strong, Raphael.
Fight well, Dmitri.

Wings snapping out, he swept off the Tower with Elena, Illium, and Jason, the four of them winging their way directly to the heart of Lijuan's operation, hoping to take her unawares. Crossbow bolts filled the air as soon as they came within range. Jason and Illium were fast enough to avoid them; Elena wasn't, but she was very good at shooting her own bolts in flight, slamming two home between the eyes. The shooters quickly grew wary of giving her a target.

They'd just crossed the border that divided their perimeter line from the enemy's attacking front, the mark pulsing hot and urgent under his skin, when Raphael saw the wave of dark gray on the lightening horizon, the line shifting to encircle the entire stage of battle.

Watch out!

Twisting sideways at Illium's warning, he barely avoided the hail of blades that was Lijuan's power, as Elena, Illium, and Jason engaged the enemy fighters that sought to disable Raphael's wings. Having materialized above him, the Archangel of China was attempting to shred him with her poisonous fire.

Coaxing the last of the wildfire inside him to the surface and drawing on the fire that lived in Elena, too, he blocked Lijuan's next barrage with ordinary angelfire and, ignoring the crossbow bolt that thudded into his shoulder, flew up, his aim to make physical contact.

Except she dematerialized without warning, her strength renewed. And when she rematerialized to the left, she managed to score him with a whip of black poison. Vicious pain stabbed through his flesh as the wildfire inside him sought to cauterize the wound and he blocked the healing—he couldn't afford to lose the last of it, of the only thing that could hurt Lijuan.

Dropping down beside him with a gloating smile, eyes virulent red, Lijuan said, "I give you one final chance to surrender, Raphael," her face a skeletal mask. "I do not intend to kill you, not any longer." She made certain not to come within touching distance. "You will be much, much more useful to me in other ways."

Raphael thought of the desiccated corpses found in her

territory, of the fighter Naasir had seen go to his death, and
knew Lijuan sought to feed on an archangel. "A very generous
offer," he said aloud, while his mind reached for Dmitri's. *You
must make sure the remainder of the Cadre knows Lijuan seeks
to feed off not only angels, but archangels.*

I'll ensure the message gets through, came the immediate
reply. *Sire, the new assault force has arrived and will swarm
the Tower in minutes if we don't do something to stop them. I've
authorized the use of any and all weapons at our disposal.*

Raphael heard gunfire and rocket booms on the heels of that
statement and knew his exhausted and wounded vampires, and
the hunters, were shooting at the enemy, while his angels, some
with broken limbs, all with injuries, filled the sky. But there
were too few of them, and too many of the strange gray-winged
angels who powered Lijuan's new assault. "What have you
become?" he said to her, unable to imagine how she could've
created this new army, silent and lethal, without anyone in the
Cadre knowing the truth.

A terrible smile. "The epitome of our evolution."

That level of power could not be held in the hands of a
nightmare.

He blasted her with angelfire without warning, wanting her
to believe his intent was another ordinary battle. Deflecting the
blows with a rain of black razors that he held back through
sheer will, she smiled again. "I will chain you in my court,
feed on you for years. You'll be the example that brings the
others in the Cadre to their knees." His shield broke, the razors
shredding his face.

Raphael!

He reached for Elena not only with his mind but his hand,
Jason and Illium clearing a path for her so she could get to his
side. *This will hurt,* hbeebti, he said, as the mad archangel
raised her hands again.

Nothing hurts when I'm with you.

Squeezing her hand, he sent an order to all his troops in the
vicinity to get out of the blast zone. If Lijuan's forces thought
them cowards in retreat and turned their attention to him,
Elena, Illium, and Jason, all the better. He'd take as many of
them with him as he could.

He met Lijuan's gaze before she would've struck again, and said, "Feed."

She froze, her surprise unhidden.

"I won't fight if you give me your word you'll call off your troops till the sun sets on this day." All he needed was a single point of contact and he could ignite the tiny amount of combined angelfire and wildfire left inside him, hopefully sending Lijuan to the hell where she belonged.

See you on the other side, Archangel.

Total calm descending on him with Elena's words, he said, "My consort also remains," knowing that was a lure Lijuan could not resist. She coveted Elena's wings for the macabre collection of angels pinned to the walls of the refrigerated space that was her museum of death. "Look down."

Lijuan's teeth gleamed in a satisfied smile as she realized whose hand he held in his own. "I will agree," she said, with a gleam in her eye, "if you give me your consort first. I wish to snap her neck, make her a beautiful corpse."

His rage violent, he felt Elena's wing just brush his as she flew up. *Contact, Raphael. That's all you need, right? Use me as a conduit.*

No! he wanted to scream as Lijuan's hand clamped over Elena's wrist at the same time that his own closed around her ankle. *Forgive me, Elena.*

I'll be waiting for you.

Refusing to let Elena die at Lijuan's hand, he reached for the flickers of flame within himself and his consort, ready to ignite them both, when something dark gray slammed into Elena hard enough to break Lijuan's hold.

At the same instant, a thousand crossbow bolts thudded into Lijuan's body.

His wings tangled with Elena's as she tumbled into him, it took Raphael several seconds to slow their momentum, and when he looked up, it was to see a badly bleeding Lijuan take bolt after bolt from the gray-winged angels, as others of the gray ones took on the enemy one-on-one.

Raphael didn't waste time wondering which unexpected ally had sent this strange force. *Attack!* he ordered his own fighters, and made the decision to use a minute amount of wildfire to neutralize the poison Lijuan had thrown at him, for he was now of more use to his people alive. *No mercy!*

A wild grin on her face, Elena lifted the crossbow she'd never dropped, one wrist ringed with bloody bruises from Lijuan's grip. *We need to fucking deify whoever the hell sent those gray guys.*

The sight of her hurt made the cold rage in him flare to icy brightness. *First,* he said, powering to Lijuan, *I need to take out the garbage.*

An archangel couldn't be killed by crossbows, but with the bolts thudding into Lijuan's body as fast as she pulled them out, she was distracted, her energies funneled toward healing herself. Her facial bones appeared and disappeared as her skin faded in and out, but when she didn't shift into her noncorporeal form, he realized that whatever power she gained from draining the lives of others, it wasn't enough to allow her to transition under this type of bloody attack.

Wrapping one hand around her ankle while she was distracted, he sent all his remaining power, power kissed with the *life* that was Elena, directly through his arm and into her bones. Her shriek splintered the sky, her lower body exploding in a blinding flash of light, her torso crumbling.

Is the wicked witch dead?

I'm not certain. He almost thought he'd seen her transition into her other form at the absolute last instant. *But even if she survived the blast, it'll have been with extreme injuries. Her body is gone.* It would take her months to regrow it, and while Lijuan had tried to make them believe she didn't need the flesh, this battle had shown she very much did.

Even if she could feed on others to speed up her healing, the way she'd opened her mouth when tugging Elena closer told Raphael she needed her physical form to feed. And he'd seen her head burst like a pumpkin as bolt after bolt thudded into it in that split second while she screamed. The gray ones were merciless fighters, but right now they were on New York's side.

And it was time for him and his own to reclaim their city.

His body's ability to store power depleted to the point of nonexistence, he grabbed the sword Illium threw at him and entered the fray, his battle cry echoed by every one of his men and women.

He didn't know how long they fought, but he was always aware of Elena and those of his Seven who fought with him. Dmitri, having held off a new attempt to storm the Tower, his view far better than those in the thick of battle, sent through continuous strategic updates that Raphael used to direct his men and women so they acted as a smooth unit. He didn't realize how far they'd pushed Lijuan's forces until they hit the Atlantic, the fighting having moved from Manhattan and over wider New York as the sun rose higher and higher in the sky.

Ten seconds later, the instant after he sliced off the head of an enemy general in a fountaining spray of red that sent the body into the water from where his people would no doubt retrieve him, for he was too old to die by beheading, he felt Jason's mind touch his. *Sire, they're lifting the flag of surrender.*

Rising immediately above the rest of his force, Raphael confirmed Jason's sighting, then raised his sword above his head in a vertical line. The message took half a minute to get through the furious fighting, but one by one his people held their blows, allowing the enemy to retreat.

"We just let them go?" Elena asked, having come up beside him. "Seriously?"

Raphael didn't blame her for her angry disbelief, his own fury colder but no less deadly. "It is part of the rules of engagement."

"But they would've killed us." It was almost a growl, her blood-streaked and battered body taut with the need to hunt down those who had hurt the people who were her own.

"If my forces had surrendered, the enemy fighters wouldn't have touched them so long as they didn't raise arms against Lijuan." Whether Lijuan herself would then have used his people for her feeds was another question, but he wasn't Lijuan, to make such an ugly breach of the rules of his people.

Contacting Dmitri and Naasir, he said, *Herd her surviving vampire troops to the pier and find them a ship. Make sure they have enough blood to survive the journey out of my waters.* After that, they became the responsibility of their own commanders, and while Raphael didn't think Lijuan had much honor any longer, he thought perhaps her older commanders had enough not to abandon their own.

"I still think it sucks." Elena pushed a strand of hair off her sweat-stained face, the brown color so wrong, Raphael knew he'd have her wash it out at the first opportunity. "I don't think that sick thing calling herself an archangel would've obeyed the rules."

"She is beyond honor and madness, a creature of true evil."

A sigh, his furious consort nonetheless lowering her crossbow. "And you're not." Scowling, she continued to watch the enemy. "Fine, fine, we'll be civilized and let them retreat, but damn it, I don't like it. They'll be back as soon as Lijuan has recovered, because it would be just too much good luck if the Queen of the Zombies was truly dead."

Of that, Raphael had no doubt. "The rules of engagement were put in place long ago, after archangelic wars no one remembers," he said to Elena, and it was also a reminder to himself of why such rules were needed. "Wars, after all, are between the archangels—yet it is the angels and vampires below us who die total deaths."

As he'd expected, the general he'd beheaded had been retrieved, while countless vampires and ordinary angelic fighters floated on the water or lay broken and bloodied across the city, their lives ended. "In those wars, it's said we decimated over eighty percent of our population. Only the archangels and the noncombatants survived and not one person ever forgot the blood that stained the hands of the Cadre at the time."

"Okay," Elena whispered, horror in her expression. "Okay, I get it now."

"Jason's squadron will escort them out of our territorial waters," he said, brushing his wing over hers. "Now we must deal with this other strange force, find out their price for this day's help."

They turned as a unit to face the city.

45

Having landed on roofs as far as the eye could see, the gray ones sat crouched like living gargoyles, their wings arched, fundamentally changing the landscape. Birds sat on the shoulders and bodies of many of them, silent and watchful.

"Have you ever seen anything like this before?" Elena asked Raphael, trying to make some sense of what she was seeing, and failing.

From what she'd witnessed in the battle as the gray angels fought around her, there was no color to them—gray eyes, pale smooth skin, hair of gray, gray wings. Yet they were humanoid, had faces with the clean lines and strong bones of the immortals. Their wings, however, had no feathers, instead formed of a leathery texture that reminded her of the wings of bats. The shape of those wings, too, was similar to the nocturnal creatures.

"No," Raphael said after a long moment, as heavy clouds passed across the sky to drop a curtain of snow on the city, the sun blotted out to cloak the world in darkness.

It created the perfect muted background for the strange angels who crouched all over New York.

"These gray ones are an enigma." Eyes of violent blue took in the eerie scene, everyone so silent it seemed impossible this was a city of countless souls. "Come."

The gray angels didn't stop them as they flew back through the snow to the Tower, Illium by their side. Coming to a stop on the Tower balcony, Elena took her place beside Raphael, their eyes on Manhattan. Dmitri flanked him in silence, while Illium acted as a winged sentry. Naasir, she realized, had to be handling the enemy vampires still in the city.

Take one step forward with me, Elena.

Guessing it to be some kind of angelic protocol, she did so without argument . . . and one of the gray ones flew toward them from a nearby building. Tall, with broad shoulders, his wings silent in the snow and his hair brushing his nape, Elena couldn't have picked him out from any of the others. It was as if they'd been minted from the same press, one after the other.

Landing right in front of them, he placed his sword horizontally in front of his body and went down on one knee, head bent.

Elena bit down hard on her lower lip to stifle her gasp. *The mark on his nape,* she said, eyes on the primal black lines of it as the male's dusty gray hair slipped to either side, *it's a mirror image of yours.*

"Sire," the unknown fighter said at the same instant, "we come as called."

Raphael's answer was accompanied by a freezing wind that swept through the deathly silent city. "None who fought so bravely should kneel."

The gray angel rose to his feet on Raphael's words. This close, Elena saw his irises weren't truly gray; they were so pale as to be barely distinguishable from the whites, but for the black pinpricks of his pupils. It should've reminded her of Lijuan, but it didn't, because where Lijuan carried death and a putrid evil in her eyes, the being that looked through those colorless eyes was near to a blank slate. As if he hadn't yet decided who he would be.

"You call me Sire." Raphael's wing was heavy against her own as they stood side by side, their bodies aligned under the falling snow that was a cold, welcome kiss on the wounds that scored her flesh. "Tell me why."

"We heard your voice in our Sleep." It was a flat, toneless statement. "We hear only the voice of the Sire or his consort." His eyes locked with Elena's.

"Elena," she said through a dry throat, forcing herself to remember this deadly creature was a friend, not foe. "You can call me Elena."

He looked at her as though she were speaking a foreign language. "You are the consort."

Okay, Archangel, I think this is more your speed than mine.

I'm uncertain these gray ones are anyone's speed. "What do you call yourselves?"

"We"—an absolute hush, the wind frozen—"are the Legion."

Elena felt her stomach drop, as if she'd learned something terrible.

The Legion.

Raphael had heard those words before, a long, long time ago. *They are,* he said to Elena, *the threat used to scare badly behaving angelic children.*

Have a nap or the Legion will come get you? Like the bogeyman?

Precisely. Except it appears our bogeyman is real. "You have been gone from the world an eon."

"Yes."

Raphael, look at his eyes. They're starting to gain color. And his hair . . .

Doing as Elena bid, Raphael saw the gray one was indeed no longer so gray. His hair was darkening into black and his irises now boasted a fine rim of blue—the same blue as Raphael's eyes. "You are now my Legion." Not a question, the mark on his face a quiet thrum that told him the truth, told him, too, that the Legion waited for his command. "Your first task is to assist my troops in securing the city and fixing the damage to the Tower."

A quiet nod, his wings folded with military tightness. "Sire."

"You are their leader. I need a name for you."

A pause. "I am not the first primary," he said at last, "but that is what I am. The Primary."

"All right," Raphael said, accepting what appeared to be a rank rather than a name. It was becoming clear the Legion was not in any way an ordinary angelic—if they were even angels—squadron. "Tell the Legion they are to obey the orders of Dmitri and Illium as if they were mine or my consort's." He pointed out the two men. "I will make the others of my Seven known to you when they return from their tasks."

"The Legion has heard and understands."

"I estimate five hundred in your squadron. Is that correct?"

"Five hundred woke to the Sire's call in urgency. Two hundred and seventy-seven need more time. They will arrive when their hearts begin to beat fast enough for flight."

Seven hundred and seventy-seven fighters who functioned as a single cohesive and apparently tireless unit, their skills lethal and their healing abilities unparalleled. He'd seen a Legion fighter beheaded, only to rise again within minutes, his head growing a new body while the old disintegrated into dust.

It was an army no other archangel would easily wish to face.

"We'll need quarters for the Legion," Raphael said to Dmitri.

"Sire." It was a quiet interruption from the Primary, and when Raphael nodded at him to speak, the male said, "We do not sleep except when it is time for us to leave the world."

"Do you eat?" Dmitri asked. "Need water?"

Another pause, akin to those of older angels who sought to mine their memories for a lost answer. "Yes"—a faint sense of surprise in his tone—"when we are awake, we do need fuel, but we can fight for many days without sustenance or rest."

I'll work out the logistics, Dmitri said mind to mind. "Though you may not need a place to sleep," he said aloud, his words directed at the Primary, "you should have a place where you can be with your men and women—" A frown. "I see no women."

"We are the Legion," came the incomprehensible answer.

Eyebrow raised, Dmitri continued. "You'll need a place where your men can gather at least."

"Yes," the Primary said after another pause, his mind seemingly not yet having shaken off the shackles of his long Sleep. "We do not . . . do well if cut off from the group so soon after waking."

"There are two warehouses next to each other not too far from the Tower," Dmitri said. "We normally use them for storage, but they can be cleared for temporary accommodation if"—a glance at the Primary—"that wouldn't be too basic an environment? They're nothing but large spaces with four walls and a roof."

"No, such will do well."

Raphael knew the warehouses could only be a short-term solution. Even with the members of the Legion rotating in and out, the combined space wasn't designed for over seven hundred winged beings. "Now that you're awake," he said to the Primary, "how long do you plan to stay this way?"

"Until it is time to Sleep again."

Okay, he takes the win for most cryptic statements.

Biting back a smile at Elena's dry assertion, Raphael said, "We'll build you a living space suited to your requirements after the repairs to the city and the Tower." Raphael owned a massive chunk of Manhattan, far more than most people realized, and it made sense to have this force around the Tower. "In the interim, you are welcome at the Tower. You are my people now."

Epilogue

Sadness had been the pulse of the city for five days following the war, as they watched flower-covered bier after bier leave for the Refuge and buried hunters and vampires who'd fallen. Elena hated funerals—not hard to figure out why—but she'd attended every single one, as had every other fighter who'd survived and wasn't confined to a sickbed. It had hurt.

The finest honor we can do the fallen is to bring our city back to life, until children play in the parks and lovers walk in the streets while angels soar among the skyscrapers and the blood kin share the kiss of life without fear. We must not forget what they died to protect.

Words a still badly hurt Aodhan had spoken, at the funeral of a vampire commander he'd considered a friend, and words they'd all taken to heart. In the past forty-eight hours, the rebuild of the city had kicked into high gear, and that was going a long way toward healing the wounds, though Elena knew it would take time for the emotional—and physical—injuries to heal.

She'd been lucky, so damn lucky that all her close friends had made it out alive, here and in the Refuge—the fighting there having ended the instant word filtered back of Lijuan's defeat. Of the injured, Ransom and Ashwini were the worst off, but they'd both be okay. Ransom had taken a crossbow bolt in the leg in the final battle, his femur snapping, while Ashwini had been slashed pretty badly with a sword across her chest. The other woman now held the Guild record for most stitches in a single sitting and was trying to avoid answering the one question to which every hunter wanted to know the answer.

If she and Janvier weren't together, then what was he doing playing (wow-mama-sex*ay*) nurse at her apartment, hmm?

The silliness of wondering about Ash and Janvier's relationship gave the tough, often stoic men and women of the Guild a much-needed emotional outlet, and if the jokes segued into more solemn conversations, that was good, too. Day by day, hour by hour, they were all finding a way to deal. For Elena part of that had meant a visit with Eve and Beth both, as well as a long squeeze-cuddle of a snuggly Zoe, a video call with Sam, and a visit to a hospital earlier that morning to fulfill her promise to a little boy who wanted to fly.

Today, she stood on a building across from the Tower with her archangel, the two of them having met there to get an overview of how the repairs were going—they'd both been working with their people until now. "Oftentimes," Raphael had said, "an archangel must stand above those he rules, but there are times when he must stand beside them."

Now, he turned to her, his leathers dusty from the work. "Astaad contacted me earlier. Once we are in a position to welcome guests, he has indicated a willingness to visit."

Elena had no arguments with that, the other archangel having done the entire world a giant favor. It had been approximately fifteen minutes after they'd returned to the Tower after the retreat of Lijuan's troops that Raphael had received a very polite call from the Archangel of the Pacific Isles. "Raphael," he'd said, "I wished to let you know I destroyed the cargo planes heading in your direction. I cannot believe Lijuan would attempt to fly such unclean creatures over my territory."

As it turned out, the holds had been stuffed with the last of Lijuan's hideous reborn so far as anyone knew. "Tell him to bring Mele along," Elena said, thinking she might actually start to enjoy this whole hostess deal if she kept getting to pick guests she liked. "Oh, you'll probably get an official update from Elijah, but I was talking to Hannah and she says they've dug out the final few stubborn reborn from their territory."

"Good. Our territory is also clean, and I think I'll speak to Eli about certain ongoing safeguards to make sure that doesn't change."

Elena nodded and drew in the crisp, bright winter air as the sounds of horns drifted up from the cabs below. God, it felt good to have her city back again. It might be a little battered, but hell if anyone was going to keep it—and the people who called it home—down. "I can't believe the Tower repairs were done so quickly."

The winter sun creating that illusion of white fire across his wings she wasn't sure was an illusion at all, Raphael walked to the edge of the building. "It's the symbol of my power."

As such, Elena thought, it could never appear weak.

"Of course," Raphael added, "the Legion is an extraordinary workforce."

"Yeah." His consort came to stand beside him, arms folded as she scowled at the sight of two Legion fighters landing on a Tower balcony. "You're sure they're not secretly planning to take over the city?"

"Yes, I feel it inside." Stroking his knuckles gently down the side of her face, the heavy bruise she'd taken on her jaw during the final fighting yet healing, he said, "You feel it, too, my suspicious consort."

She unfolded her arms. "It's like a tiny but steady pulse at the back of my mind, this awareness the Legion belong to us." Eyes of silver-gray turning to him, face solemn. "I know if I think a little too hard about the Primary, he'll appear in front of me, ready to do my bidding. And while I might be starting to get a handle on the consort thing, I'm not ready to deal with that kind of power. It's yours."

"Yes," he said, "it's mine." Elena didn't have the experience to manage a force such as the Legion, and more, she shouldn't have to. Already, she was taking on far more of the responsibilities of a consort than anyone could've expected of her so soon into her immortality. "But I hope you'll give me the benefit of your advice as I learn to deal with my new army."

A twitch of her lips, her wing sweeping across his in a silent caress. "Try to shut me up." Leaning into him, she said, "Why you, why us? I keep trying to get my head around that."

"A question to which the Primary may even now give us an answer," Raphael said, as the leader of the Legion landed in front of them.

The male's eyes remained translucent but for that ring of blue, the effect oddly beautiful, according to Raphael's consort. His hair, though, had turned totally black. His skin, too, was no longer the shade of death, but glowed golden with health, and his leathery wings had become a beaten gold except for the part where they grew out of his back.

There they were a black that echoed Elena's wings, the color bleeding into midnight blue, which then flowed into the beaten gold. The metamorphosis of the rest of the Legion was slower but no less fascinating a process. Day by day, they were all becoming painted in color—and the palette was the same.

"Sire," the Primary now said, "you call us."

"Only you. The others may continue as they are."

A nod.

"My consort has a question for you."

The Primary looked at Elena without blinking.

"Why Raphael and me?" she asked, her passionate nature inherent in the intensity of the question. "Why not Elijah and Hannah? They're older, have been together longer."

"You are *aeclari*, and the Legion may only serve *aeclari*."
Archangel?
I do not know this term, Elena. "Tell us about *aeclari*."

"*Aeclari* is you," the Primary said, as if it made perfect sense.

Do you think if I shoot him, he'll actually answer a question?

Raphael fought his laughter. *I think it's a case of asking the right questions.* "You're connected to the power that tried to fill me," he said, his skin prickling with the awareness of it.

"We are the repository. We tried to pass it to the Sire, but the Sire is not yet ready."

It was as clear an answer as he could've wished for, the whispers making sense now that he'd seen the Legion, understood how deeply they were linked to one another—as if they were one organism with many parts. "What happens when I'm ready? Do you vanish?"

"No. We are then freed to stay in the world or return to our Sleep once more. If we stay, we become alone and separate."

Raphael considered the other man's words—and the Primary *was* a man, if one who hadn't yet fully become—and placed it against what he knew of the Cascade powers gained by the rest of the Cadre. Each had to do with an ability or proclivity inherent to the archangel in question.

"You can only serve a warrior," he said, and it was no question because he felt the rightness of it in his gut. Raphael had been a warrior in one guise or another throughout his existence, from a stripling in Titus's army long ago, to fighting side by side with his own forces in the war past.

The Primary paused. "Yes," he responded at last, in that totally flat tone devoid of emotion. "A warrior who is attuned to the power of which we are formed—of the earth, of life. But the warrior must also be *aeclari*." His eyes flicked to Elena, giving Raphael the first glimmer of what that term actually meant. "And it must be the time."

The Cascade happens and Neha calls fire and ice, Elena said into his mind at the same instant. *Titus moves the earth, Astaad the sea, while creepy Lijuan brings the dead back to life. Meanwhile, my gorgeous archangel, not satisfied with, I don't know, shooting lightning bolts or something, actually taps into the energy of the planet and calls an army of bogeymen from the bottom of the ocean. Of course you do.*

The dry commentary made him wonder how he'd ever walked through life without the wit and laughter of his hunter by his side. He could no longer imagine such a cold, remote existence, the idea of it spawning an immediate repudiation in his bloodstream. Wing to wing with her, he said to the Primary, "Have others through time gained the ability to call you?"

Another long pause, the Primary turning the pages of his memory. "There have been warriors who have become attuned to the power of the earth, of life, and gained strength, but they touched only the edge of what we carry within us. It was not time for us to wake."

"Tell me your history," he said, a sudden chill over his skin, as if the answer was part of the racial memory of his people, buried deep, deep within the most primitive part of his brain.

"It was in the war that unmade our civilization that the Legion came to be. We were formed during the Cascade of Terror and bound to the first *aeclari*, our purpose to fight against the death that stalked the world."

"The reborn?" Elena whispered. "You're the antidote to their poison."

"The death took a different form then, but it was no less virulent or vicious. By the time we gained victory, angelkind was nearly destroyed, and our home hollow and dead. The Legion, too, was near death, for we are of the earth, of life. Our people, infected with the deadly toxin created by the power of an archangel of madness, made the decision to Sleep eons in the hope the poison would fade.

"When they woke, it was to find a new people had been born from the ashes of the old, and the toxin had bonded permanently to the blood of the survivors." His eyes lingered on Elena. "Madness and death reigned, until the desperation of a single individual made angelkind understand the fragile new people were their salvation, a gift from their healed world."

Raphael. Unhidden shock in his consort's expression. *I think he's talking about the birth of humanity.*

And of vampires. It was a knowledge so huge, he knew he had no hope of comprehending it in a single instant. "When," he asked, the chill he'd felt ice in his bones, "is the time?"

"Cascades come and go, are not our business, for they are part of the cycle of the world. We listen and watch in our Sleep, but wake only when that cycle reaches a crescendo, the gifts spawned in the archangels that of life and death itself, ferocious enough to rip apart the fabric of the planet." His unblinking eyes met Raphael's. "We have not woken since the Cascade of Terror."

"Oh, hell."

"Sire," the Primary said on the heels of Elena's soft imprecation, "if you would give me leave—I would rejoin the Legion."

"Fly free."

As they watched him sweep off on those wings of silence, Raphael considered the putrid darkness that had almost taken the world only days past. Lijuan's reborn had been eliminated in all affected territories, but they'd infected tens of thousands in the interim. Titus, meanwhile, continued to fight a constant trickle of disease bearers sent across by Charisemnon.

In comparison, Raphael's own strength continued to intensify day by day, until he knew that one day soon, he'd be able to wield the power carried by the Legion. "We've won this war, *hbeebti*, but it is only the first. I'm afraid this means Lijuan has not been erased from existence, for she is the epitome of death."

"Or," Elena said, "one of the other archangels holds the potential to go whackjob on us. But yeah, my money is on the Queen of the Dead."

"Lijuan won't repeat her mistakes." Raphael—the world—would have to be ready to handle a bloated monster ready to gorge herself on the life force of those she was meant to protect.

"We'll stop her," Elena said, then shot him an unexpected smile. "We're *aeclari*, after all."

"It'll be most intriguing to ascertain the exact meaning of that term." Though Raphael was in no doubt it had to do with the heartbond that tied him to his hunter.

"You mean you don't know?" Wide eyes. "The Primary was crystal clear."

"Yes, how very unintelligent of your consort not to comprehend him."

Convulsing with laughter at the way Raphael had said that without cracking a smile, Elena shook her head but couldn't get the words out. It made him smile, then throw back his head and laugh, the sight causing passing Legion fighters to pause, watch in what appeared to be shock, while the Tower troops grinned and continued on their way.

God, but he was beautiful. And he was hers.

Moving into his arms because she needed to be with him, unable to forget how close they'd come to never again touching, never again laughing with one another, she smiled and tucked her wings close as he enclosed her in his.

Cupping the side of her face with one strong hand, he held her gaze with eyes of wild, impossible blue. "I may not understand all of the Primary's words, but I know this with everything in me—the Legion would not have woken for who I was before you."

His thumb caressing her cheekbone, his face close to her own. "You have never, and will never, weaken me. You make me a better man and a better leader than I would've ever been without you." He shook his head. "You said once that you couldn't do this without me. Well, I can't do this without you, Guild Hunter."

Her eyes burned from the potent power of his words, so raw and honest and *necessary*. She hadn't known it until he spoke, but she'd needed to hear that, hear that he didn't blame her for the changes within him. "Did you know," she confessed, as the snow began to fall again, soft flakes that caught on his eyelashes, "I wake up terrified some nights and just watch you sleep?"

"No, I did not know." His cheeks creasing, his lips brushing against her own as he bent his head. "I must trust you a great deal indeed to allow myself to sleep so deeply."

That was when she understood the painful vulnerability inside her was forever. So long as Raphael existed, he'd have the ability to hurt her by getting himself injured or worse—and that was okay, because she wasn't afraid anymore, wasn't scared to live life with an open heart. Because the flip side to that awful vulnerability was an indescribable emotion that filled her up, made her happy to be alive and here, in the now.

"It's true," she murmured, as the joy of playing with her consort, her lover, her friend and mate, turned her blood to champagne, "I could've totally cut out your heart before you knew what was happening."

Their foreheads were touching now, his hand still cupping the side of her face, his chest a wall of muscled warmth against her palms. "What stopped you?"

Lowering her voice, she whispered, "I thought Montgomery might've been pissed off at all the blood on the sheets."

"Montgomery would never be something as uncouth as pissed off. Annoyed in an icily genteel manner, perhaps."

Elena knew they should get back to helping their people rebuild their city, but she reached up to trace the mark on his temple with fingers rough from the work they'd all been doing. He turned slightly into her touch as he always did, her archangel who'd never wanted her to be anything but what she was. "It looks like we've got one heck of a scary adventure coming up."

"We'll certainly not be bored."

His kiss was a branding, his wings folding back to leave them exposed, and when he wrapped one arm around her waist and lifted them into the snow-kissed sky, their mouths still locked together, she didn't protest. Though she might've smiled and blushed into the kiss at the wolf whistles that floated up, followed by the cheers.

The Cascade was in full progress. The world was becoming an insane place where rivers turned to blood and the dead walked, while archangels gained powers that made it manifest they were part of the very fabric of that world. The monsters might yet get loose again and the wicked witch was probably going to come cackling back to life to join arms with her disease-spawning best friend.

Despite all of that, at this instant, with the snow falling softly around her and her consort, their city alive, Elena didn't want to be anywhere or anywhen else. And neither, she knew, did the archangel who kissed her above Manhattan, his arms holding her safe.